IT ENDS WITH US

TALES OF THE TUATH DÉ
BOOK FOUR

TESS BARNETT

ISBN-13: 978-0-9978615-7-0

Cover Art by Jasmine Monterroso
kikissh.com

His Princely Delicates
An Imprint of Corvid House Publishing
Fantasy and Science Fiction Gay Romance Novels

Pensacola, FL
http://www.hisprincelydelicates.com

ALSO BY TESS BARNETT

Devil's Gamble

Domesticated: A Short Story Collection
In collaboration with Michelle Kay

Starbound

Left Undone

Turkish Delight

AS T.S. BARNETT

The Beast of Birmingham
Under the Devil's Wing
Into the Bear's Den
Down the Endless Road

The Left-Hand Path
Mentor
Runaway
Prodigy
Disciple

A Soul's Worth

ACKNOWLEDGMENTS

Thank you so much to everyone who's supported these boys so far! I hope you've loved being on this journey as much as I have.

1

Julien stood in the closest thing he had to a childhood home for the first time in years. The disconnected townhouse in Old Montreal still stood just as it had when he was a child—stark and creaking, smelling of parchment and gun oil. His brothers stared at him from the open hall door with the exact mix of disdain and relief he'd become accustomed to seeing on their faces. Edouard's scarred lips locked into a frown as he lifted his hands in a mocking gesture of welcome.

"Le septième fils revient," he said, never failing to remind Julien of his otherness as the Seventh Son. "It's about fucking time."

Julien dropped his duffel bag to the floor with a small sigh and stepped forward to place himself at the front of their little group, but there was no familial greeting to be had between him and his brother. "Suis-je en retard pour quelque chose, là?" He didn't want to give Edouard the satisfaction of seeming bothered.

His brother tapped his own temple on the side of Julien's missing eye and nodded toward him. "You definitely look like you lost something."

"That's a long story," Julien said, not willing to get into the details of the decision he'd made back in Tír na nÓg. "It's healed now. I'm fine."

Edouard tilted his chin toward the group behind his youngest brother, apparently not concerned with actually addressing them. "What have you brought here?"

"Trouble," Julien snorted, glancing briefly back at Ciaran and Rathgeirr. "But hopefully for everyone else more than us." He reached out to lightly touch Noah's arm and draw him forward, allowing himself a faint smile as the boy gave a timid wave. "This is Noah." Julien took a gentle hold of Noah's chin and urged him to tilt his head, exposing the crescent-shaped mark behind his ear. "He's a witch— mais yé sûr lâ. Yé apprové."

Edouard's expression noticeably darkened despite Julien's assertion that his friend was indeed a friend, but he didn't say anything, so Julien went on, stepping aside so that he could point out the fairy behind him.

"This is Ciaran—he's the gancanagh I was chasing in Vancouver." At this, more than one of his brothers did speak up with accusatory questions, but Julien lifted his hands to stifle them. "It's complicated," he said forcefully, looking at Edouard alone. If he agreed, the others would fall in line. "Yé plus une menace, Edouard. I'm certain."

"Did he just call me a menace?" Ciaran asked too loudly, and Julien was glad that Trent shushed him before he had to do it himself.

Edouard watched him in silence for a few beats, but Julien could see the growing disapproval on his eldest brother's face.

"This is Trent," Julien continued when no objection came, gesturing back at the boy. "He's human. And a friend."

Antony, Julien's second-youngest brother, was, to no surprise to Julien, the first to step closer to him with a glare and a sneering frown. "And why are there so many dangerous magical things in the fucking house?"

"Buckle up," Julien began. In front of six pairs of curious, wary eyes, he did his best to give a condensed version of the events in Vancouver, Tír na nÓg, and Lochlann, leading up to their current state—though he left out any mention of his relationship with Noah and quickly glossed over the issue of his missing eye. When he was finished, he gave them a moment or two to absorb the overabundance of information, then went on. "What matters is that I have information that says there is going to be an actual demon invasion soon—somewhere—and that said demons are going to have the help of an immortal race of warrior elf-people probably hoping to enslave what's left of mankind when the demons are done."

None of his brothers said anything for a while; they stared at him with varying levels of disbelief on their faces. Joseph, the second oldest and the tallest, spoke first.

"How do you know this information is good?"

"Well that's the thing," Julien said a little hesitantly. "I also brought one of those. He's a friend—un informateur."

"You fucking what?" Antony snapped, but Edouard shot a sidelong glare that silenced him.

"He's fine," Julien promised them. "We need to take the friends we can get in this fight; believe me. I've seen what these people can do, and Noah can tell you what the demons will do if left unchecked."

"Wait," Laurent spoke up, casually brushing Antony aside with the back of his hand, "where is this—elf? An elf?"

"The word is Alfar, but...well, you'll see." Julien turned to look behind him again. "Ciaran, it's safe to take off the glamour now."

"About that," the fairy answered with a laugh. "Can't do it."

"What do you mean, you can't do it?"

"Side effects," Ciaran said, a little more softly as he glanced over at Noah.

The witch stared at him. "What?"

"Mm. Seems I can't do magic anymore. Sorry."

Noah moved closer to him to take him by the sleeve. "You said you were fine. Now you're saying a side effect is you can't do magic anymore?"

Ciaran shrugged. "Well, but I'm alive, so..."

"Oh my god," Noah sighed. "You couldn't have mentioned before now? How am I supposed to undo a fairy glamour? I need my books."

He looked down at his bag and patted it as though to make sure it was still there, then reached out to take Rathgeirr by the front of his cloak and drag him down the hall, where he could spread his things on the floor. Joseph followed them without a word—Julien knew he wasn't about to leave a witch unsupervised in the house.

"I guess you can meet him later," Julien said.

Antony stepped in close to hiss at him. "Es-tu stupide? What were you thinking bringing these things here?" He looked over at Edouard. "Let's kill them already so we can focus on these attacks."

Laurent watched Julien with the same skeptical, questioning eyes that had been studying him since he was a boy. "It is suspicious, Julien."

"I know how it sounds," he promised them. "But in three days, the general of the Tuatha Dé Danann is going to show up here to help us deal with both of these problems, and he's going to talk about what our plan is. I'd rather not tell him we spent the whole time arguing about whether to kill our allies or not."

Edouard still hadn't spoken. He stood with his arms folded, listening, watching Julien with his scarred mouth pressed into a pensive line. Julien looked at him now, trying not to sound too plaintive.

"Edouard," he said. "If any of this Seventh Son bullshit has ever meant anything, trust me now. This is too big for us to turn away allies. Tell me what's been happening here—all of us are here to help."

Antony scoffed. "Listen to him play that card."

"Shut *up*, Antony," Hugo called from the doorway, familiar exasperation in his voice.

Edouard finally nodded. "Fine," he said at last. "Your friends can stay—as long as they understand that they are not trusted. I'm not going to put up with any bullshit."

"They don't be trouble," Julien said, and he hoped it wasn't a lie.

Edouard grunted an uncertain agreement. "Come in and get briefed," he said, and he walked back into the room where a large table was covered in printouts, maps, and a couple of laptops.

Julien paused to look back at the others, but Noah was too busy digging through his bag and mumbling to himself to catch the hunter's eye.

The witch yelled over his shoulder at Ciaran, "Can you get over here and help? I don't have a book for this."

Ciaran and Trent moved to join them, Ciaran dropping down onto the floor beside Noah and Rathgeirr. Trent stood awkwardly to the side and tried not to look at Joseph, who seemed exceptionally tall beside him.

Julien wasn't going to be any help to them, so he just followed his brothers. When he met Hugo in the door, the other man smiled broadly at him, moving in for a quick exchange of cheek kisses before thumping him on the back. "Good to see you in one piece, almost," he teased.

"Doing the best I can," Julien answered with a soft chuckle. Hugo had always been the best of them—the only one to hold onto his softness and optimism. He was also the only one Julien was honestly happy to see again.

With the war room door closed, the six of them stood around the wide table, and Edouard began.

"We've been having a rash of disappearances and unexplained deaths for months. I called the others back a few weeks ago to try and pinpoint the cause, but so far, all of our leads have died. You think it might be these demons?"

Julien nodded. "Could be. Noah's contact said that when he encountered possessed people before, they seemed like zombies—aggressive, rabid. Is that what you've been seeing here?"

"Sounds about right. At first we thought it might be a disease, but once Laurent found one in person, he could tell it had the stink of magic about it."

"Have they been coming from anywhere in particular?"

Edouard and Laurent spread the map of Montreal open in front of Julien, and Edouard pointed out the marks they'd made. "We've seen them all over. But they seem to be concentrated most around Mont Royal."

"Then I wouldn't be surprised if there's some sort of disturbance there. Noah's contact said there was some kind of portal in the town he was in. That's how they were all coming through."

Hugo let out a snort. "There's a hellmouth in Montreal?"

"Seems that way," Julien answered with a faint smile.

Arnaud spoke for the first time, his voice quiet and his hard eyes on Julien's face. "If it is possession, what do we do about it?"

"You can't be possessed if you're dead," Antony pointed out.

"We can't just kill these people," Edouard snapped. "They *are* people. We have to do something about the demon inside of them."

Julien hesitated for a moment before speaking up. "Noah has performed an exorcism before. I can ask him if he has any ideas."

"I'm not taking direction from any witch," Antony said, the word sounding like a curse on his lips.

"He's not a danger to us," Julien insisted. "He's saved my life a dozen times."

Edouard cut in before Antony could bite back. "How did you get involved with a witch in the first place, Julien?"

"He was my neighbor in Vancouver. He found me out—recognized lamia blood on my shirt. He said he wanted to help, so we sort of...fell into being partners." He glanced around the table at all of his brothers in turn. "I've never met someone who knows more about monsters and magic than he does, and if there's anyone who can help us find a solution to this, it's him."

Antony sucked his teeth in irritation. "We never needed help before."

Julien struggled to keep his voice steady. "First time for everything, isn't there?"

Hugo leaned over the table to insert himself into the conversation. "If Julien trusts him, we should at least hear him out. I care more about helping these people than I do where the help comes from."

Edouard nodded, though he gave a small, reluctant sigh. "All right. We'll see what your witch has to say."

When the double doors opened again, Noah barely heard it, nor did he look up when six sets of footsteps approached him. Sparks leapt from his hands as he pulled back from Rathgeirr with a hiss, and Ciaran swatted at him like he was scolding a child.

"Shut up, I'm doing it," Noah insisted.

"You're doing it *wrong*," Ciaran countered.

Noah scowled at him. "Well I'm the only one who can do it at all, so will you stop?" He returned his attention to Rathgeirr, who sat cross-legged and patient on the hallway floor. "Here. Again."

Out of the corner of his eye, he saw the tallest brother turn to Julien with a skeptical look, but Julien only shrugged.

"Any luck?" he asked, but Noah didn't look at him.

"Almost," he murmured, and he reached out to place both hands on Rathgeirr's chest. The alfar covered Noah's hands with his own, and they counted down from three together, and then Noah squeezed his eyes shut and said, "Réil!"

A fizzling noise crinkled the air around them, and Noah didn't have to ask if the spell worked that time. He heard the collective step back the six hunters took. Noah laughed with relief at Rathgeirr's beaming smile and reached out to thump Ciaran's bicep.

"I fuckin' told you I could do it."

"Aye, sure," Ciaran grumbled, but there was a small smile on his face, too.

When Noah turned his head, he saw their tall guard's hand at the back of his belt, presumably on the grip of a gun stashed there, but he didn't quite pull the weapon out. He stood along with the others when Julien urged them to, and the hunter guided Rathgeirr to the front of the group to present him to his brothers. Noah fought the urge to smile at the wary looks on all the men's faces—Rathgeirr cut quite an intimidating figure even to them, he was sure.

"This is Rathgeirr," Julien said. "He's one of the Alfar of Lochlannan, and it's his people that are threatening to wage war on mankind."

Not a single face in Julien's family seemed pleased, but Rathgeirr gave a little bow in greeting, looking like he didn't quite know what to do with himself.

"Why is he armed?" Antony questioned, and Rathgeirr looked down at himself.

"He'll need to give that all up," Edouard agreed. Rathgeirr dutifully removed his bow and quiver from his shoulder, then offered up the silver sword at his hip and the dagger on his thigh to the tall brother's waiting hands.

"I really am here to help," he promised them following the soft pulse in the air caused by his quick translation spell.

The oldest brother, who Noah would have pegged as being the one in charge even if he hadn't known who Edouard was from Julien's few mentions of him, looked at each of his guests with a hard eye. A younger man leaned in close to hiss some French in his ear, but Edouard pushed him aside without looking at him.

"We don't trust you," he said simply. "But I am choosing to trust Julien. Do you understand?"

Noah and Rathgeirr both nodded, but Ciaran's sigh was audible. Julien focused on him with a frown and pointed up the nearby stairs. "There's a spare room at the end of the hall. Go behave yourself. We need to talk to Noah."

Ciaran's lip curled. "I'm not going to be pushed off like a child. Tell us all what's going on so that I can help."

"No," Julien said flatly.

"Did you hear me? I'm—"

"We're not fucking around here," Edouard interrupted. "You can sit still until you're needed, or we can kill you now. Guess which one I'd rather."

Trent pulled sharply on Ciaran's sleeve and seemed to be trying to communicate his "please don't start shit" without words. Ciaran hesitated, but then he snorted.

"Fine." He turned to carry his things up the stairs, giving a quick whistle to Rathgeirr to ensure he was following.

Noah wasn't exceptionally keen on being alone with the surly-looking men, who were now all staring at him. One of them, a man with glaring eyes and a broad, stocky figure, addressed him first. "Is it true you know how to perform exorcisms?" he asked. "You've done it?"

"I did once," Noah answered.

"You could do it again?"

"I could," he said with confidence in his voice.

The man exhaled slowly through his nose, and Noah got the distinct impression he was being judged. "And you'd know a demon-possessed person when you saw them?"

"I—" Noah started, then hesitated. "Probably? They're not all exactly the same. But I know what Sabin told me."

"It seems like they've been dealing with the same thing here," Julien explained.

"Let's be sure, then," the man in front of Noah went on.

Noah glanced between him and Julien. "What's that now?"

The burlier man looked over at Edouard, and the older man nodded, so Noah was led a little farther down the hall to a door that opened onto a basement stairway. An unpleasant growling sound echoed from the darkness below.

"We captured one," the man said.

Noah gaped at him, looking between his blank face and the stairs. "You fucking *what?*"

"You said you can do exorcisms, right? So prove this is what you say it is."

"Jesus Christ," Noah grumbled, hurrying down the stairs with the rest of them following.

The basement was finished, with a single sofa and a number of bookshelves lining one wall and two doors leading off from the room. It was easy to choose the one the brothers' victim was behind—the low growl grew louder the moment Noah's scuffed sneakers touched the rug. He turned the knob and peeked inside.

A man of about forty lay strapped to a metal table in the center of the otherwise empty room, buckled securely by leather across his ankles, hips, and torso, his wrists lifted over his head. He struggled against his bonds, sticky foam pouring from the corner of his mouth, skin pale and eyes wild as they focused on Noah's face. He breathed too quickly, as if he needed more air but couldn't gasp any deeper to get it. The snarling in his throat grew louder, and he let out a stream of curses as Noah drew slowly closer.

"Uh, yeah," he said without looking back at the men behind him, "this looks about right."

"What do you want, faggot?" the man on the table rasped, spit spraying from his lips. "Get out of my face."

"Wow; uncalled for," Noah scolded. He turned back, shut the door, and touched Julien casually on the chest as he passed him to head back to the stairs. "I'll get my stuff."

Noah caught the angry brother's eyes on his hand as it left Julien— that one was Antony. Angry Antony, he reminded himself in an effort to keep these brothers straight in his head. Angry Antony and Scarred Edouard. Maybe the others would actually be normal enough to introduce themselves at some point.

He crouched down to scoop his spilled supplies back into his bag and did a quick check for the things he would need—he had salt, but that was about it. When he patted the pockets of his bag, he found the crucifix he still had from Sabin's prank. That would do. Noah approached the basement stair door and poked his head inside.

"Hey French guys, where do you keep the wine around here?"

All of them turned to look at the tallest brother, who pretended for a moment that he didn't notice, but then gave a resigned sigh and made his way upstairs, passing the witch by. Noah called out that a glass would be nice, too, and stepped back down to wait for him, but then he paused and glanced around at the other waiting brothers.

"I don't suppose you guys have any holy relics hanging around here I could use, do you?"

The stocky brother held up a finger to ask him to wait, then went upstairs himself. By the time the tallest one returned—this was getting exhausting; he was going to have to learn their names—the other was coming back down the stairs again.

Noah took the half-empty bottle of wine with a smile. "Thank you," he said. "And you're...?"

"Joseph."

"Right." Joseph the Giraffe. Got it.

The other brother returned and offered Noah a small reliquary—what looked like a finger bone, likely belonging to some saint or another, inside a small glass tube sealed at either end with hammered gold.

"Nice, man," Noah said, turning it gently in his hand. "Thank you..." he trailed off, hoping the other man would catch on, and the hunter nodded.

"Arnaud."

Arnaud. Arnaud Schwarzenegger. Easy. "Got it," he said with a smile. He took a quick breath and looked around at all of them. "Okay. So, you guys should probably not all be down here for this? It can get...gnarly. And it'll be easier if I'm alone. Honestly," he added when faced with their untrusting looks.

"I'll stay," Julien said, which didn't seem to put any of the others much more at ease. He looked over at Noah. "It'll be fine with just one more, won't it?"

Noah lifted his hands as though leveling the uncertainty. "Probably...?"

"It'll be fine," Julien answered for him. After a pause, Edouard tilted his head back toward the stairs, leading the rest of the brothers back up to the main floor.

Noah looked over at the hunter beside him and took a deep breath, holding the reliquary and the neck of the wine bottle in one hand and the glass in the other. "Here's the deal. You can come in, but you have to just sit your butt down and watch. It's going to talk to you, but you can't answer it, okay?"

Julien nodded, but Noah leaned in closer to peer into his one good eye.

"I mean it. Do not engage."

"I got it," the hunter promised him.

Noah took his phone from his pocket and did a quick search, opening a browser page to the prayer he needed and offering it to Julien. "When I say so, just read this aloud. I'll be busy and I sure as hell don't know it by heart, so this will be your contribution."

"Thanks for including me," the blond teased, and Noah smiled at him.

"You might not thank me by the time we're done."

2

The man strapped down to the table spit at Noah as the door shut behind him, but he stopped short of the slimy projectile's reach. Once it hit the ground, Noah moved closer and reached out to lay his borrowed crucifix on the captive's chest. The demon inside the man hissed and flailed, jerking his body against the restraints until the little wooden cross fell and clattered to the concrete floor. Noah gave a soft grunt of irritation and bent to pick it up, this time stuffing it underneath the snug leather band holding the man down by the chest.

"Settle down, there, friend," he said, giving the victim's stomach a light pat.

"Fuck you, faggot," the demon spat. Its voice was gravel crushed under a tire. "You think you can touch me? There are more of us coming than you can even fathom."

Noah pursed his lips skeptically as he set the bottle and glass down on the floor along with his bag. "Well, unfortunately, you're stuck in a basement," he noted. He took up the container of salt from his kit and weighed it in his hand as he returned his attention to the demon glaring at him. "So like, maybe the next ones will be harder?"

The demon fought the hold of its straps, straining the leather, and it swore at him through gritted teeth, but Noah only lifted his hands in mock surrender.

"Woo. I'm spooked. For real."

"Noah," Julien said in a tense voice from near the door. "What are you doing?"

The demon's bloodshot eyes locked onto the blond, and a cruel smile pulled its lips too wide. "Big strong hunter can't save you," it taunted. "Can't save anyone! Just a baby, a baby," it went on, its rough cackle echoing in the room.

"Shut up," Julien shot back, and Noah snapped his gaze over his shoulder.

"*You* shut up," he hissed. "So," he started a little louder, drawing the demon's attention back to him. He started a slow circle around the table, pouring salt in an uneven circle until it enclosed the trapped host. "What kind of lame demon gets caught by just some dude, anyway?" He turned the cap closed on the salt and stood looking down at the demon's glowering face with his brow knit into a sympathetic expression. "I mean, you know these guys aren't even witches, right?" he asked, his voice conspiratorially low. "Like, did you just get startled, or..."

"I am of the twelfth legion of the Great Marquis, little boy," the demon spat, lifting its chin in a sneer. "You and everyone you love will be bloody pulp under our feet."

"Ooh, man," Noah said brightly, and he planted his fists on his hips to listen. "That's fascinating. Tell me more."

"Fuck you!" it snarled. "Let me out of here!"

Noah gave a pensive hum as he set down his salt and picked up the wine bottle and glass instead, uncorking the bottle with his teeth. He spit it out beyond the ring of salt and lifted it to fill the glass. "Shouldn't you...you know, let yourself out? Or is the twelfth legion, like, the crummy one where they put the loser demons?"

"Noah, what the fuck are you doing?" Julien whispered, but the witch shushed him immediately.

The straps on the table creaked at the force of the demon's struggling, gnashing, and cursing, and Noah cast a wary glance at the spots where they attached to the table. They looked like they would hold. Probably. He took the reliquary from his pocket and dropped it into the glass, swirling it in the red wine while he approached the head of the table. The next time the demon lifted its head to shout at him, Noah plucked the vial from the glass and stuffed it into the thing's open mouth. The roar it gave made him jump slightly, but he held his ground, keeping close to the host's head.

"Yeesh, I'm sorry," Noah said. "Did that hurt?"

The demon's head thrashed back and forth, its teeth cracking the glass of the reliquary and drawing blood from its gums as it fought to push the relic back through its lips. Blood and saliva drooled from the corners of its mouth as it finally force the bone out, letting it clatter to the floor in a puddle of pink spit.

"Hey, man," Noah scolded, "those are pretty hard to come by; could you not?"

The demon's voice was thick with blood, its throat gurgling and glass cracking between its jaws as it spoke. "I will pierce your heart and devour your entrails, child!"

Noah lifted a hand to demurely cover his laugh. "What, from there? Listen, friend, I'm really only interested in big-name demons here, so unless you have somebody else you'd rather send my way, I mean—"

The table shook with the demon's growling. "I am Ongoroth of the Twelfth Legion of the Great Marquis Leraje, and when my master arrives, you and all your little fucking friends will know what suffering is!"

"Yeah, yeah," Noah sighed. "Anyway, thanks, bud." He grabbed the demon by the chin in one quick movement and poured the wine into its mouth, the glass shattering on the concrete floor as he took hold of the thing's head with both hands to clamp its mouth shut. Noah struggled to hold it still while it flailed, its body lifting as much as it could under the straps and slamming back onto the table with more force than should have been possible.

"Time to read, Julien!" Noah called, and the blond dutifully got to his feet and took a step closer.

"Exorcizámos te, ómnis immúnde spíritus, ómnis satánic potéstas, ómnis infernális adversárii, ómnis légio, ómnis congregátio et sécta diabólica, in nómine et virtúte Dómini nóstri Jésu Chrísti," Julien read from the phone's screen, and Noah wrapped both arms around the demon's head to keep it from tearing through the restraints.

The longer Julien went on, the angrier the demon became, its fingers clawing at whatever part of Noah it could reach, until it finally pulled against him once more, then collapsed onto the table. Noah waited a few beats, then slowly unclenched his grip from the host's head and leaned over to look the man in the face. His skin looked pinker, and his eyes were closed as if in sleep, his chest rising and falling at a more natural rhythm now. Satisfied, Noah straightened, his hands on his hips as he puffed out a breath and turned to look at Julien with a bright smile on his face.

"Not so bad, huh?"

Julien couldn't answer; he just laughed softly and shook his head.

Back upstairs, the other six Fournier brothers waited anxiously for them in the hallway. They all stared at Noah as he emerged and handed Joseph back his slightly less-full bottle of wine.

"Well," the witch said, "it's definitely demons. At least, that one was."

Edouard glanced at Joseph and nodded toward the basement, sending the taller man down the stairs without question.

"You're certain," Arnaud pressed.

Noah gave a small shrug. "Well it pretty much told me it was, and the exorcism worked on it, so, signs point to yes."

Another unnamed brother—the undoubtedly prettiest one, Noah noted—crossed his arms, running the fingertips of one hand pensively over his lips. "But that took so long," he said.

Noah stared at him, his breath still not entirely caught up with him from the fight of holding down the thrashing demon. "For real, man?"

The man shook his head and waved away Noah's words. "I only mean that we've been dealing with multitudes. Dozens over the last weeks." He glanced at his brothers in turn. "We couldn't possibly bring them all back here for a process like that."

Antony grunted impatiently. "So we're back to killing them."

"Wow," the last brother spoke up. "Will you chill?" This was the one who had greeted Julien kindly. Noah liked him already.

Edouard shot a glance over that silenced them both. "Now that we've confirmed that these people *are* able to be saved, that needs to be our priority."

Joseph reappeared in the stairway door with the demon's former host slung over his shoulder like a sack of potatoes, not seeming to suffer under the weight at all.

"He seems stable," he said. "I'll take him to the hospital."

Noah watched him walk down the hall and out the front door, more than one question on the tip of his tongue, but nobody else seemed concerned that Joseph was about to just carry someone down the street to the hospital, so he kept his concerns inside. The brothers continued to talk, but Noah's attention was drawn to the box he'd left on the floor across the hall—the dogs were reared onto their hind legs.

He hurried over to kneel next to the box and opened it up, scanning the letter inside. Sabin was having a problem with a spell—some sort of divination, repressed memories, maybe. Noah frowned down at the paper for a while, stretching his jaw while he scratched his cheek in thought. Then he called over to Julien, interrupting the pretty brother mid-sentence. "I need a butcher."

All of them paused and looked at him in confusion that ranged from genuine to disgusted.

"Why?" Julien asked for all of them.

"Sabin needs a sheep liver. For a spell. Is there one around?"

The friendly brother was already taking his phone from his pocket. "There's one a few blocks away. I'll find the address."

Antony scowled blatantly at Noah, but he didn't say anything, so Noah didn't have to be rude to him. Edouard looked briefly between the witch and the man who'd brought him here, and he exhaled evenly through his nose.

"You two get settled in for now. We can discuss what to do later on. Go on upstairs."

Julien didn't seem inclined to argue with the dismissal; he simply came over to Noah and scooped up his own bag, tilting his head to urge the witch to follow. At the top of the stairs, Julien took a right and opened the door closest to the loft railing, but he paused in the doorway when he realized Noah was still right behind him. He hesitated and shifted his duffel bag in his hand, glancing over at the stairs and the open door at his back before he would look Noah in the face.

"Ah. Maybe...you should stay in another room."

Noah frowned up at him. "Why? I want to stay with you. Let me see that childhood room," he teased, reaching up to lay a hand on the taller man's chest.

Julien gently pushed his hand back down. "I do too, but..." He lowered his voice and turned slightly so that his back was more toward the stairs. "Maybe it's best if we aren't...too obvious."

Noah recoiled slightly on instinct. "What do you mean, obvious?"

"I think you know."

"Are you serious right now?" Julien seemed uncomfortable with the volume of Noah's voice, but he didn't care. "You don't want your manly brothers to see manly Julien in a relationship with another guy?"

Julien shushed him and ushered him into the room so that he could shut them inside. He dropped his bag and put his hands on Noah's shoulders, frowning faintly. "It isn't just that."

"Oh, not *just*?"

Julien dropped his head briefly to sigh, then lifted it to look into the witch's eyes. "My father expects me to...continue the line, you know? Make more Fournier men to hunt more creatures. Some of the others have kids already, but since I'm the last, it's...different." He gave a small, helpless shrug. "It's not that I think my brothers would care...personally, I guess, to hear I was with a man, but it's a legacy thing, and...I know it's stupid. But I don't care about that so much; I'm going to have to deal with my father sooner or later anyway."

Noah could see that Julien was struggling, but he couldn't help the lingering frown on his own lips. "Then what is it?"

"It's...you're a witch," Julien said simply. "None of them are going to be happy if they find out I'm sleeping with...someone like that. Someone magic. We don't generally like magic."

Noah's nose scrunched in distaste, and he looked at the ground, fighting the urge to remove Julien's hands from his shoulders.

"I know," the blond said before Noah could voice his displeasure. "I'm really not trying to hide anything. I'm not ashamed of you, and I love you, and I want to be with you always, but I just...I need to find the right way to tell them so I don't just drop all of this on them. I promise I'm not trying to hide you, I just want things to go as smoothly as they can. Do you understand?"

Noah pressed his lips together and puffed out his cheeks to keep his sigh in. Julien was trying. This wasn't Travis. This wasn't only being gay in private. This was just...navigating family drama. Noah could understand that. "Well I get it," he said after a pause, looking up into Julien's frowning face. "Telling your family this sort of news is...very personal. But it sucks."

"I know," Julien agreed, noticeably softening at Noah's deflated anger.

"Can I at least sneak into your room at night?"

The blond smiled at him and moved one hand to his cheek, lightly stroking his jaw. "You won't have to sneak at all if you just give me some time. Please."

Noah took a deep breath and nodded. "Okay."

"Thank you. I promise I'll sort it out." He gestured toward the door, and Noah reluctantly followed him down the hall to the spare room, which was little more than another hallway with two sets of bunk beds against each wall.

Inside, Rathgeirr was sitting on the bottom bunk nearest the window, trying to get a look at the street outside. Ciaran and Trent were in the center of the room, and Noah entered just in time to see Trent with his arms around the fairy's waist, hefting him up off his feet and holding him there.

"You're still pretty light to me."

Ciaran wriggled until the boy set him down, then immediately scooped him up under his knees and shoulders like a bride. Trent allowed it until he spotted Noah and Julien in the doorway, at which he smacked Ciaran's chest sharply and was summarily dropped back to his feet.

"Maybe a little heavier," the fairy said with a pensive hum. "Rathgeirr, come here lad, would you?"

"What the hell are you doing?" Julien asked as he and Noah moved deeper into the room.

"I'm testing what's different," Ciaran answered without turning around. He beckoned Rathgeirr to his feet, and as soon as the alfar was standing, Ciaran picked him up and slung him over one shoulder, bouncing thoughtfully in place a few times before letting him down. "Hm. Not so bad."

Noah's brow furrowed. "Is this more 'side effects' you also

neglected to mention?"

"Oh," Ciaran said with a casual wave of one hand, "I think I've been made mortal by the spell you lot did to me, so I just want to know what my limits are now. Handy to know before I need to."

"Are you serious?"

"Don't fuss," Ciaran sighed. "It's fine. Rathgeirr, be a good lad and hit me in the face."

The alfar hesitated and glanced briefly at Noah as though the witch might advise him. "Why would I hit you?"

"Go on, boy; I'll be fine, probably."

Rathgeirr didn't move. "I...really don't want to hit someone in the face hard enough to test if they're mortal or not."

"I'll hit you in the face," Julien offered, but Ciaran scoffed at him.

"No thanks—I need someone actually strong, or what's the point?"

Noah instinctively put both hands on Julien's chest to keep him from proving Ciaran wrong. "Easy," he chuckled, and Julien snorted but stayed put.

Rathgeirr still hesitated, but Ciaran took a step closer to the alfar, jutted out his chin, and tapped his jaw encouragingly. After another reluctant pause, Rathgeirr swung. He obviously wasn't putting his full weight into the hit, but Ciaran still stumbled back a step and brought a hand up to his face. He worked his jaw to test its movement and spit a mouthful of blood into his palm, then let out a small sound of satisfaction.

"Well it's still black," he said, lifting his hand to show Trent the mixture of blood and saliva. "That's a good sign, I suppose. That wasn't half bad. I'm still pretty useful, I reckon."

Trent stood with his hands in his pockets and sighed. "Great. Glad we got it cleared up."

Noah dropped his bag near one of the empty bunks and turned back to them. "I am definitely interested in how this series of scientific experiments goes, but I need to get to a butcher. I'll get the address from...whichever that one brother is," he said on his way by Julien, not waiting for an answer in case the hunter offered to go with him. He loved Julien, but he wanted to get out into the city on his own.

"There you are," the smiling man said when Noah was back on the stairs. "C'est icitte." He showed Noah his phone so the witch could copy the address into his own map.

"Thank you—sorry, I don't know your name yet. There are so many of you."

"Hugo. And you're Noah, huh? I wouldn't have expected Julien to make friends with a witch. Maybe he's grown up a little, huh?"

Noah smiled. "It's hard to think of Julien as someone *not* grown up. But I know where you're coming from."

"I'm glad he has. He's always been so grumpy, you know? See if you can cheer him up a bit."

"I'll do my best. Hugo," he repeated with a smile. He wasn't going to need help remembering this one.

Before Noah left, he got the address for the library, and he went there first to make some copies from one of his books for Sabin. Hepatomancy would be the best choice for what he needed, Noah thought. It was a jaunt to the library, but it was a nice walk—the weather was cool, and Montreal was a pretty, old city with lots of cobblestone and brick. If they hadn't come under such crazy circumstances, Noah would have liked to do some sightseeing, but as it was, taking in the city to and from errands was likely the most he was going to get. The library was a beautiful building—all sleek glass and rounded, modern-looking chairs in open spaces. He wished he had more time to explore it. He got a few odd looks when he stood at the copier with his ancient, half-fallen-apart book splayed across the scanner, but they didn't bother him. He'd learned long ago to ignore the way people looked at him.

It felt a little like being out of the country with so much French spoken around him. Noah had learned some in school just like everyone else, but he'd gone so long without using it that now it was almost as if he'd never learned any at all. Luckily, both the librarian and the man behind the counter at the butcher shop were kind enough to speak to him in English when they noticed him struggling.

Back at the Fournier home, Noah carried his package upstairs and sat on his chosen bunk with his box, copying down instructions for the spell onto the back of a flyer the butcher had put into his bag. He folded the copies he'd made and tucked them into the box, then closed the lid and latched it, smiling faintly at the soft click it made as the silver dogs settled back into their lying positions.

"You two have a fight?" Ciaran asked, and Noah started slightly as he realized the room's other occupants were all staring at him.

He snorted and set his box down at the foot of the bed. "Surprise—turns out a culty monster hunter family probably won't like the idea of their star child being a gay witch-fucker. He's going to break it to them gently."

"Will he now," Ciaran murmured, and Noah frowned at the skeptical tone in the fairy's voice.

"Yes, he will. He said so."

"Aye, sure."

"Anyway," Noah said a little louder, "I'm more concerned about you saying you think you're mortal now. What's going on with that?"

Ciaran tugged the gold pendant from under his shirt and leaned against Noah's bunk to show it to him. "My gift from the goddess. It's cracked, see. I figured that meant I wasn't a favorite anymore. Hence the tests."

"Hm." Noah turned the pendant in his fingers, a thoughtful furrow in his brow, before dropping it back to Ciaran's chest. "With the kind of exchange the spell would have made, I guess that would make sense, assuming that the goddess you're talking about is some kind of still active spirit of some kind that's even capable of removing the blessings your people have been living with for some long, but..." He shook his head. "I'm sorry. Maybe we shouldn't have used a spell I knew so little about. There's no way we could have known the kind of consequences—"

"Pfft," Ciaran cut him off, dismissing his concerns . "You saved my life, lad. And Trent and I solved our problem. You came through in the end, after all. We're square."

Noah smiled faintly and kept his gaze to the floor, doing Trent the courtesy of pretending he couldn't see the tender look on the boy's face. "Okay then."

The dining room, it turned out, was just a big, blank room with nothing in it but a long cafeteria table and two simple benches for seats. It was attached to the kitchen by a half-wall, so Joseph was visible on the other side tending the stove. Noah had hope for the meal, since it at least smelled like real cooking, but the only things on offer were large piles of chicken breast, broccoli, and brown rice.

Julien's brothers piled up their plates, sat in a cluster at one end of the table to eat, and were already finishing up by the time the others arrived. Noah guessed he shouldn't have been surprised that they didn't want to actually share a meal. None of them except Hugo had anything but side-eyes to give their guests on their way out of the room, but Ciaran and Rathgeirr got the most blatantly mistrustful looks.

Julien still sat with them, at least. "I'm sorry about them," he said once they'd all settled with their plates. "This is just the way it's always been."

Noah didn't miss the resignation in the blond's voice. Julien had never had anything good to say about his life growing up, and he was quickly understanding why.

Rathgeirr picked up one of the larger pieces of broccoli from his plate with his fingers and held it up to Noah. "What is this called?"

"Broccoli."

"It's like a tiny tree!" the alfar laughed, shoving the floret into his mouth. "I love it."

Trent stared at him from farther down the table. "Are you actually five?"

"All this food," Ciaran said with a sneer, "but there isn't even any honey or cream in the kitchen. How am I supposed to live?"

Trent swallowed his own mouthful of rice. "Should you even still be eating that kind of crap? Or will you just get fat now?"

"Well I won't know if I don't try, will I?"

"So your answer is just to eat like garbage and see if you put on weight or not?"

"I only have so many years left now, a mhuirnín; I plan to enjoy them."

"Great," Trent sighed. "This will go well. Don't cry on me when you throw up later."

"I won't even get the chance in a place like this! It's like a prison!"

Noah glanced over at Julien, who ate the bland food without complaint or hesitation. He was probably used to it.

"I guess this at least explains how you all got so big, just eating like this all the time," he said, and Julien shrugged one shoulder.

"Food was never really about what tastes good. Just making sure you get what you need to be fit."

Noah reached over to him and gave his thigh a light squeeze under the table. "Good strategy for making handsome burly dudes, at least," he teased.

Julien looked over at him with that rare heat in his cheeks, then cleared his throat and focused purposefully on his plate. "We should probably try to get some rest pretty early tonight."

Noah smiled and released him, doing his best to enjoy his own serving of broccoli and rice. It was cute when he was shy.

Noah had a note on a scrap of paper and a long letter from Sabin waiting for him when he got back upstairs. The envelope felt heavy in his hands, so he read the note first.

Noah,

Thanks for the help. I'm excited to see everyone's face when I tell them how the spell works! >:) I'll write back tomorrow and let you know how it goes. Sorry my letter is so long, its chill if you don't want to read all of it.

This last line was hard to read, as it had been mostly scratched out, but below it, Sabin had tried again.

My letter is long because I've missed being able to tell you everything. I'm excited for you to read it.

Noah smiled so much it hurt his cheeks, but as he sat curled up on his bunk to read the letter itself, he couldn't help the tears that formed in his eyes. Without the censorship they'd suffered before, Sabin told him everything—what life had really been like in the underground bunker he'd spent the last few years in; the friends he'd made and the troubles he'd had; his suspicions about the higher-ups in his organization. He even talked about one of the boys in particular— Berlin. He told stories about the pranks he'd played on this poor person, his perfect, awful way of showing affection, and Noah felt sorry for him. He read the letter over and over again, covering his mouth with his fingertips to keep his occasional hiccup inside. His heart ached. He missed Sabin so much—being able to communicate freely with him was better than hearing nothing, for sure, but it was also its own kind of torture. Like being closer together, but still separated by glass.

"Are you okay?" Trent said uncertainly from the bunk across from him, and Noah sniffed, wiping his nose on the back of his hand.

"I'm fine," he promised. "It's just...it's nice getting to catch up with him."

"This is the kid you almost adopted or something?"

"Kind of, yeah. But some of the things he's saying in here..." Noah shook his head. "It's worrying. Can I use your laptop again?"

"Sure, if this weird halfway house has Wi-Fi."

Noah plugged in the laptop when Trent offered it to him and opened it up on the bed, giving it a minute to boot itself up. The closest router was still just named 'Lynksys 5981,' so Noah tried the password 'admin' and was promptly connected. Great monster hunters—not so great computer users. Noah settled in, hunched over the screen, and prepared to spend his night reading instead of sleeping.

"Let me know if...you know, if there's anything I can do to help," Trent offered.

Noah paused, looking over at him in mild surprise. Then he smiled. "I will."

3

By the time Trent woke up in the morning and peeled Ciaran's too-warm and too-close body away from him, Julien and the other six weirdly-like-him men had already left the house. When he'd been to the bathroom, showered, and brushed his teeth, he came back to find Noah stuffing things into his bag, another new packet of paper lying near the open fairy box.

"Are you leaving?" he asked, and the witch looked back at him over his shoulder.

"Library. I just got another letter from Sabin, and I need to figure some stuff out. Make copies. Print things."

Trent glanced over at the bunk where Ciaran was just beginning to stir. "Can I come with you?"

Noah's eyebrows lifted slightly. "I mean, I don't mind, but it'll probably be pretty boring for you."

"I just want to be somewhere normal for a while, honestly," Trent grumbled. He sat down on the bunk beside Ciaran to pull his shoes on and pushed the fairy away by his face when he tried to put his arms around his waist. "Go back to sleep. You're not coming."

"Why not? Give me a tick to put some clothes on, and—"

"Because if you go, then it's a field trip, and if everyone's going then Rathgeirr will want to come, and that defeats the purpose of this being a normal fucking thing. So go back to sleep. I'll bring you back something sweet."

25

"Agreed," Ciaran chuckled, and he pulled Trent's head close enough to press a kiss to his cheek before dropping back down onto the pillow without further argument.

He and Noah headed out onto the street once they were ready, Noah leading the way with a map open on his phone. Trent paused when they reached the main road at the end of the neighborhood.

"I think we can take the green line to get there quicker than walking," he said.

Noah stopped to look at him. "You know your way around Montreal?"

"Not really," he shrugged. "I came on school trips a couple of times, and the library is really nice, so I went a lot."

The witch laughed. "What a nerd."

"Fuck you."

"Thank god you said that though; it took me forever to walk yesterday. Lead the way."

Trent found the nearest metro station with the help of Noah's map, and he paid for them to ride with his dwindling supply of Canadian money. He tried not to think about what he and Ciaran were going to do when it actually ran out—assuming they survived the coming elf/demon apocalypse, that is. That would be future Trent's problem, he guessed.

Once they reached the library, Noah promptly spread his notes across one of the long tables near the public computers. He looked up the sections he needed and wrote down titles and Dewey decimals for Trent to fetch. Trent was glad to have something to do, though the collection of books in his arms wasn't exactly comforting—demons, Judeo-Christian mythos, occult studies, and a couple of titles Trent couldn't even guess at. He set them all on Noah's table for him and sat nearby while the witch pored over them, scanning each page deliberately and occasionally pushing an open tome toward Trent and directing him to get a copy made of this or that page.

With new papers added to the notes Noah had brought with him, and more than one book open on the table between them, Trent sat back in his seat and pulled his glasses from his face to wipe the lenses clean with his shirt.

"So, what is this we're looking at, exactly?"

"The demon we saw in Lochlann," Noah answered without looking up from the book he had in his lap, the spine propped up against the edge of the table. "Ashmodai. A.K.A. Asmodeus, apparently. One of the seven Princes of Hell. This one is the Prince of Lust. That's pretty hot."

Trent slipped his glasses back onto his nose so that he could better stare at the witch across from him. "The demon."

Now Noah did look up. "I mean, if he wasn't a demon; you know, the whole..." He made a gesture around his head to indicate the horns of the man they'd seen in the King's hall. "Woosh, and the veil and the long hair and everything. It was pretty sexy, right?"

"Uh-huh."

"Anyway," he went on, gesturing as if to brush off the thought, "apparently he's waging war on everyone on Earth, so I thought we should probably deal with that. And in a letter I got this morning, Sabin said he was behind the town he was in with all the people who were possessed, and *also* he's pretty sure he's helped some boss-type woman in this program he's in *summon* this demon. Which, in case you couldn't guess, is a pretty stupid idea. He didn't know what he was doing, but I saw the circle he said he drew for her, and..." He puffed his cheeks out in a sigh. "It also seems like one of the boys Sabin has been working with is someone that Ashmodai wants for...something? And he's also a demon? But he's nice? Oh and all this is on top of the fact that the Alfar, the immortal Viking warrior elves, are going to help them do it? Like, all of this is such bad news that I almost don't even know what to do with it."

Noah pushed his book back up onto the table and slumped over it, his arms dangling helplessly beside him as his cheek mushed against the open page. "I thought Sabin was safe," he said softly. "I thought he'd be fine in his secret underground government bunker or whatever the hell, but if he's dealing with all this too, and his friends are involved, I just...ugh," he sighed, turning his face into the book so that his voice was muffled by the paper. "I'm so worried about him."

Trent sat uncomfortably in his chair, unsure what to say that could possibly help the situation. He didn't know Noah very well at all, really, and even if he had, he wasn't very good at...empathizing. Thankfully, before he could say anything awkward, the witch lifted his head, took a deep breath, and forced a smile onto his face as he pulled the book into his lap again.

"But moping about it won't help. Think you have one more copy-making trip in you?"

By the time they left the library, Noah's bag was stuffed with folded papers. He followed Trent with one sheet still in his hand, scanning it as they walked, but when Trent turned to head back into the metro station, Noah stopped him with a casual hand on his elbow.

"Actually, I have another stop to make, if you want to come. I need more particular stuff than the supplies I have back at the house. I asked around last night and heard about a place in town to buy some stuff I can use."

Trent hesitated. "You mean witch stuff?"

"Yeah." Noah leaned a little closer to him with a cajoling smile. "Also, I'm running low on these fairy mushrooms I paid the guy in Belfast with and I don't know if this place takes barter, so I was maybe hoping I could lean on my rich kid friend a little bit?"

Trent frowned at him and leaned back instinctively to replace the distance between them. "I don't have infinite money."

Noah's expression softened. "You seemed like you didn't want to talk about it before."

"Yep," Trent agreed. "Still don't. Come on," he added quickly, "let's go get your witch crap."

Noah led them with his phone in his hand, and they walked together in silence, but Noah glanced at him out of the corner of his eye so often that Trent finally snapped at him.

"What?"

"Nothing," Noah lied, shrugging and tilting his head slightly as he looked over at the other boy. "Just...sometimes it's good to talk about stuff, you know? Even if there's nothing you can do about it."

"There's nothing to talk about," Trent insisted. "My dad kicked me out because it's disrespectful of your parents to like dick I guess, so I took what I could, and now I'm on my own. That's it."

Noah visibly winced, and it made Trent's stomach hurt to think the witch was pitying him. "Sorry," he said. "That's really rough."

"It is what it is," Trent answered without looking at him. This wasn't a conversation he wanted to have.

Noah leaned forward a little as they walked to try to catch his eye. "It's okay to admit when things are hard, Trent."

"It doesn't change anything to complain." Noah started to speak again, but Trent cut him off. "Are we almost there?"

Noah frowned, but he let it go and just looked back down at his phone. "Yeah," he said, more softly. "Almost there."

The storefront Noah stopped in front of was all glass, the display full of stained glass lanterns, herbs hung to dry in bunches, candles, and statuettes. The recessed red door sat underneath a hanging wooden sign, the golden script "Charmant Sortilèges" glimmering on a blue paint background. A five-pointed star had been drawn on the glass above the doorknob, surrounded by Hebrew letters, and underneath, a phrase in classic-looking calligraphy—*Boutique spécialisée en magie blanche et sapiences traditionnelles.*

Both of them stood looking at it for a few beats while Noah tucked his phone back into his pocket.

"Well," he said cheerfully, "my French sucks, but I know 'magie blanche' is white magic, so that's a good sign, right?"

"I guess?"

Noah pulled the door open and went inside with a smile on his face, barely bothering to hold the door for Trent behind him. The walls of the shop were lined with shelves, each one piled high with glass jars—some labeled and some not—or incense or candles or pentagrams or...were those animal parts? Ginger that tasted like peppermint and kept him from getting seasick was one thing, but this was real witch eye of newt stuff, and that was entirely different. Trent stood as close to the center of the room as he could, keeping his hands tucked inside his pockets while Noah circled the room, touching vials and jars and scooping up handfuls of herbs in baskets to bring them to his nose for a deep sniff.

"You know I said I'd go to the library because I wanted to go somewhere normal, right?" Trent pointed out while Noah held a jar of unidentified liquid up to the nearest light.

"This is normal!" the witch countered. "Ish," he added with a light laugh. "Don't worry about it; these things don't bite. I just need a few things. I'll only be a minute."

"It's already been so much longer than a minute."

"I'll hurry, okay? Simmer down."

Trent gave a silent sigh, but he waited while Noah finished searching every shelf in the place. With armfuls of his chosen goods, he finally looked back at Trent and waved him over to the counter with his head. Trent's high school French was only marginally better than Noah's, but he managed to make it through the transaction without the cashier laughing at him, so he considered it a success. He lamented the limited number of bills remaining in his wallet as he handed over payment for the witch's choices, but he kept it to himself.

"Thank you," Noah said earnestly once they were back on the street, both of them carrying plastic bags full of unknown ingredients. "Really. This stuff is to help all of us, but you still didn't have to pay for it." He nudged Trent with his elbow and smiled sidelong at him while they walked. "You're nicer than you let on."

"I'm really not," Trent assured him.

"Whatever you say. Anyway, you'll be happy to know that the next stop is a perfectly normal butcher shop."

"I didn't know there was a next stop. Why are we going to a butcher?"

"Sabin needs sheep livers for a spell he's doing, but since he's sort of on lockdown in the middle of Louisiana somewhere, and it's supposed to be a secret spell, he can't really ask his jailers for them."

"You're right. That's totally normal."

Noah shrugged. "I mean, the *butcher* is normal. I figure that's about the best you can really expect with the way our lives are right now, right?"

Trent scoffed quietly, turning his face toward the street so that Noah wouldn't see his faint smile.

Back at the house, Trent tempted Ciaran away from the bunk room with a honey bun he'd picked up on the way home to keep him away from Noah while he worked. They wandered the house together, the only sound between them the crinkling of Ciaran's plastic wrapper. The place seemed far too empty for how many people were staying there—something about it felt hollow. No artwork broke up the stark whiteness of the walls; no rugs hid the years of scuffs on the floor; no spare furniture filled the space. There was nothing. Just hallways full of closed doors that neither Trent nor Ciaran were exceptionally keen to try to open.

They found some milk in the refrigerator downstairs, at least, so Ciaran helped himself to that, and they sat on a bench in the lonely mess hall while Ciaran licked the last bits of sticky glaze from his fingers. Trent hesitated to speak and ruin the rare quiet, but he couldn't keep his worry inside any longer.

"Are you...okay?" he asked, softly, as if someone might hear him caring. "With all of this. The...spell and everything. You're feeling okay?"

"Ach, I'm fine," Ciaran snorted, pausing to take a long swig of milk. "We discussed it already, didn't we? No problems at all. We'll get this war business sorted, and then we'll away to Greece."

Trent shook his head and leaned his elbows on the table with a small sigh. "Just like that, huh?"

"Aye," Ciaran said. He reached out and took up the boy's hand, drawing it close so that he could kiss his knuckles. "Just like that. It's not worth fussing, a mhuirnín. Things will go as they go. As long as you're right beside me, we'll end up all right somehow."

Trent's cheeks warmed, and he pulled away and wouldn't meet Ciaran's eyes. "Now my hand is sticky. Thanks a lot."

The fairy gave a low chuckle that spread the heat deeper into Trent's skin. "I'm going to get the rest of you sticky in a minute."

"Not when we're sharing bunk beds you're not," he grumbled.

Ciaran scooted closer to him on the bench and leaned over to murmur close against his ear. "Just you wait."

4

Julien sat on the old bed in his room, aching down to his bones but still upright. He'd brought another possession victim back to the house in the afternoon and helped Noah perform the exorcism, which had gone as well as could be expected. But it took longer than the first. Noah didn't want to say that it took a lot out of him, but Julien could see it in his face. It was possible to help people this way, but Laurent had been right—this was too inefficient. It wouldn't solve their current problem, or the one that was soon to come. They would have to come up with a better solution.

For now, Julien struggled to listen to the witch who sat beside him with a packet of papers in his hands. His clothes were filthy—just because the demons were their main problem, that didn't mean they were the only things that needed killing around Montreal—and he hadn't had anything to eat since breakfast, but Noah had pulled him upstairs the moment he came in the door and told him it was important, so he was trying to pay attention.

"Look at this. I got this from Sabin this morning," Noah said, pushing the papers into Julien's hands.

The hunter frowned down at the page, skimming the messy handwriting, and he looked back up at Noah with confusion on his face. "Your kid...has a crush on some other kid?"

"What?" Noah said. He looked over at the page Julien was reading and snatched it away again. "No, no, not that. Don't look at that." He leaned over Julien to flip through the papers for him and find the right one. "This one. The part about the demons."

Julien paused to rub at his eye with one knuckle before trying again. His frown deepened the longer he read—demon summoning, bargains, kidnapping? "This is...complicated."

"Yeah, no shit," Noah agreed with a dry laugh. "I tried to look up what I could about this guy and figure some things out, but I think I need more information from Sabin directly. From what he said, he had a literal angel with him it sounds like, and that was the only way they could effectively deal with the possessed people in those numbers. I don't happen to know any angels, so I think we're out of luck there. And that's not even considering how adding the alfar to this shit pot is going to make it so, so much worse."

Julien sighed and let Noah take the papers back from him. "Lugh will be here tomorrow. He won't be happy to hear we've made no progress, but maybe we can come up with something better once we have everyone in the same room."

Noah carefully folded the letter back up, as if he was afraid any more of his young friend's feelings would escape. "I don't suppose you've talked to your brothers yet, and I can stop sleeping in the other room? Rathgeirr snores."

Julien shifted guiltily on the mattress. "Yeah, it...it hasn't really come up. We've all been busy, and—"

"Sure," Noah said without looking at him.

"Noah, I'm sorry. I really will tell them soon. It's just...with everything going on, it's hard for me to start an argument on purpose on top of all that."

"I get it," Noah assured him. "But I don't like feeling like I'm being hidden."

"You're not," he promised, reaching over to cover one of the witch's hands with his. "I'm sorry. I will tell them."

Noah paused, and then he glanced over at the blond out of the corner of his eye, a sly smile playing at the corners of his lips. "But these doors have locks on them, right?"

"Yes?" Julien said, frowning, and Noah cast his eyes over to the closed bedroom door, where the click of the lock sounded from across the room. Realization thumped into Julien's chest, and he tensed. "Noah," he started carefully, "we shouldn't; it's an old house, and...things...make noise, and if one of my brothers knocks—"

"Then tell them it's been a long, frustrating day, and you're jerking off." Noah was already kicking off his shoes and crawling up to kneel on the bed, his shirt up and over his head a moment later.

Julien swallowed hard at the sight of the lean, pale skin exposed in the dim light of his room, trying to ignore the tightness growing in his belly. "Noah," he tried again, "I haven't showered—I'm pretty sure I've got blood on me. You really don't want to—"

The witch pushed him down onto his back and smoothly moved to straddle his hips, slender fingers already working on his belt buckle.

"Oh, I really do," he purred. "You're not the only one it's been a tense day for."

With Noah half naked on top of him, pulling at the button of his jeans, Julien was helpless. His hands were on the witch's hips, keeping him close while Noah bent over him to bite a few kisses along the line of his jaw.

"We have to be quiet," Julien whispered, knowing he didn't have to voice his surrender. "Please."

Noah's tongue brushed the blond's earlobe, and he murmured, "Worry about yourself being quiet."

Julien bit the inside of his cheek as Noah freed his erection, stroking him with an easy, eager hand. He ran his unoccupied fingers underneath Julien's shirt, pushing it up past his stomach to his chest and leaning back just enough to let the blond sit up and pull it free. He pulled Noah down to him with one hand at the back of his head to catch him in a kiss, the other fighting to unfasten the witch's belt. Noah only let out soft, muffled whimpers into the kiss, but each one sent a jolt of suspense up the hunter's spine. He knew he should have pushed Noah away—should have insisted that this wasn't the time or place—but he had no defense against this man.

He lifted Noah with him as he sat up, causing a quiet bubble of laughter, and he turned the smaller man onto his back, urging him to pick up his hips so that Julien could tug down his jeans and toss them away. He spread the witch's thighs with a gentle hand and bent over him to taste his lips again. Noah writhed underneath him, desperate for Julien's firm grip around his cock, scratching blunted fingernails against the hunter's sides as he pushed up into his touch. Noah was so beautiful like this—his back curved into a steep arch, pale nipples begging to be bitten, muscles tightening with every gasp. Julien looped an arm under the small of the witch's back and left kisses over the soft skin of his stomach, keeping him lifted slightly from the bed. Noah twitched underneath him as the blond's tongue touched the line of his hips, and Julien hesitated, unable to ignore how close he was to the witch's erection.

Even the notion of performing oral sex on another man sent a wave of embarrassment through Julien as soon as it crossed his mind. He'd certainly never done it before—but Noah had done it to him, hadn't he? It hadn't seemed strange then. It wasn't fair to think of it as strange, was it? If Noah had been a woman, would Julien be hesitating now? Putting someone else's dick in his mouth was farther along the spectrum toward 'gay' than Julien had ever considered himself, and that shouldn't—didn't—matter to him, but that didn't change the fact that it was completely foreign to any experience Julien had thus far. But if Noah wanted him to do it, he should, shouldn't he?

He realized with a start that Noah was looking down at him, cheeks flushed, breath still shallow but a faint, understanding smile on his lips.

"Julien," he said softly, "you don't have to do anything you're not comfortable with."

"No," the blond insisted. "I want to." He pressed another kiss to Noah's stomach so he wouldn't have to look him in the face, and he began to stroke him again as he inched a little lower. But what if he did it, and he was awful? What if the whole thing was ruined because Julien had no idea what he was doing? There was no way this would be the witch's first blowjob—and no way Julien could hope to compare to the experience of...someone more skilled.

When Noah began to laugh, Julien realized precisely how long he'd been doing nothing but staring at the other man's dick in his hand. Heat flooded his face, but he fought the urge to retreat.

"I'm sorry," Noah said, hiding his laughter with one hand. "You just look so serious. I promise, you really don't have to; it's okay."

Julien's grip tightened on him, causing a hitch in his breath that cut his next laugh short. Noah expected him to fall short in this. Expected him to hesitate. To pull away. So with one slow, warning brush of his tongue, Julien took the witch into his mouth. Noah gasped sharply, his thighs tightening against the hunter's shoulders and his head falling back against the pillow. The witch's hand moved in startled, jerking movements down to touch Julien's head, fingers fastening in the blond hair but not pulling. Julien did his best to move smoothly, taking Noah as deeply as he dared and letting his hand make up the difference. It was a strange sensation, but the way Noah whined and bucked underneath him, panting and whispering the hunter's name, was intoxicating.

Noah was doing a progressively worse job of being quiet the longer Julien went. His fingers scraped into the sheets and against the hunter's scalp, and his breath caught in his chest, hips lifting to press deeper into Julien's mouth.

"Julien, if you—I'm—fuck," the witch breathed. "I'm gonna—"

Julien almost pulled back on instinct, but he didn't have time. Noah's grip tightened in his hair, and with a half laughing, relieved cry, the witch's head fell back and his back arched as each pulse of his orgasm spilled bitter fluid into the back of Julien's throat. He wasn't ready for it. He coughed as he retreated, sitting back on his heels and covering his mouth with a closed fist to stifle it. Below him, Noah had slumped into the mattress with his head to one side, his pale skin flushed and his chest heaving for air. His fingers slowly unclenched and flattened against the sheets, and when he opened his eyes and looked up at Julien with a slow, foxlike smile, the hunter took him by the legs and flipped him effortlessly over onto his stomach.

Noah laughed, helping to situate himself on his elbows once he landed, but when Julien hiked him up onto his knees and pushed down on the space between his shoulder blades to arch his back, the laughter died, sucked up into a gasp. Julien didn't hesitate now. He left a few bites, a little rougher than he intended, on the skin of Noah's back and ass, and when he spread him open with firm hands and ran his tongue over him, he was rewarded by a startled, quivering moan barely muffled by the pillow. Noah pushed back shamelessly against him, urging him on with whispers and pants and lowering his face to the mattress, hands lacing together as his arms curled behind his head in an attempt to steepen the arch of his back.

"Fuck, Julien, please—please, I want you inside me," he begged, and the hunter had no argument to give. He straightened and moved in close, taking hold of Noah's hand and guiding it underneath them so that the witch's hand could smooth the now-familiar slick liquid from his spell over Julien's cock.

Julien tested the readiness of the man under him by sliding a single lubricated finger inside of him, but Noah whined and reached back to slap plaintively at the blond's thigh.

"Fuck me already," he commanded, so Julien complied. He laid a steadying hand on Noah's hip and eased into him, forcing himself to wait through the hiss the witch gave as he adjusted to the intrusion. When Noah sighed and rolled his hips against his lover's, Julien began to move, bending to wrap an arm around the smaller man's waist so that he could taste the flushed skin of his back.

There was no pretending they were being quiet now. Noah whimpered and moaned and planted his palms against the headboard to gain purchase that allowed him to rock back against Julien at the pace he demanded from the hunter. Julien kept up with him despite his own shallow breath. Noah was too tight around him, too wanting, too shivering in his cries. There was no way Julien could last. When Noah pushed up onto his hands and took hold of the top of the headboard so that he could take what he wanted with more force, Julien was helpless, unable to pull his attention from the lean muscle that shifted under the pale skin of the witch's back.

"Don't you dare come yet," Noah panted, throwing a glance over his shoulder that made the blond go weak.

"Pas de promesses," Julien answered with a tight chuckle in his throat, but he did his best, hands touching whatever soft skin he could reach and finally dropping to catch himself on the bed as he fell over the younger man's back. He pushed into Noah as deeply as the stop of his own hips would allow, shifting until he found just the right angle to make the witch attempt to muffle his moan in his own bicep. Noah's grip on the headboard failed, so he settled for arching low into the mattress again and letting Julien take him.

"God, Julien, just—just like that—fuck, I want your come in me, please—"

Noah didn't have to finish the thought. Julien gripped him so tightly he worried he might bruise him, a tight groan escaping his own throat as his cock pulsed deep inside the other man, each wave rocking him forward a little, so that when he could finally relax, he had to force himself back onto his heels to release his softening erection and allow Noah to collapse onto his belly on the mattress. Julien eased himself down beside the witch, the muscles in his legs complaining from the prolonged tension, and he put a hand in Noah's slightly damp hair and inched forward to kiss him.

"Not sorry," Noah said with a sleepy smile on his lips, and Julien chuckled.

"At least if they heard, I'll have a good opportunity to tell them the truth."

"That's positive thinking."

They laid together for a while, Noah's head tucked underneath Julien's chin like it was made for the space and his fingers curled loosely between them to toy with the blond's chest hair. Julien almost dozed off, but he stirred when Noah sat up. He bent down and placed another kiss on Julien's lips, then hauled himself over the larger man's body so he could put his feet on the floor.

"I guess I'll leave you to your manly straight man business," he teased. Julien rolled over and wrapped his arms around the witch's waist, impeding his attempt to reach for his discarded pants.

"I love you," he murmured against Noah's skin. "I'll tell them."

"I know you will," Noah promised. He turned and stroked Julien's hair, then bent to kiss his temple. "And I love you, too. Let's find some food, tough guy."

5

Julien spent the following day out in the city, in almost constant communication with his brothers, searching for any sign of the sort of thing Sabin had mentioned—a portal, or a nest, or anything that looked like it might be the source of the demons or their way into this world. Arnaud had acquired crucifixes and supplies of holy water for each of them to use, but since they were trying to keep the hosts alive, their options were limited to damage control.

Three people made it back to the house over the course of the day, all of them captured by Edouard and Joseph, and Noah dutifully performed the exorcisms with Julien's help, but it was exhausting him. Still, when they finished, he simply smiled, waved goodbye to Julien again, and shut himself in the bunk room upstairs to return to his notes. He told Julien he'd been trying to put out feelers among his fellow witches online, but without giving too much away about their situation, there didn't seem to be much for them to do except for what they were already doing.

On top of that, another day had now passed, and Julien still hadn't said a word to any of his brothers about the reality of his relationship with Noah. When he returned to the house with Arnaud in the evening, he spotted Noah at the foot of the stairs, clearly trying not to watch him too closely. Julien could guess what the look was for. he wanted to be able to sleep next to Noah, too—and they'd already wasted two nights. This was supposed to be the day Lugh arrived, so it was likely to be their last chance for even the relative quiet they'd enjoyed since arriving in Montreal.

His other brothers trickled in, all of them just as weary, famished, and frustrated as Julien himself, but when it was time for them all to file into the dining room, Julien caught Hugo by the elbow and pulled him to the far end of the hallway.

"I need to talk to you," he said in French, keeping his voice low.

"Are we conspiring for takeout?" Hugo asked with a tired laugh. "I'm in. After the day I had, the last thing I want is Antony's burned chicken."

"No, listen—Hugo, if I tell you something, I need you to tell me what the others will say."

His brother laughed. "You think I know better than you?"

Julien allowed himself a faint smile, but he shook his head. "This is important. You know Noah, the witch I brought with me?"

Hugo furrowed his brow and pursed his lips, looking at his little brother like he thought he might have hit his head. "Julien, you've both been here for three days already. Yeah, I know him."

"Right," Julien sighed. "I know. I know. But here's the thing. You see—he and I...even though he's a witch, he's...more than a friend to me."

Hugo nodded his understanding. "Like a best friend?"

"Well—yes, but no."

"Ah, so like a partner."

"Yes precisely," Julien agreed quickly, tapping his brother on the shoulder. "A partner."

"But you said that already. Who cares?"

"Hugo, you don't understand—"

"I'm getting hungry enough to eat Antony's cooking now, Julien; can we go?"

"You're not understanding me," Julien insisted. "Noah is my best friend, my partner, my..." He trailed off and rolled his hands as though his brother should be able to extrapolate his meaning, but Hugo only stared at him in hungry impatience, so Julien sighed and dropped his hands back to his side. "He's my *boyfriend*, Hugo."

Hugo had leaned his head to look past Julien at the dining room door, but now he snapped his gaze back to his younger brother's face. "Boyfriend?" he echoed. "What, for real?"

"Yes, for real."

"But...you're not gay."

Julien ran a hand through his hair and gave an awkward half shrug. "I didn't think so," he admitted. "It's complicated."

Hugo lowered his voice to match Julien's hushed tone. "How long have you two been together?"

"Not...that long," Julien said.

"Is it serious? If it's not serious, you probably just shouldn't say anything."

"It is serious," Julien said immediately. "I love him," he went on. A twist of embarrassment grew in his gut, but he was determined not to let Noah down again.

Hugo took a deep breath and let it out in a sigh, his lips pulling into a grimace as he rubbed a hand over the back of his neck. "He's a witch, Julien. And you know Edouard is going to tell you about all the sons you're supposed to have."

"I know, I know. That's why I told you first."

"Well, why don't you just keep quiet about it? Once this is over, and we all split up again, you can just ignore Father and Edouard until they die."

Julien shook his head. "I shouldn't have to hide him. This is my life, no matter what they think—and I get to decide who I spend it with."

"Ahh, Julien," Hugo sighed, reaching up to lay a hand on the other man's shoulder. "Such youthful innocence."

"Fuck you, Hugo," Julien shot back, but his brother was laughing. He slapped Julien's arm and took a step backward toward the dining room.

"Well, I think you knew how it will go before you asked me. But I'll back you up if they start yelling."

Julien grumbled his thanks and followed him down the hall, where everyone else had already found places along the table. He saw Hugo wink at Noah as he passed him, and the witch looked up at Julien in confusion, but he waved it off. He took a seat on the bench in between the two groups, and once everyone had settled, Julien steeled himself and loudly cleared his throat.

"I have something to tell you," he said. All of his brothers were watching him, but Julien kept his eyes on Edouard, who lifted a curious brow at him. "Noah and I are in a relationship. A romantic relationship," he clarified immediately.

He expected the slight recoil of surprise he saw in each of his brothers. Edouard's normal frown deepened into a scowl, and near the end of the table, Antony leaned forward with a sneer on his face to direct his disgust at Noah directly. Julien could feel eyes on him from his end of the table, too, but he didn't turn to see.

"I'm not going to stop seeing him just because he's a witch," he went on, forcing himself to hold Edouard's stern gaze. "I trust him with my life, and I don't want to hear any shit about passing on legacies or how important it is to make another Fournier like me. I love him, and that's it," he added firmly.

Laurent gave a faint snort but had the decency to hide it behind his hand and play it off as a cough. Joseph barely seemed to be listening— he was staring down at his plate with his hands in his lap, as if he was trying to decide if it would be rude to continue eating during this discussion.

Edouard leaned an elbow on the table and stared over at Julien. "You know you have a responsibility to this family. To the world."

"I don't *care*, Edouard," Julien sighed. "I can hunt monsters until I die whether I'm a father or not, and some of *you* can try to make seven boys if you feel that strongly about this shit."

"But he's a witch!" Antony snapped, gesturing broadly across the table at Noah. "Are you stupid? You're sharing a bed with an abomination!"

"Shut your mouth, Antony," Julien growled.

"It's bad enough you brought all these *things* into the house, and we're expected to treat them like guests!"

Hugo slapped the table in front of Antony to get his attention and pointed an accusing finger at him. "They *are* guests, and the witch has been helping free people from possession for three days already, so maybe you should open your eyes!"

Antony stood and leaned on the table to point all the way down at

Rathgeirr, who frowned, as though surprised to be included in this argument. "*That thing* is one of the things we're supposed to have to fight! And you want me to sit down and eat dinner with it!" He moved his hand to indicate Ciaran, the next target of his tirade. "That one is a known killer! Julien was actively hunting it himself just a few weeks ago! And now our brother is sleeping with a witch, who we're letting bring spellbooks and supplies and God-knows-what into our house?" He locked his gaze on Julien with a scowl. "Maybe it's Julien we shouldn't trust anymore."

"Antony, that's enough," Arnaud cut in.

"He's lost his mind!" Antony shot back. "How do you all sleep at night knowing what's under our roof?"

"Antony," Edouard growled. "Go cool off."

Antony glanced at each of his brothers, nostrils flaring in rage, but then he lifted his hands. "When one of these *creatures* gets us all killed, it'll be too late to tell me I was right." He shoved his plate away from him, spilling rice onto the table, and stalked out of the room. Julien did his best not to sigh too loudly, but Hugo did it for him.

Edouard turned his attention back to Julien now. "This isn't something I can just ignore, Julien."

Arnaud interrupted before Julien could respond. "Edouard, we have more important things happening right now. Let's deal with those first."

Edouard remained silent and frowning across the table at his youngest brother, but after a long pause, he nodded. "It can wait," he said. The "but not forever" was unspoken, but Julien heard it nonetheless.

His brothers cleared out of the room quickly after that—mostly from the universal Fournier trait of simply avoiding uncomfortable personal situations—and Julien was left sitting a short distance away from Noah and the others, passing the awkward silence by staring down at his plate.

Finally, from the end of the table, Ciaran called out, "Why didn't you just move him into your room when we arrived and deal with it if they noticed instead of giving a speech? Fucking idiot," he added with a laugh.

Noah shushed him and reached over to slap at his hand, then

scooted down the bench to rub Julien's arm, which successfully prevented him from going across the table at the fairy.

"It was very sweet," Noah said quietly, offering him a reassuring smile. "Not...exactly what I thought you meant when you said you'd tell them, but sweet."

Julien kept his eyes on his half-eaten food. He *was* an idiot.

Ciaran didn't let him wallow. "And anyway, where the hell is my son? Isn't it the third day? Or did losing my magic make me forget how to count?"

Julien's eyes narrowed slightly. That was decidedly more pressing.

6

Ciaran was bored out of his mind. The whole house was on edge since Lugh hadn't shown up yesterday, but they had no choice but to carry on like normal—which meant the human hunters going out and doing all the work, and Ciaran being left on house arrest with Rathgeirr. The alfar seemed satisfied to sit on his bunk by the window and watch YouTube on Trent's laptop or eat bowl after bowl of cereal from the kitchen, but Ciaran was getting antsy.

He was still adjusting to his new bodily state—it was a different feeling, somehow, even though not much seemed to have changed about him physically. He grew tired more easily, perhaps. It was hard to put his finger on, but he didn't feel ill, and he'd tested picking things up around the house and found his strength only slightly wanting, so he kept his thoughts to himself. Trent was stressed enough.

Noah was visibly anxious, too—he sat with Rathgeirr all morning, studying some of the books they'd stolen from the library in Falias, but he kept looking at the small box on the bed beside them, as if he hoped every moment he might have missed its latest message.

Ciaran was more irritated that Lugh was late.

In the middle of the afternoon, when the humans had gathered to reconvene and compare notes in their dedicated conference room, three loud knocks sounded at the front door, but it opened before anyone had time to answer them.

Ciaran saw his son in the doorway from the foot of the stairs, and he crossed the hallway to meet him as the brothers began to appear from behind the closed doors of the war room. "About time, mo mhac."

Lugh looked down at him, apparently unmoved by the scolding. "It has been three days," he pointed out.

"Actually," Julien said, "this is the fourth day we've been here."

"And thus three full days have passed since you left. It wasn't an estimation, an duine."

The hunter did a good job holding in his sigh. "I'm glad you're here now," he said, and the relief on his face was obvious. He turned to face his brothers, who Ciaran was satisfied to see all noticeably hesitant to get very close to their new visitor. Ciaran could brush off being called a "thing," but he suspected the same childish tantrums wouldn't be directed at his son. Though a part of him hoped they would—the one named Antony deserved to have his head put through something hard.

"This is Lugh Lámfada," Julien said, addressing his family's tense faces. "General of the Tuatha Dé Danann. He's convinced his people to help us, I hope?" he added with a glance up to Lugh.

"As agreed."

"And these are my brothers." The hunter introduced them all in turn, but Lugh didn't even try to feign interest. He nodded politely, then looked pointedly down at Julien.

"I assume you have news for me."

The others had come downstairs to investigate the noise, and Ciaran waved Rathgeirr along to join them as everyone filed back into the room so that Lugh could be apprised. More than one of the humans cast skeptical looks at all three of them, but before anyone could object, Lugh was already addressing them.

"Tell me what you've been dealing with here."

They all waited while Julien got him caught up on the situation in Montreal—the nature of the possessed people they'd come across, Noah's effective but inefficient exorcism method, and the increasing numbers present in the city.

"But we've had no luck locating the...entry, or whatever they're using," Julien finished. "We don't know how many there actually are or where they're coming from."

"That is likely a problem that must be solved at the source, and that source may not be in the city at all," Lugh answered, his eyes skimming the maps and pins on the table. After a moment, he returned his attention to Julien again. "The Tuatha Dé Danann are ready to sail for Lochlann at my order. I sent scouts ahead when you left Tír na nÓg, and they've confirmed that the Lochlannan have been on the move already. Some smaller vessels have left the island and sailed South, but we don't yet know their destinations—have you seen any here?"

"None except the one standing there now," Arnaud said dryly.

"The bulk of their forces have yet to depart," Lugh went on. "If we can cut them off and stop the two main forces from meeting up at all, that would be ideal." He turned to Rathgeirr, who stood up a little straighter upon being noticed. "Do you have any idea of the potential numbers we're dealing with?"

The alfar paused. "You mean...*everyone*? Well, they won't send everyone I suppose, but—the soldiers...each city has four Yfirmaður, and each commands at least fifty ships. A snekkja will hold about forty men, a skeid about sixty, and a busse eighty, but the fleets may be made up of different numbers of those, so it's hard to say exactly."

Laurent leaned a hand on the table and stared across the table at Rathgeirr in disbelief. "So what you're saying is that we're looking at a fighting force of at least thirty-two thousand, and maybe double that."

Rathgeirr looked apologetic, but all he could offer was a small shrug.

"That is a great number of ships," Lugh said with a frown.

"A great number *more* than you have?" Edouard asked.

"I have little over five hundred birlinn, and I'm sure they are neither swifter nor better built than those of the Lochlannan. And my men are not naval fighters. It would be better to catch them farther North, before they can get the full force of their numbers behind them, and run them aground. If we can't pin them down on Lochlann itself before they embark, we'll have to engage them somewhere we can corral them."

He pushed some papers off the table out of his way, ignoring Edouard's muttering of irritation, and exposed a world map that had been unrolled at one end of the surface. He spread it flat before him and tapped a part of the ocean between Greenland and Russia. "Lochlann is here," he said, "in what's called the Barents Sea. Depending on where their destination actually is, they may sail past Éire to reach the mainland, or they may pass closer to An Íoslainn to get to North America, if that is indeed their goal. Either way, they will pass through the Norwegian Sea, which is a broad enough passing that I wouldn't count on being able to effectively block it." He addressed his next question to Julien, which visibly rankled the eldest brother. "Do we know where the demons' leader is now? Where they may try to meet?"

"No idea," the hunter admitted. "If those are the kind of numbers the Alfar are providing, for all we know, the demons we've encountered here might just be stragglers."

Noah spoke up from the door, where he and Trent waited and listened. "Sabin might know more," he said. "But I haven't heard back from him yet."

"We don't have very long to wait," Lugh answered. "The Lochlannan will not dally."

"I can write to him again," the witch promised. "Just give me time to get an answer." Without waiting for permission, he hurried back down the hall, footsteps rushing up the stairs.

Lugh watched him go, but then frowned at Julien. "We cannot wait for information that may not come."

"I know. Can we at least put it off until the morning? The kid is the best potential lead we have. If he doesn't have an answer, we can reevaluate then. I don't want you to have come here for nothing."

"I won't have," Lugh said simply, and he finally turned his gaze on Ciaran. "Are you fit after your injury? Can you fight?"

Ciaran considered himself lucky that Noah had run off when he had, since he definitely would have called Ciaran out and told his secret if he'd still been there. "I can fight," he said.

"Then you can sail. I'll need every man I can get." He looked to Rathgeirr, his eyes scanning him quickly as though sizing him up. "Will you come? Can you fight your own people?"

Rathgeirr paused, reaching up as though he meant to finger the bowstring he expected to find at his chest and then forcing his hands back down to his sides when he found it missing. He nodded. "They're in the wrong. I haven't seen much of the human world yet, but...I want to see more. And they would destroy it. So I'll help you."

"Good."

Trent's hesitant step forward from the doorway made Ciaran turn.

"I'm coming too," he said, glancing uncertainly between father and son.

Lugh's eyebrows lifted slightly. "You, lenab? You'll be killed," he said flatly. "Better you stay far away from the fighting, as before."

"I'm not staying behind again," the boy insisted. With tension in his shoulders and a frown on his lips, he looked Ciaran in the eyes with such determination that it startled him. "I'm not letting you go off to some war without me."

Ciaran smiled at him, his voice soft as he answered, "I wouldn't dream of leaving you, a mhuirnín."

Lugh said nothing, but the glance he gave Ciaran said enough—this was ill-advised, and he wouldn't be responsible if something happened to the boy. That was fine. It wasn't Lugh's job to keep Trent safe—it was Ciaran's, and he'd do it gladly.

Lugh steered the conversation back to business by speaking to Julien again. "Is there anything you need from me with regard to what's happening here? I can't leave you any soldiers, but if I'm staying until tomorrow in any case, perhaps personally, I—"

Antony interrupted him with a snarl. "Nobody asked you to come in here and try to take everything over, creature."

Lugh paused, and he subtly straightened as he turned his gaze to the glaring young man with the air of someone absolutely unaccustomed to being interrupted. Ciaran fought to stifle his grin.

"Have men fallen so far they've forgotten how to hold their tongues in the presence of their betters?" Lugh asked in a low, dangerous voice.

"Antony," Julien scolded, "do you want to solve this problem or don't you?"

"Why is it *you* who gets to decide how we solve it? We don't need this thing to do it for us!"

"Boy," Lugh spoke over him, "in these past three days, I have raised an army of immortals thirty thousand strong and ready to sail at my command to defend *your* human cities. What have you accomplished in the same time?"

"Not much," Edouard cut in before Antony could spit any more venom. He looked around the table at his younger brothers and spoke through a tight jaw. "I like this just as little as any of you, but the situation presented to us is...desperate. We have to focus on the goal— and that is to protect the people."

"But Edouard," Antony almost begged, "to rely on magic—"

"I don't see you presenting any other fucking options, Antony! What do you suggest, eh? If you think of a way to win this fight by bitching about it, you let me know—but in the meantime, maybe we ought to at least listen to the offer of the man with the soldiers! Beau cave," he finished with disgust.

Antony finally shut his mouth. He shoved away Hugo's hand when the other man tried to pat his shoulder and stood with his arms folded, silent but glaring across the table at Julien.

Lugh allowed a single beat to pass, then returned his attention to Julien as if the interruption had never happened. "Perhaps personally I can be of some help. You said you've been capturing some of these people and releasing them once they're cured—but you're still none the wiser as to their numbers or plans?"

"Well," Julien began with a shrug, "the hosts don't remember anything once they wake up, and the demons themselves aren't very talkative."

Lugh tilted his head slightly. "How persuasively have you asked?"

From farther down the table, Laurent said, "I wouldn't think a demon could be intimidated."

"Anything can be intimidated," Arnaud answered with a dry chuckle. "He's right. We should try."

Ciaran didn't bother voicing the very high likelihood that the witch actually performing these exorcisms wasn't going to be keen on the sort of aggressive asking they were suggesting. It wasn't his business. He backed away from the table while the others kept talking and took Trent by the hand on his way out, walking back toward the stairs with him.

"Wait," Trent said, though he still walked next to the fairy, "why are we leaving? Aren't they still talking about important things?"

"Not to me," Ciaran shrugged. "You heard it—you and I are leaving in the morning, bound for Lochlann. The rest is details."

Trent frowned at him as they entered the bunk room upstairs. "Are you going to tell Lugh about your magic?"

"Oh yeah I will," Ciaran snorted. "Are you joking? What for?"

Trent took a seat on the bunk they'd been sharing, his brow furrowed in concern but his eyes not meeting Ciaran's. "You were so convinced we were all going to die just going to that island at all. And that was when we were trying to be friendly. This is a hundred times worse than that. Don't you think with how dangerous this is, you should be sharing information?"

"He's not asking me to come along to do magic," Ciaran scoffed. "He just needs more people to hit Lochlannan in the teeth. That I can do. I don't need magic to fight."

Trent stared up at him. "Last time you were in a fight, didn't you get fatally stabbed? Or did I imagine that part?"

"Nobody's ever called you sweet, have they?"

"You're not taking this seriously."

Ciaran let out a light sigh and dropped down beside him. "What would you have me say, a mhuirnín? I've got to go."

"No you *don't*," Trent insisted. "Tell Lugh you're mortal and useless now and you're going to sit here and eat chocolate bars until you're fat."

Ciaran wrinkled his nose. "I'm not going to—"

"I swear to God, if you try to argue about getting fat right now."

The fairy leaned back on his hands, turning his head to press his cheek into his shoulder so he could look at Trent. "Don't fuss so much. Let's have an adventure before we settle down, eh?"

"I've had enough fucking adventure with you already!"

"Well," Ciaran tried a little more softly, "one more." He reached a hand out to lace his fingers through Trent's. "Last one; I promise. After this, it'll be nothing but your preferred variety of landscape and lots of filthy, filthy sex."

Trent stared blankly at him. "Is that what you think being a person is like?"

"Well isn't it?"

Trent sighed and tugged out of Ciaran's grip to press the balls of his hands into his eyes.

"You worry too much, a mhuirnín. Try to make the best of a bad situation, eh? Think about all the new experiences you'll get to have."

"Sure. Great."

Ciaran sat up and took the boy by the wrists to uncover his face, smiling gently at him and leaning in to press a warm kiss to his lips. "It's enough for me that you offered to come."

Trent pressed his mouth into a firm line and kept his eyes on the space between them rather than looking his lover in the face. "Yeah, well. If I'm not there, you'll just do even dumber things."

"That's the spirit," Ciaran chuckled, and he pulled him in again to kiss the reluctant smile that formed on his lips.

7

"This is a terrible idea."

Noah stood in the front hallway near the door to the basement stairs, looking up at Lugh, who was currently holding a thrashing, drooling man by the neck high enough that the toes of their shoes barely scraped the wood floor. Edouard, Arnaud, and Julien stood by, but it was Julien who spoke to him.

"Noah, we need information. We need to know how to fight this, and if your friend doesn't answer—"

"So you want to *torture* this person?" Noah gestured at the suffering man, held so casually by his scruff like an animal. "Have you forgotten this is a person?"

"Of course not," Julien sighed. "Nobody said torture."

"Nobody said we wouldn't," Arnaud muttered.

Lugh was already moving toward the stairs. "I didn't catch it for nothing."

Noah reached after him as though there were anything he could do to stop him, then let his hand slap back to his side. "What is it you think I can do, anyway? I could maybe make up some kind of serum, but this is a demon we're talking about—who's to say it would even work? It's hard enough just getting these things to tell me their names. I don't know if you've looked at me lately, but I'm not exactly intimidating."

"We don't have very many options left," Edouard pointed out. "We have to try something."

"And I've never met a creature I couldn't break," Arnaud added.

Noah couldn't help his glare. "This isn't a *creature*; it's a person with a spirit inside it!"

"Then we'll try to only break the spirit," Edouard said, and he and Arnaud stepped through the door to follow Lugh into the basement.

Julien moved to go with them, but he paused to touch Noah's arm. "You don't have to do anything you don't want to do. But we can't do nothing."

"I want it on record that I don't like this at all," Noah called after him.

"Noted." Julien shut the stairway door behind him, shutting Noah out of the process.

Noah scooted his fairy box close to the wall so that he could keep an eye on it, but his ear was against the door for the better part of an hour. He could hear the thing down there, distantly growling, and the voices of the brothers, sometimes yelling. Rathgeirr noticed him on the way to the kitchen and waited with him, but he was clearly more curious than concerned.

When Noah heard footsteps on the stairs, he backed away from the door just in time to avoid having it open onto his face. Lugh and the three brothers filed out into the hall, Arnaud wiping something off of his hands with a rag. Noah thought he had a cut on his hand, but he couldn't get a good enough look.

"It talked," Arnaud said bluntly. "You can send it back home now. Said it's name was Strega."

Noah shot a questioning look up at Julien, who touched his shoulder and nodded.

"He's okay, Noah. No permanent damage."

"No permanent—for fuck's sake," Noah spat, brushing the blond aside and hurrying down the stairs with his bag of supplies in hand. The man on the table had no flailing or frothing left in him—he lay slack, eyes wide open and head fallen to the side, a little dried foam at the corners of his mouth. What the fuck had they done to him?

Noah checked him for injury, but could find none. He guessed "no permanent damage" was the best he could hope for. At least it would be easy to perform the exorcism now. He spread his salt, placed the crucifix, consecrated the wine with the now well-chewed bone from the reliquary, and held the demon's mouth shut with one hand once he'd poured it inside, his phone in his free hand so that he could read the Latin aloud.

The body jerked and seized in his grip, arching away from the table and shuddering violently against the straps, but then it finally relaxed. Signs of healthy color returned to the man's face, and his eyes fluttered shut as he settled against the metal table. Noah sighed as he picked up his bag and headed for the door again. Someone would still need to take this person to the hospital.

When he reached the top of the stairs, he found everyone standing in the hall waiting for him—Rathgeirr was even returning with Ciaran and Trent. Edouard's usual frown showed a touch more worry than usual, and as soon as Noah appeared and dropped his bag, he folded his arms and took a slow breath before beginning.

"This demon didn't seem to know where their leader was planning to appear, but we did get some information. These...Alfar have apparently agreed to help the demons come into this world physically—not just by possessing human hosts. This isn't a problem we could have anticipated," he added grimly. He turned his eyes on Rathgeirr. "Is that the sort of magic your people could do?"

The alfar frowned uncertainly. "I don't know of anything like that in particular, but the demon came to King Huldrekall some weeks ago; if the scholars have been working on such a spell since then, it's very possible."

Edouard glanced down at the floor briefly, as though that wasn't the answer he wanted, then looked back around at his brothers. "The demon mentioned a portal. Somewhere they'll be able to come through once the spell is done."

"Are we assuming that's somewhere near Mont Royal?" Laurent asked. "Since they've seemed more concentrated in the area."

"I think that's a safe bet. Tonight we'll start scouting the area more closely. Set up a grid." He turned to Noah with a reluctant scowl. "Does a witch have a way of finding something like that if we can't?"

Noah puffed out his cheeks. "I mean, I can try to scope out if there seems to be a high density of magic around there, but I can't say I've ever gone demon portal hunting before."

"Well?" Antony snapped. "What are we waiting for? Let's find this portal and figure out how to close it before the rest of the damn menagerie shows up."

Arnaud snorted. "For once, I agree with Antony. Let's not waste any more time."

The men split up again to gather their weapons and head back into the city, but Noah stopped Julien with a hand on his arm.

"Should I come too?"

He shook his head. "We have some equipment that can track magic ourselves, and you'll just throw it off. For now, it's probably better if you stay here and wait to hear from your friend. Get some rest."

Noah's brow creased into a frown. Julien had been going out every day since they'd arrived, and usually again at night. He'd been bruised and exhausted every time Noah saw him. "When are you going to rest?" he asked softly.

Julien covered Noah's hand with his and gave it a light squeeze. "When this is done." He offered the witch a faint smile before releasing him and taking the stairs to his room two at a time.

Noah looked back at the non-hunter portion of their group with a sigh. Ciaran had his hands on his hips as he looked up at his much-larger son.

"Should we be staying to help deal with this?" he asked, but Lugh immediately shook his head.

"I need you and Rathgeirr with me. We will have to leave this portal to the men."

Noah bent to scoop up his box from its place near the door and ran his fingers over the delicate silver hounds, who stubbornly refused to rear and deliver him news. It had been too long. Why was it taking Sabin so long to answer? Had something happened to him? Worry gnawed at Noah's gut. He didn't let the box out of his sight for the rest of the evening.

Long after dark, none of the Fournier brothers had returned to the house, so Noah eventually went to bed—not that he really got any rest. He didn't really worry about Julien being out late; he knew the hunter could handle himself. He did worry that he was going to be dead on his feet before long, though. And it was no big victory to be laying in Julien's bed at last without the blond there beside him. But he couldn't stop thinking about Sabin. The boy had been so communicative, and now...nothing.

He kept the box on the nightstand and stared at it until his eyes finally fell shut.

Almost as soon as Noah had drifted off, a sudden click woke him. The dogs had moved. Noah sat up and almost dropped the box in his hurry to pull it onto the bed and get it open. He expected a letter inside—new information, an update on his progress, maybe questions—but the only thing laying in the dark velvet was a small note, torn from a page and bearing just two words.

Send dirt.

Noah stared at it for a few beats, his half-asleep brain taking its time firing to life. If Sabin needed dirt, then he wanted to perform the teleportation spell they'd talked about for years—dreamed about, if Noah was honest. He'd been trying to send Sabin components almost since he left, but he doubted many ever made it to him. The key ingredient was soil from your destination. Sabin needed dirt. And a slip of paper like this with no explanation meant that something was wrong.

Noah flew from the bed and fell to his knees in front of his bag across the room, digging through his ingredients for a few rarer items Sabin was likely to be short on. He shoved them into the box and snapped the lid shut as he found them like a cashier sending groceries to be bagged. As soon as he was finished, he plucked an empty mason jar from his kit and slammed the bedroom door open, holding the fairy box under his arm as he rushed down the stairs and out the front door. He twisted the jar open as he went, crossing the street barefoot and wearing only a worn pair of yoga pants. He fell to the ground in the neighbor's tiny front yard, scraped a couple handfuls of dirt into the jar, sealed it, and went back inside as fast as he could manage. He dropped the box on the war table, laid the jar carefully inside, and tore a corner from one of the printed maps to write on the back.

Prepping the circle now. Hang on.

As he went back upstairs to get dressed and gather his supplies,

Ciaran poked his head out of the door down the hall.

"Oi," he called. "What's the racket?"

Noah stopped short. "Oh—will you help me?" He returned to Julien's room and pulled on a shirt without waiting for an answer, but he yelled louder into the hallway, "I have a list of things I need to have for this spell but the circle takes ages to draw."

Ciaran appeared in the open door a moment later, also only half-dressed. "What spell's this now?"

"Hold on." Noah grabbed his phone from the nightstand and called Julien. He tucked the phone under his ear and dug jars and packets from his bag while he waited, shoving them into Ciaran's confused but willing hands. When Julien picked up, Noah didn't bother greeting him. "So, if I was going to draw a circle on the floor that may or may not leave a permanent mark, is there a place you guys would rather I do that?"

"Uh. Why?"

"Sabin. I got a note from him, and he wants to come here. He knows the spell, but there has to be somewhere for him to land, so I have to draw something to receive him."

Julien paused for just a moment. "You can't do that at the house."

"Julien, if Sabin says he needs me, I don't give a shit about what your—"

"No," he cut in, "I mean you *can't*. The house is protected against things like that. I—actually, hold on. I'll send you the address of a little safehouse I've used before. Meet me there."

"Okay. I'm leaving now." Noah hung up on him and shoved his phone into his pocket, then tugged on his shoes. Trent and Rathgeirr were awake now and peering over Ciaran's shoulder while Noah went frantically around the room gathering supplies and books, mumbling to himself and counting on his fingers. He needed to hurry. He had to have everything, and he had to get the circle drawn, and with Sabin waiting for him—

When he was pulling yet another filled notebook from his bag in search of the right one, Rathgeirr knelt beside him and reached over to take a light hold of his fingers, which Noah hadn't realized were trembling.

"What do you need, Noah?" he asked, and the calm tone of his voice took a little of the tension from the witch's gut.

Noah took a long breath, then smiled and handed the alfar some candles and chalk. "Thank you."

By the time Noah finished, Ciaran and Trent had dressed themselves and seemed to be waiting for instruction.

"Better than sitting around at the house," Ciaran said with a grin, and Noah smiled.

"I want to come, too," Rathgeirr piped up.

Noah made a soft, uncertain sound. "I'm not very good at glamours, and with how difficult it was to take the last one off, I'm not sure if I should."

"It's night now," Rathgeirr said. "Don't worry about me. I can follow without being seen."

"Good enough for me."

They all left the house with hands and pockets full of spell ingredients, candles, a couple of books, incense, and the right notebook. As soon as they were outside, Noah turned to ask Rathgeirr how he planned to stay out of sight just in time to see him jump up to grab the edge of the house's lowest eave, his feet barely touching the brick before he disappeared onto the roof. That was certainly one way to do it.

Noah kept his box under his arm as they walked, following his phone's directions to the address Julien had sent. It wasn't a long trip, really—but every second was torturous. Sabin was waiting for him. Sabin was coming. He was really coming. He was going to be here soon.

When they reached the rusted door in the alley that Julien's address had led them to, Noah stopped to put his phone away, and he jumped when Rathgeirr dropped down next to him with a bright smile. Julien was waiting by the door, so as soon as it was open, they all went inside.

It was more of a safe hovel than a safe house, really—just a small, empty warehouse room with a cot and a beaten-up footlocker in one corner. Even so, it looked big enough to draw the circle in, so Noah didn't care about the rest. He directed Ciaran and Trent, who were on candle-placing and incense-lighting duty, from his notes, and then he set to work with his chalk, working on hands and knees on the concrete floor while Rathgeirr followed him, holding the book open to the right page so the witch could copy the design.

Julien stood out of the way, but Noah could feel the hunter's eyes on him even before he spoke. "So this is...teleportation?"

Noah didn't look up at him. "Yes. It's a really difficult spell. It needs a lot of specific things, but I've been sending them to him little by little as I can. I've been waiting to get him out of that place since I got his first letter." He paused to draw the notebook in Rathgeirr's hands a little closer to his face so he could check a detail, then returned to his work. "If he's ready to do it, then I don't want to make him wait."

Julien made a sound like he was holding back his magic-related concerns, but Noah didn't care about his magic-related concerns, so he just focused on his circle, and the hunter had the good sense to keep quiet.

By the time he finished, the others had settled in against the walls to wait. Noah stood and took the book from Rathgeirr with a smile of thanks, then carefully checked every inch of the diagram against his own drawing. When he was satisfied, he took a seat at the back of the room with his box beside him and tore a page from the notebook.

Ready on this end. See you soon.

He shut the lid on the fairy box to send the note, then waited. He stared at the circle and willed it to do something. Anything. But it didn't. So he waited, his heart in his throat.

Minutes passed. Rathgeirr settled on the floor adjacent to him, and Ciaran and Trent sat opposite, both of them curiously watching the circle as well. But the circle wasn't activating. Had he done something wrong?

Noah got up and checked the circle again, checked his notes, checked the cardinal directions and the placement of the candles. Everything was right. So he sat, and he waited. Julien took a seat on the cot and dug through the old footlocker, but the only thing he found were some crusty, bloody old bandages and a couple of handgun magazines. He put those in his coat pocket.

More minutes passed. An hour. Two. Noah sat with his arms wrapped around his knees, subtly rocking while he stared at the dead circle on the floor. Periodically, he tore a new sheet from his notebook to send Sabin another note.

Is everything okay? Do you need something else?
Here's a drawing of the circle in case you lost it.
I can get more dirt if you need it.
Is something wrong?
I'm ready when you are.
Please answer me.

No matter how many messages he sent, the circle was still, and so was the box. Ciaran and Trent fell asleep on each other's shoulders, and Julien offered Noah his place on the cot, but the witch just shook his head and held onto his knees a little tighter. Sabin was coming. He had to be coming.

At some point, Noah dozed off with his forehead on his knees, but he jerked his head up at the sound of a small click from his box. Morning light had begun to peek through the pair of squat windows near the ceiling, illuminating the clouds of dust they'd kicked up in the night. Rathgeirr lay curled up in the corner with his cloak over him like a blanket, and even Julien had fallen asleep sat up on his cot with his back against the wall. How long had it been?

Noah opened the box and retrieved the small note he found there, and he blinked his tired eyes once or twice to make sure he was reading the words properly.

Sorry. Overslept. Drawing the circle now.

Julien and the others must have heard the noise, too—they were all staring at him now. Noah read the note one more time, then laughed and let his head drop forward.

"Is everything okay?" Julien asked, but Noah just stretched to hand him the note. The hunter looked down at it, paused, and then snapped his eyes back up to Noah. "He *overslept?* Voyons donc, tu me niaises?"

"You're serious?" Ciaran sighed. "Fucking teenagers."

"At least he's up now," Noah said, trying to be cheerful through his lingering worry.

"Then now that your lad's finished his beauty rest, this is really happening?"

"I hope so."

Trent looked grumpily over at the fairy but kept his complaints to himself, just settling back against the wall with a huffing sigh.

Noah closed his box again in case Sabin needed to send anything else, and he paused to stretch before sprawling his legs out in front of him to wait. They still had a way to go before Sabin would be ready, if he was only just drawing the circle—but Noah didn't say that out loud. He just stared at the marks on the floor and chewed the rings in his lips.

After a while, a soft spark formed at the center of the circle. Noah's breath caught in his chest, and he scrambled to his feet, his stomach in knots and his heart in his throat, and he watched. Sabin was coming.

8

The chalk outline on the floor began to smoke, lighting in the center and spreading slowly out toward the edges. Noah stood as close as he dared, barely sparing a glance at Julien as he moved to stand beside him.

"Ah, Noah," the hunter murmured, "is the room about to catch fire?"

"It's just a spell; don't worry."

"Magic fire is still fire, isn't it?"

"Julien, it's fine," Noah insisted, just in time for the rim of the circle to burst to life, bright flames licking eagerly toward the ceiling. Julien took a step back, but Noah held his ground, squinting through the heat but refusing to turn away. He needed to see.

Beyond the flames, six silhouetted figures took shape. Noah fought the urge to move closer—he had to wait. As soon as the fire began to die, he saw him. Sabin. The boy was older, taller than when he'd last seen him, with more piercings in his face, but...it was really him. The air left Noah's lungs, and he took a step toward the circle, careful not to disrupt the edges in case he interfered with the spell. Sabin's hair was pulled back from his sweaty face into a haphazard ponytail, and dark circles made his eyes look sunken. His own box was tucked tightly under one arm, and as soon as the flames sank back into dark wisps of smoke along the chalk circle, he moved forward.

"Noah?" he murmured in a low, strained voice, his legs failing him as the box clattered to the floor.

"Sabin!" Noah called out in alarm. The boy's knee hit the concrete, but before he could drop, Noah was at his side, easing him to the floor and cradling him in his lap.

Noah held the boy close with an arm around his shoulders and pushed some stray hairs from his face, but Sabin's eyes were closed. Noah whispered his name and tapped his cheek, then shook him gently by the shoulder, but he didn't respond. He was out cold.

A boy with a blue mohawk pushed his way through the group in the circle and knelt beside them. He frowned down at Sabin's sleeping face.

"For fuck's sake!" he spat. He looked up at Noah with worry in his brown eyes.

"I told him it was too soon to do something like this."

Noah barely heard him. He checked Sabin's forehead for fever and laid a hand on his chest to feel his heartbeat. He was pale and damp with sweat—and even unconscious, weariness creased his brow. Noah spared the other boy a glance before looking up at Julien, who had at some point knelt beside him and put a hand on his back.

"We need to take him back home," Noah said in a rush.

Julien gave a soft swear and cast a quick look around the room before answering. "Noah, my brothers aren't going to—"

"Your brothers can fuck themselves, Julien! I'm taking him back whether you help me or not."

The hunter only hesitated a moment more before he gave a quick sigh and turned around, hunkering down closer to the floor so that Sabin could be loaded onto his back. Noah lifted him with the other boy's help and settled his arms over Julien's shoulders. The blond stood, hooking his hands under Sabin's thighs, and shifted him up a little higher to get a better grip on his legs.

As they rushed to the door, Julien paused, and he and Noah realized at the same moment that the other newcomers were trying to follow them. A blond-haired teen was right at Julien's back—a frowning boy with large, feathered wings.

"Ah," Julien began uncertainly, "you should all wait here. There are more of you than I expected."

"We really don't have a lot of time to hang around," the blond boy said urgently, but Noah was already out the door. "And I don't think we should be separated."

"Relax, kid," Julien muttered, bouncing Sabin up a little more on his back. "My place isn't far from here. I just need to..." He hesitated and passed another look over the unexpected crowd. "...prepare my brothers." He threw a glance over his shoulder to Trent. "I'll text you when I'm on my way back," he said.

The boy with the mohawk moved to follow them, and Noah waved him along with them, assuring him it was fine. He barely heard the blond boy's last objection as Julien kicked the door shut behind them.

The hunter knew the back streets of Montreal well, so they were able to make it back to the house without passing too many morning pedestrians on the sidewalk. Noah followed along beside him, occasionally reaching up to touch Sabin's arm or his back, reassuring himself that the boy was real. Halfway there, Sabin gave a few wet coughs, and vomit poured over Julien's shoulder and down his front. The blond stopped walking, as if he needed a moment to process what had just happened, but then he just gave a sigh through his nose and kept walking while Noah tried to clean Sabin's face on the move.

On the front step of Julien's house, he poked his head in to listen once Noah opened the door. There was no sign of movement from inside, which meant his brothers were either still out or had finally gone to sleep, so Julien moved quickly and quietly up the stairs at the back of the hall. With Noah's help, he dropped Sabin from his back onto the bed in his room. While the new boy tucked Sabin under the blanket, Noah turned to his bag and tore threw it in search of the items he needed. Once he had the jars in hand, he snatched a bit of cloth from a side pocket and rushed back to kneel next to the bed. Tears fell freely from his eyes, and he sniffled as he wet the cloth, pausing to wipe a trail of snot on the back of his arm. He didn't look up when Julien put a gentle hand on his shoulder.

"I'll go take care of the others," he said softly, and Noah nodded without taking his attention from Sabin.

He spread the cloth on the mattress and spilled some herbs from a jar along the center, then wrapped them up tightly and dripped sweet-smelling oil into the fabric, pausing frequently to touch Sabin's chest, his arm, his face. It really was him. Noah laid the bundle carefully on Sabin's forehead and tucked the blanket up closer around his chin. He sat on his heels and watched the boy sleep, one hand resting on his arm, until he realized with a small start that the other boy was still standing by.

Noah forced himself to stand, and though his eyes were still wet, he smiled at the boy who'd so quickly rushed to Sabin's aid. Sabin had mentioned that one of his companions was someone he felt close to. "You must be Berlin," he said.

The boy just stared at him blankly for a few seconds. He pointed at himself, then began to laugh. He laughed so hard that he doubled over, and as he wheezed with his hands on his knees, he put up one finger to tell Noah to wait.

Noah's brow wrinkled in confusion. "So you're...*not* Berlin?"

With one hand still on his knee, the boy let out the last of his laughter, and as he straightened, he wiped a tear from one eye. "God no," he said. "Berlin's the angry-looking black kid with all the tattoos." He flashed Noah a bright smile. "I'm definitely much nicer and wittier than he is." He paused, then lifted his shoulders as though reconsidering. "Well, *nicer* depends on who I'm talking to, I guess."

"Well, you're talking to Noah," he answered with as much of a smile as he could manage with Sabin unconscious in the bed behind him. If this wasn't the kid Sabin had a crush on, where had that kid been when he'd almost hit the floor? "Thanks for helping him here, not-Berlin."

The boy put a hand to his own chest. "Jett. And you didn't have to tell me who you are," he added. "I could have guessed as soon as that fire went down. Haven't ever seen Sabin look so...well..." He did his best not to smile too broadly. "Tender might be too embarrassing a word. He'd be mad at me if I said that. But we've all heard about you."

If Noah was honest, he was a little disappointed this *wasn't* the kid Sabin had written him about. He was cute. "I won't tell him he looked tender if you don't," he promised. "What happened to you guys, anyway? I haven't heard from him in a couple of days, and then I get this emergency note, and he shows up like this?"

Jett looked past him at Sabin and frowned, setting his hands on his hips. "Everything happened, I guess. We'd been dealing with some ghost kids that could hypnotize us, so he'd been using a lot of magic to keep us from being able to hear anything. Then the regression spells, with the livers—I know you heard about those. Then fighting monsters, and running, and then Marla asking him to do *another* circle for summoning demons and shit, and...it was a whole thing."

Noah sat on the edge of the bed and wrapped his hand gently around Sabin's fingers. "He did all that," he murmured. "He's come a long way from doing card tricks."

"I bet he still does a mean card trick," Jett said, and Noah smiled just a little. "Anyway, he was already looking pretty wiped, and then when we had to book it out of the swamp, I was practically carrying him. It was all kind of a clusterfuck."

"God," Noah sighed. "The poor kid. Don't tell him I said that, either," he added with a quick glance up at the boy. "But none of the rest of you seem half as beat up. There are so many of you—weren't you all fighting?"

Jett reached up to muss his own hair, shrugging one shoulder as he answered. "We were. But I guess some of our powers just don't drain us the way his do. And, honestly, most of us aren't nearly as useful as he is."

Noah's expression slowly tightened into a faint scowl. "So just use him up until he has to be carried? Until he passes out?" He struggled not to grip Sabin's hand too tightly.

Jett shifted his weight on his feet, at least having the decency to look uncomfortable. When he spoke, his voice was low, and it lacked the teasing tone he'd had thus far. "I never intended for any of this to happen. He's saved my life...I mean, probably more than once. But you're right. We should have been keeping a closer eye on him."

"He could *die*," Noah spat. "And then after all that, using a teleportation spell on...Christ, however many of you there are, he—" He stopped himself, forcing a deep breath into his lungs so that he didn't resort to shouting.

"Die?" Jett moved closer to the bed so that he could look Noah in the face. "Wait, he could *actually* die from using too much magic?"

"Of course he could! Where do you think magic comes from? It's *in us.* If he hadn't passed out when he did, even a card trick could have—and you all just—" Noah pressed his lips together and shook his head, distracting himself by checking the compress on Sabin's forehead. "Whatever. I'm just glad he's here now."

"I had no idea," Jett said, soft and sincere, but Noah still didn't look at him.

"Seems like something you ought to consider when making drastic requests of your friends, but what the fuck do I know, I guess."

Jett was quiet for a long time, allowing Noah to settle a little as he watched Sabin's sleeping face. When he did speak, it was quiet, as though he didn't want to interrupt. "I'm sorry," he said. "You're right. And when he wakes up, I'll apologize to him, too. I'm just glad our mistake didn't...didn't turn into something that couldn't be fixed."

Noah sighed. This kid didn't deserve his anger. Sabin was his friend—and he was clearly worried about him, too. So Noah looked back up at him and offered him a small smile. "Turns out you are pretty nice," he muttered.

Jett let out a snort. "Thanks. The next time we fight a giant toad monster, I'll tell him to take it easy."

Noah paused. "A giant toad monster? What kind? How big?" He stopped and held up a hand. "You know what—never mind. That can wait. Can you hand me the moringa oil from my kit over there? It's the yellowy one in the square jar."

The boy seemed happy to be given something to do. He crouched on the floor to dig around for the jar with a smile. "I mean, it's a pretty awesome story. Daring close calls and shit." He rose with the oil in his hand and turned to place it in Noah's waiting palm. "I can see where Sabin learned a lot of his magic from," he said while Noah unscrewed the jar. "Sabin has so much stuff like this. Do you keep spiders in tanks, too?"

"Not lately," Noah chuckled softly. "Been too homeless for a little while now." He dipped two fingers into the jar and touched traces onto Sabin's forehead, his lips, and the hollow of his throat, then pulled down the blanket and lifted the boy's shirt to leave the skin-warmed oil on his chest and stomach. "I tried to teach him what I could, before...well, before he was taken from me. I wish we'd had more time, but...he's really come into his own. He was just a kid when

I lost him, and now look at him." A small, sad laugh escaped him. "He's so grown up."

"I also won't tell him you said that," Jett teased. "Honestly, I've not known him for long—maybe a month. But he's impressive," he added, making no attempt to disguise his peeking under Sabin's shirt. Noah tucked it back down and pulled the blanket up over him again.

"I'm a little surprised I haven't heard more about you in his letters," he murmured, glancing back at Jett with a smirk.

"Eh," he shrugged, "I've only been around a month. It would've happened if I had more time."

Noah laughed softly. "Is that so?"

Jett winked at him with a grin on his face, but then he let out a small laugh and waved a hand between them. "He wouldn't want anything to do with me. I'm a mess." He leaned over a little closer to Noah and tucked a fist under his chin. "But what about you? If I'm around more than a month, will *you* write letters about me?"

Noah snorted at him. "Sorry, but are you even legal?"

"I'm older than I look," the boy promised.

"Well, you're cute, but I'm with the blond who carried Sabin here—Julien."

"Ah, that doesn't surprise me," Jett said with a sage nod. "I think you and Sabin have the same taste in guys. The serious tough guys. I get it."

"Great," Noah chuckled.

"Uh, also," Jett went on a little more quietly, "don't tell him I know. He's not told any of us, and I don't think anyone else knows. I don't even know if, uh—" He glanced at Sabin as if he might hear. "—if his interest knows. Sabin doesn't seem to be one for traditional tokens of affection."

"Yeah," Noah said softly. "That's not a big surprise."

A quiet knock at the door interrupted them, and Julien stuck his head in. He glanced between them and spoke in a low voice so as not to disturb the sleeping boy. "The others are here. I'll get them set up in the bunks. Do you need anything?"

Jett pushed away from the bed and dusted off his hands on the pockets of his jeans. "I'll go back to the others so you two can have a minute. He won't want anyone else seeing him like this, anyway.

We'll keep it our secret, okay?" He gave Noah another wink on his way to the door, and the witch smiled. He wasn't so bad.

Julien was still waiting by the door, so Noah gently shooed him away. "I'm fine. Go find Lugh; he'll want to know about this."

Julien nodded and shut the door as quietly as he could on his way out. Once Noah was alone in the room with Sabin, he settled in on the floor beside the bed with his arms folded under his chin. He made sure the compress stayed damp and warm and the blanket stayed tucked snugly around the boy's body, and then he hid his smile in the crook of his elbow. He was really here.

9

After a while, Noah finally let his eyes drift shut, satisfied that Sabin wasn't going to disappear. He was stirred by the sound of the boy's soft, waking intake of breath, and when Noah lifted his head, he smiled to see Sabin pull the compress to his nose and inhale deeply.

"You always liked the clary sage the best," Noah said softly.

Sabin sat still for what almost seemed like too long, just breathing in the scent of the oil and herbs in his hand, but then he snapped bolt upright in the bed, nearly throwing the blankets off of him as he struggled against the restriction of the sheets as if they were a straitjacket. Noah moved to sit at the edge of the bed when the boy audibly gasped, the rush of oxygen sending him into a swaying slump. Noah caught him by the shoulders and gently pressed him back toward the mattress, quietly shushing him.

"Easy, kiddo," he murmured. "Seems like you've had a rough time."

Sabin settled against the pillow with his eyes scrunched slightly against the dim light of the room. He slowly cracked them open, seeming to take a few moments to bring his surroundings into focus, and then he finally looked Noah in the face.

"Noah?" His voice cracked as he spoke, shooting a warm pain into Noah's heart. When Sabin tried to sit up again, Noah helped steady him, gently pushing the spilled hair out of his face to get a better look at him and doing his best not to let his own tears spill.

"I'm right here," he said through a tight throat. "Don't push yourself."

"Where are we?" Sabin asked in a voice rough with sleep, and Noah smiled and stifled a soft hiccup.

"You're in Montreal," he managed to say. "The spell brought you here."

"Montre—" Sabin began, but then he let his head fall back, his whole body dropping heavily to the mattress with Noah's guidance. "Oh my god," he groaned. "I need you to send me back."

Noah laughed, turning his head to wipe some stray tears that were threatening to fall from his chin onto the sleeve of his shirt and smiling as the boy's grip tightened on his arm. "It's not so bad," he said thickly.

"Someone must be blackmailing you to say that."

"This is Julien's family's house," Noah corrected him gently. The temptation to go along with the joke was strong, but there were too many Quebeckers in the house who already didn't like him. "I'll show you around properly when you're back on your feet."

Sabin just laid on the bed for a few beats with a slightly sour look on his face, and Noah couldn't help his soft, choking laugh. Sabin was actually here—actually talking to him. He was fine. He was safe. When the boy opened the blue eyes that had once stared at Noah so defiantly in the street, now peering up at him with a faint smile, Noah's heart constricted.

"Stupid," Sabin said, "why are you crying?"

Noah tried to breathe and hiccupped instead. He bent over the boy, wrapping his arms around his head and pulling him into the tightest hug he thought he could stand. He touched Sabin's hair and sniffled into his shoulder, taking a few shaky breaths before he could find his voice again. "I can't believe you're really here," he whispered.

Sabin didn't answer. He stayed still for a breath or two, then began to pull away from Noah's grip.

"Stop crying on me," he said, a cavalier tone in his voice that he obviously hoped the older man would believe. He didn't. He'd heard that false spite too many times to buy it now. Noah reluctantly loosened his hold, allowing the boy to retreat. "I'm fine. This should be a happy thing. Not a bunch of blubbering."

"I am happy," Noah said immediately. He moved his hands up to cup Sabin's face, a smile on his face that couldn't come close to showing the relief he felt all the way down to his bones. "I'm so happy." Laughter spilled out of him, and he smoothed Sabin's hair again, unable to keep from looking at the young man the boy he'd known had become. "Your voice broke," he added after a pause, feeling another welling of tears pricking his eyes.

Sabin forced out a small laugh. "Sounds pretty good, huh?" Despite the boy's clear efforts, his eyes reddened, and faint pools of tears began to form at the edges. He brought up an arm between them in an attempt to hide his face and tried to pull away again, clearing his throat to cover the tension of his voice, but Noah only laughed at him.

"You called me stupid, and look at you," he chided gently. "I guess we're both stupid, huh?"

The boy finally let out a tight sob, and he curled in on himself like a child, his breath ragged and shaking. The sound broke Noah's heart.

"Oh, kid," he whispered as he scooted down onto the bed to lie beside him, clutching him close under his chin with gentle, stroking fingers in his hair. "It's all right," he promised, his own voice staying steady now that Sabin needed it to be. "I'm here. You're safe." He held the boy while his body shivered, rocking him gently and letting his cheek rest against his hair. He held his own eyes shut tight, allowing the last of his tears to fall as Sabin's arms finally found their way around Noah's torso, hands curling into the back of his shirt.

Noah waited until they'd both found a normal breathing rhythm again, and once Sabin's grip on him loosened just a little, he leaned back to look the boy in the face. "So I'm waiting for my apology for you making me think you were in trouble and then going the fuck back to sleep."

Sabin gave a small snort. Noah let him go when he sat up, glancing down at the boy's fingers as they guiltily twisted the tearstained fabric of his shirt. He reached over to the nightstand for a tissue and handed it over as he sat up next to Sabin, tucking his knees up to wrap his arms around them. He smiled as Sabin blew his nose and took a deep, steeling breath.

"I didn't mean to; I must have passed out," he said. "Noah,

everything's gone to shit. I don't know how much the others have told you, but we were all right about Marla. She left us out there to die, and she took Cole and Alistair with her. I think she's going to give them to the demons. Cole, at least." He rubbed at his head as though working away an ache. "Jett said they were going to Antarctica, but..." Sabin exhaled so deeply Noah worried he might be deflating.

Then Noah paused. "Antarctica?" he echoed, leaning away just a little so he could look down at Sabin's face. "The demons are meeting in Antarctica?"

"It seems that way." Sabin let out another great sigh, and Noah softened. He'd been having an even rougher time than Noah had imagined. The boy reached out to take Noah's hand, and he drooped over to lean heavily against the other man's shoulder. The simple familiarity of the gesture warmed Noah's chest. "Was I right though?" Sabin asked. "Do you think you guys can help us?"

"I hope we can all help each other," Noah answered softly. "It hasn't exactly been a cakewalk here, either. But we'll sort it out now that we're all together. Even just you knowing where the demons will be is huge—Lugh will be glad to hear it."

"I really thought I'd done enough, but..." Sabin looked down at his lap, the ring in his lip twitching with the anxious movement of his tongue. "I feel like shit."

Noah frowned down at him. This poor kid. How much of the burden had the others laid on his shoulders for him to give all he had and still feel like he'd failed them?

The bedroom door handle gave a soft click, and Sabin straightened instantly, both of his hands clutching Noah's tight as Julien peeked inside. Noah caught him giving Sabin a brief look up and down before he opened the door a little wider with his elbow, his hands occupied with two large mugs.

"I thought I heard you up," he said. "Tout baigne?" He lifted the mugs slightly but didn't come any closer, as if he still thought he might be intruding. "This is tea, if you want it."

Noah waved him inside, thanking him with a smile as he took one of the mugs for himself with the one free hand the boy allowed him. "Sabin, this is Julien. Julien, Sabin."

Julien gave Sabin a faint smile as he held the remaining mug expectantly out, but the boy just stared up at him with a flat expression, clearly studying him and making no move to reach for the offered drink.

"Sorry, Noah," he said without taking his eyes from Julien's, "does your boyfriend speak English?"

Julien paused, looking mildly taken aback as he glanced at Noah. He frowned as if he might actually be doubting whether he'd spoken English or not. "Uh. It's tea," he tried again.

"Sabin," Noah said, not falling for this act at all. Sabin had pushed back against every boyfriend Noah had during their time together, and he guessed this wouldn't be any different. "Julien made you tea. Wasn't. That. Nice. Of him."

"Is that what he's saying?" the boy asked, his voice innocent as he took the mug but his face a dead stare up at the blond. "Sorry; I don't speak French."

Julien's nostrils flared a little. "I wasn't—"

"Sabin's just tired," Noah cut in, not missing the squeeze Sabin gave his hand. "He's still pretty sleepy, so he's probably just not hearing things right," he finished with a pointed glance at the boy beside him. "I think that's definitely what's happening, right, Sabin?"

"Excusez-moi?" Sabin lifted the mug in Julien's direction and spoke insultingly slowly. "What's in the mug? Is this tea? T-E-A?" He gave an exaggerated shrug and shook his head as though the communication situation was hopeless.

Julien simply stared down at him, and Noah could see his gears turning, weighing the choices of being polite to Noah's beloved guest or putting him out on his ass. Noah couldn't be positive which decision he landed on, so when Julien opened his mouth to speak, Noah went first.

"Hey Julien, you know what—I bet Sabin's hungry, and I could go for something myself. Would you maybe go see if there's anything good in the kitchen?"

Julien's jaw worked slowly before he answered. "Sure," he said through tight lips, and he kept his good eye on Sabin until he left the room, shutting the door just a little hard behind him.

"Are you kidding me?" Sabin asked almost before the door was shut, making no attempt to lower his voice. "*That's* the guy you picked?"

Noah almost spilled his tea, he turned on the boy so fast. "What are you talking about? All he did was bring you tea, and you gave him so much shit! What's the matter with you?"

"What's the matter?" Sabin repeated, disgust in his voice. "*He* is clearly the matter, Noah. I mean, for starters, he's straight. Don't think I've forgotten that little tidbit from your letter. And now he's failed my test. Dude's clearly got a temper. He looked like he was ready to lose it. That's the sort of guy that gives you a black eye."

"Sabin," Noah sighed, his expression softening. The boy had seen the worst of what it had been like with Travis—the shouting, the bruises, the excuses. For all Noah's coaching and encouragement and advice, he'd proven himself to have pretty poor judgment when it came to choosing boyfriends himself. He forgave too much. He knew that. Sabin clearly knew it, too. It put Noah's stomach in a pleasant knot to see the boy so ready to stand up for him—even if it meant irritating Julien.

"I know I haven't...always made super good choices," Noah said. "But this is different—it really is," he insisted, anticipating the boy's objection. "You were baiting him. Anybody would get annoyed. And, you'll notice, he didn't even do anything about it except go to get you more food. When you got here, he carried you on his back for, like, eight blocks. You threw up on his shoulder. He's a good guy."

"Is that why I smell like Labatt?" Sabin grumped, and Noah frowned at him. "You've said it's different before," the boy went on, scowling down into his tea. "And anyone can act nice for a while. That's not hard. I was a kid last time, but I'm not anymore. I'm not going to let that sort of thing happen again."

Noah didn't quite manage to hide his smile. "I know," he said. "But this really is different. You also read the part in my letter about him going on some, like, epic hero's journey to some forbidden island somewhere and losing his eye to save my life, right? If a guy like that ever raises a hand to me, you have my permission to hex his balls off."

Sabin glared across at him for a few beats, and Noah saw the same little punk who'd been doing magic in the streets of Vancouver.

"He's a Quebecois, too," the boy went on. "That's, like, two strikes right there. I mean, he even *looks* French before he opens his mouth."

"Dude," Noah said more quietly, leaning in a little closer to drop his voice through his laughter. "Wait until you meet the rest of them. He has six brothers, and they are fucking *French*."

Sabin tried not to smile and failed, finally leaning back against the headboard and taking a reluctant sip of his tea. "Does he call his dick a baguette?"

"Real talk, the French mostly comes out when he's irritated, and it's pretty hot actually. But—but but but." He scooted up to sit more snugly against the headboard with him, their knees touching. "I want to talk about you, here. You know, Jett helped me get you home, and so I actually assumed he was that kid Berlin you mentioned."

Sabin snorted into his mug at the mention of Berlin's name, splashing tea up onto his lip.

"I want to hear about the real one. Tell me the deets."

Sabin wiped at his mouth and blew into the tea to cool it rather than looking Noah in the face. "There's not really anything to hear."

Noah nudged the boy with his elbow. "Come on. I've waited for years to talk crushes with you."

Sabin took a deep breath with both hands on his mug. "I mean, there really isn't anything to hear. I was just wrong about the things I sent you in that letter. It was all just in my head. He's a dick, anyway," he added with spite in his voice.

Noah cringed a little but tried to keep his voice cheerful. "I'm sorry, kid. That's rough. Was he at least not dickish about...you know, telling you that?"

"I think I came on too strong." Sabin swallowed and looked up at Noah with a faint, forced smile on his lips. "I mean, a scary witch coming after you? I guess it's normal to freak out a bit about that. It's whatever, though."

He paused, setting his mug on the nightstand so that he could turn to face Sabin properly. "Scary witch? He said that to you?"

"I mean, he didn't use those words exactly." Sabin gave a snort. "You know the go-to word is usually *freak*. But that's just because people aren't imaginative."

A weight settled on Noah's shoulders. Sabin had been taken from him so that he could be somewhere with other boys like him. That's what the man had said. He'd said Sabin would be included. Safe.

Accepted. Noah had let Sabin go because he'd thought he was going somewhere where he wouldn't have to feel like this again. Instead, he'd been thrown into dangerous situations, used for his magic by his teammates until his body gave out, and now he'd been called a freak by one of the people just like him?

Anger boiled in Noah's belly, and he struggled to keep it down. "This kid," he said slowly, "called you a freak? You told him you liked him, and he called you a *freak?*"

"Like a million people have called me a freak, Noah. It's not that big a deal. *And* he's Catholic, so *everyone* is a devil worshiper. It was stupid of me to even try."

"It—" Noah stopped himself, balling his hand into a fist and tapping his knuckle against his mouth as if that would help keep the anger inside. Sabin had dealt with too much vicious abuse from his foster parents for Noah to stomach him taking it from people that were supposed to be his teammates—his friends. He took a quick breath and looked Sabin in the eyes. "I want you to tell me the truth. Right now. Did he put his hands on you?"

"Did he—?" Sabin paused as realization came over his face. "This isn't the same," he said, too quickly. "Like, he shoved me. He didn't beat me up or anything."

"This time is different, huh?" Noah said quietly, echoing the boy's own concerns about him. He let out a humorless laugh, shaking his head as he turned to climb out of the bed. "No," he said. "No, no, no, no. Nope."

Sabin grabbed Noah by the sleeve of his shirt, but he brushed the boy's hand away. "Hold on, where are you going?"

"He doesn't get to make you feel like that," Noah answered simply, and before he finished crossing the room, the bedroom door slammed open to let him out into the hall. He stepped quickly toward the bunk room, calling out, "Berlin!" as he approached the door and threw it open.

The room was a little crowded now with five new people in it. Trent and Ciaran seemed to be on babysitting duty while the group of boys clustered close together to talk among themselves, though Rathgeirr lingered at their periphery with a curious look on his face.

The blond with the wings was standing with his arms folded, grumpily addressing the other tired-looking teens. Noah was satisfied to see the startled looks on their faces as he came through the doorway.

"Everybody who just had their asses teleported here, get where I can see your stupid faces," he snapped. "Like right fuckin' now."

The boys exchanged a few concerned looks, but they all rose and shuffled over to stand in front of him like children who knew they were about to be scolded. Ciaran followed, leaning against one of the bunks with a smile on his face like he was eager for gossip. Noah scanned each of their faces, locking eyes with the dark-skinned boy who lurked at the back of the small group. Berlin.

"You," Noah said. He crooked a finger at him, then pointed at the floor directly in front of him without moving his eyes from the boy's. "You come here. Right now."

The other boys all turned to look at him, but Berlin obeyed, holding Noah's gaze and moving to stand in front of the smaller witch with a surly jut of his chin.

Noah did his best to keep his tone in check, but it was difficult with the boy staring down at him so smugly. This kid was twice Sabin's size—and he'd thought he could push him around. Noah knew his type. A bully. "I need you to listen to me," he said in a low voice. "You don't get to call him a freak. You don't get to make him feel that way. That word had better not even leave your fucking mouth where I can hear it, do you understand me? And if you ever lay hands on him again, I will turn you fucking *inside out*. That's a promise you don't want to make me keep."

Berlin stared at him, seemingly unmoved, though he matched Noah's quiet voice. "Is there another word for someone who puts snakes in my bed?"

"Are you serious?" Noah hissed. "All the shit you've seen on your stupid missions, and the thing that tips the fucking scales for you is *pranks?* You're just like the rest of them. If you knew the damage you'd done—" He stopped himself, briefly shutting his eyes and taking a quick, deep breath to force back the tingling in his skin. He was about to do something he'd regret.

He heard the boy's next breath—subdued, but heavier, like he was trying hard to keep still, and Noah could see the goosebumps prickling on his dark skin as the faint, crackling sensation of ozone flowing from the witch reached him. When Noah looked up into Berlin's eyes, he didn't look so smug anymore. He was afraid.

Good.

"You don't have to like him," Noah said evenly. "But you do have to not be a dick about it. He's your teammate, and he's supposed to be your friend. I'm not going to have this conversation with you again." He leaned around the Berlin's broad shoulders to point an accusing finger at rest of the boys, who all hung back awkwardly. "As for the rest of you, Sabin's doing fine, not that you fucking asked. You all ought to be ashamed for letting him get this bad. Fucking children," he finished with a frown, and then he turned his back on them, slamming the door behind him and standing in the hallway to put his face in his hands.

"Did he pee his pants?" Sabin said from nearby, and Noah jumped. The boy was leaning weakly against the wall, so Noah moved over to him and pulled him into a tight hug on the pretense of helping support him.

"I'm so sorry," he murmured into the other witch's hair. "I'm sorry for all of this. I'm sorry for letting them take you, and for everything that's happened since, and...I'm just so sorry. It shouldn't have been this way. I shouldn't have—" Noah stopped to breathe, but it turned into another soft hiccup.

Sabin sighed softly against him. "Stop," he said, a false annoyance in his voice that Noah knew well. "No more crying. Apologizing about that stuff so much makes me feel bad. There's nothing for you to apologize about. I mean, other than ruining my reputation just now," he added with a small groan. "He's gonna think I went crying to you now."

Noah snorted out a soft laugh, slowly leaning back from the embrace but leaving his hands gently on Sabin's shoulders. "If it helps any, I'm pretty sure he did pee a little, there at the end."

Sabin looked up at him with an exhausted smile. "Good. But I really don't want to face any of them right now."

"Oh, you're mistaken if you think you're not staying in the room with me."

Heavy bootsteps sounded on the stairs, and Noah looked over in time to see Julien rounding the corner with a bag of takeout boxes in one hand. He spotted the pair and gave what Noah considered a very gracious smile, considering his last conversation with Sabin.

"Did you still want something to eat?"

Sabin turned his face to the wall and tried to sniff away the last of his feelings, but when he looked back at Julien, he at least sounded a little more subdued. "Hey Pierre," he called. "What's in the boxes? Cigarettes and croissants?"

"Oh, I'm sorry," Julien shot back. "Do you not like poutine? I'll just throw this out."

"Hey hey hey—" Sabin pushed away from the wall and made straight for the food as if drawn forward by the promise of gravy and cheese curds, his stomach growling audibly. But as he reached for the bag, the knee he'd landed on before gave out under him, and he stumbled forward.

Before he could hit the ground, Julien caught him around the middle, easily scooping him back upright with his free arm. Noah rushed to help him, holding the boy by the waist to urge him back toward Julien's room.

Sabin kept his mouth shut, a faint touch of embarrassed heat in his face, until they reached the bedroom door. Then he said, much louder than necessary to ensure Julien could hear, "See? I told you he smelled like Labatt."

Noah reached back to take the boxes from Julien, whispering, "We're working on it," as he kicked the door shut and left the hunter empty-handed   in   the   hallway.

10

Once Julien had made his food delivery to Noah and the little pissant the witch for some reason seemed to adore, he tried to catch a nap in Hugo's room and was too soon kicked out upon his brother's return. He didn't dare step foot back in his own room and risk the wrath of Noah's kid, so he was on his way downstairs to find somewhere else to sleep when he met Lugh in the hallway.

"There you are," the hunter sighed. "You need a cell phone. Noah's friend is here—and all his friends. They're upstairs."

"Then it's time to find out what they know," the fairy answered curtly. He was already walking, so Julien cast a longing glance toward the study door, where a soft couch waited, then let out a faint sigh and followed him back up.

Julien directed the fairy to his room, and when Lugh opened the door, they found Sabin on the bed in a post-poutine coma while Noah sat up at the small desk across the room, a book open on his lap.

"Oh, you're here!" Noah said in a hushed voice. "I was going to try to find you, but..." He hesitated and looked over at the sleeping boy with a smile far gentler than he deserved. "I guess I lost track of time."

Lugh let a beat of silence pass, clearly not pleased with that answer. But instead of scolding, he just stepped over to the bed and looked down at the boy until he stirred.

Sabin stared up at him, blinking away the sleep in his eyes and swallowing hard once the fairy came into focus. "Oh," he said quietly. "You're big."

"So they say," Lugh answered dryly. "You're the little witch who's been fighting demons?"

Sabin edged upward into sitting on the mattress, seeming wary of taking his eyes from Lugh's face. He swallowed before answering. "Uh...yeah?"

Noah closed his book and leaned over in the chair to catch the boy's eye. "You don't have to be nervous, Sabin. This is Lugh. He's here to help."

"I'm not nervous," the younger witch said immediately, the slight crack in his voice causing Julien to fight a smirk. "Who said I was nervous?" Sabin clambered up to stand on the bed so that he could look the fairy straight in the face.

Lugh gave a short snort that may have been amusement. "I have questions for you. When you fought the demons before, there was a portal that they came through?"

"Yeah, that's right. Hidden in a room in a community center."

"It was hidden," Lugh repeated. "But you could see it? You knew it for what it was?"

"Yeah, once we found it," Sabin shrugged. "I mean, it was...five, six meters across? It looked a bit like a tunnel, but it was full of something...black. Not really smoke. Not really liquid. It's hard to explain. But it definitely looked, uh...demon-y."

Julien frowned. A five or six meter hole in the ground was something he and his brothers should have been able to find. Lugh glanced back at him with a frown that said he was thinking the same thing.

"And how did you close it?" the fairy went on.

"It just...closed up on its own. Cole and Bastian were able to, like...banish the demons out of people, I guess. And when the demons all went back through, I guess they chose to close it. Then it was just dirt."

Lugh folded his arms and dropped his gaze with a small, pensive sound. "That is unfortunate. I'd assumed there was some magic you'd done to seal it." He glanced over his shoulder at Julien. "That makes this worse."

"Great," the hunter sighed.

"I mean, there might be magic to close it," Sabin said. He looked over at Noah with a hopeful expression. "I bet we could find something. Right?"

Noah gave a slow, uncertain shrug. "I've been doing some reading on it since I got here, but...it's not promising."

Sabin turned back to Lugh, standing up a little straighter. "We can keep looking," he promised. Where had this version been when Julien was just trying to feed him?

"I trust you will," Lugh said, giving the young witch a quick glance up and down. "Are you well enough to—"

"Yes," Sabin cut him off eagerly.

The fairy nodded, and he led the way down the hall at Julien's direction, opening the bunk room door in search of the other boys. Julien knocked on each of his brothers' doors in turn, rousing them all and ushering them down to meet with the others. The war room was packed almost to capacity, but Julien's brothers and the new arrivals seemed eager to distance themselves from each other, so both ends of the table were more cramped than was really necessary. Lugh stood at the center so that he could address them all.

"I need to know what you know about the demons," he said first, his attention on the gathered boys. "I need to know where their leader is, how to close their portals, and how to kill any that come through. Do you know these things?"

The boy with the glasses—Milo, Julien had learned on the way over—stood a little closer to the table to answer. "We think Antarctica. I found a significant amount of information on the area after Marla left us in Louisiana." His voice was raspy and strained, and he paused to cough before carrying on. "Maps, all sorts of satellite readings spanning several months. She'd clearly been watching the area for a long time. Whether she was doing it for herself or for Ashmodai is anyone's guess, though."

"Antarctica?" Laurent echoed from across the table. "How are we supposed to do anything about something happening in *Antarctica*?"

"That is another issue," Milo agreed, his voice cracking slightly.

The boy beside him fussed over him, and Julien spotted Noah slipping quietly out of the room.

"It's moot if we have no goal," the fairy said. "We know where Ashmodai is, then. How can he be killed?"

Every set of eyes at the table turned toward the blond boy, whose white-feathered wings shook faintly under the attention.

"What's your name, boy?" Lugh asked, and the teen stood up a little straighter.

"Bastian."

"Then, Bastian—we need to solve the root problem. I can sail to meet the Lochlannan, but I can't fight them forever. Ashmodai is the cause of this conflict, and without knowing how to stop him, all of this is nothing more than talk."

Bastian swallowed hard, looking uncomfortable at how far he had to crane his neck to look at the man addressing him. His mouth opened and closed again, grasping for words that wouldn't come, until a boy with a blue mohawk stepped in for him, resting a hand on the table and leaning over it to catch Lugh's attention.

"Don't bother worrying about how to kill Ashmodai," he said. "Hey there. Jett. How ya doin," he said, giving the fairy a quick two-fingered salute. "We can handle that part once we get to him—after we get our friends back. Cole will be the only one who can do it."

Bastian turned on him. "What? Are you stupid? I'm not letting Cole go up against this guy."

Jett gave a shrug. "I mean, have fun if you want to give it a shot. But to kill a demon prince, you'll either need an archangel or another demon. And I don't see any feathers coming out your pocket. So unless you're hiding something from us, Cole is our only choice."

Antony spat out a curse. "Where did you people even come from? Why do you know so much about it?"

"Because I'm a smart guy, okay?" Jett shot back.

Antony sneered. "With that haircut?"

Arnaud cuffed the back of his younger brother's head. "Just shut up. Just for today. We're finally making progress; don't fuck it up."

Lugh spoke over them, his deep voice stern enough to silence the table. "That is only one answer we need. Ashmodai is not the only demon." He directed his question to Jett now, since Bastian wasn't as helpful as Julien would have expected the one with the wings to be. "What do you know about demons who come to this plane without a host? Of their own accord?"

"As of right now, there's no such thing," Jett answered."Demons can't come to this plane in body—only in spirit. And even then, it's difficult. They have to find places where the barrier is weak. The portals are built so that corporeal things can be moved from this plane to that. It's usually one way. They planned to take Cole through it."

Lugh seemed satisfied to have the attention of someone who actually had answers, and Julien couldn't blame him. "Unfortunately," the fairy said, "the demons' physical presence seems to be the situation we will soon face. A demon we captured told us that the Lochlannan have agreed to use their magic to allow the demons to pass." He nodded toward Rathgeirr, but then carried on, and the alfar seemed relieved not to have to answer any questions himself. "Apparently they will use the portals to do this."

Jett smiled a little, his hands on his hips as he cast his eyes to the side as though considering. "Ah...that is clever, isn't it? Things certainly seem to be making sense now."

"I had some hope one of you might know how to kill them, so that we might have a chance of dealing with this problem, but it seems that hope was in vain," Lugh said with a brief, disdainful glance toward Bastian.

"Oh, I definitely know how to do that part," Jett said casually.

"Are you fucking kidding?" Berlin snapped, but the other boy wasn't intimidated.

"Well, if it makes you feel any better, Berlin, I *don't* know how to shut the portals. So you can worry about that part, okay?"

"Tell us how to kill them," Lugh cut in, his tone far sharper in the face of so much bickering.

Jett huffed at Berlin before answering. "Once on earth, demons aren't much different than humans. Are any of you ordained by chance? You'll need holy weapons. Usually having a priest anoint them with holy water will do the trick, but there are ways to make them stronger."

Julien sighed. "Tabarnak, that will be easy to explain at St. Joseph."

"You or one of your brothers should get ordained. It comes in handy."

"We'll get on it," the hunter answered dryly. "What do we do in the meantime?"

"Well if the portals are about to become two way streets, then it seems like we should be sorting out how to close them."

"We haven't even been able to *find* the portal," Julien said. "We haven't seen anything like what Sabin described. Just possessed hosts."

Bastian finally spoke up, his voice a little too loud, as if he was excited to actually have something to contribute. "We heard that for months before we got to Trumbull, possessed people had been gathering in the town where the portal was. Congregating. Just waiting on us to get there."

Lugh turned his attention from the boy to speak to Julien instead. "The portal wasn't the only source, then. You may not have missed it after all; it may simply not be here yet."

"But it must be coming," the hunter insisted. "There've been so many."

"The Lochlannan are already on the move," Lugh pointed out. "We have to assume that they'll get the portals open before we can stop it, since we don't know where, or how many, they may be. Closing the gates is the priority, and then you," looking at Julien, "can concern yourself with putting down the strays."

"Dieu merci," Hugo said with a laugh. "Finally, something we know how to do."

Noah returned with a steaming cup in his hands, and he stopped at the end of the table to place a gentle hand on Milo's back, offering him the mug with an encouraging nod.

"Make sure you drink it all," Julien heard him murmur, and Milo glanced up at him with a surprised lift of his eyebrows, but he nodded and offered a smile and quiet thanks in return.

"That leaves the question of the portals themselves," Lugh continued. "If we don't know how to close them, who may?"

"They've been opened before," Jett said. "A long, *long* time ago. Men closed them, though I have no idea how. The information must be somewhere, though. I don't imagine the people who figured it out would just die with something like that. They must have passed it on."

Bastian elbowed Berlin, forcing him a little closer to the edge of the table. "I think Berlin might have a good place for us to start."

The tattooed boy sucked his teeth in irritation, casting an irritated glance at his friend, but he begrudgingly answered. "There's a monastery outside of Tübingen, Germany. I stayed there as a kid. If we ask, they can at least supply us with weapons. And maybe they know something about the portal stuff, too."

Edouard spoke now, loud enough to be heard across the table. "It's as good a place to start as any."

"Bebenhausen?" Laurent said. He leaned his hands on the table surface to peer over at Berlin. "Are you talking about The Benedictine Order of the Holy Vessel of Solomon?"

"Yeah, that's them," Berlin grunted without meeting the other man's eyes.

"I didn't think they still existed," Laurent went on with clear interest on his face. He glanced around the table at his brothers. "They were supposed to be an order of holy knights. If we can get help like that, it's worth it to try."

Lugh nodded his agreement and turned his attention to the boys. "You all will go, then?"

Bastian's voice seemed a bit more certain now. "We work as a team," he said with a quick look back at the others. "So we'll go together."

Lugh gave a soft grunt of acceptance. "I can provide the way."

"Are we really trusting this to the children?" Edouard asked skeptically. "Surely one of us ought to go."

Julien couldn't help his scoff of disbelief. "Edouard, you threw me in a river to fight a rusalka when I was thirteen. Are you serious?"

"Regarde ce gang de caves," Antony agreed, gesturing broadly at the group of teens across from him. "We're supposed to just trust these magic fucks are going to do as they say?"

Lugh hadn't taken his eyes off of Bastian. "Should we trust you? Are you children?"

The boy stuck his chin out a little, the feathers on his wings faintly fluffing. "We're young, but we aren't stupid. We've fought plenty of awful things. And we want these demons defeated as much as any of you. Why would we double cross you?"

Berlin wasn't so diplomatic. He shouted across the table at Antony,

"How many demons have you fought so far, fuckface?"

"I was putting down monsters while you were still sucking a tit, colon."

"Yeah, that wasn't my question, was it?"

Antony scoffed at him. "You're acting quite grateful considering we're letting you stay in our home."

"I don't *have* to be grateful if you're only helping us so we can kiss your asses, all right? That's not how helping people works."

Lugh dropped one hand heavily onto the table, making the sturdy wood tremble under his palm. "If they will go," he said, frowning at one end of the table and then the other, "we should let them. I have no more time to waste arguing." Once he was satisfied by the following quiet, he straightened and went on. "I will open the way so they may use the sídaige conar."

Milo made a soft, excited sound, and he took a step forward with his mug in his hands to look up at Lugh with wide eyes. "A fairy road?" he asked, wonder in his voice. He already sounded much healthier, and the sound put a warm smile on Noah's face.

"Yes," Lugh confirmed. "It will get you there the fastest."

Milo turned to the large boy next to him and whispered excitedly to him, clearly no longer listening.

Lugh exhaled through his nose with one hand on his hip, seeming to consider for a moment. "Five days," he said. He raised his eyes to each of the boys in turn. "In five days, my ships will pass near the Tasman Sea. If you can be on the coast there, I will carry you the rest of the way."

"We'll do it," Bastian said right away, his chest puffing a little despite the glare of the dark-skinned boy beside him. Milo turned back to them with a curious crease in his brow.

"Five days? Is five days going to be enough time? Isn't this island you're going to near the Arctic Circle?"

"It's enough time for my ship," the fairy answered simply. "Be on the southern coast at dusk of the fifth day," he added with a pointed look at the blond. "I can provide you with the means to signal my ships when it's time."

At the other side of the room, Antony opened his mouth again with an argument on his lips, so Lugh spoke first—and louder.

"Gather what you may need. I will give you the day to recuperate," he added as an aside in Sabin's direction, "but we must not waste time. In the morning, I expect you to be ready to leave."

"I'll sleep extra recuperatively tonight," the young witch promised.

Lugh tilted his head toward the door to dismiss the boys, then returned his attention to Julien's brothers. Julien watched their guests go with a faint frown. These kids showed up with very little, and they were about to send them back off on their own—apparently to face a secret government organization as well as a demon prince. While Edouard and the others were distracted, Julien slipped from the room and gave a quick, sharp whistle to catch the group before they went upstairs.

"You boys want some weapons?"

11

Having Sabin at the house—even Julien's family's weird, lifeless house—was like a dream. In some ways, the boy was very different from the one Noah remembered. He was more confident and more grown up. But mostly, once Sabin had some rest and some food and they had a free afternoon ahead of them, it was almost as if he'd never left. They swapped stories, laughed, and just sat together in Julien's room with music playing loudly from Noah's phone.

The only time Sabin left Noah's side was to go and fetch his own kit from the bunk room and plop on Julien's floor with it. He dug through the bag with both hands, then pulled free a polished silver mask with thick, frowning lips and sharply-carved eyes. Smooth lapis lazuli formed intricate shapes across the broad forehead and beneath the eyes, like a mask upon a mask. He held it carefully in both hands as he offered it to Noah, who received it with just as much reverence.

"This is the mask of the Kalku—the bog witch we killed in Louisiana," Sabin explained. "I...thought it would be safest if Julien and his brothers held onto it. I'm not *positive* she's not still in there. It seems like dudes like them would be able to keep it safe if that's the case. But don't you dare tell him I said so," he added with a petulant glower, and Noah smiled.

"I'll skip that part," he promised.

With the mask tucked safely into Julien's desk for now, Noah helped himself to Sabin's kit, checking his reserves and ingredients and finding them wanting. It didn't take much convincing to get a *little* more money out of Trent, and Julien told them which bus to take to get back to the shop without walking for an hour, which was helpful.

Sabin managed to restrain himself reasonably well in the shop, though Noah could tell he was tingling with excitement. How long had it been since he'd been able to just go out into the city on his own and go shopping? Noah was glad to scour the shelves with him, chatting about tricks they'd both picked up during the time they were apart, smelling herbs, and choosing the best bits of stone and wood and bone for Sabin to take with him. He kept a little cash left over, though—their next stop would be the grocery store.

Sabin didn't even wait until they were back on the bus to open his first packet of Jos Louis and shove it whole into his mouth. They made the trek back to the house, arms laden with bags of ketchup chips, cans of Crush cream soda, some Coffee Crisp, and as many boxes of Jos Louis as they could afford. They only thing they couldn't track down was Nanaimo bars, prompting Sabin into another tirade about "fucking Montreal," but Noah found it hard to take him seriously with red velvet crumbs on his cheek.

Sabin devoured his food at dinner. For a second, Noah was a little grateful that Sabin had been put up by someone else for a while—he wasn't sure he'd have been able to afford to feed the growing teenager.

The rest of the boys seemed to be constantly bickering—with Julien's brothers as well as with each other. They never had kind words to say to any of their comrades. They always just tore each other down. Hugo, at least, tried to be welcoming, but by the time Antony and Berlin almost went across the table at each other, Noah was done. Bastian, the one who'd been calling himself the leader this whole time, even yelled at one of the other boys and stormed out. Lugh seemed to be taking a liking to Sabin, though, which warmed Noah's heart a little. The kid could do worse than being on the half-giant's good side.

Julien kept his distance from them, even after dinner. Noah wished he'd make more of an effort, but he couldn't blame him for avoiding Sabin's smart-ass mouth when he was running on so little sleep. He also couldn't complain about the extra alone time with Sabin, especially when he was going to lose him again so soon.

When they'd both settled on Julien's bed and sat sharing one of the bags of ketchup chips, Noah fidgeted with the blanket a little, trying not to voice what was really on his mind. Finally, when he felt Sabin's knowing, waiting eyes on him, he spoke up.

"I don't know why you have to go with them, anyway," he said in a rush. "All those other kids are assholes, and they almost got you killed before, and they clearly don't appreciate everything you do for them, and you could do just as much good against the demons staying here with Julien and I." He paused, then consciously shut his mouth and gave a small huff through his nose.

Sabin seemed surprised by the older witch's outburst, but he ate the chip in his hand with a weary smile. "Staying here with you would be the best," he said. "And you better not think that's not how this is gonna end, but..." He paused and sighed lightly. "I have to go."

"But they're all so *awful*," Noah argued. "Except Jett. I like Jett. But other than him, they're just...I thought you guys would all be friends, teammates, whatever, like, supporting each other and fighting monsters and shit. But none of you even seem to like each other."

"Yeah," Sabin agreed. "Right now we're all pretty awful. But we weren't originally. Marla's really messed us up. I mean, I'd had my suspicions, but she wasn't always terrible. And some of the others, like Milo and Cole, really did see her as a mother figure, I think. Turns out, when someone like that tries to murder you, it puts a strain on your other relationships. And there are a hundred other awful things that have happened. But in the end, they're still my friends. My shitty, stressed out, dickhead friends." He snorted softly and turned his eyes to Noah, clearly hoping he'd lightened the mood.

Noah slumped back against the headboard beside him and laid his head on the boy's shoulder with a slow, heavy breath. "I can't argue with that," he admitted softly. "Just...be good, okay? Come back to me."

"When I get back, I think we should go get tattoos. I was able to do my own piercings, but there was no way in hell I was gonna give myself a prison tat."

He snorted. "I know a girl in Vancouver. It's a promise."

Sabin chewed his chips loudly into Noah's ear until the older man finally leaned back from him. At least now the boy was free, and they would be able to keep in touch until they could get back to each other again. They *would* get back to each other. He had to trust in that. Until then, Noah could at least scold him for not keeping up with his yoga and meditation.

Noah didn't sleep well—he spent a lot of time watching Sabin curled up peacefully in the bed, and he found Jett in the kitchen when he went downstairs to have a cup of tea, which was a welcome reminder that not *all* of Sabin's teammates were shitty dickheads. Maybe Sabin could date him, instead. Berlin certainly hadn't done anything that impressed Noah.

In the morning, they made a strange gathering on the Tour de Lévis—Julien, Noah, Ciaran, Trent, Rathgeirr, and Lugh, as well as all six of the boys, each of them loaded up with their weapons and supplies. Lugh stood at one side of the stone tower with Bastian, to whom he offered a small stone pendant carved with swirling knots.

"This will open the way for you when you're ready to return. The word is 'aroslaici,'" he said, but when Bastian reached to take the token from him, Lugh kept a firm hold on it to draw the boy's attention to his eyes. "This is a rare and powerful artifact—and I am expecting it back."

"Yes sir," Bastian answered—pretty bravely, Noah thought, considering.

When the gate was open, Noah grabbed for Sabin one last time while Lugh instructed the others, hugging him as tightly as he could without a care to whether he'd be embarrassed. "Take care of yourself," he whispered into the boy's hair. He did his best not to cry again, but he let a single sniffle escape him as he reluctantly released the boy he wanted so badly to keep next to him. This was Sabin's decision—it had to be. And when he came back, they'd go and get tattoos.

Sabin gave him a sad but sure smile, and he winked at him before turning his back to him to follow the rest of the boys through the open portal. Jett was waiting for him, and as they walked together, the boy put a light hand on the back of Sabin's neck and leaned in to speak into his ear. That was promising. Noah smiled faintly and forced himself to exhale slowly as Julien took a gentle hold of his hand.

Lugh didn't waste any time in opening a second door. Ciaran, Trent, and Rathgeirr stood ready, their own bags slung over shoulders. Noah gave Rathgeirr a (significantly less-intense) hug goodbye, which seemed to startle him, but the alfar smiled and wished him luck. Even Trent muttered a goodbye on his way through. Noah considered that a step in the right direction.

"Good luck storming the island!" he called before their figures disappeared into the blackness of the gate.

Lugh lingered just a moment, and he reached out to thump Julien lightly on the shoulder. "Good luck, an duine. We'll meet again."

He nodded. "I'll take care of things here."

The fairy seemed to accept this answer, and as he stepped beyond the threshold of the portal, it snapped cleanly shut behind him, leaving Noah and Julien to stand alone at the top of the aging tower.

Julien touched the witch's cheek, wiping away a stray tear with his thumb. "He'll be back before you know it," he promised.

"I hope you're right," Noah sighed. He hesitated, glancing around at the city sprawled around them before looking back up into Julien's face. "So," he began quietly, "I know we have a lot to do, and the world is ending and everything, but...do you know anywhere good to get breakfast? I want you to take me on a date in Montreal."

The hunter's eyebrows lifted in surprise, but after a pause, he smiled.   "You   like   crepes?"

12

Trent was on a boat again. Almost as soon as they'd arrived at—wherever the fairy road had taken them, it all just looked like farmland to him—Lugh had hurried them to the coast and loaded them onto his ship. Trent had spent more time on that goddamn boat than he'd ever wanted to, and now he was willingly climbing back in. He must be an idiot. Noah had at least sent him equipped with a supply of the strange peppermint-ginger tablets that had kept him from puking his guts out before, but Trent had brought along a box of regular old Dramamine too, just in case.

At least, Lugh had assured them, his scouts reported that the storm surrounding the island had dissipated, so it shouldn't take nine days to reach anymore. That was better than no good news, Trent guessed. He still sat as close to the center of the boat as he could and left Ciaran to enjoy the sea air from his place at the bow. Rathgeirr sat near him with a sympathetic frown, but whenever he tried to offer words of comfort, Trent just shushed him. The alfar passed the time instead by fussing over the new brooch securing his cloak, refastening the shining silver circle of knotwork that matched the pattern on the fairy general's shield. It had been a gift from Lugh—a sign to the rest of the army that he was a friend.

Trent was already about to reach for a second bit of ginger when Rathgeirr suddenly rushed past him, knocking Ciaran aside so that he could lean against the front of the boat to look out. Ahead of them, a long line of ships had appeared at the horizon, skimming the dark water so lightly they barely made any wake. Trent stood with one hand on the mast to get a better view as they approached. This number was only the tail end of the fairy ships—Lugh's vessel was faster, and he sailed beyond the coming row into a much larger mass of swift ships, men's voices lifting in a chanting cheer as their general passed.

The ships around them were larger than Lugh's—much longer, and each with tall sails as well as sets of oars along the sides. There must have been thirty or forty men on each one. At the head of the group, one massive, ornately-decorated ship led the way across the cold, barren ocean, and it was only when they caught up to this one that Ciaran dropped the sails and helped secure Lugh's boat to the side. The three kings of the Tuatha Dé Danann stood waiting on the deck for Lugh to board, so Trent stayed put. He'd been around the fairies enough to know a human wouldn't be welcomed in a council like this. Ciaran waved him over a little closer to the edge as he climbed up, though, so Trent lingered nearby, his fingertips on the railing so he could peek over like a mermaid watching her chosen sailor.

The kings had seemed pleased to see Lugh, but when Rathgeirr recounted for them the numbers he'd given before, their faces fell. The one with thick braids in his beard—the High King, Ciaran had called him before—spoke first.

"We can't possibly surround them if we're outnumbered. How are we supposed to contain that many ships?"

"We can't," Lugh answered simply. "A defensive position isn't feasible. We have to attack them."

"Attack the Isle of Lochlann?" one of the other kings scoffed.

"If we attack, they will be forced to defend. They will have to leave soldiers here to defend their cities. And the more people they leave, the fewer there will be to enter the world of men."

The three brother kings exchanged concerned glances with each other, and Trent shared their uncertainty. They were so outnumbered they couldn't hope to defend against the numbers the alfar had, so the answer was to...attack them head on? The thought made his stomach hurt.

Even so, the High King returned his attention to Lugh, and he nodded. "It's agreed."

Lugh didn't wait to be dismissed. He returned to his place at the helm of his own ship, and as soon as Ciaran had freed them from the kings' longship and dropped the sails, they started North again with the whole of the fairy navy at their backs. Maybe Trent should have asked if he could hitch a ride on one of those, instead.

They didn't have to go much farther before Trent began to really, really wish he could have stayed home. More ships than he could count, each built of dark, ashen wood with snarling dragons at the head, sailed smoothly through the thick, rolling cloud of black smoke that preceded it, stretched so far across the ocean that Trent couldn't see either end of them. As soon as the ships came within sight of each other, deep, heavy drumbeats began to sound from the dark vessels in a grim rhythm that brought up goosebumps on Trent's skin. Ciaran held tight to the leather grip of his shillelagh and strapped his shield to his arm, the silver face of the boar on its front still shining despite its numerous scratches. Rathgeirr took his bow from his shoulder and glanced into the quiver at his back to do a quick count.

All around them, the fairy ships rowed swiftly toward the line of waiting longboats, and archers stood along the rails with arrows nocked, waiting for the order to release. At Lugh's shout, a hundred arrows flew from either side of their boat, arcing toward the approaching ships with a loud hum. Too many of the arrows were diverted, crashing against a shimmer of silver light that seemed to encompass the whole of each alfar ship, but some pierced the veil and the men beneath it, bringing up cries of pain barely audible over the rush of the waves.

The sound of the arrows was lasting too long—when Trent lifted his eyes, he saw the mass of black firing back toward them in a cloud like a swarm of insects. He didn't have time to wonder what to do. Before he could form a single thought, Ciaran had snatched him by the arm and pulled him down low to the floor of the ship, drawing up his shield to cover them both. He braced but still jerked downward as arrowheads buried themselves in the thick wood, more landing in the bench on both sides of them. He stood with Trent behind him and swung his shillelagh once, snapping the arrows that stuck out from the boar's face so that the feathered ends clattered into the bottom of the boat.

Trent startled at a sharp whinny at the side of the ship. Lugh's horse stood with water washing over its hooves, but it didn't have to wait long for the fairy to climb into its saddle. He pulled his spear free of its leather, the tip bursting to life with yellow flame, and shouted at Ciaran.

"Get through their line!" The horse shook its head and snorted, bursting to run, and Lugh pointed the way toward the island with his spear. "I want that bow on Lochlannan soil!"

Ciaran urged Trent into the small space between the benches where he'd spent a good portion of their last boat ride, then took his place at the helm and steered the ship to follow the thumping hoofbeats of the Enbarr.

Trent forced himself not to cower completely, though he was positive he wasn't going to be of any use. The seas grew rough around them, the crashing waves seeming to pass harmlessly by the alfar ships only to hit the fairies all the harder. Trent was sprayed with foam more than once, but Ciaran sailed on. Rathgeirr stood on the edge of the boat as steadily as if it were solid ground, firing his arrows toward the enemy ships one by one with a sharp gaze. Lugh's spear was a blaze of light on the smoky water, forcing up screams wherever it passed.

"Trent!" Ciaran's voice called out over the fury around them. "Drop the second sail! We have to break through!"

"What?" Trent shouted back. "How?"

He pointed at one of the ropes knotted securely to a metal cleat along the hull. "There!"

Trent forced himself over the bench and took hold of the rope, tearing it free and almost losing his grip on it in the process. At Ciaran's yell, Trent pulled with his whole body weight, hauling the heavy canvas loose to catch the last scraps of wind. As he held the rope taut, a sharp whistle sounded near his face, but a glint of light made him flinch, and when he opened his eyes, he saw the two halves of the arrow that had almost struck him, and Rathgeirr with his sword in hand. The alfar gave him a quick smile and a nod, then pulled one of the used arrows from the nearest bench and fired it back.

Trent did his best to hold tight to the rope, not really having any idea what he was doing. Their boat scraped the side of one of the larger alfar ships with a creaking crash, and for the first time, this close to the others, Rathgeirr hesitated to shoot. He stumbled when the ship's bow smashed back into the water, finally allowing them to pass beyond the line of dark longships. They weren't the only ship to make it—the alfar ships were too long to turn quickly, so dozens of fairy boats passed through the fjords beside them and crashed onto the rocky beaches with a heavy thump.

Ciaran moved forward immediately, tossing their bags of supplies to Rathgeirr on the shore and dragging Trent onto the beach alongside him, barely getting him free of Lugh's ship before it retreated of its own accord, sinking back under the surface of the water. Its master appeared moments later, touching his spear to each boat as it emptied and setting it to burn.

"What the hell is he doing?" Trent asked, unsteadily held upright by Ciaran's arm around his shoulders.

Ciaran watched the crumbling ships with a grim frown. "He's making sure they know we aren't leaving."

Beyond the edge of the fjord, the tallest of the alfar ships were still sailing, almost too far away to see, now. Lugh's horse reared to a stop in front of the High King, who stood with his brothers on an outcropping of rock nearby.

"Huldrekall is leading the largest ships," Lugh said without preamble. "They don't intend to stop for us. With your blessing, Ard Rí, I will take some ships to hunt them down. We must not let Huldrekall reach this demon."

"Of course," the king answered, already waving the other man away. "Choose your men. We will begin the assault here."

Lugh's ship surfaced a short distance from the shore, and the general pointed out a handful of men standing by, who made for the shoreline without hesitation. Ciaran moved automatically to join them, but Lugh lowered his spear to block him.

"Not you."

"What do you mean, not me?" Ciaran spit, looking up at the larger man as if he'd offended him.

Lugh urged the horse a step closer and leaned down to speak to his father in a lowered voice. "We are outnumbered here," he said. "Traditional tactics will not suffice. I need people who can be where the Lochlannan are not looking and strike where they are weak. Can you do that, Scal Balb?"

Ciaran frowned, but after a moment, he nodded. "I can."

"Good." Lugh dropped from his horse onto the boat, allowing the animal to run free into the ocean, and as soon as he was at the helm, he and the men he'd chosen were sailing from the island, accompanied by a handful of other ships equally loaded with soldiers.

Standing under his own power on the shifting sand, a cold wind biting into his damp skin as he clutched his bag to his chest, Trent realized he was trembling. He jumped when Ciaran touched his arm and only relaxed a little under the warmth of the fairy's smile, but he followed where the others walked. At the High King's direction, the mass of the army began to set up camp along one of the tall, bleak cliffs. The misty ruins that Trent knew hid the city of Falias were far beneath them, but still close enough that it made Trent nervous.

The sheer number of people around Trent overwhelmed him. There were crowds of fairies everywhere—mostly men, but some women too, all working with quick, practiced hands to raise tents, carry supplies, and build fires along the windy coast. Lugh had taken dozens with him as well. It hadn't struck Trent until this moment what an army of thirty thousand people actually looked like.

Ciaran guided him with a hand at his elbow, Rathgeirr following along behind, and at the crest of the next hill, one of the fairy's brothers called out to him. Cu, Cethen, Airmed, and Ciaran's father were setting up their places with the help of a few bustling servants. Ciaran exchanged laughing greetings and hugs with his siblings, and Airmed even grabbed Trent around the neck for a brief squeeze, but when she released him and found herself faced with Rathgeirr, she hesitated before giving him a quick, polite curtsy instead.

"What now?" Trent asked while Ciaran dropped his bag in the dirt. He accepted a bundle from one of the servants so that he could pitch their own simple tent. "I get that this isn't a blockade or whatever anymore, but so now we're just going to sit here?"

"Everyone's been sailing for days," Ciaran said with a shrug. "They need rest and food. The Lochlannan will take time to get their own ships back safe to port, and then they'll have to decide what to do about us." He laid out the canvas that would be their roof and deftly raised it into a more rooflike shape on its poles, as if he'd done it a hundred times. "Still—we'll need to become a threat pretty quickly, or we'll just be wiped out, I suspect."

Trent frowned at him. "Is that what Lugh meant by non-traditional tactics?"

"Yes," he answered simply, crouching to pin the tent securely into the ground. "Falias will be empty of soldiers except for the city garrison, likely, and if we're lucky, the others will think about saving their own cities before they come to Falias's aid."

Cu appeared behind Ciaran, slapping his back with a laugh as he rose. "Are you talking about doing some damage to the city? That's what I came for!"

Ciaran tossed his bag into the small tent, then paused when he turned back to Trent. "Just stay here for now. Please," he added quickly. "I'll need to see what the Ard Rí has to say."

"Sure," Trent answered, his tone subdued. He watched Ciaran go off with his brothers, all three of them already talking amongst themselves, and then he spread the blanket they'd been given over the hard ground and took his place in the tent to wait. What the fuck were either of them doing here?

13

The Ard Rí actually seemed happy to see Ciaran, which was a pleasant surprise. He greeted the three brothers kindly, but there was no point to a long briefing. Everyone present had taken part in enough wars to know the situation. So the High King assigned Ciaran command of a dozen men, including his younger brothers, and sent him away with a single order.

"Let them know we're here."

Ciaran promised Trent with a kiss that he would be back by morning, assured him that he would be fine, and slipped back out of the tent before the boy could put up too much of a fight. He checked the buckles on his armor and secured the leather strap of his shillelagh around his wrist as he returned to meet his brothers at the first descent of the hill leading down from the camp. He stopped them both a fair distance from the men waiting for them.

"I ought to tell you both something," he said in a low voice. Once they'd both turned to face him, he went on. "That spell that the human witch used to bring me back, after the battle at Mag Dúshlán. It took something from me. I can't do magic anymore. I'm still fit, but...I think I've been made mortal?"

"What?" Cethen breathed. "How?"

Ciaran pulled the golden pendant from under his shirt and held it out to them, displaying the deep black crack in the carving.

Cu gave a soft whistle. "Don't like the look of that at all."

"Doesn't seem promising, does it?" Ciaran chuckled.

Cu tilted his head to peer at him. "But you still came."

"I can still fight," Ciaran insisted. "And I still want to end this nonsense once and for all so I can go back to *not* being here."

Cethen let out a quiet sigh, watching his eldest brother with concern creasing his brow. "Bráthair, if you're sure, but..."

"I'm sure. Don't tell athair—the last thing I need is him finding one more reason to tell me I'm useless. As long as I can still fight, I'm going to. You lot...may just have to cover for me a bit on the magic front."

"Not the first time we've covered for you," Cu snorted.

"And not likely to be the last," Ciaran agreed with a chuckle. "Thank you. Now let's go. Step one is to have ourselves some horses."

They gathered the rest of the men, Ciaran tapping Rathgeirr on their way, and spent the time until dusk scouting the area around the city. They drew close enough for the disguising mist to give way, but skirted the city itself, crouching low to walk through the tall grain in the surrounding fields. The solid ramparts were lit at intervals with bright torches, and cloaked figures stalked the perimeter—though not as many as Ciaran had feared. They'd left behind a light guard, just as Lugh expected.

The alfar patrolled their sections of the wall with frustrating regularity, but when Ciaran saw a gap, he led the group toward the wall, their movements barely rustling the grain around them. He stopped near the rear of the city, where the field was split by a road that led from the closed gate. The stables would be near there—he'd ridden down this same road with Trent not so long ago. The men squatted together in a line along the shadow of the wall, and Ciaran addressed them in a hushed whisper.

"The gate opens by magic," he said. "We won't be able to go in that way."

"I can open it," Rathgeirr spoke up.

"They're still sure to notice if we just open the front gate and walk in, lad."

"Then how are we getting the horses?" Cethen asked.

Ciaran turned, scanning the thick stones of the rampart, and he slid his shillelagh through the loop in his belt to free his hands. He reached up to run his fingertips along the edges of the closest stones, leaning his weight back on his heels to test the grip.

"It'll do," he murmured with a nod, and the others seemed to catch his meaning. "Cu, you stay outside. Give us some time, and then get their attention. We'll need their eyes on you and away from the gate."

Cu gave a quick nod and slipped away through the field again on his own, back toward the thin grass and rocks of the gate.

"Rathgeirr," Ciaran went on, "when you hear Cu, open up for us."

"Yes." The alfar almost seemed to melt into the shadow of the stones as he made his way closer to the narrow road.

Ciaran offered his remaining brother a brief smile. "On with it, then." He took a firmer hold of the wall just above his head and hefted himself up, the other fairies following him straight up the side of the tall rampart. At the top, Ciaran paused with his eyes scantly over the edge, skimming the broad wall for guards and hauling himself up at the corner of one of the low towers. He risked crossing the rampart to check their location in the city below and found the marketplace, empty of bodies now that night had fallen.

With his back flattened against the tower, he waved the rest of his men up one by one, each one dropping to the ground inside the city with a silent step. He had to snatch one of the younger ones by the back of his collar and drag him back behind a rack of spears as a guard passed by, pressing a hand to the young man's mouth to keep him silent until the alfar passed. Then he pushed him along, called up the last of them, and finally went himself, his boots finding the packed earth of the marketplace. The others had tucked themselves close around the cloth-covered wooden stalls out of sight of the guards above, so Ciaran gestured to them to follow and made his way carefully through the market alleys.

He stopped with a hand behind him to halt Cethen as an alfar carrying a torch walked the path in front of them, but as soon as he'd gone, the fairies slipped through to the long, covered stables beyond. They passed rows of dark, thatched-roof homes and came to a stop at the towering wooden doors of the stable. Two men lifted the heavy beam barring the doors and laid it aside, allowing them all to slip into the shadows within.

Before the horses could startle, Cethen made his way down the corridor, gently touching each animal's neck or muzzle and whispering soothing magic to them. Cethen had never had a soul for battle—but for charming horses, there was no one Ciaran would trust more. He waved the rest of the men behind his brother, and they began to open the stall doors, swiftly taking up ropes and slinging them around the animals' necks to guide them out. Ciaran kept his place near the door to watch for any guards while the others mounted their chosen horses, each with two or three other leads in their hands, and then they all waited in tense silence for any sign from Cu.

Somewhere on the ramparts, a deep, bellowing war horn blew, and voices outside the stable began to shout. " Ævintýri," the warning came, carried torches flooding toward the gate as Ciaran watched from the door. He waved the men forward, easily settling himself on the back of the horse Cethen offered him, and when he kicked the stable door open wide and gave the call, they rode out, hooves pounding full speed through the quiet marketplace. The last fairy to leave the stable hit a lit brazier with his sword, spilling hot coal into the dry hay and igniting a blaze that swallowed the wooden stalls so quickly that Ciaran could feel the heat of the flames on his back before he even reached the rampart.

The stones of the closed gate gave way before them, revealing Cu standing on a boulder outside the wall, pounding his shield with the pommel of his sword and shouting taunts at the alfar who were swiftly gathering at the edge of the wall. The noise was amplified, as if dozens more warriors lurked in the thin trees behind him, and the alfar dropped from the wall to approach him with weapons drawn.

Ciaran reached him first. He hauled his brother up behind him with a tight grip on his forearm and didn't bother trying to hide his smile as Cu let loose a whooping laugh that echoed across the field. He raised his shield to block an arrow that would otherwise have struck Ciaran's shoulder while they rode, but they met no further resistance—the fire in the stable would be spreading quickly, and Ciaran could already hear the shouts of the Alfar, forced to return to the city to stop it from taking over the homes nearby.

He spotted Rathgeirr on a horse close by as they gave the city a wide berth, making certain they weren't being followed back to the camp. It would be hidden from sight by magic, but that wouldn't stop an Alfar soldier from putting two and two together if a whole pack of horses suddenly vanished into the hill.

When they did make it back, they led the horses through the rows of tents and campfires to the sound of laughter and welcoming shouts. The three kings met them as they dismounted, several servants coming to take the animals away for care and feeding. Ciaran accepted the High King's nod of thanks with a polite bow, then made for the spot where Trent waited. He brushed by him with a hand on the flap of the tent, wasting no time in unbuckling his belt and loosening the straps on his armor to remove it.

"I told you I'd be back," he said, hoping for Trent's sake that he didn't sound as tired as he felt.

Trent settled cross-legged in the small space near him. "So the secret to a successful war campaign is stealing horses?" he asked with a mild scoff. "You're a horse thief now?"

Ciaran paused with his armor still in his hands, then pressed his lips together and gave a serious nod as he set it aside. "Aye. *Now* I'm a horse thief. Yes."

"You're hilarious," Trent answered flatly. "I'm glad you're enjoying yourself now that we're in the middle of a war."

The fairy gave a light sigh and took his place beside Trent, tugging off his boots and tossing them into a corner. "Listen, a mhuirnín. Long ago, I ran away. Because I was selfish." He laced his fingers together in his lap and looked down at them, not quite wanting to meet the other man's eyes. "I wasn't thinking of how I'd affect anyone. I just wanted to get out and live my life and be...*away* from all of them. I did it for ages, and look where it got me. People died because of me—literally, directly died because they touched me, and I didn't care. All of this not caring almost got you killed, in the end. The best thing that's ever happened to me, and all I've ever done is get you into trouble."

Trent slumped a little next to him and leaned his elbow on his knee, his chin in one hand. "You picked now, after you've turned mortal and useless, to have a conscience?"

Ciaran snorted softly. "Not a conscience, maybe." He looked over at the boy and reached out to brush his fingers over his cheek. "But if there's something I can do that will help to keep you safe and make a better future for us, I'm going to do it. Even if I am mortal and useless now."

Trent hesitated, a faint flush blooming under his cheeks, and he forced his gaze away from the fairy's. "That's stupid," he grumped. "You're stupid."

"Aye, likely," Ciaran chuckled. He leaned closer and turned Trent's face to him with a light touch so that he could press a kiss to his lips. Trent gripped his forearm with clinging fingers, and the fairy retreated just enough to whisper to him. "Come lay with me, a mhuirnín."

Their bed was only a pile of blankets and furs on rocky ground, but with Trent tucked into the crook of his arm, Ciaran didn't mind it. He kept the boy close to him, kissing him and touching his hair. Trent slowly relaxed against him, sighing softly under the fairy's lips, but he tensed again when Ciaran's hand traced down his back to give his ass a firm squeeze and tug him closer.

"Are you serious right now?" Trent whispered, his eyes darting toward the closed flap of the tent.

Ciaran ignored his protests, dipping his head to give the boy's chin a soft bite. "It's been days since we were alone together," he murmured, a smile crossing his lips at the shiver his tone made in the other man. His hand went under Trent's shirt, chilled fingers flattening against his warm skin, and he lapped at the line of collarbone exposed at his neckline.

Trent shuddered, his grip tightening on Ciaran's tunic and his dick stirring against the fairy's hip despite his complaints. "We're in a military camp right now on Viking Elf Island," he hissed, only managing to sound distantly irritated. "Does the constant threat of death turn you on or something?"

Ciaran smiled against Trent's skin and slid one hand between them to grip his growing erection, relishing the soft hitch in the other man's chest. "Why?" he asked, touching a kiss to the corner of Trent's lips. "Doesn't it you?" He tugged at the waist of Trent's slacks and snapped the button open.

There was no fighting him. Trent clung tightly to the fairy's back, his breath held tight in his throat so that he could hold in his moans as his lover stroked him with firm, familiar fingers. His own hands fought with the lacing on Ciaran's trousers, and soon they were both panting into the other's shoulder, fighting for air as their hands moved desperately between them. Ciaran held the smaller man close against him, tasting his lips eagerly and refusing to let him pull away even when his hips bucked helplessly. Trent finally gave a strained, tight-jawed cry into the fairy's kiss as his orgasm pulsed into his hand, and he soon felt the heat of Ciaran's own climax spilling messily over his fingers, the groan in the fairy's throat almost succeeding in rousing him again.

When the haze over his vision cleared, Trent realized that he'd gotten semen—from one or the other of them, or both, he didn't know—all over the front of his shirt, and he let out an irritated scoff.

"Ugh," he grunted into Ciaran's neck. "This is one of maybe three shirts I still own."

"Just wash it in the river like a good wife," the fairy rumbled against the smaller man's hair. "Will you do mine?"

"I'm going to drown you in the river," Trent promised.

Ciaran smiled, turning Trent's face toward him with a gentle hand and laying a long, warm kiss to his lips that the boy didn't have the heart to pull back from.

14

Maybe they were looking in the wrong place. Julien had spent the better part of the day searching the park and woods around Mont Royal, as had his brothers, and they were no nearer to finding the actual door the demons hoped to use than they had been three days ago. Since the others had gone, Noah had been free to come with him. The witch had been glad to explore even this small part of the city—especially since they'd all split up, and he wouldn't have to put up with any of the Fournier brothers except for Julien himself.

Arnaud had dug a handful of consecrated items from the armory—and gracefully not mentioned the missing weapons Julien had given away—but they consisted wholly of two crucifixes, five small bottles of holy water, and six steel daggers. Joseph had gladly given up his chance to carry one, as he never got close enough to anything to fight with something like a dagger. It meant they were likely to have to carry a possession victim back to the house with a bullet in their leg, but that was better than dead, Julien supposed.

He walked the paths surrounding the Cimetière Notre-Dame-Des-Neiges with Noah at his side, the witch murmuring to himself and slowly wringing bitter-smelling oils over his hands, which he laid on this or that stone or bench as they went. Each time he would frown and shake his head or lead them quicker down a turn in the lane, but they never came across anyone Noah even suspected was possessed. Lugh had said the Alfar were on the move, so where the hell were they? This directionless searching was wearing on everyone.

They did get derailed from their mission when Julien crumpled underneath a slick-skinned, black creature that leapt at him from the eaves of one of the larger mausoleums. It was almost shaped like a person, but its hands and feet were webbed and toothed with serrated spines that latched onto the flesh of the hunter's arms. Julien put a rip in his coat tearing the thing off of him, and while he grappled with its slippery limbs and dodged its broad, angler fish mouth, Noah stood by with a groan of frustration on his lips.

"Oh, that's a...a zad...fuck, I can't remember. Hang on," he said, holding up one finger while he pulled his phone from his pocket to type.

Julien shoved the creature away from him and got his boot onto its neck, but in exchange, it wrapped its long, sharp fingers around one of his thighs.

"How many digits does it have?" Noah called over to him.

Julien grunted as he hit the dirt from the struggling monster's pull, but with his legs fastening around at least one of its limbs to pin it down by the shoulder, he was able to sink one of his larger knives into its neck. Deep blue blood spurted from the thing's moist skin, staining Julien's shirt and almost getting in his mouth. It thrashed against him for a few brief moments, but when enough of its blood had seeped into the soil, it went still, its arms and legs finally thumping back to the ground. Julien nudged its webbed hand with one boot once he got to his feet.

"Four," he answered as he got to his feet.

"Zadavi!" the witch said with a triumphant smile on its face. He stepped over and picked one of the broken spines from the hunter's legs, making him wince. He brought it close to his face for inspection. "Oh, I'm gonna keep these," he mumbled to himself, and he crouched to gather a few more from the corpse before Julien hauled it away to a dumpster at the edge of the cemetery's grounds.

They hadn't stopped to eat, only shared some granola bars as they went, and that had been hours ago, now. Night had fully fallen, and the day's worth of seeking spells was clearly taking its toll on Noah, but the witch kept on without complaint, still smiling whenever the hunter happened to catch his eye. Julien didn't say it, but he was glad just to be somewhere with him.

"So, there are seven of you," Noah began, "and you guys split up into pairs when we left, right? So, if I hadn't been here—before you knew me—would you have just been out of luck when this sort of thing happened?"

Julien shrugged one shoulder. "Not that we're all together like this very often, but yes. I was usually alone."

"The more I hear about your family, the more I dislike them."

When they reached the end of their section of the grid Laurent had drawn up on the map and had to move on, they hopped the tall, iron fence to get into the cemetery proper. The paths here were a little more worn than the gentle walkways through the park, and there were fewer lights, but Noah kept their way lit with a small blue flame carefully controlled in his palm.

"Why do I spend so much time in cemeteries with you?" the witch teased, and Julien snorted softly.

"You said you wanted to go on more dates."

"Cute."

They walked for close to an hour, both watching the periphery of the light for signs of movement or the scent of magic—or anything else that had even a slim chance of guiding them in the direction of the portal.

"God, this place is huge," Noah sighed. "Like, half of this town seems to be cemetery. Is everyone in Quebec buried here?"

"Most of Montreal is buried here," Julien agreed with a shrug. "My grandfather and three of my uncles are buried here. And many more before them, too, I guess."

"But not your dad, right? He's still living, isn't he?"

"I shouldn't say 'unfortunately,' but yes," Julien grumbled.

"And why isn't he here where the world is ending?"

"He wouldn't see it that way. This is just another problem—and the world is always full of problems, he says. As soon as all of us were of age, he left this part of it to us. He's somewhere in Southeast Asia, the last I heard. Thailand, maybe. I don't know where any of my uncles are. When my brothers' children are grown, we'll be expected to travel, too. Then they will stay in Canada in our place."

"That's one way to run a family, I guess. So you haven't seen him in a long time? Edouard seems like he's pretty settled into being in charge."

"He is," Julien grunted. "Very settled. My father left when I was around twenty, so..." He shrugged one shoulder. "Fifteen years. I don't miss him."

The witch softened slightly. "Do you think you'll be buried here?"

"Me? Pfft." Julien glanced over at him in the flickering light. "I'm going to live forever; don't you know that?"

Noah laughed and shook his head. "Maybe we should go home. If you're making jokes on the job, you're clearly sleep-deprived."

Julien was tempted to agree with him. But before they had the chance to discuss it, they turned the corner close to a building cut into the side of a dark cliff face, and Noah put a hand on his chest to stop him. A low metal gate guarded the entrance, which was an arch of glass with mosaic angels flanking the door. Above it, in a small alcove of rock, a statue of Mary was nestled overlooking the courtyard, her hands clasped to her chest and her eyes raised to heaven. Julien recognized it—this was the columbarium, where urns of ashes were stored.

"Do you smell that?" Noah whispered, inching a little closer to his side.

Julien took a couple deep breaths, but the air only smelled like night in the city, trees and dust, and the dried monster blood on his shirt. He shook his head, and Noah looked up at him in disbelief, his own nose scrunched as if touched by something sour.

"Really? That's demon," he said. "It's stronger than it's been on the people you've brought home."

Julien frowned and moved ahead of him to scan the front of the building. Near the corner, hunched under an outcropping of rock, a figure stood stock still, staring at the stained glass in the archway. Curling horns grew from its head, curling up toward its forehead, and feathered black wings shuddered around its back, twitching as if eager to move.

"Is that it?" Noah hissed behind him. "He's not...frothing. How do you tell if someone's possessed? We can't just attack someone for being in the cemetery."

Julien's good eye narrowed faintly. This looked like just another person to Noah—but he could see it for what it was.

"That's not someone possessed," the hunter murmured. "That's a demon."

Noah stepped up behind him to speak at his shoulder. "What? Are you sure?"

The figure turned its head toward Julien, its eyes catching the faint moonlight like a cat, and it opened its mouth, showing too many sharp teeth and releasing a terrible, growling hiss.

"Pretty sure." Julien urged Noah back and shifted his feet, bracing his boots into the path. He may not have been armed ideally for fighting demons, but he still knew how to stab something in the heart.

As soon as he reached for the blessed knife at the back of his belt, the thing shrieked and rushed at him, clasping onto his shoulders and forcing him back across the courtyard with massive, beating wings. Julien fought to stay on his feet as he was scraped backward, his own grip latched onto the front of the demon's clothes to keep him at least arm's length away. This creature was stronger than Julien—but he was used to fighting things stronger than him. He dug his heels into the ground and heaved his body weight against it, twisting one of its arms into a tight hold so that he could use the knife from his belt to cut into the meat at the base of its wings. He drew blood, and the demon screeched, clawed fingers scraping his shoulder as it lifted him by his own grip on its arm and flung him back into the nearby bushes.

The air was knocked from Julien's lungs as he landed, but he turned to right himself with a deep breath. At the edge of the courtyard, Noah was scrambling on the ground with a piece of charcoal in his hand, murmuring to himself as he scratched out the edges of a circle. In the moment it took Julien to look at the witch, the demon was on top of him again, pinning him to the ground and forcing the knife out of his hand with a few solid slams of his wrist into the dirt. The hunter had to take hold of the demon's head to keep its teeth from fastening onto him, one hand holding it by the neck and the other attempting to avoid its claws long enough to pat the ground in search of his knife.

"Julien!" Noah called. "Bring it over here!"

"Bring it over here, he says," Julien muttered with thick saliva dribbling onto his cheek. "Sacrement." He brought up his foot to plant it on the demon's chest, his hips lifting from the ground in his effort to heave the creature off of him. He pushed to his feet and barreled into the demon, his arms locking around its neck from behind. It's wings still flapped loudly near Julien's head, almost lifting him from the ground, but the injured one was just weak enough for him to fight the pull. With a grunt of exertion, Julien hurled the snarling body across the courtyard toward the circle Noah had drawn. As soon as the demon crossed the edge of the circle, it slammed into an invisible barrier on the other side and crashed to the ground. It slammed its shoulder against the cage formed by the spell as if it hoped to break it—and the look on Noah's face told him that wasn't impossible.

"This is temporary," the witch said in a rush. "Let's do this quick."

Julien glanced back toward the bush where he'd lost his knife, but as he took a step toward it, Noah reached out a hand and whipped the handle of the blade into Julien's palm. He flipped it in his hand and approached the circle while the witch murmured incantations at the edge of the circle, trying to nail down the right spell to keep the demon from continuing to smash against the circle's barrier. Beads of sweat formed on his forehead and his fingers trembled—it was clearly taking most of his attention just keeping the walls up and the thing contained.

While the demon continued to beat wildly against Noah's hold, Julien circled it, and when he saw the chance, he reached beyond the edge of the circle and snatched the creature by its injured wing. It hissed sharply at him, shrieking and fighting his grip, but Julien hauled it to the ground with his full body weight and swung, planting the dagger into its chest. It jerked against him and clawed the air, barely missing his face, and its wings left swirls of dust as they beat against the ground. The demon locked eyes with him, teeth bared like an animal, and then its body gave out and collapsed into the flat courtyard, almost immediately breaking into chunks of black ash that settled on the path. Julien got to his feet, kicking one of the piles into dust and looking over at Noah as the charcoal circle faded from the pavement, its power spent. Both of them were breathing hard, though

Julien was substantially dirtier.

They didn't have to speak to know that they both understood what a real demon showing up meant.

They were the first ones to get back to the house. Noah led the blond upstairs to the room they could share again now that Sabin had gone, and gathered some jars from his kit while Julien stripped off his coat and shirt. The pierced skin in his thigh was barely noticeable, but the demon had gotten his shoulder pretty deeply. Noah pulled his knees up under him on the bed once Julien sat down and scooped up some of the poultice of ground herbs and oils from his mortar bowl.

"You know," he said as he smoothed some of the mixture over Julien's largest cut, "it was pretty hot seeing you throw that thing around."

Julien snorted. "Glad you're turned on by seeing me get my ass kicked."

"Is that what you call getting your ass kicked?"

The hunter gave a small shrug and winced slightly at the movement in his shoulder. "Just part of the job. It happens."

Noah paused, settling back on his heels, and he reached out to brush his fingertips over some of the varied, ragged scars on Julien's chest. "You never once even questioned getting involved in this fight, did you?" he asked softly. "The demons and the Alfar. There's a problem, a threat, and people are in danger, so here you are."

Julien turned his head to hide the faint heat he felt in his face. It was embarrassing to be praised so gently. "This is just the way it's always been," he said in what he hoped was a casual way.

"That's what I mean," Noah said. "It's so much a part of who you are that you don't even think about it. You just...help. Whenever someone needs it." The witch smiled at him and leaned forward to press a warm kiss to his scruffy cheek. "I just thought you should know that I see it."

Julien let out a noncommittal scoff and kept his face turned away, but when Noah set down his poultice and climbed into his lap, that drew his attention. The witch kissed his lips and his jaw, then moved closer to speak in a low voice near his ear.

"When do you think your brothers will be back?"

Julien's hands went under Noah's shirt of their own accord, gripping the witch's waist and pulling him tighter against him. He nuzzled the smaller man's neck and tasted the faint salt of sweat there. "Not sure," he murmured against his skin. "Do you think you're about to make a lot of noise?"

Noah smirked down at him and rolled his hips, drawing a quiet grunt from Julien's throat, and then the witch's fingers went to work on his belt buckle, tugging it loose with practiced ease. But as soon as Noah slid down to his knees on the floor between Julien's thighs, the front door slammed downstairs, and irritated French echoed outside the bedroom. Julien sighed and leaned back on his hands, jumping when Noah leaned close to give his erection a soft bite through the rough fabric of his jeans.

"We'll pick this up later," the witch promised.

Julien grunted as he stood, pausing to refasten his belt and tuck his dick into the waistband of his jeans until it calmed down, then gingerly pulled his shirt back over his head.

"I'll tell Sabin the demons are here," Noah said, already climbing back up onto the bed with his box and a pad of paper. "Let him know we'd appreciate them getting back to us quick on those weapons and portal-closing issues."

Julien nodded and left him, and as he rounded the top of the stairs, he saw Edouard, Joseph, Arnaud, and Antony, all arguing in the hallway.

"This is pointless," Antony snapped. "We need more information. I'm sick of just going for long walks in the park every night and getting nowhere!"

Edouard wasn't listening to him—his gaze clipped over to Julien as he came down into the corridor. "Any luck today?"

"Bad news," Julien answered. "We saw a demon in the flesh today. Not just a possessed host. The gate must be open now—wherever it is."

"Tabarnak," Antony swore.

Arnaud frowned. "Then we need to find these—Alfar? Who are supposed to be opening it. Guarding it. We can't fight an endless flood of demons, even if we do get the weapons your witch's friends promised."

"No, we can't," Julien agreed. "I killed the one we came across today, but if I'm honest, I'd be hard-pressed to take on more than two at a time. Also, judging by what Noah said, even these still just look like normal people. I could see its real face, but he couldn't."

Edouard put his hands on his hips and looked down at the floor, sighing softly through his nose. "That's going to make things more difficult. We'll need to stick together from now on—I won't have anyone getting regular people involved through carelessness," he added, and he didn't have to look at Antony for Julien and Arnaud to know they were talking about him. "Julien can spot them for us."

"As long as they don't come up on his right side," Antony sneered.

"Fuck you, Antony," Julien spat.

"Fuck you."

"Enough!" Edouard shouted, and the younger men obediently stilled. He turned to look over his shoulder at Joseph. "Call Hugo and Laurent back. We need to discuss how to proceed."

With more plans made and maps marked up, Julien went back upstairs to quickly strap a fresh bandage over his shoulder and retrieve his coat, and he found Noah huddled over handwritten pages spread over the blankets.

"The monks say they need more time on the weapons," he explained without looking up. "But Sabin sent me the method for closing the portals. It's...complicated. I need a lot of stuff, and it needs to charge. It's a huge spell." He hesitated, and Julien could see the unspoken uncertainty on his face. "I'll...I'll need to take some notes."

"I'm going out again." Julien gave the witch an apologetic smile when he finally lifted his head. "No more time to waste wandering. I'll try to be back before dawn."

"I'll be here," Noah answered with false cheer in his voice, but he still smiled when Julien bent down to kiss him.

Julien led his brothers back to Mont Royal and through the pathways of the Cimetière Notre-Dame-Des-Neiges, along the same trails he'd walked with Noah earlier in the evening, until they reached a broad causeway lined with marble mausoleums. Joseph tapped Julien's shoulder and pointed toward one at the far end of the lane, its stone door cracked and half fallen away. When Arnaud approached and hauled the broken fragments away, they were faced with at least a dozen hunkered figures, each with rustling black feathers, standing shoulder to shoulder and turning to glare at the intruders.

Between the seven of them, the nest was easy pickings.

15

By the morning of the second day, half of the Tuatha De Danann camp had split off from the first and made their way toward the next city inland—Findias, Ciaran said. The more trouble they could be, the better, and harassing both cities at once would force the alfar to split their attention.

"But what for?" Trent asked over a breakfast of porridge and dried fruit. He sat with Ciaran and his brothers at the closest fire to their tents, all of them cross-legged on blankets tossed haphazardly around the burning wood. "What's the goal? They already left soldiers behind instead of going to meet the demons, like Lugh said. Are you guys really planning to attack a city full of civilians? Why?"

"To burn it down, most likely," Ciaran answered, shrugging one shoulder.

"That's a what, not a why," Trent pointed out with a frown. "There are just regular people in there. They didn't ask for this war."

Ciaran snorted and swallowed his mouthful of porridge. "Few people ever ask to go to war, a mhuirnín. If we make enough of a fuss here, whomever King Huldrekall left in charge in there will likely withdraw the people to Murias, and we'll either set up camp inside the city ourselves, or raze it and move on to the next. That's just the way these things go."

Trent stared down into his bowl, not bothering to hide the scowl on his lips. "You're way too okay with this."

Ciaran leaned an elbow on his knee to look over at the boy. "What would you have me do? Here we are. I don't plan on cutting down any cowering children, but we have a purpose, and I aim to see it done."

"And what am I supposed to do this whole time?" Trent answered in a more hushed voice, grateful that Ciaran's brothers seemed satisfied to chat with each other rather than listen in. "Just wait around in camp and hope a bunch of these people don't show up and murder everyone while you assholes are off trying to murder all of them?"

"You stay where you're safest, Trent," Ciaran said with a soft sigh. "That's here in the camp."

"But I'm useless here!"

Ciaran stared at him for a beat, and Trent could read his face without a word being spoken—you're useless everywhere. "You're not trained for this," he said instead, which didn't make Trent feel much better. "Or used to it. Just let me protect you, will you?"

"I came all this way. If I'm going to be here, I want to help somehow. There has to be something I can do. Ever since this whole thing started, all I've done is sit around and watch people stronger than me, more magical than me. I know I'm not a soldier or a witch or whatever, but I have to be able to help someway, right?"

"It's enough that you want to, a mhuirnín," Ciaran said gently. "Airmed doesn't fight either—I'm sure she'd love to have your help dressing the wounded. That's something you can do *here*."

"But I—"

"It's not an argument I'm going to have," the fairy cut him off, more firmly. He set down his bowl and stood, giving a quick whistle to hurry his brothers along. "We need to be off. Promise me you won't do anything rash while I'm away. Please."

Trent felt like a pouting child as he frowned up at Ciaran, snorting and turning his head away. "Fine." Once they'd gone, he grumpily scooped up the bowls they'd left behind and helped one of the servants empty and clean them before going to find Airmed. He wasn't a healer, either—but she might be able to find *something* he could do.

She wasn't the only one tending to injuries. Ciaran's father also stalked the tent where a few men who'd suffered arrow wounds on the way to the island still lay recovering, and a handful of other men and women walked between the rows of cots at Airmed's direction. When she spotted Trent, she approached him with a smile, wiping oils from her hands.

"Hello there! Are you ailing? I have some time if there's anything bothering you."

"No, I'm...I'm fine. Ciaran said I..." He sighed, running his tongue along his lower teeth in frustration before going on. "Ciaran said you might have something for me to do."

"Oh! Aye sure I could find some work for you, if that's what you're wanting. Do you know anything about medicine?"

"Not really," he admitted, embarrassment settling in his stomach like a bitter weight.

"Well, that's fine," she assured him, reaching out to give his arm an affirming squeeze. "Always something to do, regardless. Come along."

Trent followed her, and she set a number of tasks to him—rolling strips of bandages, grinding herbs into paste, scrubbing linens in the nearby lake. He didn't consider himself above manual labor, despite how often his father had drilled into him that such work was "not for people like us," but it still felt like being left behind with the children to know that Ciaran was off fighting for his people against some terrifying enemy, and Trent was doing laundry. It didn't feel like an equal contribution to the war effort.

"I wish there was more I could do," he finally said to Airmed while they hung bedding up to dry over a few low, thin branches. She'd been casting glances at him all day while he moped and scowled, but she'd graciously allowed him his space to pout until he was ready. "Everybody else is so goddamn magic and powerful and whatever bullshit, and my most useful skill is doing taxes. Do you guys even have taxes?"

"I'm afraid not," she answered with a kind smile. "But not everyone is a fighter, are they? We all have our strengths and weaknesses."

"Yeah, well everyone else's strengths seem a lot more helpful than mine."

"You've been plenty helpful. Don't fret. Cian's right—the best thing you can do is stay safe at the camp and not make him worry for you."

"Great," Trent muttered. As if Ciaran was the only one who worried.

"I do have a concern for poor Rathgeirr," she said, a little more quietly. "I wonder if he's really all right, being made to fight his own people. It must be hard on him."

Trent grunted a vague agreement, but he wasn't really sure what she wanted him to say. At least Rathgeirr had a role to play in this at all.

By the time Ciaran and the others rode back into the camp that evening, Trent's hands were reddened from scrubbing, but he didn't complain. Ciaran looked far more weary than him—apparently they'd spent the day setting fires in the Alfar's fields that couldn't be put out except by magic, harassing and chasing off the slaves who worked the land, and sniping at guard patrols from the backs of their stolen horses. Ciaran only led one group of many like his own—taking shots at the city and its people where they could and scattering before they could be struck back. Trent wondered if the Alfar considered it unfair.

Trent brought Ciaran his dinner in one of the same wooden bowls he'd had his breakfast in, and the fairy thanked him with a smile, taking a brief hold of Trent's hand to kiss his knuckles. Trent sat beside him, but Ciaran was too busy discussing the next day's plan of attack with his brothers to have time for conversation, so Trent just ate his sweet potatoes and gruel with Rathgeirr fidgeting beside him. Airmed passed to and fro nearby on her way from the physician's tent to her own, and each time she went, Rathgeirr did his best—but failed—to act like he wasn't looking at her.

"I didn't expect her to be here," he said quietly, stirring his pottage rather than eating it and casting his black eyes up toward the distant tent as its flap fell shut again.

"What?" Trent asked, a little surprised the alfar was talking to him. "Who?"

"Airmed," Rathgeirr whispered. "I didn't think—I don't know why I wouldn't have thought—it makes sense that not only warriors would—" He stopped himself and gave a light sigh. "I only—she's lovely, isn't she?"

"I...guess so?" Trent agreed halfheartedly.

"I don't know much about the customs of the Ævintýri," he sighed. "How do I approach her? Should I offer a gift? In Falias, it would be customary to present her with a bouquet of nootka, but I would have to speak to her father, or...her eldest brother," he finished more quietly with a wary glance over at Ciaran. "And he threatened me the last time it came up, so I would rather not...remind him of this issue until I'm sure she has even noticed me."

Trent stared at him, uncomfortable at the expectation of sympathizing. He never knew what to say to people in these kinds of situations—but a couple of days ago, he'd called the alfar stupid for something he'd already forgotten, and it had seemed to hurt his feelings, so guilt forced him to at least listen now. "I'm really not the person to ask about this," he said as politely as he could.

Rathgeirr's shoulders drooped slightly, but then he paused, and he turned to Trent with renewed hope on his face. "You were with her all day, were you not? Has she said anything about me?"

"Uh. Actually, she said she was worried about you having to fight your own people. She wondered if you were okay with it."

Rathgeirr looked down into his bowl, his sharp canines visible in his unrestrained smile. "That is...good news." He turned to face Trent more directly and beamed over at him. "Then, do you think I should? Approach her, I mean. Do you think she would...look kindly on me?"

"Listen," Trent answered uncertainly, "I don't know anything about this kind of stuff. Ciaran just showed up at my apartment and did whatever he wanted and now I've ended up in a war zone, so I'm not the best person to ask for advice, here."

"But you're human," the alfar answered easily. "So it shouldn't surprise you that he did whatever he wanted, right?"

Trent snorted at him. "Look, you really need to quit this shit about humans, okay?"

"No, no," Rathgeirr said immediately. "I told you—I don't think we should be using the humans as slaves, either. Really. You ought to be protected."

"That's not any better!" Trent snapped. "We're not animals." He paused at the wilted look on the other man's face and huffed a sigh through his nose. "Humans have gotten along on their own for literally thousands of years without some superior race babysitting us or treating us like pets."

Rathgeirr went silent for a while, looking down into his bowl with a pensive frown. When he looked up, he spoke in a much softer voice. "I am sorry," he said, so earnestly that Trent felt a little bad. "I hadn't thought of it that way. The wider world is still new to me, and I am...still learning. But...I hope that you and I are friends, Trent," he finished, a soft crease in his brow.

Trent groaned. "Yeah, yeah," he sighed, pushing his food around his bowl so he didn't have to look the alfar in the face. "I guess we're friends."

"It's difficult to change what you've heard your whole life," Rathgeirr said. "The Alfar do only think of humans as animals. They're the same as sheep or goats—they're useful to you, and a man may count his wealth by them. And they've been slaves here for so long, with no way to escape and nowhere to go, I can't imagine they ever even think of fighting back."

Trent paused, his spoon stilling in his hand. He looked over at Rathgeirr, who had peacefully returned to eating his meal, and he frowned. Maybe there *was* something Trent could do.

16

Noah didn't sleep much through the night; he spent the hours reading Sabin's notes over and over again, trying to make sense of the scope of what needed to be done. How had the monks done this themselves, so long ago? Was this method even confirmed? Had they used witches back then?

Was this even something Noah was capable of?

When he set aside one of his books and pulled Sabin's copied notes back over to him from their stack on the nearest bunk bed, a folded paper heart bounced out close to his knee. He'd noticed it when the boy had first sent the packet, but the spell had taken precedence then, and his name on it hadn't been in Sabin's handwriting. He picked it up now, turning the piece of paper over in his hand. It had Noah's name on it, but he didn't recognize the writing. He unfolded it carefully so it didn't rip and flattened out the seams against his thigh.

A gentle witch fate brought aligned with me,
His eyes aglow with warmth and smile fair.
My witch has made my soul to be laid bare,
So long untouched yet yearning to be free.

What shall I call him, then; what shall I be?

To whom shall I send my soft unvoiced prayer
That a man so kind should see fit to share
A moment or two with someone like me?

But how can I hope, how can I dare reach
With trembling hand, for lush porcelain skin?
When faced with perfection, dare I begin?
For since I first saw it, so I have planned
To touch and caress that ass like a peach
'Last to hold grace in the palm of my hand.

Noah stared down at the name written in swirling calligraphy at the bottom—Jett. His face actually grew hot for a few passing seconds; he'd never gotten any kind of love note from someone before, and this was...a lot grander than that, even if it was about his ass. That kid was trouble. Noah smiled and laid the gently-smoothed paper on the bed beside him, then tore a sheet from his legal pad and stuffed his own note into the box he'd left on top of one of his piles of books.

Tell Jett I said thanks. He's cute, but still too young for me. I hope everything's good on your end. Miss you.

When Julien finally returned, they both passed out for a few hours, but it wasn't restful sleep for either of them.

Trent had left Noah his laptop to use in his absence since he wasn't likely to have any use of it on the island of Lochlann, so the witch spent his morning questioning fellow witches on the few online resources he knew of—asking questions about demons and leylines and trying not to give away too much of his problem. If he could avoid too many people knowing some kind of invasion was potentially coming, that would be best.

Noah groggily followed Julien downstairs when the blond came to fetch him for breakfast, and sitting at the long table was even more awkward without any of the other non-hunters there with them. Noah sat at one end of the bench with the rest of the brothers at the other, feeling exceptionally out of place. He focused on his open book on the table, comparing the list Sabin had sent him to the ingredients in his herbal compendium and doing measurement conversion math in his notebook. Julien smiled at him as he set down Noah's plate of eggs and toast and took his place beside him, so Noah thanked him and took a bite of the toast, but he couldn't help the queasy feeling in his stomach. Edouard was looking at him—he could feel it. It didn't take long for the oldest Fournier to clear his throat.

"Julien, we really have to talk about this," he said, and Julien looked over at him while he swallowed his mouthful of eggs.

"Talk about what? I thought we were going to scout for the portal along the Côte-des-Neiges tonight."

"That isn't what I mean. We have to talk about *him*."

Noah glanced over at him out of the corner of his eye, unwilling to fully look up from his book.

"There isn't anything to talk about," Julien insisted.

"I think there is," Edouard countered immediately. "You don't really think this can continue? I can overlook some indiscretions and...experiments, but you're really too old now to be—"

"Are you serious?" Julien interrupted. "Experiments? *Indiscretions*?"

"Julien," his older brother sighed, "this family has survived to do the work we do for five generations because we have all always put the work *first*. All of us. You're throwing those years spent training you back in Father's face."

"Ah, va chier," Julien sneered, "when have I ever stopped working? I was on my own for years, doing what *Father* trained me to do! This doesn't have anything to do with the work, and you know it."

"It has to do with the *continuation* of the work. If you don't continue the family line—"

"Alors quoi, Edouard?" Julien lifted one hand and let it thump back to the table in frustration. "Emile and Théo aren't doing the work *you* trained them to do? Joseph's daughters, they aren't going to do the work? Arnaud, how old is Jérôme now? Seventeen? Is *he* going to do the work?"

"Of course he is," Arnaud answered without hesitation.

"Julien," Edouard cut in, "you know that *you* more than any of us have a responsibility to carry on the name."

"We don't even know that it works that way!" Julien shook his head. "I'm supposed to give up the person I love and find someone willing to have *at least* seven children with me, then hope that it was all worth my time, and my youngest son ends up with his whole family either pushing him or resenting him, is that it?"

"Fucking ungrateful," the other shot back, leaning one elbow on the table to point an accusing finger at his youngest brother. "You know what gifts you have, and not to even try to pass them on to the next generation is irresponsible!"

Arnaud held up a hand before Julien could answer, his voice significantly calmer than the others'. "On top of what Edouard is saying, Julien, it's a liability having him here."

Julien heaved out a sigh. "Again because he's a witch? He's helped us so much already! If you can't take my word for it and trust him, you should at least be able to see that."

"It isn't that," Arnaud went on. "It's *because* you're saying you love him that he shouldn't be here."

"What are you talking about?"

"Edouard's wife isn't here, Julien. My wife isn't here. Because you can't have your mind on two things at once, and your mind will be on your witch for as long as he's here. Send him away, at least, so that you can focus on the work we have to do."

"You're joking," Julien scoffed. "How do you think we're going to close this demon portal without him? How do you think we would have even gotten this far without him?"

Arnaud lifted his hands in brief surrender. "I just don't want you making stupid choices in the heat of the moment."

Julien tensed on the bench beside Noah, his shoulders rising and falling in a tightly controlled breath. "I *don't* make stupid choices."

"Being with him at all is a stupid choice!" Edouard snapped. Julien bit back with a curse, and Arnaud knocked his fist firmly on the table to cut them off.

"Julien," he said evenly, "the whole family has always asked a lot of you. We know that. And no matter what Edouard says," he added with a pointed frown at the older man, "you're our brother, and we care if you're happy or not."

Hugo had been staring down at his plate so far, but at this, he looked down the table toward Julien and offered him an eager nod of agreement.

"So," Arnaud continued, "is it possible that you might...you know, marry and have children anyway, and you and Noah could...be discreet?"

Hugo stopped nodding. "C'est pas de farces, Arnaud!"

"I'm not joking."

Noah curled his arms around his stomach, his appetite lost, but Julien pushed his plate away in disgust.

"Ben là! I'm not talking about this anymore."

"Don't marry, then!" Arnaud tried again. "Stay with your witch and just find a woman to have your children."

Hugo stared at him in disbelief. "Where do you think you'd find a woman like that?" he asked in a hushed voice.

Noah folded his book closed with his notes inside and tucked it up under his arm, then swung his legs out from under the table and walked swiftly out of the room. He couldn't listen to this anymore. Instead of returning to Julien's room, he went the opposite way down the upstairs hall and shut himself in the bunk room, where he could spread his papers out over the floor. This spell needed a lot of attention—he couldn't waste his focus on arguing with some culty family that was never going to see him as a person regardless of what he did. They could say what they wanted about him. Whether it was because he was a man, or because he was a witch, or whatever. They didn't matter. What mattered was getting this demon gate closed before the Alfar could let too many through. And Julien was still defending him. He wasn't going to listen to them. They'd been through too much together for Julien to take their bullshit to heart now.

He hoped.

Julien stepped inside the room after a while to check on him, but Noah put on his brightest smile.

"I'll be ready to hunt more demons whenever you are. I just need to get this sorted out right now."

The hunter frowned uncertainly at him, but nodded and left him to his work, so Noah threw himself into it, pretending he couldn't hear the passing voices outside the door. He spread Sabin's letter out in front of his lap to read it again and check it against his notes to make sure he hadn't missed anything, and he'd almost put the morning's conversation out of his mind when another knock sounded on the door. When he looked up, Hugo was poking his head inside with a friendly smile on his face.

"Can I come in?" he asked. Noah didn't really want to speak to any of these people, if he was honest, but he didn't have the heart to refuse the only one who'd had even one kind word to say to him since he arrived, so he waved him in. Hugo moved to the bunk nearest the witch and dropped down heavily onto the mattress with his elbows on his knees, fingers laced loosely between them.

"I wanted to apologize," he said after a brief pause. "For the way the others are."

"It's fine," Noah lied, waving away the apology with one hand. "Julien clearly knew to expect this kind of pushback. I trust him. And I'm...proud of him for telling you all about us, even knowing the kind of shit he was going to catch for it. He could have just kept us a secret."

"I'm glad he didn't." Hugo glanced toward the door, then leaned in a little closer to Noah and dropped his voice. "Julien has always had a lot on his shoulders. I'm sure you know. He never thinks about himself, you know? It's always been the job, the job. Honestly," he added with a laugh, "before you came along, I wondered what kind of woman would ever put up with him long enough to have seven kids, you know?"

Noah smiled, just a little.

"Anyway, I'm glad to see him putting himself first for once. Putting a person first, instead of always work, work. You know? He might be a Seventh Son of a Seventh Son, destined monster slayer," he said in a stuffy, dramatic voice, "but he's still a man too, you know? The others forget. But I wanted you to know I'm on your side. You've helped us when you didn't have to, and you've been kind when the others have been fucking rude. So I appreciate it."

Noah lowered his head to snort out a soft laugh, and he nodded before looking back up at him. "Thanks, Hugo."

Hugo leaned back on the bed and gave his knees a solid slap before he rose. "En tout cas. Just don't listen to their bullshit, and it'll all turn out okay, eh?" He thumped Noah on the shoulder in what he probably thought was a friendly tap but lurched the witch forward so suddenly he almost had to catch himself with his hands on the floor. Noah watched him go with a faint smile. They weren't all so bad.

Julien came in a while later to let Noah know he was leaving, but when the witch stood to join him, he put a hand on his shoulder to still him.

"You stay in," Julien said, and Noah frowned at him.

"Because of those assholes? I don't care about them, Julien," he said, trying to sound firm. The hunter watched his eyes with a soft expression that felt exposing, and he touched Noah's cheek with one calloused hand.

"Not because of them," he said gently. "Because you have this spell to do. That part is your job—we can do ours. Once you've got it figured out, you can come demon hunting with us again," he promised.

"You know how to woo somebody," Noah teased. He slid his fingers into the blond hair at the back of the hunter's neck and pulled him down into a kiss. "Be careful," he whispered near Julien's lips. His eyes briefly cut over to the open door, where Edouard had paused to scowl at them, but then he tugged Julien close again and kissed him a little more deeply. He let one hand slip around to give the blond's backside a squeeze that made him jump, and when he leaned back, he just caught Edouard stalking from the doorway. Noah was sad to have missed the look on his face.

Julien smiled at him with faint pink tinting his cheeks, and Noah reluctantly let him go. He had studying to do.

17

Ciaran came back bloody the next evening. The cut in his side seeped black, so the men with him hadn't been suspicious, but when he settled inside the tent where Trent waited for him, he let out a pained grunt and flopped heavily into the blankets.

"This definitely hurts more than it ought to," he admitted in a mumble against one of the furs. "This mortal business isn't all it's cracked up to be."

"Who could have possibly given you the idea that being mortal was going to be better?" Trent asked, already lifting the fairy's shirt to check the injury.

"Ach, I'm fine," he insisted, though Trent hadn't asked. "Airmed gave me something to put on it. Said it would help. Not worth a fuss."

"Literally nobody is fussing over you." Trent took the vial of oil from Ciaran's open hand and popped the cork out to pour a few drops into the wound. He hissed, but soon settled against the blankets with a sigh of relief.

Trent recorked the vial and set it aside, sitting back near the wall of the tent and frowning down at the other man. He'd spent the day being gently ordered by Airmed—which meant more menial jobs and more scrubbing in the lake—but his mind had been on Rathgeirr's words the night before. The humans in these cities never considered fighting back. Why would they? They'd all been here for generations, and even if they were to try to escape, where would they go? They'd all just be gathered up again, punished, and put back to work. It felt insulting to think, but they just didn't know any better than what they already had.

"Ciaran," he began after a while, and the fairy tilted his head to peer sleepily up at him with a soft hum of acknowledgment. "I think I've figured out a way that I can help."

"How's that?"

"I think...I need to get inside the city."

Ciaran paused, then sat up on one elbow to look more directly at him. "Inside the city," he repeated.

"Yeah. If I can get inside, then I can talk to the humans there, and I can tell them what it's like away from this fucking island. I can tell them there's...another way. The Alfar aren't prepared for their slaves to fight against them, but they might—if they even had the idea that they could."

The fairy's brow furrowed. "That's not the worst idea in theory, a mhuirnín, but you couldn't possibly. It's far too dangerous for you to go anywhere near Falias. You do stand out, remember. They'd know you as an outsider in an instant."

"So what? Because it's dangerous, that means I shouldn't try? Like what you're out doing every day is so fucking safe?" he added with a light poke to Ciaran's wound that made him cringe and swat at Trent's hand.

"*I'm* doing what I've been doing for ages," he argued. "Trent, I know you're feeling out of place, but this isn't the answer. If you're only patient, then when this is over, we—"

"I've *been* patient! I'm tired of sitting around!"

Ciaran sighed, and he pushed himself up to sit beside the other man and reached up to touch his hair. "I know you are, lad. And honestly, I'll have this argument with you a hundred times rather than have you go back to being depressed, but...this can't be the answer. How could I do what I need to do if I'm afraid for you?"

Trent scowled down at his lap, refusing to look the fairy in the eyes. Ciaran had to do what he needed to do. Because he's used to this. He's trained for it. He's been doing it for ages. He couldn't be distracted by worry. Fine.

He took a slow breath. "I understand," he said. "You're right."

"Thank you," Ciaran answered, and the relief in his voice tightened Trent's stomach with guilt. He pulled the boy in closer to him and kissed him, his hand resting lightly at the side of Trent's neck. Trent melted into him, his fingers clutching at the fairy's shirt.

Trent had to do what he needed to do, too.

When Ciaran urged him down onto his back, Trent let him without argument, his arms around his lover's shoulders and his mouth open to his kiss. Ciaran's injury didn't seem to bother him now—his cock pressed against Trent's hip with the same insistence as always, and he supported himself over the smaller man easily, his fingertips running a trail up Trent's stomach that drew up shivers wherever they passed. Trent slid his fingers through the fairy's messy hair, still a little damp with sweat from the day, and gripped the back of his tunic, tugging it up and over Ciaran's head with a little assistance.

"Tá mo chroí istigh ionat," Ciaran whispered against the other man's lips, and Trent found himself faintly smiling into the kiss. He turned Ciaran's head to nip at his earlobe and murmur into his ear.

"I don't understand that shit."

Ciaran's chuckle rumbled in his throat, and he bent to press a long kiss to Trent's teasing lips. "I love you," he tried again.

"Better," Trent mumbled, already kissing him again. The fairy almost snapped one of Trent's buttons getting his shirt off, earning himself a smack, but Trent lifted his hips obediently when Ciaran sat back to pull his pants down and toss them away. He dropped down beside Trent to kick off his boots and remove his own trousers, jumping a little when the other man's teeth bit lightly at one of his nipples while he was distracted.

"Feisty today," Ciaran said with a smile, and he took hold of Trent's thigh to pull it over his hip and close the distance between them. He left bites on his lover's neck and shoulder, guiding Trent into a steady, rolling motion against him that caught the boy's breath in his chest and caused him to clamp his arms tighter around the fairy's shoulders. Ciaran's body was hot against him, the friction of his cock against Trent's keeping him from taking a full breath.

Trent didn't want to resist him today. He didn't care if someone outside heard them. He just wanted him. He loved him. No matter what else happened, Trent could at least settle that sure calm in his chest and hold tight to it. When Ciaran leaned over him to pat around in the bag stuffed at the back of the tent in search of the bottle of lubricant they'd brought with them, Trent bucked up against him and kissed his jaw, his chin, his lips—whatever he could reach. Ciaran's longing groan against him made his stomach churn with anticipation, and he let the fairy spread his legs and settle between them without shame. He held tight to the furs near his head and sucked in a sharp breath when Ciaran's slicked fingers entered him, pushing back against the intrusion in search of more of the pleasant burn he wanted. Ciaran fell over him again, kissing his parted lips and brushing the spot that made him jump with expert fingers.

He didn't make Trent wait long—the boy's ragged breath and twitching, neglected dick demanded his attention. When Ciaran took hold of him, Trent couldn't help the shuddering moan that fell from his lips or the bite of his fingernails into the other man's back as he gripped his lover tight to him again. Ciaran pulled his hand free and almost immediately pushed forward again, easing his cock inside the other man as slowly as he could manage. Trent's head fell back to the blanket, and he tugged Ciaran deeper into him with legs tightened around the fairy's hips. Ciaran whispered something against the corner of Trent's mouth, but the boy didn't have the presence of mind to ask what it meant. He just kissed him, a whine in his throat as Ciaran began to move within him, hand stroking him in time with the thrust of his hips.

Trent kept the other man close to him, hoping his eagerness and his clinging didn't give him away. He wanted Ciaran against him, inside him, more now than he ever had, perhaps—because he'd made up his mind to do something stupid. Trent kissed him, allowing the moans in his throat to be heard without restraint. Ciaran set the pace Trent urged him toward, both of them panting and clutching, kissing and touching, until they lay spent beside each other, limbs tangled and lungs burning with lost breath.

Trent splayed his hands over Ciaran's chest, attempting to still their trembling, and he leaned in to give the fairy another long, slow kiss.

"I love you," he murmured softly, and Ciaran smiled, his thumb brushing gently over the other man's waist.

"I love you, a mhuirnín," he answered without opening his eyes.

Trent didn't voice what he really wanted to say next—*I'm sorry.*

With Ciaran fast asleep under the blankets, Trent eased himself from the tent and into the cold night wind rushing through the camp. He passed by dying fires and quiet rows of tents, walking quickly so that he didn't lose his nerve. When he reached the edge of the camp, a man standing watch caught him and stopped him with a short whistle.

"Where you off to, lenab?"

Trent forced himself not to scowl at him. He didn't know this person, but he guessed word of the only human in the camp got around. "Just going for a piss," he muttered, passing by the fairy with what he hoped looked like a casual step.

"Don't wander too far, now. Spell only goes as far as the treeline."

"Got it," Trent called back. He ducked behind the closest tree to break the guard's line of sight, then allowed himself one more slow breath. This was the right decision. This would help—this was something Trent could do. Something *only* Trent could do. And hopefully, it wouldn't end with him getting murdered.

He wasn't sure exactly when he passed out of the invisibility spell protecting the fairy's camp, since he walked past the edge of the trees without so much as a tingle, but he had to assume he was exposed by the time he entered the sparse grass of the field outside the walls of Falias. He circled the city a fair distance before drawing too close, just in case he was spotted walking a direct line from the camp to the city, then began his approach with his heart pounding in his chest.

It wasn't hard to be noisy and noticeable on his way; Trent wasn't a naturally graceful person, and he doubted he would fool the keen senses of an Alfar for more than a second. The torches atop the ramparts grew brighter the closer he came, but before he considered himself particularly near, he stopped short as the tip of an arrow sunk into the dirt scant inches from his shoes.

"The next one won't miss, outsider," a stern voice called.

Trent lifted his eyes to the wall and saw the alfar at the top of the rampart, another arrow already nocked and pulled back to his cheek.

"Be still."

He raised his hands in surrender, and another man he hadn't noticed appeared at his side, taking him by the back of the neck and forcing him easily to his knees with one hand.

"I'm not armed," Trent said quickly. "Please."

"Why is a pet of the Ævintýri off its leash?" the alfar sneered.

Trent hunched his shoulders in a flinch at the sound of the guard's voice, trying to play the role of a frightened human servant—it wasn't difficult. His heart beat so fast it almost hurt. "I—I went for firewood and got lost. I couldn't find my way back to camp. Please don't hurt me—I'm...I'm nobody—"

"You're useless if you can't even take us to them," the man holding him muttered, and he dragged Trent back to his feet, the edge of his knife already pressed into the side of his throat when the guard on the rampart stopped him with a shout.

"Bring him here," the other called, sliding his arrow back into its quiver.

Trent was forced forward by the push of the hand at his neck. A steep set of stairs opened up in the side of the wall as they approached, allowing the guard to lead Trent up to the top of the wall. He stood in front of the guard who'd fired at him, knowing better than to look him in the face. The way to stay alive here was to be what the Alfar expected him to be—and that was a groveling, subservient slave.

The guard took him by the chin and forced his gaze up so that he could inspect him. Trent caught a glimpse of his black eyes and the thick lines of drawn down his face like tears of charcoal before he clipped his gaze downward again.

"He looks different from the others," the guard murmured. "The Ævintýri have been collecting more exotic animals." He turned Trent's head this way and that, pushing his thumb over his lips to expose his teeth. "Healthy enough." He moved to speak over Trent's shoulder to the other guard. "He'll make a fine gift for Prince Hathuwulf."

Trent's heart dropped into his stomach. An Alfar prince was not someone he'd ever expected—or wanted—to meet. This wasn't going well. What the hell had he done?

The alfar at his back put his hands on Trent to search him, but Trent hadn't brought anything with him. He nodded to the other, who was obviously his superior.

"Keep to your post," the officer said, and he led Trent ahead of him by the scruff of his collar, walking him at a brisk pace down from the rampart and into the city. Trent stumbled once, and the alfar hefted him easily back upright to keep him moving until they reached the door of a longhouse still lit on the inside.

The officer banged on the entrance with his free fist, and once the door opened, he shoved Trent inside, no longer caring that he almost fell to the ground. An older human man stood by the door, bowing low and waiting to be addressed before speaking.

"Clean him up," the officer ordered, "and dress him properly. I'll be coming to collect him in the morning. And chain him," he added in a rougher voice. "I won't have him escaping and letting in his Ævintýri masters."

"Of course, herra," the man said instantly.

The alfar didn't wait to see his orders obeyed; he turned and let one of the other slaves shut the door behind him, leaving Trent in a long room full of nothing but piles of hay for beds, a few tattered blankets and wooden buckets, and a single large fire. Trent watched the man who approached him, both of them wary, but then the slave waved over a couple of the women nearby, who wasted no time in stripping Trent of his clothes and scrubbing him with thick rags dunked in a bucket of cold water. He was sure he needed a bath after spending days in the camp, but this wasn't how he would have asked to get clean again.

"What is this place?" Trent asked. None of the other humans answered him. "Who are you? Do you work for the prince?"

The only reply he got was a rough drying off. One of the women presented him with a pair of plain trousers and a simple blue tunic, the same as the rest of them wore. As soon as he was dressed, the older man approached him with a limping step and led him to the wall farthest from the door, where he was chained to the floor by his wrists and ankles.

"Please, talk to me," Trent begged, but the man only spared him a brief, sympathetic glance before leaving him. Trent slid down the wall to the floor, his chains clunking heavily around him. This was what he expected would happen, right? He'd done it. He was here—and he hadn't been murdered yet. Even so, as he sat looking at the slaves settling in on their beds of hay, he couldn't help thinking that he'd done an incredibly stupid fucking thing.

18

At some point, Trent dozed off with his head resting against the wall, but the light of dawn pouring in through the slits in the wood woke him. The others in the longhouse were already moving, tending the fire and going about their business. The man from the night before offered him some bread and a cup of water, which Trent thanked him for. Many of the men and women who'd slept in the room with him filed out before Trent was even fully awake, until only the older man and a small handful of others were left behind. They set about cleaning up the house, scooping out some of the older hay and laying down fresh bedding—or at least, what counted for bedding here. Even if Trent had tried to help, he only had about a foot of leeway on the chains keeping him.

"Is this what you do?" he asked, hoping at least one of them would answer him. "You take care of these quarters?" None of them looked at him, so he tried again. "Do you even get to leave the house? Do you get to leave the city? Or is this all your life is? Do you just do whatever the Alfar tell you, and that's it?"

Finally, one of the women whipped an angry glare in his direction. "You're the same as us, so why don't you stop acting so high and mighty? The Ævintýri let their men get mouthy," she muttered, returning her attention to scrubbing the pot in her lap.

"I'm not the same as you," Trent insisted. "No other humans are the same as you. Away from this island, humans aren't slaves. We're free. The whole world is free."

"He's lying," the woman said when one of the younger girls paused to look over at him. "That can't be."

"That kind of talk is dangerous," the man cut in, his limp preventing him from turning too quickly to face the new captive. "Keep that up and you'll see what happens to foolish young men who dream of freedom," he spat.

"You don't understand," Trent sighed. "I'm trying to tell you—"

He was stopped short by the door thumping open, and all eyes turned to the alfar who'd brought Trent here the night before. The other humans went silent and still, hands clasped in front of them and eyes respectfully lowered.

"Bring him to me," the officer said simply, and the head slave made quick work of the locks binding Trent to the floor. When Trent stood in front of him again, the alfar took him by the shoulder to turn him around and back again. He gave a grunt of approval, then walked Trent out of the longhouse without another word. Trent glanced backward at the doorway, but none of the slaves even raised their eyes to look at him.

They walked through the city with the alfar's hand tight at the back of his neck. Trent passed through the inner ramparts, and he recognized the part of the city where he'd stayed with Gunvard, and the Great Hall where Ciaran had first met with King Huldrekall. They didn't stop at either of them—not that Trent could have found a friend there even if they had. Instead, the officer led him to another large longhouse with thick animal carvings surrounding the doorway and pushed him through the front door.

An alfar in more casual clothes looked up from a writing desk near the door, his eyebrows lifting in silent question at the intrusion. He had an air like a head of house—and a busy one, by the unimpressed look on his face as he scanned the soldier in front of him.

"I have a gift for Prince Hathuwulf," the officer said, his tone significantly more polite than Trent had heard it thus far.

The butler-looking alfar rose, his hands clasped lightly behind his back as he approached Trent. He looked him up and down like goods for sale, then gave a small hum. "Wait here," he said. "We shall see if the prince is taking audience today."

They waited a long while. Once, Trent risked peeking up at his captor, hoping to at least see if he was looking impatient or if this was normal, but the alfar caught him with raised eyes and cuffed him sharply on the back of the head. Trent didn't see the other one return, but he heard him speak from across the room.

"Prince Hathuwulf will see you," he said, and the officer pushed Trent forward through the house to follow the steward.

The room Trent found himself in was warmer than the rest of the house. A large fire burned in the center of the floor, its smoke drifting up and through a narrow vent hatched into the roof. A heavy wooden table with seats for four took up the majority of the room, its surface covered with papers, scrolls, and a single silver cup, and in the largest chair sat an alfar who could only be Prince Hathuwulf. Trent only caught a glimpse of him before remembering to lower his eyes as he was presented. His black hair was held back from his face by braids strung with silver beads and pulled into a knot at the back of his head, the rest falling loose down to his shoulders. He was handsome, in the strange way the Alfar were, and he watched Trent with sharp but weary eyes. He didn't get up when they entered.

The officer beside Trent bowed deeply, his firm hand forcing the boy's head down as well. "Yðar Hátign," he said, "it is my honor to present you with this gift, captured from the invading fairies."

Hathuwulf's voice was low and steady—the sort of voice that didn't need to be raised to be obeyed. "It is a strange sort of gift, to assume your prince wants for slaves."

The officer's grip tightened on the back of Trent's head. "Highness, my intention would never be to—"

"Enough," the prince cut him off evenly. "Let me see this gift."

The soldier pushed Trent's shoulder, so he moved forward, coming to stand closer to the prince's chair and the light of the fire. Hathuwulf leaned his elbows on the arms of his chair and tilted his head to look up into Trent's lowered face. A heavy silver torc with matching wolf heads hung around his neck, matching the delicate embroidery at the collar of his dark tunic and a number of small silver hoops hung through piercings in his long, pointed ears. He paused, his black eyes narrowing slightly as he studied Trent's face.

"I accept your gift," he said after a tense silence, and he waved the soldier over with one hand, sliding one of the heavy silver rings from his finger and offering it to him. "You have my thanks, soldier. Be well."

The guard accepted the ring in an open palm and bowed even deeper than before, then swiftly excused himself, taking a few steps backward before turning his back to leave the room.

Trent stood as still as he could, his eyes on the floor. The Alfar king had threatened to murder them all just for showing up last time—how was a prince going to treat an enemy captive? Hathuwulf settled back into his chair, his fingers laced loosely over his lap, and he watched Trent for a while before he spoke.

"I know you, don't I?"

Trent hesitated, his brow furrowing. He wasn't sure if he should look up, or if he was going to be scolded for actually talking, or what this person expected of him—but there seemed to be a high probability of being murdered for doing the wrong thing.

"You may speak," the prince said. "I saw you in the Great Hall some time ago, when your fairy master came to beg the aid of my father."

"That...was me. Yes," Trent agreed. This didn't feel like the right time to correct him on the "master" issue.

"And now," Hathuwulf went on, "having taken advantage of our island's hospitality, your master returns to burn the fields that feed her people."

Trent froze. He definitely didn't have a good answer for that. But before he could build up too much panic, the prince gave a light sigh and waved him back a step so that he could stand.

"It isn't your doing, I suppose." He stopped close in front of Trent, but the boy didn't lift his eyes beyond the thick leather belt and the sheathed dagger at the alfar's waist. "What is your name, child?"

"Trent," he said, glad to finally be faced with a question he knew the answer to.

"Trent," the prince repeated softly. The name sounded strange when the alfar said it, like his mouth wasn't used to making that sort of sound. "How do they treat you—your fairy masters? You may answer."

Permission to reply and the *ability* to reply were different things. Did he tell the truth? Did he make something up? This man hadn't shoved him yet, so that was promising, Trent guessed, but an Alfar prince probably wasn't exceptionally sympathetic to the cause of human freedom. Playing it vague was probably the best option, at least until Trent had a better sense of how likely this person was to murder him.

"I'm...not treated badly with them," he said. At least if he was called out later, he could still say he told the truth. The fairies *hadn't* ever treated him poorly, really. Not by Alfar standards, anyway.

Hathuwulf gave a soft, pensive hum, folding his hands behind his back. He was uncomfortably close and uncomfortably tall. "Do you think they treat you as well as the heir of the Alfar might?"

"That depends on how well the heir of the Alfar treats his servants," Trent answered, then immediately clamped his mouth shut and closed his eyes. He half expected to be smacked again, but the prince only exhaled softly in amusement.

"You're a clever one, aren't you? I'll be clear. If you tell me what you know about the invaders destroying my island, I can make life for you here very easy indeed."

Trent's stomach tightened. This wasn't at all what he thought he'd be dealing with when he formed this stupid plan in his head the day before. He'd thought, maybe, being Chinese and interesting-looking might keep him from death long enough to get into the slave quarters, but it seemed that had worked a little too well. And now this prince recognized him. Obviously Trent couldn't betray Ciaran and the others—but if he didn't give this prince *something*, was he going to throw Trent in a dungeon somewhere to starve to death? Maybe Ciaran had been right. Maybe this had been a completely stupid, dangerous idea, and he should have just stayed in camp and helped Airmed roll bandages and do laundry all day.

The prince spoke again before Trent could. "You're conflicted," he said quietly. "That speaks to your character as well as that of your master. Very well." He lifted one hand, and somewhere deeper in the house, a bell sounded. A moment later, an older woman in a slave's blue dress entered the room. "Skathi," the prince greeted her, not unkindly, "please show our new arrival to his place. Make him comfortable."

"Of course, herra," the woman said with a bow. "By your leave."

"I hope you'll consider what I said, Trent. We'll speak more later."

The old woman urged Trent out of the room with a light hand on his arm, and together they walked back through the entry hall and into the attached slave house, where a few low beds lined the walls around a small, unlit fire pit. They were simple, but they were a huge step up from piles of hay on the floor.

"The one on the end there is free," the woman said with a gesture toward it, and she offered Trent a faint smile before beginning to bustle around the room. "You're lucky to have been brought to the house of Prince Hathuwulf. He's a good master. Some aren't so kind. I'm Skathi, as you heard—the head matron. You'll meet Jensi and Keldan later. There are others, but they're still back at home."

Trent took a seat on the bed at her urging and accepted the new blanket and the cup of warm goat's milk she offered him—which didn't taste as disgusting as he feared. This wasn't the prince's home?

The woman paused in front of him, and when he looked up at her, she gave a friendly lift of her eyebrows. "Have you really come from the fairy camp?"

"Yeah," he agreed, holding the cup in his lap with both hands. "But I wasn't a slave there. The Tuatha De Danann don't keep slaves."

Skathi tilted her head at him with a frown. "Don't keep slaves?" She scoffed, as though the idea were preposterous. "Who does their washing and cooking?"

"I mean—they have servants. But they aren't human. They're fairies, too, and they're paid. Most humans don't live where the fairies do—they live in the outside world, and they aren't *anyone's* slaves there. Away from this island, the rest of the world is just humans, living however they want."

It was a rose-tinted explanation of how things *actually* were in the rest of the world, of course, but since his poorly-thought-out plan wasn't going as he'd expected anyway, maybe the best choice he had right now was simply to tell as many humans as he came across that there was another way. He searched the woman's face for signs of hope, or curiosity, but she only held her hands together in front of her and softened into a warm, motherly smile.

"That's a nice dream, isn't it?"

"It's not a dream!" he insisted, more harshly than she deserved. "There's literally a whole world out there where humans are free and do whatever they want. My family had enough money to live in an apartment with maid service and a man to guard the door. The building I lived in was taller than ten of these houses on top of each other. *That's* what the human world is like."

Skathi watched him in silence for a few beats, then reached down to take away his cup and touch her hand to his forehead as though she expected him to be feverish. "Well," she said cheerfully, "wherever you came from, I'm sure you had a rough night. Get some rest and wait until His Highness decides where he wants you."

She left him before he could argue any further, so he sighed and slumped back against the wall beside his assigned bed. He looked out over the slave house, nothing but bunks and a dented cauldron hung over a cold fire, and he pushed his hands hard against his face. All he'd accomplished was getting himself actually enslaved—with absolutely zero exit strategy.

Trent did get a little sleep on his cot, but later in the day, Skathi woke him and put him to work. He was given a bucket and a brush and told to go from one end of the house to the other—stone floors got dirty easily. When that was done, he was tasked with bringing firewood in from a shed outside and starting a fire for the evening in the prince's bedroom, so he brought the wood, piled it up in the center of the pit so it looked like a campfire—then stood and stared at it for a while. He had no idea how to make a fire without matches. He'd never been camping. He looked around the room, hoping for guidance, but it was just a bedroom. The only furniture in it was a small table and chair, a washing basin in the corner, and a massive bed, its headboard posts carved into ox heads. It was thick with plush furs that looked far warmer than anything in the slave house.

There probably wasn't much chance of finding a lighter anywhere nearby. Would it be cheating if he went into one of the rooms that already had a fire and carried a lit chunk of wood into here? Maybe he could take a piece to light?

"Did your last household not teach you how to build a fire?"

The prince's voice made Trent jump, dropping the small chunk of wood he'd been considering stealing fire from the kitchen with, and he turned to see the alfar with one hand on the now open door.

"I—no," he admitted, remembering a little late to drop his gaze to the floor. "I don't know how."

Hathuwulf passed him by without comment, drifting the door shut gently on his way in, and he took a small stone and a scrap of metal from a drawer of the desk. He crouched by the waiting wood, and in one easy movement, ignited the bits of kindling underneath the logs. When he rose, he held the flint and scraper out to drop them into Trent's waiting hands.

"No magic required," he said flatly, which didn't do anything to help Trent feeling like a useless idiot.

He peeked up enough to see the prince turning up his sleeves to expose slate-colored forearms, the basin in the corner filling itself with steaming water as he approached it.

"Have you considered my offer?" Hathuwulf asked, turning his back on the boy to wash his hands and face in the warm water, but Trent didn't have an answer for him. If he told this man what he wanted to know about the fairies, they'd be wiped out. They'd only done as well as they had so far because they'd been using hit-and-run tactics—even Trent could see that.

The prince turned back to him, drying his face with a cloth from the table and crossing the room with unhurried steps. He stood close to Trent and touched under his chin to lift his face.

"You could have a room of your own," the prince said. "Access to my private baths. More food than you could hope to eat. Fine clothes." He tilted his head slightly, his knuckle firm under Trent's chin. "If only you tell me where to find the fairy camp and help me put an end to this conflict."

Trent swallowed hard. Prince Hathuwulf was a good master, Skathi said. People whose slaves called them good weren't likely to just...murder people, right? He wasn't getting anywhere talking to the slaves themselves—but maybe he could get somewhere by talking to an heir. He forced himself to look up despite the way Hathuwulf's steady black eyes put a chill in his skin.

"I can't do that," he said, his voice more firm than he'd expected.

"I doubt your master deserves such loyalty from you." He sighed through his nose and let his hand drop, watching Trent's face for a moment longer. "Perhaps if you can't be cajoled, you can be compelled. As easy a life as I can give you, I can also give one unfathomably worse. You realize that, don't you?"

"Then neither of us would be happy."

Hathuwulf paused. "You don't speak very much like a slave. How you look me in the eyes like that—you address your master in this way in the place you came from?"

"In the place I came from, I'm not a slave," Trent answered. He held his hands in tight fists at his sides to keep them from shaking. "I came here to help the Tuatha De Danann stop you people from making war on the whole planet."

The prince stared at him, his expression unreadable. "Is that so?"

"I know about the king going to meet a demon in Antarctica," Trent went on, the words falling out of him now. "I know about your plans to help him open portals everywhere so more demons can come through and take over everything."

Hathuwulf ticked an eyebrow. "And you presumed to come into my house and beg me to be merciful, is that it?"

"Well—" Trent stopped, swallowed, and tried again. "I didn't...actually know I'd be in your house. That was just luck, I guess."

The alfar prince watched him in silence, then took a calm seat in the chair by the fire. He sat looking into the flames, his elbows perched on the arms of his chair, and Trent stood by, not sure what else he was supposed to do. He didn't dare try to leave without being dismissed.

When Hathuwulf spoke again, his voice was softer. "I counseled my father against this war," he said without moving his eyes from the fire. "We've been prosperous here for a thousand years, and yet now he seeks war with the outside. Glory and blood, because this creature Ashmodai promised him victory," he said with a slight sneer in his voice that didn't quite touch his lips. "Our people have always valued glory and honor above all else, but my father isn't here to see what his greed has done to the people left behind. Scorched fields, slaughtered herds, and attacks from the shadows by men we once called our kin." He exhaled slowly. "I wonder if this is the glory he had in mind."

Trent frowned at him, risking taking a half step closer. "None of this is going to end well for your people. Even if you beat the Tuatha De Danann here, even if the people working outside with us *don't* close your demon portals, there's no way you can take on the whole world. It's a different time now."

Hathwulf gave a small snort, but Trent couldn't tell if it was amusement or frustration. He looked up at the boy across the fire. "I believe you aren't a slave, with a mouth like that."

"You said yourself it's been a thousand years since any of the Alfar left this island. The world out there isn't the one you think it is. This place hasn't changed, but everywhere else *has*," Trent promised him. "You think it'll be like the old days, where you'll just roll some ships up to a little coastal village, do some raiding, and sail on home again? Do you know what a camera is, or a cell phone? Do you know what the Internet is? Do you know what a *missile* is?"

The prince's eyes narrowed faintly, but he didn't speak, so Trent felt emboldened to go on.

"You might be able to do cool magic, but you're delusional if you think the population of this island has a chance against the seven *billion* humans out there."

"Perhaps the fairies should have taught you how to better hold your tongue," Hathuwulf said pointedly as he stood from his seat.

Trent took a step back on instinct as the alfar approached him, trying not to look like he was shrinking under the prince's gaze—even though he definitely was.

"Your situation is precarious at best," the prince said, his tone even but his threat clear. "Do not make me regret what kindness I have shown you thus far. You may go," he finished.

It wasn't a request, and Trent knew it, so he decided not to push his luck. He gave the prince a small bow and backed away before leaving like he'd seen the others do, then hurried back to the room where Skathi had put him that morning, his heart feeling like it was going to pound its way right up his throat.

He didn't have much chance to recover before the old woman found him again and put him to work doing laundry—under her supervision, of course. For dinner, he was given the same bowl of porridge and salted fish as the other slaves and sent to bed as soon as the kitchen was clean. Trent curled up on his side with his back to the room, his thin blanket tucked up close around his chin. The fire kept the room mostly warm, at least, even if the straw that made up his lumpy mattress was hard to settle into.

He missed Ciaran.

19

Noah woke up wrapped in a blanket on Julien's bed, but he was almost positive he'd passed out on the bunk room floor sometime in the late morning. He nuzzled his face closer into the pillow and took a deep breath of the scent Julien had left there. It almost made up for having to listen to his brothers earlier in the day. When he lifted his head and rubbed the sleep from his eyes, he spotted the silver dogs on his box reared up with a message, so he crawled across the bed to drag it toward him from the floor. No more drawings or instructions this time—thank God, Noah thought—just a letter from Sabin.

Hey Noah,

This monastery is the tits. They have a secret library with a poorly conceived lock that's full of super old books. I'm working my way through them. We have weapons ready for you, but apparently making holy weapons takes more time than we thought. We're sending yours back to you so you can get started, but we'll have to hang around for a bit longer to have ours done. We'll be ready to send them over at 3:00 our time, so be ready at the fort.

Sabin

Noah washed and dressed himself, replied to Sabin with thanks and a request that he *not* get kicked out of the monastery for snooping (but do send anything cool that you find), then went downstairs to find Julien. He didn't want to tell the boy how nervous he was about the spell he'd been tasked with—he was sure he had enough to worry about on his end, and there was no sense adding to it.

Edouard assigned Joseph and Arnaud to accompany them back to the Tour de Lévis to collect the weapons, which was an awkward trip for Noah to make, but he just kept to the back and tried to let the brothers forget he was there. Arnaud's suggestions that Noah be Julien's dirty little secret had left a bitter taste in his mouth, but at least Joseph seemed to just be the silent type. He'd much rather deal with the silent type.

They stood at the top of the Tour de Lévis and waited while Noah sent Sabin another quick note to let him know they'd arrived. The sudden snap of the gate opening startled him, and Noah half hoped that Sabin would come himself to deliver their weapons—but instead of any of the boys, a duffel bag flew from the black opening in the air, landing hard against the back wall of the fort's rooftop. Joseph had to dodge the next one, and a minute later, a pile of long daggers clattered to the floor at the base of the gate—followed by a halberd, which rang loudly as its blade struck the stone.

"L'ostie des enfants," Arnaud muttered as the door flickered shut again.

Julien bent to pick up the halberd, weighing it in both hands and looking over at Noah with a confused frown. "What in the hell are we supposed to do with this? We have to ride the Metro."

Noah lifted both shoulders and held them in a long shrug. "Maybe we could stash it somewhere here?" he suggested. "Come get it at a better time?"

"Like fucking when?" Julien mumbled to himself, but he went down the stairs to find somewhere in the old fort to hide the cumbersome weapon.

Joseph and Arnaud tucked the pile of daggers away in one of the duffel bags, which were apparently full of boxes upon boxes of ammunition—*that* was what the brothers had decided to send to be blessed by an ancient order of holy monks? The bags were easy to carry back to the house without drawing too much attention to themselves, at least.

Once they had them at home, the dining room table became a

scene Noah had seen countless times on Julien's apartment floor. Guns were everywhere in pieces, each brother sat at the bench carefully cleaning and oiling their weapons to make certain they would be reliable when it counted. Julien had frequently spread himself out on the floor back home and silently checked his weapons—probably more frequently than they really needed it, but Noah suspected that it was the closest thing the hunter had to meditation, so he'd always been happy to sit by and quietly share space with him. He suspected he wouldn't be such welcome company at the table now, though. It had taken him a long time to get used to the presence of guns at all, and they still made him uncomfortable, so he left the hunters to it and returned to his work in the bunk room.

He opened Trent's laptop on one of the beds that didn't have papers on it and answered some messages he'd received from a handful of fellow witches he knew online. He'd been put in touch with a couple that actually lived in Montreal, so he was eager to make contact with them in person and see if he could get their help in preparing this portal-closing spell. He organized his notes while he waited for their decision, but when he checked his email later, the replies he got made his heart sink. It had been a mistake to mention that he was staying with a family of monster hunters.

No fucking way, one email said. *I'm not coming within a hundred feet of any of those Fournier assholes.*

Are you safe there? Those guys are dangerous for people like us. I'd get out fast if I were you, another said.

Fuck them. One of them murdered my cousin, and nothing ever fucking happened.

Noah stared at his screen, his shoulders slumped. He guessed he should have expected this kind of answer. Julien himself had admitted a long time ago that he'd killed witches before—ones that had been doing horrible things, he said. It was obvious the hunter was wary of Noah's magic, but even early in their friendship, he'd apparently judged correctly that *this* witch was no real threat to anyone. The others, Noah guessed, weren't so discerning.

Noah was on his own, then.

He borrowed a bit of money from Julien, who had to sneak the cash out of a hidden lockbox under the stairs, and went out to make yet another trip to the shop for supplies. He had a list now—a substantial one. The woman behind the counter smiled a little uncertainly at him as he piled jars and candles and bundles of herbs in front of her, but she softened when Noah thanked her earnestly in bad French.

He wished he'd brought a backpack. The paper bags he carried weighed his arms down on the trip back, but at least he could set them on the floor of the bus.

The bunk room just belonged to Noah now—his notes, drawings, books, and jars covered almost every inch of the floor by the time he sorted through his new ingredients, leaving only enough room for the door to swing open. Noah set out his supplies on the map of Montreal he'd stolen from Laurent, arranging the packets he would need to prepare and charge in their correct order, but without the portal's location to center them on, it felt a lot like just shuffling papers. He could prepare the tools—but they would be useless.

Julien appeared after the sun set, the sweat on his brow telling Noah he'd already been out for the day.

"We're going back to the cemetery. Will you come?"

Noah hesitated, looking out over his haphazard spread to take stock of himself, and then he nodded. "Okay. Okay, um—yes. Let me—yes. I'll be down in a minute."

Julien smiled softly at him. "Don't work yourself too hard."

"As if you're one to talk," the witch muttered as he scooped up some of his tokens and stuffed them in his pocket.

He met the rest of them downstairs, a little impressed at how unarmed the group always managed to look while carrying *so* many guns, and he followed the brothers out of the house and back the familiar way toward Mont Royal.

"So," he began, catching Julien's attention, "you guys are planning on just using those guns to fight demons, like...in the middle of the park?"

The hunter shrugged one shoulder. "They're the most effective weapons we have."

"But guns are loud," Noah pointed out. "And super illegal. And there are *seven* of you. That's...you know, seven times as loud and illegal. I really doubt the cops are going to go easy on you even if you tell them, 'oh, it's cool; it's because we're out here fighting demons, don't worry about it.'"

Julien frowned faintly as if the prospect hadn't crossed his mind. "We *do* know some of them personally, but you're right."

The witch sighed. "How you guys got by for so long *without* using magic, I don't know. How about you just let me know when you're all about to start shooting, and I'll make sure the noise doesn't get out. I'm glad you all thought this through so well before we left."

Julien let out a soft chuckle through his nose and caught Noah's fingers in his while they walked, just for a moment. "That's why I keep you around, mon raleur."

"Mhm," Noah hummed, but he smiled over at the blond just the same.

Noah didn't recognize the place Edouard led them to—Montreal was a new city to him, and he'd really only seen this area after dark—but it looked like it was close to where he and Julien had met the first demon. He followed along at the rear of the group, the men ahead of him spreading out into a line that reminded him of a search party. It kind of was a search party, he guessed—the most murderous one ever, but still a search party. After they'd been walking a while, Antony stopped them with a sharp, quiet hiss, holding out his hand and then pointing toward a cluster of trees near a lane that separated the cemetery from the park. In the dark, Noah could just barely make out a huddled mass of human shapes, standing too close together within the trees with their bodies subtly trembling. The first one had been this way, too—maybe being in the real world this way was overwhelming for them.

Noah tapped Julien's shoulder and pointed wordlessly ahead of them to indicate he was moving forward, and the hunter nodded. Noah skirted the copse of trees as silently as he could and dropped to his knees on the nearest path, beginning to mark out circles in charcoal so that the brothers could use the traps if they needed to. Keeping up more than one was going to be tricky—but hopefully these culty monster hunters could at least be efficient.

He missed the first gunshot, and he swore as the demon's screeches echoed through the dark, but he recovered quickly, moving away from the traps and throwing up a sound-muffling spell over as large an area as he could. These stupid shits were just determined to get arrested.

The brothers *did* prove to be efficient—and, if Noah was honest, all seven of them together were pretty impressive. Joseph seemed to be missing, but Noah saw a demon jerk backwards and crash into the brush, a bullet hole visible in his chest before he collapsed into ash. Joseph wasn't too far away. The others seemed to fall into a rhythm, even as more and more people appeared to face them—bullets struck knees, demons shrieked and fell to the ground, and then the hunter would finish them with a dagger to the heart. They all just looked like people to Noah, and more than once he turned his face away when a demon had their eyes on him as they died. They weren't just people. He knew that. Julien could see them—and Julien would never attack someone who was just a person.

As soon as Julien made use of the first trap Noah laid, knocking a demon into it to hold it while he was forced to deal with another on top of him, Hugo took notice, and soon Noah was dripping sweat and leaning against a gravestone for support while he kept three barriers up at once. Thankfully, the killing blows didn't take long.

When the area went silent, the last demon's cry fading into the night, Noah let the sound spell drop and put his hands on his knees, doubling over to puff. He had no idea how many demons that had been. The brothers had killed them all—but this *still* wasn't a portal. There was no opening in the ground, no black hole. Not even a prickle on the back of Noah's neck that might have told him something powerful was nearby. Just woods, graves, and demons. They couldn't go on like this.

The hunters reconvened, talked briefly amongst themselves, and then carried on deeper through the cemetery, Julien glancing back to Noah and urging him to follow with a quick tilt of his head. He obeyed, though his body ached a little. If the others could keep going, Noah sure as hell wasn't going to be the first one to complain.

As they passed out of the trees and into the more open graveyard, Noah paused. At the far end of the clearing, standing among the gravestones as still as a statue, was an Alfar. He was tall and slender, his dark robes brushing the ground underneath a hooded, fur-lined cloak. Black hair spilled loose over his shoulders down to his waist, and he held a wooden staff as tall as he was in one hand, silver accents barely glinting off the gnarled wood in the dim moonlight.

Noah's heart constricted under the alfar's steady black gaze, but he still called out for Julien in a hushed voice. He dared to move his eyes from the staring figure as the hunter approached, and by the time the brothers had each been hissed at and rushed over, the alfar was gone.

"I saw him," Noah insisted. "One of the Alfar."

More than one of the brothers cursed, but Edouard focused them with a sharp, quiet whistle. "That means we're on the right track," he said. "We keep going."

Noah spread some abremalin oil onto his palms from the vial in his pocket and spread his hands toward the ground, hoping the alfar was a magical-enough creature to leave behind a trail he could follow. Laurent had a small device in his hand that flickered bright green when he stood too near to Noah, so he clicked his tongue and moved farther away so that it could give a more accurate reading. They found demon stragglers in the darker parts of the woods as they went, which the brothers were easily able to put down, and Noah got the feeling they were being watched more than once, but despite their careful checks, they reached the iron fence of the cemetery without another sign of the man they'd seen. Dawn would be coming soon, so Edouard admitted defeat and called the excursion, allowing the exhausted group to return home for some rest.

"For fuck's sake," Hugo sighed almost as soon as the front door shut behind them. "Are we sure this portal exists at all?"

"The Alfar wouldn't be here if it wasn't at least going to exist soon," Noah said.

Antony crossed his arms over his chest with a grunt of disgust as he turned to face Noah. "What is the point of bringing this thing with us if it can't even find what we're looking for?"

"Who the fuck are you calling a thing?" Julien snapped.

Antony gestured at Noah with both hands, as though the answer should have been obvious, but the witch only let out a small sigh. The others were at least able to keep their disdain silent or civil— but *this* brother, in particular, Noah really could have done without.

"We're letting this witch live in our house and do his magic here, and for what?" he shouted. He turned on Noah with a sneer on his lips. "If you're not even good at hunting down your own kind, why should we trust that you're doing what you say you're doing at all?"

Noah recoiled with a snort. "Excuse me? My own kind? The *demons?* Fuck you."

"*Magic things*," Antony answered, hatred in his voice. "How do we know you're not jerking us off and trying to protect them?"

"Are you stupid?" Noah shot back before he could stop himself. "Where were you tonight? How was *any* of what I did protecting those demons?"

"It was convenient that you didn't see that alfar until it was too late for us to do anything about it."

Edouard raised his voice over the bickering. "Antony, fucking enough! Go sleep off this idiocy."

Antony leaned so close to Noah's face that he could smell the hunter's sweat, green eyes scanning the witch for signs of betrayal. "I'm going to keep a closer eye on you, witch," he promised in a low, dangerous voice.

Noah didn't waver. He kept the other man's gaze until he retreated and stalked toward the stairs, then called out after him, "Let me know at the end of the week how many times I've scratched my ass," earning himself a venomous scowl. Noah turned to the remaining brothers with one hand on his hip, the other lifting and dropping again in frustration. "I hope you guys know, by the way, that I reached out for help closing this portal and got shut down because— *surprise*—no witch in town wants to help the family that kills them for no reason. So maybe, just fucking maybe, you ought to reevaluate your murder filters."

Hugo, at least, was good enough to look upset by this news, but Edouard only sighed.

"Everyone get some rest," he said. "We'll talk about where to go next once everyone has had some sleep."

Julien took Noah by the hand a little too tightly, and he led them up the stairs to his room, slamming the door behind them and wincing as he jerked his coat off too roughly for his still-tender shoulder. He was seething, but he seemed determined not to speak too soon and risk raising his voice. Noah could guess the cause.

"Don't worry about Antony," Noah said as gently as he could, taking a cross-legged seat on the bed. He was pretty irritated himself, but it wasn't going to help anything for both of them to just be sitting around mad at some idiot. "He's not going to do anything. He just wants to feel big, and I'm an easy target."

"I don't want him anywhere near you," Julien said, roughly, as though the words had been waiting to escape him.

"Are we doing this again? Come on, Julien. I can take care of myself."

The hunter hesitated, then gave a heavy sigh and slumped down on the bed beside him. "Désolé," he said in a much softer voice, though it still sounded strained. "I know," he promised. "I know you can. It's...stupid. But with Antony, I...I worry more. Not because I think he'll hurt you, but...never mind." He shook his head and looked away with a frown. "It's stupid."

Noah chuckled and laid a hand on the larger man's knee. "I like to hear your stupid ideas."

Julien huffed softly. "I told you that I wasn't going to get upset anymore thinking that you were going to...leave," he ended awkwardly.

Noah stared at him, unable to form words for almost a full minute. "You're worried that...I'm going to *leave you*? For *that*?"

"I told you it was stupid," the hunter grumped. "It's just that once before, when we were young, for a little while I was seeing this girl, and then she met Antony, and..." He shrugged without looking up.

The witch couldn't help his soft laugh. "I really, really don't think you have anything to worry about, Julien. A, he's a complete asshole, and B, if he stole one of your girlfriends once, doesn't that mean he's straight?"

Now Julien looked at him. "I was straight too, Noah."

"Oh." He snorted. "Right. I forgot how irresistible I am, I guess." He cupped Julien's stubbled cheeks with both hands and leaned in to kiss his frown. There was so much insecurity under this gruff monster hunter exterior. So much uncertainty. It was sweet—and even sweeter that Julien was actually trying to share it with him and get over it, rather than letting it fester until he exploded. "Don't worry," he said against the other man's lips. "If he even tries to make a move, I'll hex his dick off."

The blond hesitated. "Is that something you can do?"

"Let's hope you never have to find out," Noah purred in reply, enjoying the subtle tension in the hunter's shoulders. A click from the box on the nightstand drew his gaze, and he leaned across Julien's lap to pull it closer to him. He flipped the small latch between the rearing dogs and opened the lid, expecting a note from Sabin—but instead, an origami tulip lay lightly on the black velvet.

"What is that?" Julien asked as Noah lifted it, and the witch sighed. "I think...this is probably from Jett."

"Jett? The mohawk kid?"

Noah was already unfolding the paper flower, doing his best not to tear it in the process. "He sent me a...kind of a love letter the other day. It's nothing," he followed up immediately with an exaggerated shrug.

"A love letter?" Julien echoed, doing a good job of keeping his voice steady considering the conversation they'd been having immediately previous to this.

"Well it was more of a...poem. About my butt. I'm pretty sure he was joking," he went on as the flower finally began to unfold into a more sheetlike shape. "I told him thanks, but even if I didn't already have the best boyfriend ever, he's Sabin's age. That's weird."

"Hm."

Noah gave the blond a smile and flattened the letter open on the bed beside them, holding it out so that he and Julien could read it at the same time.

My dearest Noah,

Though our time together was short, it was filled with passion and promises. I, however, will not be able to fulfill those vows we whispered to one another in the comfort of the night. Though the warmth of the bittersweet tea we shared will carry me through the coldest of winters, the season of our hearts has changed. I hope that you are able to move into your own spring and hold our memories close to shield yourself against the chilled winds of sorrow until your summer comes.

Keep your head and your dreams high, and do not debase the beauty of your lithe body or your voluminous heart by pursuing me further. I will remain but a fleeting vision of your youth, and I hope that you will cherish that, just as I cherished you for these few ephemeral days.

Unfortunately no longer yours,

Jett

PS: Please ask Lugh if he would be interested in the whirlwinds of my affections upon your next meeting.

Noah gave a slightly longer sigh as he reached the end of the letter. Julien took it from him to scan again, and the witch lifted a hand as if providing the letter itself as proof that Jett was ridiculous.

The hunter's brow formed a faint crease. "Vows we whispered to one another?" he read aloud. This time he did a slightly worse job sounding careless, and it almost broke Noah's heart.

"Julien, you know he's just teasing. Look—he's basically asking me for Lugh's number at the bottom. We chatted over tea the night the boys were here, and that was it. You know that, right?"

"I know," the blond promised him. He folded the letter in half, ruining the creases that had once made it a flower, and offered it to Noah. He looked the witch in the face and took a soft, even breath. "I know."

Noah smiled and took Julien's face in his hands again to kiss him. The paper fell to the floor as Julien reached for Noah's waist instead. Noah smirked into the kiss and eased backward, drawing Julien down to the mattress with him. Sometimes a good distraction was the best medicine.

20

Noah hadn't come out of the bunk room all day. When Julien checked on him, he was bent over one book or the other, mumbling to himself while he ground herbs in his bowl or wrapped twine around pieces of carved wood. It was probably better he did all that in here rather than where the others could see him—Julien had heard enough arguments about the use of magic to last him a lifetime, and having Noah at least temporarily out of sight kept new outbursts to a minimum.

Julien opened the door one last time before sunset and found Noah right where he'd left him—on the floor among his papers and jars. It was a picture that would have made Julien himself uncomfortable not so long ago, if he was honest—a witch in the midst of unknown spellwork involving a number of some unidentified totems. He couldn't say he wasn't still wary of magic, after all he'd seen in his life. But this witch—just this one—only made him feel warm.

Noah looked up from the floor with dark bags under his eyes, his hands working steadily on the mortar and pestle in his lap. "Is it time to go?"

The hunter frowned at him. "Are you sure you're up for it? T'as l'air pas mal fatigué."

"This is just...a lot. I'm okay." He used the nearby bed frame to push himself up, but when he rose, he wavered for a second as though he'd stood up too fast.

"Why don't you stay in tonight?" Julien said, one hand on the witch's shoulder. "Get some rest. There's no sense in exhausting yourself. You're going your part."

"And, what, you guys are just going to shoot demons quietly?"

"Don't worry about us. Promise me you'll put that away and get some sleep. Just for tonight."

Noah didn't look pleased about the idea. He peered over at Julien with his lips pursed into a skeptical frown, but then he let out a sigh and looked down at the floor, scuffing the wood with one bare foot. "Fine."

"We'll muddle through without you somehow, mon raleur." Julien smiled at Noah's sleepy, dismissive shooing and shut the door on his way out.

Even the air of the park and cemetery surrounding Mont Royal seemed stale. Julien was sick of it. He didn't even know anymore how many nights they'd spent out here, looking for a portal that they *hoped* was actually nearby. And the longer they looked for it, the more pissed off everyone got. Without Noah to accompany him, Julien was left on his own again when his brothers split up to search—not that he minded. He'd had too many blissful years without having to listen to Antony's complaining that putting up with it now was wearing on his patience.

He walked the outline of the forest, skirting the quiet playground near the Lac-aux-Castors with his eyes scanning the trees for signs of movement. How was it possible that they'd scoured almost every inch of Mont Royal and not found a gaping black demon pit? As he was considering turning back, a mild splash from the still lake water caught his attention, and he followed the sound with his eyes. Just within the edges of the lights lining the sidewalk, something slipped into the trees.

Even at this distance, it looked big. Taller than Julien, easily, and standing on thick, digitigrade legs. It had spotted him, too. At least, it seemed so—the creature had flaking horns curling out from where its eyes should have been, weighing down a sharp, triangular face with no lips to hide its bared teeth. The end of its heavy, scaled tail twitched in the dirt, and it settled into a crouch that moved the bony spines in its shoulders. Whether it could see him or not, it definitely knew Julien was there.

The hunter spared a quick glance around the area, grateful that the park had become mostly deserted as the sun set. He dropped the duffel bag over his shoulder onto the closest bench without taking his gaze from the demon and reached behind him to take the blessed knife and the Colt from the back of his belt. Noah wasn't there to completely muffle the noise, but the attached silencer would have to do. Julien shifted his boots in the grass and gave a quick, sharp whistle, jutting his chin toward the creature.

"Aweille."

The thing made a horrible, growling roar, showing a long black tongue, and it rushed him, bounding across the park on its clawed hands like a monstrous gorilla. Julien fired, his bullet finding its intended place in the demon's gut, but the creature didn't stop. It just leaked blood onto the grass and pavement as it barreled toward its prey. Julien braced himself to meet it, but the demon hit him like a truck, knocking the wind from his lungs and lifting him off the grass. He buried his knife in the meat near its neck, earning a vicious howl from the beast and stars in his own vision as he was slammed brutally back down to the ground.

Julien focused enough to fire again as the thing reached for him, burying another shot in its chest. It hissed in pain and snatched Julien up by one leg, flinging him so hard against the park bench that he was sure he cracked at least one rib. Before he could get his bearings, the demon released his ankle, instead grabbing him up by the back of his coat with both clawed hands. Julien twisted in the creature's grip and shot another round into its chest. This one found its home in the thing's heart, and the demon shrieked, flinging Julien away from it with one last burst of fury. The hunter only caught a glimpse of the demon's scaly skin burning away to ash before his beaten body hit the lake.

The water chilled Julien's skin, and he winced out some bubbles as his ribs protested his attempt to make for the surface. He kicked with his legs and pushed with the arm that hurt slightly less to move—but something felt wrong. He wasn't making progress. He stilled a moment, lungs burning, and was sure that he was being pulled subtly downward. Julien turned to look toward the bottom of the murky lake, squinting through the darkness. To anyone else, it would probably have been impossible to see, but Julien's remaining eye was still good enough to make out the ring of deeper black in the low pit of the rocky bottom. Faint wisps of heavy smoke seemed to pool around the edges of the circle, moving easily despite the press of the water above.

This was the portal. No wonder they hadn't been able to find it.

Julien grunted with effort as he renewed his swim, forcing his aching body to push hard enough for his head to break the surface of the water. He still felt the lingering tug on his ankles all the way to the shore, but as soon as he pulled himself up on the concrete bank, it faded. He allowed himself to lay still on the path for a minute or two, catching his breath and gingerly touching his ribs, and then he hauled himself to his feet. He needed to let the others know. Unfortunately, a quick pat of his pockets told him that his phone had been lost to the depths of the lake—possibly even to Hell itself—so he retrieved his abandoned bag of weapons and made his way back to the house.

Noah was the only one at home when Julien returned. The hunter was eager to get back to the portal to keep an eye on it, but Noah insisted on wrapping his ribs and making him drink a foul-smelling tonic the witch mixed up before they left. Despite Julien's grumbling, his torso felt much better almost immediately.

"So it's actually *in* the lake?" Noah asked once they were on their way again. He still had bags under his eyes, but finally seeing progress seemed to have invigorated him.

"At the bottom," Julien answered with a nod. His still-damp pants clung unpleasantly to his legs as he walked, but he hadn't wanted to take the time to change them.

"Clever fucks," the witch muttered. He had his phone out to take notes while they walked, which meant that Julien occasionally had to guide him by the shoulder to keep him from walking into a lamppost—but it was an exercise Julien was used to from his nights in Vancouver with the studious witch at his side.

Once they reached the edge of the park, they circled around to the dark cafe in the pavilion, hoping to stay out of sight during their approach. Demons probably lurked in every copse of trees across the lake, and killing them wasn't the pair's purpose tonight.

"I just need to get the coordinates as exact as possible for the spell," Noah said under his breath as they crouched at the edge of the building, the lake just in view beyond the metal railing of the cafe's balcony. "Do you think I could get out to the middle of the water? It was in the middle, right?"

Julien shushed him without answering and pressed him tighter against the wall with a gentle hand. A thick mist had begun to wash over the paved edges of the lake, seeping down from the treeline and over the still surface of the water. It rolled smoothly across the ground until it covered the pavilion from the woods to the parking lot, and then it settled heavily over the area, almost hiding the entire park from view—but Julien still saw the movement in the trees, the dark fog disturbed by slow, purposeful footsteps.

"Alfar magic," Noah whispered. He dug quick and silent in the small bag thrown over his shoulder and retrieved a small vial with an eyedropper, then tilted his head back and let a single droplet fall into each of his eyes. He blinked a few times and hissed softly through his teeth, exhaling softly as he tucked the vial away again. He caught Julien's questioning look and grinned. "Rathgeirr helped me. We don't all have special monster hunter eyes."

They both went quiet as a tall figure emerged from the trees, walking steadily toward the water with a gnarled wooden staff in his hand. Long black hair, dark clothing, and slate grey skin. This was the alfar Noah had described—the one who had been watching them. Who was he?

The alfar stood at the edge of the lake now, holding his staff in both hands in front of him. He tapped the foot of it against the path once, twice, and again, then lifted the staff over his head, his back arching subtly with the slow, circular movement of his arms.

Julien could almost feel the prickling of curious excitement on the skin of the witch in front of him, but the sight laid a pit in the hunter's stomach.

A faint rumble ran through the ground and into the foundation of the building where they hid, and below them, the alfar took a half step back as though bracing himself and hit the foot of his staff on the pavement one last time, then spread his arms, his staff remaining upright in front of him. It slowly rose without his help, and with its movement, the mist over the lake parted. The water itself followed, until it floated in the air a dozen feet above the bottom of the lake, a faintly rolling mass of water that still dripped softly onto the damp stone below.

"Holy shit," Noah breathed. He edged ever so slightly closer to the corner of the building, and Julien put a warning hand on his shoulder.

The alfar took his staff from the air with a casual gesture and started down the slope toward the bottom, where the open demon portal lay dark and shifting. He walked until he stood at the edge, then crouched at the stone rim, balancing with the help of the staff. He leaned his ear close to the thick smoke as though listening, and then rose, gripping his staff in both hands once again. He leaned forward over the smoky precipice and dripped the bottom of his staff beneath the moving layer of black. He stayed that way for a few long, tense seconds, and then his body twisted, his knees bending to accommodate the sharp arch of his back. A deep sound like a sudden, heaving shout echoed from the bottom of the lake, and the alfar slammed the staff back down again.

This time, instead of sinking into the pit, it seemed to hit something solid, and a pulse rippled out from the point of impact, sparking a bright ring in the air that quickly burned away the smoke over the surface of the portal. The alfar's body shook, but he held firm to his staff until the way was open, and bodies began to crawl from the now clear depths. Men and women with long, black-feathered wings and sharp horns darted from the pit and into the trees, along with gruesome creatures of different shapes and sizes, all of them doubtless headed for one of the mausoleum hideaways Julien and his brothers had found in the cemetery. This time it was Noah who had to reach back and keep Julien in his place.

After scarcely a minute, the alfar stumbled back, and the way crashed closed again in a shower of sparks, immediately overtaken by the same thick smoke as before. He stood at the edge of the portal, shoulders moving with heavy breath, and then he slowly turned back toward the path. As soon as both of his feet were on the concrete again, the water dropped back into place, waves sloshing over the edges of the man-made shore as the lake settled into stillness once more. The alfar exchanged brief words with one of the winged demons who had lingered, and then disappeared back into the wood, the grey mist retreating along with him until the park stood just as empty and quiet as before—as if nothing had happened at all.

"Fuck me," Noah said softly, and the admiration in his voice put Julien's hackles up.

"Let's get your coordinates and get the hell out of here," he muttered.

"The fucking lake," Edouard spat. "All of this wandering around, and they hid the thing at the bottom of the *fucking* lake." He sat hunched over the kitchen table with the others along the bench beside him, every single one of them tired and irritable. Even Antony was quiet; he still had a scowl on his face, but he looked more likely to put his head down and take a nap than to shout.

"It's ingenious," Laurent muttered, mostly to himself. "We'd have no way of looking underneath the water for it. And why would we think to? I wouldn't have considered the possibility that they would have access themselves, if not for the magic you described."

"This was *insane* magic," Noah agreed, seeming far more lively than any of them appreciated. "Even aside from holding open a literal portal to Hell, moving a fucking lake out of the way and just keeping it there *while* you hold open a literal portal to Hell is—" He stopped and shook his head. "I've never heard of anything like it. But it tells us that the alfar is the key—the portal isn't *open* open. He's got to keep going out there and opening it. So if we can get rid of him, then we can close the portal whenever we want, because it'll be only one-way again, right?"

"Supposedly," Julien agreed. "If we can trust a kid with a blue mohawk to be our source on Hell magic."

"We don't have any choice," Edouard sighed. "We only have so much to go on." He ran a hand over his scarred face and let it drop back to the table with a thump. "At least we know where to find this alfar now. Everyone get some sleep. Tomorrow night we'll put an end to this."

Seven people had to move much more slowly through the park to stay as quiet as Julien and Noah had been on their own. The brothers formed a ragged group in the trees, listening for any movement that might mean demons, but the grounds were quiet.

When the lake came into view beyond the woods, Joseph stopped Edouard with a hand on his shoulder, and they all went still. There were voices nearby. Beyond the trees, the alfar stood on the path along the edge of the lake, flanked on either side by two others who looked to Julien like soldiers—one of whom had a heavy shield slung on his back and stood with more authority than the others. Guards for the magic user, maybe?

Each brother found a thick tree to press his back to, and Edouard risked a glance around the edge to get a better look at the gathering in the distance.

"Well," Hugo whispered, "either we found them, or we found some other weird cult."

Edouard put a finger to his lips to shush the younger hunter and lifted his hands to sign instead—another skill their father had drilled into them at a young age, precisely for situations like this. *Five of them. Four armed.*

Let's go, Antony returned with an impatient gesture.

Laurent gave a light snap with his fingers to draw the others' attention. *We may not get another chance like this. We need to be cautious. Split up. Surround them. Attack as one. Kill the one with the staff first.*

Edouard pointed to Laurent to indicate this was the plan of action, then waved them all forward. As they stretched out into a line in the trees, preparing to surround the pavilion where the alfar stood, the one holding the staff turned to face the building as if he'd been waiting for them to make their move.

"You've finally arrived," he called, his voice low and clear. "I expected more from the men who've been killing so many of my demons."

"Go!" Edouard snapped at the others, but the moment they moved forward, the alfar lifted his staff and slammed the bottom into the stone beneath him, cracking far too loudly through the thin night air.

A pulse of light expanded from the point of impact like a shockwave, washing over the paved path and benches until it reached the brothers themselves. The touch of the light made them stumble, and each hunter faltered, clutching at their heads with both hands. Only Julien stood stable, looking between his brothers with growing concern.

"What's wrong with you?" Julien snapped, but none of the others answered him. He shook Joseph by the shoulder and got nothing in response. He looked over at the alfar and found black eyes watching him with a curious tilt of the head.

All around him, his brothers' arms went slack and their bodies still.

"All but one," the alfar's voice echoed softly. "How curious."

Julien's brothers lifted their heads to look at him, and he took a step back from them. This was not good. At his left, Laurent lifted his pistol to his brother's chest, but Julien knocked his hand away so that he only fired into the dirt. Antony came at him from the other direction, swinging his fist and clipping Julien in the chin before he could move out of the way. So not good. When Antony swung at him again, Julien knocked him in the jaw, sending him stumbling backward to put some distance between them, and he ducked underneath Edouard's dagger before taking off toward the road.

He ran as fast as he could, dodging between the trees at sharp angles as he raced back toward the lights of the city and still getting grazed in the thigh by a bullet anyway. He sucked in a sharp breath and clenched his jaw through the pain with the sounds of his brothers' footsteps too close behind him. When he put his hands on the top of the iron fence of the cemetery and forced himself over with a grunt, landing unsteadily on the lit sidewalk outside, he carried on for another block before he leaned against the alley corner of a building to listen.

They weren't following him.

That wasn't good either. Was it worse? They weren't going to kill him, but now they would be held captive by the alfar—or they'd be dead as soon as they got back to him. Julien put his hands on his knees to catch his breath, grimacing as he pushed against the wound in his leg. What the hell had that spell been? What had he done to them?

A few pedestrians watched him out of the corners of their eyes as they passed. He was drawing attention—and he couldn't help them without a plan. He had to assume he *could* help them. With one more puff of breath, he eased away from the wall and made his way back to the house, limping more the farther he went.

He made it all the way upstairs and to his bedroom before too much blood had soaked into his pants, and he shut the door quietly so as not to wake the witch that lay sleeping in his bed. He got his coat, boots, and pants off with only minimal wincing, but his opening the door again to fetch the first aid kid finally woke Noah up.

"You guys are back early," he mumbled with his face still half buried in the pillow.

"It's just me," Julien answered softly. "The others are...ah...tabarnak," he sighed. This was so fucking not good.

"Are you bleeding? You're bleeding—sit down." Noah urged him back onto the bed and went to get the first aid kit himself, settling down on the floor so that he could reach the deep cut in Julien's thigh. "What the hell happened?"

"We found the alfar," he said. "But he did something. With the staff he had. Some kind of magic. The others, they were...hypnotized, or something, and they attacked me. So I ran." He frowned down at Noah while the witch cleaned his wound. "I shouldn't have left them."

"What else were you supposed to do?" Noah took some oil from one of his jars with his fingers and rubbed it lightly along the edges of the cut. He was frowning, too, despite his words. "There's no way you could fight all six of them on your own."

"I might have to," Julien sighed.

"You said he used the staff—the same one we saw him with yesterday?"

"Ouais."

The witch paused as he set down his jar of oil and exchanged it for regular non-magic bandages. "Do you think it's what Ciaran was sent after before? The thing that's supposed to control people's minds?"

"Maybe. It did seem like they were being controlled. They wouldn't speak to me."

"I wonder why it didn't work on you," Noah mused, his hands working deftly to wrap the linen around Julien's thigh. "Do you think it's a Seventh Son thing? Or maybe the protective magic Airmed put on your patch?"

"I don't know," the blond admitted. "I'm grateful either way."

Noah taped the bandage snug with a frown on his lips. "What do we do now?"

Julien rubbed his hands roughly over his face. Noah wouldn't be able to join him on any hunts now. Whatever the reason the staff hadn't worked on Julien, it was no indication it wouldn't work on witches—and aside from how worried Julien would be personally if Noah was hypnotized and taken somewhere, the alfar having a human witch at his disposal was not something he wanted to happen. Ever. At all. Noah would just have to stay away until Julien dealt with this problem—or, until he found the portal so that they could put an end to the whole thing.

If the staff was what controlled them, then the staff would be the key to undoing...whatever the alfar had done. The one who'd cast the spell was the leader. Julien just needed to find him again.

And do what? he thought with a heavy sigh. The city was filling with demons, the alfar had been here for days—at least five of them. And now Julien was all alone.

"We need to leave," the hunter said at last. "My brothers may already be coming. I don't know what the alfar plans to do, but I don't want to be here waiting when he decides to do it. We can go to the safehouse we used before."

"You sit," Noah insisted. "I'll get our shit. I hope that cot fits two people."

"It doesn't," Julien answered in a soft snort, and the witch threw him a faint smile over his shoulder on his way out.

The floor of the small warehouse still bore the faint charred chalk marks of Noah's summoning circle, which he scuffed out more completely on his way by. Both he and Julien were loaded down with what supplies they could carry from the house—including Noah's spell components, books, box, and notes, more first aid supplies, and a large duffel bag of ammunition and weapons. They piled their belongings in one corner and sat side by side on the narrow cot by the wall.

"I got all the totems in position around the city today, at least," Noah offered. "So I can close the portal once, you know...the coast is clear, I guess."

A minute or two of silence passed between them.

"I lost my phone in the lake," Julien said, rolling his head on the wall he leaned against to look at the man beside him. "The only one I could find in my room at home was my old Nokia. It still charged when I plugged it in, and I've had the same number for a dozen years, so I'm hoping it'll do."

"Are you serious? Show me."

Julien grunted as he bent over with still-sore ribs, and he offered the witch the small grey brick masquerading as a cell phone once he found it in his duffel pocket.

"Oh, snap," Noah laughed, tucking his feet up onto the edge of the cot. "Snake 2. This is high tech software you've got here."

"Har har."

"Will you give me my own custom ringtone? Ooh—do you have any girls' numbers in here from back in your wild younger days?"

"Not likely."

Noah set down the phone and leaned against the blond's shoulder with a tired smile, allowing the night's exhaustion to sink thoroughly into both of them. After a moment, he peeked up at the larger man's face.

"Everything's...gonna be okay, right?" the witch asked in a quiet voice. "I mean...if things are tough here, and the boys are off on their own—and who even knows what's happening with Ciaran and Lugh and the others..."

Julien reached over to cup Noah's cheek and pull him a little closer, laying a long kiss on the top of his head. "Everything will be okay," he promised.

Noah sighed softly into his touch. "Okay. Right. Of course it will." He sat up and offered the hunter a faint smile. "Let's rock-paper-scissors for the cot."

21

Ciaran shifted his grip on the shillelagh strapped to his wrist, the blue roan horse beneath him huffing and fidgeting as though it could sense his impatience. When he'd woken up the previous morning and found no sign of Trent, it hadn't been hard to guess what the boy had done. Ciaran had spent two days fighting to put enough pressure on the city's inhabitants that he could convince the Ard Rí it was time to push harder—and now he sat mounted with his brothers and the army of the Tuath Dé at his sides, the sky still a short time away from the slow brightening of dawn.

"If he's in there, we'll find him," Cu promised, but Ciaran didn't answer him. He rolled his shoulder to test his shield arm and set his grim gaze on the distant walls of Falias. If Trent meant to get captured, then he was either dead already, or he was inside the city. Ciaran would burn it to the ground if he had to.

When the Ard Rí gave the call, the men on the ground moved first, pouring down the hill toward the city. Ciaran gripped his horse's reins so tight he heard the leather squeak as he watched the sparse light of torches in the city below. Rathgeirr opened the broad gate in the ramparts to allow the army through, and then shouts of war echoed back up the hillside. The Ard Rí began the charge of the mounted forces, but Ciaran and his brothers overtook him.

By the time Ciaran reached the open gate, the men on foot had cleared the way for the horses, pushing back the guards in the streets and setting fires in the market stalls. Ciaran caught an alfar soldier in the temple with his shillelagh as he passed, sending him to the ground to be trampled by the horses who followed. He stood up in his stirrups to scan the rooftops ahead and get his bearings while panicking women rushed their families away from the fighting. The slave quarters were at the far end of the market.

With a whistle, Ciaran called his brothers with him, the sound of hooves pounding on the streets through the rows of thatched-roof homes. The fire they'd begun in the stable days before had destroyed it and a few houses nearby, but Ciaran rode through the cinders without a second look. He left his horse behind near the doorway to the longhouse and kicked the door open by the latch, bringing up his shield as he entered—but there was no one inside. Ciaran spat out a curse and stalked the length of the house, checking the makeshift beds and each corner of the room before giving up and returning to the street.

"If no one is in there, they've *all* gone somewhere," Cethen assured him. The three of them tore through each home they passed, forcing back alfar soldiers when they found them and shouting at civilians to flee before setting each house to burn as it was emptied. One of the alfar caught Ciaran in the meat of his arm with an arrow, but Cu put his sword through him, and Ciaran broke the arrow to pull the head fully through his bicep with a cringing grunt.

Finally, once they breached the inner ramparts, Ciaran found a small cluster of cowering young humans hiding out behind a longhouse. More people had begun to flee, the alfar guards holding the line against the fairy invaders to allow them more time to escape through the back gate, but before these slaves could run, Ciaran snatched one of them by the back of his blue tunic and dragged him up to his feet.

"I'm looking for someone," he said, forcing as much civility into his tone as he could so that the boy would stop flinching long enough to answer him. "Have you seen a human here—someone new, with black hair and strange eyes?"

"Herra minn," the slave answered in a trembling voice, his hands raised to hide his face, "I don't—I haven't—"

Ciaran dropped him without waiting for him to finish, shoving him in the direction of the fleeing alfar women. He kept searching, Cu and Cethen beside him, and he grabbed every blue tunic or dress he spotted to question them. Eventually, a young woman pointed toward the largest house in the city, a compound with its own protective fence beyond the great hall.

"He—I saw a boy taken to be given to Prince Hathuwulf!"

Ciaran left her in the street and ran, the heat of the fires that now burned across the ramparts reaching his back, and he broke through the gate of the royal compound with Trent's name tearing from his throat. Cu and Cethen checked the small slave house and found it empty, so the three of them pushed through to enter the longhouse, Ciaran calling for Trent every time he turned a corner into another empty room.

When he came through the back of the house near the rampart, he turned to the flood of people escaping by the open gate, guided by alfar soldiers shouting orders over the burning chaos. A handful of them were mounted, and near the gate, an Alfar man sat tall in his saddle, scanning the faces of the passing civilians—and in front of him, holding tight to the horse's thick mane, was Trent.

Ciaran nearly screamed his name, calling to his brothers to give him a horse, but as he made for the gate, one of the burning homes broke in front of him, charred logs collapsing into the street and ashes from the thatching of the roof spitting up a cloud of cinders. By the time Ciaran made it around, the horse and its riders were gone—escaped beyond the rampart gate.

"Cian—more soldiers coming!" Cethen called, but Ciaran lingered, staring toward the walls for any sign of Trent until Cu snapped at him to pay attention.

Ciaran joined them, but he kept looking back toward the gate. Had Trent seen him? He hadn't been struggling—had that been the prince he rode with? Why hadn't he tried to hide, or escape? He hadn't even called out—but he must have known Ciaran would be looking for him.

He fought until his limbs almost gave out, doing his part to put down the last of the remaining alfar and secure the city, but as soon as the din of battle faded and the cheers of the Tuath De sounded through the streets, Ciaran took the first horse he found by the reins and hefted himself into the saddle.

"And where are you going?" Cu asked, reaching out to grab the horse by the bridle before Ciaran could lead it off.

"I'm going after him!"

"Aye sure just go straight into them on your own; that's wise."

"If I don't go now, he'll be taken to Findias and be lost all over again!"

"Cian, look at you!" Cu sighed. "Let me see you lift that arm."

Ciaran scowled down at his brother and raised his shillelagh over his head—or rather, he tried. It weighed him down. The wound in his bicep had torn open wider, and he didn't even attempt to number the bruises and scrapes he'd suffered. His whole body ached. With a snort of disgust, he let his arm drop back to his side.

"We'll get him back," Cu said earnestly. "Make sure he's got something to come back to."

Ciaran didn't answer, but he dismounted and walked beside his brother back to where the rest of the Tuath De had begun to tend to the wounded and gather captives. He watched the humans cling to each other, many with tears on their faces while they watched the fairies pass them by. They must have expected to be killed, or worse. Who knew what they'd been told by their masters about the Tuatha De Danann?

Ciaran laid down his shield and shillelagh near the still-standing great hall, where the three kings had convened to discuss the day's outcome.

"The alfar we'll keep, of course," Mac Cuill was saying as Ciaran and his brothers let themselves inside. "At least until we can reach an agreement with King Huldrekall. But the humans—"

"They aren't any good as bargaining chips," Mac Cecht advised. "They breed too quickly for the city to miss only the number remaining here."

Mac Gréine grunted softly, one hand running over his beard in thought as he listened to the counsel of his fellow kings.

"Use them," Ciaran interrupted, drawing the kings' eyes to him. He took a few steps closer to them and offered a cursory bow, but he didn't wait to be questioned before continuing. "These people have been slaves their whole lives—if the Tuath De grant them mercy and freedom, they may help us fight their former owners. Arm every man who's willing, and let him share what he knows."

Mac Cuill's lip curled slightly. "These are servants—not soldiers. And mortals, besides. What use will they be against the Alfar?"

"Every man deserves the chance to fight for his freedom," Ciaran countered. "Or should our people have given in to the Fomorians so long ago, judging them too strong?"

"Their intelligence might be worthwhile," Mac Cecht said, tilting his head toward his brothers. "They would know the workings of the island better than we."

Mac Gréine hummed his agreement and nodded toward Ciaran. "Astute, Scal Balb. We will consider it."

"And when do we move on to Findias?" Ciaran pressed.

"Patience. Haste will be our enemy. See to the men—and tell your father I will need a report of the wounded."

Ciaran almost spoke up again, but Cu slapped him on the arm with the back of his hand and tilted his head toward the door, so Ciaran followed him with a frown on his lips.

Airmed patched him up and left him by one of the fires back at camp later in the day—a number of men had been left inside Falias to sort through the remains, search for survivors, and tend to the new captives, but Ciaran and many others were eventually released to rest. He sat on a downed log that served as a bench and looked into the fire while servants and physicians bustled around him. He'd let Trent get away. He'd lost him. Hadn't been able to reach him in time. Now he was inside a brand new city, with tall ramparts and fresh soldiers. Apparently in the care of an Alfar prince who carried him out personally on his own horse. What had happened in the single day Ciaran had been forced to wait?

He looked up when Rathgeirr took a seat beside him. The alfar's brow was knitted in sympathy, and he hunched his shoulders slightly as he leaned forward with his hands on his knees to look Ciaran in the face.

"Your brother told me that Trent was given to Prince Hathuwulf," he said, and Ciaran tried not to scowl at him. The idea that Trent could be "given to" anyone turned his stomach. "He is King Huldrekall's eldest son and heir. He is a good man," Rathgeirr assured him.

Ciaran gave a skeptical snort and turned his eyes back to the fire.

"I wanted to tell you. If Trent is in Prince Hathuwulf's house, he won't be mistreated."

"I don't want him to be a slave in *anybody's* house," Ciaran spat, and the alfar grimaced.

"I'm certain. I just thought...you would want to know that he isn't likely in actual danger. He can still be brought back."

Ciaran glanced sidelong at the other man and let out a light sigh through his nose. "I appreciate the thought, Rathgeirr. Thank you."

The alfar nodded, but he lingered. "My father was not in Falias. Nor my brother. I think they must be with King Huldrekall." He hesitated, glancing down at the bark of the log that made their seat. "I...fear for their safety, being pursued by Lugh. My father is a good scholar and physician, but...he is not a warrior. And my brother is strong, but the Alfar have not gone to war during either of our lifetimes."

"Lugh won't have forgotten the hospitality Gunvard gave us. And if your brother is anything like you, I'm sure he'll keep his head when it matters."

Rathgeirr paused, but then he smiled, and he gave a small nod. The alfar touched Ciaran's shoulder as he rose, and he left him to his brooding. The smell of food reached him as cauldrons bubbled on fires nearby, but he had no appetite. The only thought in his mind was the image of Trent seated comfortably in front of a Lochlannan with a commanding air, looking like he had no intention of being anywhere else.

22

Trent opened his eyes blearily to the sound of shouting in the house. For a moment, he didn't even move—he was too exhausted from being run around the house from dawn until dusk the day before. Cries and commands drifted in from the outside, and he sat up to put his feet back into his shoes. The others rushed around the room, gathering up what they could, but he went to the narrow window to see into the courtyard. In the distance, smoke rose from the far side of the city, and if he strained, he could hear the same sound of metal on shield that had seemed so loud in the cavern in Tír na nÓg .

He could hear Irish voices and see figures storming the inner rampart. The fairies were here. Ciaran was coming.

The other slaves hurried out of the room, Skathi urging him to follow, but the small group parted instantly when Hathuwulf appeared in the short hallway, a leather and chainmail chestpiece visible beneath his dark cloak and a heavy sword at his hip. Trent looked up at him and blanched slightly under his black gaze.

"You told me he wasn't your master," the prince said in a low, even voice, "but Cian mac Cainte has come for you even so." He took a step closer, but Trent moved backward on instinct. "I won't give up so dear a prize."

Trent hesitated, glancing toward the window. Maybe he could run.

If he called out, maybe Ciaran would hear him. Maybe *someone* would hear him. He swallowed down the fear rising up his throat. He couldn't. He hadn't accomplished anything yet. If he didn't even help anything, what had all this been for? He looked up into Hathuwulf's face with his heart about to break through his own ribs.

"You'd better hurry, then."

The prince considered him for a brief moment, his black eyes fixed on Trent's, and then he turned to leave, calling to Skathi to take the others and make for the rear gate. Trent followed them, but when they reached the door of the longhouse, Hathuwulf put a hand on his back and guided him away from the others. He lifted Trent easily onto the front of a sturdy, buckskin-colored horse and mounted behind him, arms encircling the boy to grip the reins as he kneed the animal into a run.

Outside of the prince's grounds, soldiers waved along a river of Alfar and humans who fled with their scant belongings wrapped in blankets, some of them carrying nothing at all. Trent expected to be carried through the crowd, but Hathuwulf lingered, his horse trotting back to the tail end of the escaping citizens. He made certain that Skathi and the two young men from his household were safely out of the gates, and when one of the Tuath De appeared from an alley, sword ready to strike at a couple of unarmed stragglers, he pushed Trent's head down with one hand to double him over and get him out of the way of the arrow he fired into the fairy's chest.

Trent thought, once, that he heard Ciaran's voice—but he couldn't go to him. Not yet. He didn't dare look back and risk seeing him. He would definitely lose his nerve.

The prince was the last out of the gate, and even as he followed the crowd that made their way across the charred fields away from the city, he frequently paused to stand in his stirrups and scan the long line of worn faces. When people lagged behind, he shouted to the other mounted soldiers, who stayed at the rear to aid anyone who needed it.

Trent behaved himself, holding onto the horse and occasionally glancing up to Hathuwulf's stern face. This man wasn't what Trent had expected. He clearly cared about his people and their welfare—his actions today had made that clear, even if he hadn't shown thoughtfulness in their conversation the night before. Maybe Trent had been just as guilty as the others when it came to the way he thought about the other races—though he hadn't enslaved anybody lately, so he still had that over the Alfar. Maybe it was worthwhile to try harder to get through to Hathuwulf himself.

The ragged refugees arrived at the walls of Findias with their prince at the head, his simple call to the guards opening a broad entry in the ramparts to allow the group to file inside. People spread out into the streets, settling wherever they could find shelter or help, and Hathuwulf rode deeper into a city not entirely untouched by the conflict—there were burn marks at some of the guard posts on top of the outer rampart, and Trent could smell the same bitter scent of scorched wheat as had taken over the grounds surrounding Falias.

Hathuwulf finally dismounted at the gate to a tall greathouse, a human trotting up to take the reins of his horse as Trent eased himself uncertainly back onto solid ground. He followed the prince inside, where they met an older-looking alfar with worry creased permanently into his forehead.

"Ráðherra Kothran," Hathuwulf said, weariness palpable in his voice, "Falias is fallen. Distribute what supplies we have to those who need it, and prepare for me a report on the status here."

"Of course, Yðar Hátign."

The prince started to cross the room, then seemed to realize that Trent was still following him. He glanced down at him with a thin frown. "Find Skathi," he said simply. "There is much to be done."

Skathi found Trent first. The woman patted his shoulders as though checking him for injury and smiled to see him unhurt.

"Come along," she said, waving him after her on her way into the city.

"So, where are we?" Trent asked her as they walked.

"This is Findias. Prince Hathuwulf is the true ruler here—we'd only moved the household to Falias while King Huldrekall is away. I can't say I'm glad to be home under these conditions," she sighed. "But Prince Hathuwulf will take care of us, I'm sure."

Trent frowned, but he didn't have time to answer. Skathi put him to work with the other men from Hathuwulf's house, handing out food, water, blankets, and various other supplies from the storage in the Great Hall. He tried to broach the subject of human freedom and the outside with the two young men, but neither of them seemed interested in listening to someone who'd come to the island with the people who'd just burned one of their cities.

By the time he was allowed to stop and eat something himself, late into the evening, Trent was dead on his feet. There were so many people—and the fairies had destroyed their homes. There were no good sides in this war.

Trent almost fell asleep in his bowl of porridge, but Skathi still tasked him with cleaning up the prince's bedroom, which had been empty in his absence. It barely needed it—the floor had a few muddy bootprints on it, and dust had settled into the crevices of the snarling wolf heads carved into the bedposts, but at least Trent knew how to make a fire now. It still took him a few tries.

He passed Hathwulf in the hall on his way back to the slave house, looking worn down and walking toward his room with heavy steps, but he didn't look at Trent as he went by. His day had probably been as tiring as Trent's, in its way.

The beds in the slave house here were a little more cramped than where they'd come from, but they were softer. Trent could have fallen asleep on a rock, he was so exhausted—so the straw-filled pillow and fur blanket almost felt close to luxury.

The next day, Trent was put to work again. He did his part to clean up the house under Skathi's direction, then was sent back into the city to give what help he could to the refugees. He sweat from the effort of carting supplies to and fro even in the chilled air, his body still sluggish and stiff from the past two days of work. His hands were scratched and sore, but he tried to keep up with the other young men as they moved through the city. Trent had been a slave for two days, and he already didn't know how the others dealt with the monotony on top of everything else—but he was glad, at least, to see that Hathuwulf was making efforts to take care of his people.

Hathuwulf had sent a cart of hay to the large arbor at the center of the marketplace so that beds could be made for the refugees, and a handful of alfar soldiers oversaw the slaves charged with arranging them. The bales of hay were massive—Trent struggled to get his arms around a corner of one, let alone drag it from the back of the cart. He stumbled when something sharp struck the backs of his knees, and he turned to see one of the guards glaring at him with a long leather strap like a horse whip in his hand.

"Move faster, or you won't earn your dinner, þræll," the alfar snapped.

Heat rushed to Trent's face, and before he could stop himself, he'd opened his mouth. "You look like you've been eating enough dinners for both of us, fatass."

Everyone in earshot went suddenly still, and Trent's heart fell into his gut. The alfar guard's dark eyes widened in shock, and then he had Trent by the scruff of his shirt, forcing him down to the ground.

"Hold him!" he growled at the nearest slave, and a man Trent didn't know knelt in front of him.

Trent saw the sympathy in his eyes, but the man didn't look at him. He only tugged Trent's tunic free of its belt and pulled it up close to his head, holding the boy close to the ground by his shoulders. Trent pulled against him instinctively, but the slave held him fast, his voice little more than a breath in Trent's ear.

"Better to be still, son," he whispered. "Or it'll be worse."

Trent heard the shifting of the alfar's boots behind him, and his whole body tensed. The man's hands tightened on his shoulders in anticipation, and Trent squeezed his eyes shut. He was an idiot. A fucking idiot.

The first lash was like a burn across the soft skin between his shoulders, sharp and hot, and Trent snapped his jaw closed to keep from biting his tongue. The second came fast. Trent's heartbeat pulsed painfully through his skin, and his breath quickened under the third, fourth, and fifth strike, each one delayed just enough to allow the throb of agony to subside. He trembled, feeling the warm streaks of blood forming streams down his sides.

When the next blow should have landed, a voice stopped it— Skathi.

"Herra minn!" she called, and Trent heard her hurrying steps approaching from behind him. "Forgive me, herra minn," the woman said in a rush.

Trent peeked over his shoulder. The alfar had actually lowered his strap to listen—being the head slave in the prince's house must have been worth a moment's pause, at least. Trent could barely focus on her. His head swam and his torn skin hurt so much he thought he might throw up.

"This þræll is the property of my master Prince Hathuwulf," Skathi went on. "He would not be pleased to see him punished this way." She gave a deep bow with her hands clasped in front of her.

The alfar hesitated, then let out a snort and gestured to the man holding Trent down. He was released, but when he put his hands on the ground to push himself up, his arms shook with the effort. Jensi and Totti, the two young men from Hathuwulf's house, appeared to help him to his feet, and they half carried him away from the arbor while Skathi apologized again to the sneering guard.

"Foolish creature," the old woman scolded Trent as they walked, but there was warmth in her voice.

Trent was deposited back in his bed, one of them men helping remove his belt and tunic so that he could lay on his stomach, and Skathi settled beside him with a damp cloth in her hand. Even the care she gave him stung. Trent hid his face in the fur blanket beneath him so that it could absorb the tears he couldn't hold in. He never should have come here. He should have stayed at the camp and done what Ciaran told him. Just stayed put and stayed safe. Fucking idiot.

When Skathi had finished cleaning his wounds and dressed him in a clean tunic, she gave his hair a gentle pat, called him foolish one last time, and left him to rest.

He rubbed his face into the fur to clear away his tears and laid scowling across at the wall. The longer he sat there, the angrier he got. This was exactly why he *shouldn't* have stayed behind with Ciaran like a good, useless little human. Because things like this were happening here. Because someone could get whipped on the spot just for insulting an alfar's pride, and nobody even thought to do anything about it. Because there wasn't anything they *could* do about it, except beg for mercy by using the name of some other, more important alfar.

Fuck these guys. He couldn't feel sorry for himself. He came here for a reason, and he needed to see it through.

23

With his back complaining loudly at him, Trent pushed himself out of the bed and made his way slowly out of the slave house. Skathi had warned him about wandering the premises when he had no work to do—better just to mind your business, she said—but he *did* have work to do.

Despite his tough talk, he still hesitated when he stood outside Hathuwulf's door. The bar for a *good* master seemed to be pretty low. But this one, at least, had been decent to him. He had to try. Trent put his hand near the wood, took a deep breath, and knocked.

He waited for so long, holding his breath, that he was forced to exhale without an answer. He tried again, a little louder. Still nothing. So he steeled himself, then pushed open the door and stuck his head inside. The room was empty—a fire burned in the center of the room, and the desk in the corner sat strewn with papers and a map of the island, but the bed was still made. Hathuwulf wasn't here.

Trent eased the door shut with a frown, half expecting the prince to be lurking behind him when he turned his head, but the hall was empty, too. He could hear Skathi in the kitchen but saw no sign of the alfar owner of the home. Quietly skirting the woman cleaning, Trent snuck through the house to the rear exit and slipped outside. Maybe the prince was getting some air, or visiting the stable, or—

He stopped short when he rounded the corner of the house and found a stone bath sunk into the ground, much like the one Ciaran had taken him to outside Gunvard's house. The important difference was that this one had Prince Hathuwulf in it—his arms spread over the rim of stone and his black hair pulled back into a knot to keep it free of the water and show more of the silver jewelry in his ears. He'd let his head loll back and his eyes shut so that he could relax into the steam, but a few damp-looking reports sat on the ground near his resting hand. The water only came to just below his dark nipples, so when he breathed, Trent saw the subtle lift of thick muscle that rippled the surface. He tried to carefully circle the hot spring so that he could address the prince face to face, moving with hesitant steps this close to him.

"If you're not careful, I'll start to think you're a spy," Hathuwulf rumbled softly, and Trent jumped, narrowly avoiding putting his foot in the water as the alfar lifted his head. The prince watched him with those steady black eyes and waited until he'd found stable footing. "Skathi tells me you got into trouble in the city today. Are you well?"

"That's a funny way of saying someone *whipped* me," Trent muttered.

"They wouldn't have done it if they'd known you belonged to me. They know I don't allow it."

"So it's just some slaves who get tortured. Great."

"Did you want something, Trent?" the prince asked pointedly.

He swallowed and tried to keep his hands still at his sides. This wasn't what he'd come here to do. "I...wanted to talk to you."

Hathuwulf stared at him. "And you thought you'd just wander over and find me," he said dryly. "You really are a terrible slave." He settled a bit deeper into the water, clearly not concerned with holding a conversation while naked in a bath. "Go ahead and talk, since you're already here."

Trent shifted on his feet, daring to take a half step closer to the alfar. "I wanted to tell you that...you're not what I expected."

The prince put his hands under the water to rub a scoop of hot water over his face, his weary sigh barely audible. "Is that so?"

"I came here thinking I *would* be a spy. That I'd get the slaves to fight, or if I couldn't, maybe I could at least find out whatever I could in the city, escape somehow, and take what I found back to the Tuatha De Danann. I thought the Alfar were awful. Villains, I guess. Monsters. And a lot of you suck, don't get me wrong. And keeping slaves is fucked up. But the fairies aren't innocent either—I know that. And...the people I've been helping here, and...you," he added awkwardly, "you don't...seem like much of a villain at all."

Hathuwulf ran a hand over his face to brush away the excess water. "I'm sorry to have disillusioned you, Trent, but in case you haven't taken full stock of the situation, I have too much on my mind to discuss philosophy with you." He splashed more of the hot water over his chest and under his arms, clearly hoping Trent would take his blunt words as the dismissal they were, but Trent didn't let up. He couldn't.

"That's not what I mean. I'm saying I don't think it's right for your people to be wiped out, even if some of you are terrible, just because your dad made a stupid choice and the fairies don't like it. But that's what's going to happen even if you win here. You can't take on the word outside."

"So you've said." The prince sat back against the edge of the bath and finally looked back up at him. "And why should it matter to you? Even if you are telling the truth—even if the humans are as numerous and as advanced as you say, and this isn't simply a lie to fool me into sparing them—why should you *want* to avoid destroying a threat like the Alfar?"

"Because I'm not a genocidal asshole, man," Trent spat, and the subtle narrowing of the prince's dark eyes made him pause. This probably wasn't someone who was used to being addressed so casually—and definitely not by a human. Trent lowered his voice and tried again. "These aren't just soldiers you've got here—they're families. I know you care about protecting them. I've seen it. But war never benefits anybody who's not the one giving orders."

Hathuwulf watched him in silence for a few beats, then gave a quick, quiet exhale through his nose. "I've let you say your piece."

He stood, the hot water running suddenly down the length of his body, and Trent panicked, staring down at the grass with an intense frown to avoid seeing more than the glimpse he got. Hathuwulf bent to scoop up a simple light robe from the ground and pulled it up over his broad, damp shoulders, and he tied it around the waist before addressing the boy again.

"I won't hear any more of this, Trent. Your situation may have been different where you came from, and I have been accommodating—but here, you must learn to know your place."

Trent took another step forward as the prince gathered his papers and turned to leave. "But if you just—"

Hathuwulf paused, and the glance he threw over his shoulder was so sharp that Trent's resolve withered into silence.

"It is unseemly for a slave to wander his master's house," the alfar said in a low voice. "Return to your quarters and stay there until Skathi has work for you." He didn't wait for an answer before returning to the house—which was good, because Trent didn't have the voice for one. He just watched the man's back disappear through the doorway and sighed. What was he supposed to do now?

Trent didn't sleep well—not just because of the fresh wounds in his back. He missed Ciaran, and he wished the fairy had been there even to scold him for his stupidity. Maybe he'd misjudged the prince. Caring about his own people didn't mean he cared about humans. Trent buried his face in the furs that covered his bed and shut his eyes, hoping his back would stop aching at least long enough for him to fall asleep, but almost as soon as he felt himself sink into unconsciousness, he was startled by a firm hand on his shoulder. He blinked, and in the darkness, he could just barely make out Hathuwulf's grey features.

"Show me," the prince whispered. He pulled Trent out of bed, barely waiting for him to pull his boots back on before throwing a dark cloak over his shoulders and urging him out of the room. When Trent tried to ask what was happening, Hathuwulf shushed him with a finger to his lips and led him from the house and off of the grounds, pulling him by the hand along narrow alleys and past patrolling guards. His brief touch opened a slim exit in the rampart, and they slipped through together to head toward the rocky coastline.

Trent stumbled on the slick stones as they made their way down, so Hathuwulf lifted the smaller man over his shoulder and made his way lightly down the rocks to the water, where he deposited Trent in a long, narrow boat with a single mast. His boots splashed in the water as he shoved the boat away from the beach, and then he hopped in himself once the craft began to float. He took up the oars and rowed until the outline of the shore began to fade into the darkness, and then he stood and leaned over Trent to drop the sail. Trent's stomach lurched at the sudden rocking movement, but he covered his mouth with one hand and swallowed down his bile.

"What's going on?" he asked, thankful his voice sounded steadier than his stomach felt.

Hathuwulf sat down in front of him, allowing the boat to drift farther from the island while he hunched slightly to look Trent in the face. His mouth was set into a firm line, his stern face ashen in the moonlight.

"Show me the human world my people face," he said, and Trent hesitated, staring at him in confusion as water lapped idly against the sides of the boat.

"Really?" he managed after a moment. "In this boat? Isn't this island in the middle of nowhere? It would take days to get to a real city."

"This is Norðanvindur," the prince said, as if that explained anything. When Trent didn't look impressed, he went on. "It goes where I want it, when I want it. And I want it to take me to the human world. I want *you* to take me to the human world," he clarified.

"And how exactly does that work?"

"Tell the ship," he answered simply.

"...Tell the ship."

"Tell it where you want to go. Picture it in your mind, and the ship will bring us there."

Trent glanced up at the sail uncertainly. "Is that...a thing I can do?"

"I can't do it," the prince admitted with a subtle shrug. "I don't know any of these human cities."

"I thought you didn't believe me anyway."

Hathuwulf's frown softened, just a little, and so did his voice. "I never take a risk when the potential cost is more than I could bear," he said. "I can't take the chance that you're telling the truth. Show me."

Trent nodded, but he didn't really know how to fulfill the prince's request. Assuming the boat worked as advertised, how was he supposed to choose what to show him? Vancouver came to mind immediately, of course—but as he imagined the view from the water, he wondered if it would be impressive enough. He was only likely to get one shot at this. Then he paused. Coastal cities. Of course.

He closed his eyes, holding onto both sides of the boat for stability, and he tried to picture the skyline in Victoria Harbour leading into Kowloon Bay. He was glad that Noah had spent so long drilling the whole "clear your mind" thing into him during their last trip. It was almost easy to put aside the rocking of the boat and the Alfar prince staring at him and instead focus on the golden lights of Hong Kong's skyscrapers, almost seeming to grow out of the water themselves. He felt the boat begin to move underneath him, and his stomach protested, but he did his best to keep his mouth clamped shut. When he couldn't stand it anymore, he finally leaned over the side of the boat to vomit, but as he coughed, caught his breath, and raised his eyes, he realized that he'd thrown up in Victoria Harbour.

Hathuwulf was already standing at the front of the boat, one hand steadying himself on the rope hanging from the sail as he stared up at the buildings across the bay. Lights of every color shone reflections onto the dark water, spotlights idling back and forth into the low, grey clouds, and nearby, a brightly-lit yacht drifted by them, music and laughter pouring from the deck. The prince didn't move for a long time.

"This is the human world?" he asked, so softly Trent almost didn't hear him.

"This is one city in the human world," Trent answered. "There are a hundred more just like it or bigger. We have cars—machines that we ride in father than any horse. We have planes to fly us anywhere we want. We have smart phones, computers the size of your hand that let you talk to anyone anywhere on Earth and look up any information you want to know about anything. We have bombs that could destroy a whole city this size in a second. That's what humans are like now," he said, hoping he sounded earnest. "That's what you'd be up against."

The alfar shook his head, silently watching the city as their boat coasted through the harbor. "I tried to tell my father it was foolish," he said at last. "If I'd known just how foolish..."

He turned his back on the city and sat back down with his elbows on his knees, looking slumped and defeated. Trent actually felt a little sorry for him. The next time Hathuwulf spoke, he sounded for the first time like he was just talking—not commanding, or directing, or demanding. He sounded like a man instead of a prince.

"The Alfar were once great. Feared. Respected." He laced his fingers in his lap and looked down at them. "It was my grandfather who decided to stop the raids on the outside world and hide us away on our island. He saw what was coming even then. When he took ill, and my father became king...I knew even when I was young that he was waiting for an excuse." He gave a small snort and shook his head. "Ashmodai gave it to him. And now our whole way of life is threatened."

The prince was silent for a minute more, but Trent didn't know what to say to him. It was, admittedly, difficult for him to focus while his stomach was threatening to give up the last of the food in it.

Hathuwulf looked back up to Trent's face, his expression already set back into its stony normalcy, as if he'd made a decision. "Thank you, Trent," he said, and the next thing Trent knew, the boat was moving again. He barely had time to register the change before the hull bumped gently into the beach outside Findias.

Trent tried to stand, and his stomach didn't seem to come with him, but Hathuwulf caught him before he fell into the rocks and helped right him on solid ground. He led Trent by the hand back up to the city and into the house, where he left the boy at the doorway to the slave quarter without another word. Trent sat down on his bed to pull off his boots, moving slowly so that his stomach could settle. He didn't know what had just happened, really—but at least the prince seemed to believe him now.

24

Julien's prehistoric phone woke him up, buzzing loudly on the floor until he was able to reach it and squint at the green and black screen. He didn't recognize the number, of course—anyone who might have been calling him was either sleeping on the cot next to him or under the thrall of some magic staff spell. He frowned at the phone and lifted it to his ear anyway, pausing to clear the sleep from his throat before answering.

"Bonjour, hello?"

"Bonjour," a woman's voice began, continuing in cheerful French. "I'm calling to speak with Julien Fournier?"

"Ouais, c'est moi," Julien answered, grunting softly as he sat up on one elbow.

"My name is Isabelle; I'm calling from BMO."

Julien paused. He barely had $50 in his Bank of Montreal account. He hardly ever used his debit card, and his sole credit card had gone unused for years.

"I just need to verify some potentially fraudulent charges on your account," she went on. "Did you attempt a purchase with Green Cabs Dunedin, in Dunedin, New Zealand?"

"New—" Julien stopped himself, then, with a scowl, he stretched his arm to dig his wallet out of his pants pocket, his phone tucked between his ear and his shoulder. He flipped open the wallet and snorted at the empty space where his credit card used to be. New Zealand. God damnit—that little shit. Sabin must have stolen his card at some point without him noticing, and now he was using it to go who knows where and buy who knows what—

Julien paused. The boys had said they were going to help their friends. They had taken so little with them, and now they were headed to Antarctica on their own. Of course they needed supplies. He sighed softly through his nose, then spoke again.

"Ouais. I did. I'm on vacation," he said, his eyes squeezed shut as he imagined the interest charges he'd be paying for the next ten years.

"Okay! Thank you for confirming. If the charge didn't go through, please try it again, and I'll release the card for use. If you let BMO know in advance next time you plan to travel, we can avoid this inconvenience in the future."

"Of course. My mistake. Thank you."

"Not a problem, Monsieur Fournier. Thank you for choosing BMO, and I hope you have a great vacation."

Julien thanked the woman again, then slumped back onto the floor and let his phone thunk to the concrete beside him. Noah lifted his head to rest his chin on the edge of the cot and peer down at him.

"Are you on vacation?" he mumbled, reaching out to brush his fingers over the blond's bare shoulder.

"Your kid is on vacation. With my credit card."

The witch cringed. "Sorry."

"It's fine."

Noah leaned off the cot with his weight on his hands to kiss Julien's stubbled jaw. "Thanks for not getting Sabin arrested for fraud."

"I'll get it out of him in labor when he gets back," the hunter rumbled. "At least he won't freeze to death."

Noah slid down fully onto the floor so that he could curl up at the other man's side. "I'm worried about him. I know he's doing the right thing, but—I wish he could have just stayed here."

"He'll be fine," Julien assured him, turning his head and placing a kiss on the witch's hair. "They have a lot going on between them. I'm sure they'll manage."

Noah sat up, shaking his head as though he didn't want to think about it too much, and folded his body over his legs in a long stretch. The next time he spoke, he was muffled by his knees. "So what do we do next?"

"Figure out how to break the alfar's spell, I guess," Julien sighed as he pushed to his feet, dragging his duffel onto the cot so he could paw through it for his packed change of clothes.

Noah straightened and twisted, resting both palms to one side on the floor, then he paused and glanced around the room. "And...is there a *bathroom* of any kind in this place, or..."

Julien shrugged. "I never stayed here long-term. I usually just pissed in the alley."

"Great," Noah answered cheerfully. "Cute. I love it."

"Sorry," the hunter said absently. He gave a small snort as he rotated his arm—ribs didn't feel great, but they were much better than the night before. "I'll have to draw the alfar leader out somehow," he went on. "I have to get that staff and...break it, probably."

Noah turned to twist in the other direction. "You think you can just, like, smash it on the ground? It looked like pretty sturdy wood to me, even if it's not protected somehow."

"Well I have to do something," the blond grumped. He pulled his clean shirt over his head and reached for his last remaining pair of pants without holes in them. "If you have any ideas, I'm all ears."

"If *I* could get hold of it—"

"No," Julien cut him off. "You're not going anywhere near it."

Noah crawled up onto his knees and reached back for his heels, curving his back in an arch that on any other day would have driven Julien to distraction. "So you're the one who knows all about magic, then?"

Julien paused, staring down at him uncertainly. "No," he admitted.

The witch straightened again, planting his hands on the floor in front of him to arch his back in the other direction, then lifted his hips and stretched his heels toward the floor. "It's a magic staff, is all I'm saying. I can probably help."

"I won't risk it happening to you, too." He fastened his belt buckle and pulled on his coat. "Laurent always kept a tracker on Arnaud said he wandered off on his own too much otherwise. He's sure to have a backup receiver in his room somewhere. If I can find that, then I can take one of the tranquilizer rifles in the armory and go after them."

Noah finally got to his feet, moving to stand in front of Julien. "I didn't think you guys would have things like tranquilizers."

"We probably don't," the blond said with a light sigh. "Poisons and such sometimes, so I'm sure there are empty darts there, but just putting things to sleep isn't normally what we do."

"Maybe I can put something together? A sleeping potion or something, but injectable."

Julien paused and peered down at him. "Do you...make a lot of injectable potions?"

"Well—no," he admitted. "But something that affects the bloodstream might be even quicker than a drink, right? I'll see what I can do."

A faint smile touched Julien's lips as he imagined the face Antony would make if he heard them discussing putting magic tranquilizers into one of their decidedly un-magical guns. Noah dug in his bag for his toothbrush and did his best without water.

"Didn't you tell that one kid with Sabin that you were a terrible shot? You let him take your big rifle, right? So is this really the best option?"

The hunter frowned. "I *am* an awful shot. But it's the only option I can think of."

Noah smiled around his toothbrush. "Then I'll make extra."

The two of them stood at the corner of the block for a long while, staring down the street at the front door of the worn townhouse. There was no way the alfar was going to just forget about Julien—but they could hope he didn't have enough access to the others' memories or minds to find out the location of the house. Were the other brothers puppets, or were they conscious servants now? Noah had no idea how the mind control spell worked, and he wasn't about to head back to the woods to ask—though the thought was tempting.

Julien led the way down the sidewalk with Noah close behind, listening for anything out of place on the quiet street, but they made it into the front hallway without any trouble. They split up at the entrance, Julien heading downstairs into the armory to gather up the air rifle and as many empty darts as he could find and Noah grabbing a few herbs and jars he'd left behind and tossing them into a backpack. As Noah was not keen on getting ambushed, he intended to hurry.

Even the witch could tell it was too still in the house. Julien stalked the upstairs hall with suspicion creasing his brow, but nothing appeared, even as they both slipped into Laurent's room and shut the door swiftly behind them.

This room was more lived-in than Julien's had been. Maps covered all four walls, each one marked with circles, notes, and pushpins, and the small bookcase by the bed was bursting with worn paperbacks and reference tomes stuffed in any way they would fit. The surface of the desk lay hidden underneath printouts, notebooks, and scattered pens, and the wastebasket was overflowing with crumpled papers. The rolling chair even had a mesh lumbar support strapped to it, Noah noted with a smile. Laurent might actually be his kind of person.

While Julien dug through the footlocker by the bed, Noah set to work searching the desk drawers. At first, all he found was more of the same—notepads, packs of sticky tabs, boxes of pushpins—but when he opened the bottom drawer, he spotted a half-used bottle of clear gel and what was clearly a silicone masturbation sleeve. Noah snorted and pushed the drawer closed again. Poor dear. Julien wasn't the only lonesome monster hunter.

Julien made a soft sound of triumph from across the room and crouched down by the nearest outlet to plug in his prize—a palm-sized hunk of plastic that looked almost as advanced as the device Julien was now using as a cell phone. The simple screen lit up once it was plugged in, and after a thoughtful pause, a ping appeared at the center between a long string of coordinates. Julien rose to compare the numbers to the map of Montreal stuck to the wall, and he tapped his finger on a tiny slip of land toward the north of the city, in the middle of the St. Lawrence.

"Arnaud is here. The bastards are right in the middle of the park—not even trying to hide."

"If the alfar took him with them, that's promising, right? It means they're alive."

"Probably," Julien agreed. "I still need to get there sooner rather than later."

"I'm going too," the witch insisted, but Julien shook his head.

"Not until I figure out what to do about that staff."

"Fine," Noah sighed. "Let's gather up our shit and go back, and I can work on those tranquilizers."

"What would I do without you, mon râleur?"

"Die young, I imagine," Noah answered on his way out.

Julien stopped at the front door with his ear to the wood, keeping Noah behind him with a gentle hand. When he was satisfied there was no one waiting on the other side, he gave the witch a nod and opened the door to leave—then immediately stopped. Something wasn't right.

He heard the click from a distance, followed by a loud shot, but he still didn't quite move in time. The .30 caliber bullet hit the meat of his shoulder, knocking him onto his ass and back into the house before it put a ragged hole in the wood floor behind him. Noah swore, and Julien kicked the door shut just as another round hit it, splintering the wood and sending sharp pieces into his calf.

"What the fuck is that?!" Noah shouted, and Julien grimaced through the pain in his shoulder as he moved to shove the witch down against the wall and close to the floor.

"Joseph," he answered, his voice worryingly weak. Blood poured from the missing chunk of flesh in his arm, and Noah moved to cover it with his hands, whispering a spell Julien had heard many times before in an effort to stop the flow. He'd had too little sleep and too many injuries over the last few days to be losing this much blood. But he couldn't stay here—he had to get up, had to get out, find Joseph—

"For fuck's sake!" Noah snapped, and Julien followed his gaze to the stairs at the end of the hall, where Laurent stood with his Ruger leveled at his brother's chest. Julien couldn't force his body to move fast enough—but he didn't have to. Noah released the wound on his arm and raised his hands toward Laurent, then jerked them back in a quick, grasping motion that brought the other man tumbling forward down the stairs in a series of painful-sounded crashes.

The witch stood, and with another gesture, he lifted Laurent from the floor by one ankle, leaving him to dangle awkwardly in mid-air with his dropped gun out of reach.

"I've got him, if you can—"

"I'm coming," Julien insisted, pausing only to tug the largest bit of wood from his skin before he pushed himself to standing with his remaining good arm. He reached back to take one of the spare darts from the case at his hip and approached Laurent with a limping step. He had to move out of the way of his swing, newly armed with one of the knives on his belt, but he managed to rush close enough to get his arms around his brother's neck. It took a few more seconds of lashing out at Julien, who tried to keep out of the way of the slashing knife, but then Laurent began to slow, and his arms went slack, allowing the blade to clatter to the floor.

Noah waited a few beats after he went still, then lowered him gently into a heap on the floor. Julien kicked the weapons away from Laurent's hands and turned back to the front door, inching along the wall to peek out the window. He couldn't see Joseph, of course—but he couldn't be too far. There wasn't good line of sight here anywhere except one of the nearby rooftops, maybe. He would probably move and try again the next time Julien left the house.

"So, what do I do with him?" Noah asked from where he knelt beside the unconscious Laurent, and Julien had to pause a moment to focus on what he'd said. Too much blood gone.

"Basement," he managed. "The table. The—"

"Demon straps, got it," Noah cut him off. "Sit down before you pass out, please—I'll be right back." The witch tried to lift Laurent onto his shoulders, but the taller man was too heavy, so Noah gave a preparatory huff and then lifted him again with a spell, the tension visible in his arms as he led him carefully through the doorway to the stairs.

Julien tried to follow, but Noah hissed at him, so he stopped and allowed himself to slide down the wall to the floor. He focused on pulling the remaining splinters from his leg with the hand that still worked—the one attached to his injured shoulder had become difficult to move. It was a struggle to breathe, and his eyelids had grown heavy. He saw Noah reappear at his side, but the witch's voice was muffled as if he were talking from underwater. Then the only thing Julien could see was the blackness that started at the edges of his vision and quickly overtook him.

He woke up in his bed upstairs, his whole body sore. He felt the familiar scratchiness of bandages soaked in dried blood against his shoulder and leg and didn't dare try to move either of them. It even hurt to turn his head in search of Noah. Julien didn't have the breath to try to call out to him—he was too drowsy. But the door opened a few minutes later, and Noah returned, holding a bottle of pills and a glass of water.

"Oh, thank god," he sighed, hastily setting the items on the nightstand and sitting down beside the hunter. "You know I hate it when you lose consciousness," he scolded, but there was a smile of relief on his face. "Here. Take one of these. Antibiotics." He twisted the bottle open and helped Julien lift his head enough to swallow one of the large pills. "I won't accept you going through a bunch of fairy challenge shit and then dying from infection."

Julien snorted softly since he didn't have the strength to laugh. "Where's Laurent?" he asked, his voice sounding dry despite the drink of water.

"Tied to the demon table, right where I left him. He's awake now, but I think I got all of his weapons, and if those straps will hold down a possessed person, I'm pretty sure he's not going anywhere." Noah shrugged his shoulders and shook his head with a humorless chuckle. "Not that that helps me have any idea what to do with him."

"We need to undo the spell on him," Julien croaked, and Noah stared flatly at him.

"Oh, okay. Let me just consult my book on how to counter mind control by ancient viking elf artifacts. Oh wait—"

"I get it," Julien sighed. "But there has to be something. Is he lucid?"

"Kind of?" Noah answered with a faint, uncertain cringe. "I mean, I only went to check on him a couple times, and he just watched me. Didn't say anything. It was a little creepy. I almost covered his face with a towel or something."

Julien sighed and stared up at the ceiling. His brain was still too foggy for this problem.

"Well, I'll try to figure something out," Noah said, laying a hand gently on Julien's forearm as he rose. "You just...stay here and try not to get hurt any more. If you die, your brothers are just shit out of luck because I'm not going after them," he went on, already on his way out of the room. He paused to smile at Julien as he eased the door shut.

Julien couldn't argue—and he didn't want to. He barely kept his eyes open long enough to hear Noah's footsteps growing fainter down the hallway.

Noah stood in front of the closed door in the basement, his arms folded across his chest as he chewed pensively on one fingernail. A spell caused by an artifact—Julien probably had the right idea that the best solution would be to break the staff itself, but since they didn't have access to it and couldn't guarantee it could be easily broken even if they did, that option was sort of...not an option. Noah had some experience with things like fetishes or bags that could be hidden and affect a person from a distance, but this wasn't really that, either. And the chances of Noah being able to make something that was *stronger* than an Alfar relic were, to put it lightly, pretty fucking slim.

He wished he could have asked Lugh, or even Ciaran—but they were definitely out of contact for the near future. Sabin had his hands full and probably wouldn't have an answer anyway, and Julien was barely conscious. Noah was all alone. Except for Laurent, he guessed. Not great company.

Noah took a deep breath, let it out in a huff, and dropped his hands back to his sides. He had to try something. And if that didn't work, he'd try another thing. And if the other thing didn't work, he'd probably kick something, and then he'd try a third thing. There just wasn't another option. They couldn't leave the house again with Joseph out there waiting to snipe them both in the brain, anyway.

He opened the door long enough to confirm that Laurent was still creepily staring at him, gave a little wave, then shut him in again and headed back upstairs. There had been some mention of the staff in one of the books Rathgeirr had brought him from the library in Falias, so that was as good a place to start as any. He settled on the floor of the bunk room and pulled the heavy tome into his lap, lifting it open with both hands and skimming through the list of spells at the beginning.

He still had to consult the rune primer Rathgeirr had left him, since his reading of the Elder Futhark was spotty, but he found the page he wanted and did his best to read it from the scant notes he'd taken. Unfortunately, none of the Alfar work was simple—every spell's workings was hidden inside a story, and Rathgeirr had had to explain almost all of the tales they'd read together. Noah just didn't understand a lot of the cultural references. He hunched over the book and frowned at the runes, sounding them out and writing them in more readable text onto one of the notebooks he had scattered around the room.

"I go to the...wood. To the...wet? Wet forest? To win a magic staff, with which I will tame you, maid, to do my will." Noah frowned down at the words he'd written and shook his head. That didn't help at all. He knew the gambanteinn *existed*. But how did it work? He huffed and tried to get a little farther down the page.

"I write thee a charm...spell? Charm. Charm. I write thee a charm, and three runes...within, I guess. Longing and madness and lust. Yikes." He paused. "But what I have written, I may yet...*unwrite*, if I have a need? Unwrite is good; tell me more about unwrite, book." He leaned a little closer, as if that might help make the spell's meaning clearer, but there was very little else. Something about three horns of...filth. That was vague. Should he feed Laurent something? Some *filth*? Use these runes? But use them how?

Noah groaned in frustration and fell back onto the floor with his arms splayed, the book still weighing down his crossed legs. He would just have to go with his gut and try some first thing, he guessed. So he shoved the book off his lap and bent over it to copy down the specific three runes listed, then pushed himself up to standing and made his way downstairs with his arms full of jars from his kit.

Laurent was right where Noah had left him—that much, at least, was still going according to plan—and he still kept silent eyes on the witch as he circled the table and set his supplies on the floor.

"So, I'm gonna try some stuff," Noah said, glancing at the trapped hunter out of the corner of his eye. "Sorry in advance if it sucks for you, but I don't have much to go on, here." He straightened and planted his hands on his hips to quickly look his captive up and down, then stepped closer, hesitating with his hands over Laurent's chest.

The hunter didn't move, didn't speak—he just stared. Noah would have almost rather been spit at and called a faggot.

He tried speaking the words from the runes, watching Laurent's eyes for any change, but got nothing. That was expected. He tried taking his jar of sea salt and rosemary oil and marking the runes one by one on the hunter's forehead, and again got nothing but a creepy stare.

"I'm going to figure you out," Noah promised—but he did lay a spare bit of cloth over Laurent's face before he tried anything further.

Julien rolled on his mattress just enough to check the time. He'd been asleep for two hours already, but he felt like he could have slept for twelve more. He didn't have the option—it was evening now, and the rest of his brothers were waiting for him. He hoped. With a stiff grunt, he pushed himself upright and paused to take a breath, assessing the state of his battered body. The cut in his thigh from the previous night was closed, at least, thanks to Noah's oils, and the punctures the wood had made in his calf were manageable. He would have to take it easy with his shoulder, though. That wasn't going to mend quickly—and if he wasn't careful, it could not mend properly at all.

Good thing he wasn't about to have to go out and shoot a rifle, or anything.

He sighed and stood all the way up, gingerly placing weight on his wounded leg and only wincing briefly before he started out of the room. His arm should really have been in a sling, but that was a medical luxury he didn't have time for tonight.

The house was quiet, so Julien picked his way down the stairs and toward the basement door, leaning his good arm against the railing to take some weight off his leg on his way to the lower floor. When he reached the room where Noah said he'd kept Laurent, the door was shut, so he pushed it open and looked inside to check on the witch's progress.

Laurent was still strapped to the table, but now his unbuttoned shirt had been pushed to his sides beneath the straps, and his pants had been pulled down to his knees, so that his whole torso lay exposed on the table, coated with some sort of fluid and marked with chalky, reddish runes. Noah squatted over him on top of the table, hands slick with oil and hair damp with sweat as he let his palms rest on Laurent's marked stomach. Soft, tired laughter fell from his lips, and as Julien's entrance caused a creak from the door hinge, both Laurent and the witch turned to look at him.

"Oh hey!" Noah panted. "I did it!"

"Hello," Laurent offered, his voice sounding dry.

Julien stared, swallowed, and forced himself to take a slow breath. "Great job," he said, though his grip on the door handle was too tight. Noah didn't miss it.

The witch dropped down from the table and scooped up a bit of cloth that had fallen to the floor, then laid it modestly over Laurent's exposed dick before he started to unfasten the straps. "Turns out it's pretty involved, surprising nobody, I guess," Noah said. His hands shook a little as they fought with the ratchet buckles, but he kept his voice light. "But I think I've got it now."

Laurent sat up to help him with the lower straps as soon as his chest was free, then slid to the floor and hastily did up his pants, glancing awkwardly over at his brother.

"And they have to be naked?" Julien asked, hoping he didn't sound as irritated as he felt.

"Well," Noah began with a shrug, "the spell sort of...is that kind of control? I mean, not, you know, leading them by the dick or anything. It's hard to say without Rathgeirr to help me, but in the book, it's kind of like, taking over their base urges? Longing and madness and lust, it said. So, the purification oil has to go, you know...everywhere like that." He wiped his hands clean on the cloth Laurent had left behind and gave both men his best bright smile. "But now that I know what to do next time, it won't take so long! That's good, right?"

Julien and Laurent exchanged a brief look, and then the older brother cleared his throat and edged toward the door.

"I'm going to...get cleaned up," he muttered, flattening himself against the door frame to squeeze by and hurry up the stairs.

As soon as he was gone, Julien turned his frown on Noah, but he was determined to keep his voice steady. This was magic—just magic. It wasn't worth his jealousy, and the witch didn't deserve his anger.

He was helping. He'd tired himself out helping—again. And he was planning to keep doing it. So Julien took another breath before he spoke.

"So it's...going to be the same method for all of them?"

Noah cringed as he nodded. "I'm not looking forward to it. But now that I know this works, I don't want to waste time trying other stuff, you know? So you just...bring them to me, and I'll get them right again."

"Right," Julien sighed, and Noah approached him to lay a light hand on his uninjured arm.

"I know that face. But I promise you, there is *nothing* sexy about this. Believe me."

"I do," the hunter promised. "That doesn't mean I'm excited about you having to touch every single one of my brothers' dicks."

Noah snorted softly. "Especially when I haven't even gotten to touch *your* dick in days. It's not fair." He leaned up to press a gentle kiss to Julien's lips. "I'll make it up."

The blond let his hand close around the smaller man's wrist. "Don't distract me when I have to go hunting," he murmured against Noah's kiss.

"Oh, don't mind me," Noah teased, sliding by him to head up the stairs. "I'll just be alone, in bed, having some quiet time to myself until you get back." He poked his head back around the corner when he reached the top. "And take another antibiotic at ten!"

Julien frowned petulantly after him, then spared a glance back at the oily mess the witch had left on the table before taking the stairs again himself.

Laurent was waiting for him in the war room, but he didn't really meet Julien's eyes as he came in. "Joseph will still be waiting outside," he said. "My memory is hazy, but I remember both of us being sent after you. The others were kept behind for some reason."

"Well, then let's go get them back," Julien said simply, but his brother gave him a quick look up and down.

"You're in no state to go anywhere. You'll have to let me handle Joseph."

Julien gave an indignant snort, but had no argument to give. He was already a little lightheaded just from standing up for this long. He tilted his chin toward the outside hallway. "Noah is making some tranquilizers. You can use those."

"Perfect." Laurent left Julien behind, and after a few minutes, Julien met him coming back down the stairs with a handful of darts in his hand. Laurent took up the rifle Julien had dropped earlier, then reached for the handle of the damaged front door.

"Shouldn't you at least go out the back? Both of us can't get shot."

"The front door is safer," Laurent said. "He'll expect you to avoid it, so he'll have set up somewhere he can see you leave through the rear. I'll need to circle him." He didn't wait for Julien's agreement; he just slipped out the door and clicked it shut behind him.

Julien sighed, leaning his tired weight against the railing. He hated feeling useless—he should have been more careful trying to leave. And if Laurent was wrong about Joseph's strategy, he wasn't likely to be able to dodge their brother's shot the same way Julien had.

He listened near the front window, expecting any moment to hear the distant thump of Joseph's rifle—but barely ten minutes had passed when a heavy knock sounded at the door as if it was being kicked, and Laurent appeared when Julien opened it. Joseph was unconscious on his back, the taller man's toes almost dragging on the steps.

Laurent was rarely wrong, Julien thought with a faint smile.

Noah hadn't meant to fall asleep, but as soon as his head hit the pillow, he was out. He was only jerked awake again by Laurent knocking heavily on Julien's door and jerking a thumb toward the stairs when Noah opened it.

"Joseph is in the basement," he said, not looking the younger man in the face as he spoke. If Noah had known all it took was an unsatisfying handjob to get Julien's brothers to be brief and polite with him, he would have considered it a long time ago.

"I'm coming," the witch promised, though his legs felt heavy underneath him as he followed Laurent out of the room. He needed sleep. But Julien needed Joseph back more—so he trudged down to the basement. Laurent left him behind to go join Julien, and Noah got to work.

It was a much quicker process this time, but no less tiring. It was, however, a little less awkward—Joseph had come to his senses, taken a moment to assess the situation once he was let up from the table, and then he nodded at Noah in thanks and clapped the witch on the shoulder before bothering to pull his pants up.

25

Julien didn't need much persuasion to go to bed rather than head back out that night. Laurent and Joseph were both drained, Noah was dead on his feet, and Julien himself should probably have been in the hospital. The only thing they would accomplish going out now would be getting killed—so the four of them went as quick and quiet as they could back to Julien's small safehouse. It probably wouldn't be long before Laurent and Joseph were missed; either the alfar already knew the spell had been broken, or he'd grow impatient waiting for them to return. Either way, none of them were keen to risk sticking around.

The warehouse room was big enough for all of them to find a patch of floor to pass out on between their piles of bags and supplies, though not for any privacy. Noah insisted that Julien take the cot, since he was injured, and the hunter didn't argue much.

In the morning, Julien awoke to the witch leaning over him, peeling away the taped bandage on his shoulder. "I'll redo this, but it looks a lot better. I'm getting good at this healing magic stuff, thanks to you," Noah added with a smile. "Maybe if you keep this up, I'll get as good as Airmed."

"Better," Julien agreed, and he dutifully rose at the witch's direction so that his various injuries could be attended to. His shoulder still wouldn't really move, but it wasn't nearly as throbbing as it had been the previous night, and standing up hadn't made him dizzy, so that was progress.

From their places on the floor, both Joseph and Laurent eyed their younger brother skeptically, but neither commented on his now limited usefulness. When Laurent happened to lock eyes with Noah, he moved away immediately, turning his back to focus intently on eating his granola bar and scrolling on his phone.

"Think Laurent learned something about himself yesterday?" Joseph muttered in French as he leaned closer to Julien, a faint, teasing smirk on his lips.

Julien frowned at him but refused to acknowledge the possibility, as that line of thinking was sure to lead him to jealousy and distraction. He didn't need either.

"So," Laurent began loudly, clearly hoping to cut off any taunting that might arise, "there doesn't seem to be anything in the news about the gunfire near the house yesterday. That's lucky."

Joseph scoffed. "Lucky. I'm not stupid enough to set up somewhere I'd be traced."

"Lucky you didn't turn stupid when you were mind controlled, then," Laurent muttered. "Anyway, I have Arnaud's location, at least, and Julien seems to have found my backup tracker, so we'll be fine to split up. And with the darts that—the witch made," he stumbled, feigning distraction by fiddling with the tracker in his hands, "getting the others knocked out won't be a problem. They seem effective. The issue will be getting them *back* once they've been knocked out. I have to assume that they'll still be kept close to the alfar and his guards, so we're unlikely to have the chance to just go in and carry them out of the woods."

"That staff he used," Julien cut in. "I know it. The fairies called it the gambanteinn—and you've seen for yourself what it does. If we can break the staff, we should be able to break the spell."

Laurent gave a pensive hum and scratched at his cheek. "That isn't much of an improvement. That still will require us to get close enough to—"

"It'll break if I shoot it," Joseph offered, and both brothers paused to look over at him. He shrugged one shoulder. "Won't it?"

"Can you hit a target like that from a safe distance?" Julien asked.

Joseph snorted at him. "Can I hit a target like that," he echoed in a derisive tone.

"We'll need to keep it still long enough," Laurent went on. He glanced over at Julien's injured shoulder. "Perhaps we need a distraction—or bait."

"You want me to be *bait?*"

"You're hardly fit for anything else. And the alfar will be expecting you to come. If Joseph and I hang back, he may even think we're dead."

Julien frowned but didn't argue. "Fine."

"I'll prep everything we'll need," Laurent said with a nod, the issue decided. "We can go after dark."

Julien could almost move his arm in half a circle by the time he stepped foot in Mont Royal again, and he didn't limp when he walked. Noah really was good—in the past, Julien had been regularly incapacitated for a week or more. If his family wasn't so stuck in their way of thinking, they could have vastly increased their efficiency by partnering up with willing witches long ago. But Edouard wasn't likely to listen to a suggestion like that.

He glanced down at the tracker in his hand, powered by the battery back in his pocket, and followed the path that would lead him nearest to the coordinates. Noah had come along despite Julien's misgivings, taking up a place with Joseph so that he could silence the sound of his rifle when the time came. Since he and his brothers had split up, they'd fitted themselves with radio earpieces from the armory, so that Julien heard Joseph's voice confirm he was in position and Laurent assure him he was standing by.

"I have eyes on the leader," Joseph murmured. "Four guards. No demons yet. I can see Arnaud and Edouard, but not the others. Keep your guard up, Julien. They may circle you."

"I'm watching," he muttered just loud enough to be heard. He heard movement in the trees ahead and slowed his pace, tucking the tracker back into his pocket. In a small clearing, the darkly-clad figures of the alfar almost blended into the night, but Julien could see their outlines sharply. He stopped where he was when the one holding the staff turned to face him.

"You came back, human," the alfar said, something like amusement on his grey face. He tilted his head slightly as he looked across the darkness at Julien. "Do I have something you want?"

"Turn him to his left," Joseph said quietly in his ear.

"You know you do," Julien answered evenly, lifting his hands to show that he was unarmed. He took a few slow steps to the right, craning his neck as though he was trying to see over the alfar's shoulder. "I don't want to fight my own family."

"How do you avoid the same fate?" the alfar asked. "What are you? What magic keeps you?"

"Didn't think you'd care about a human," Julien muttered, inching farther until the alfar was forced to shift his stance to face him fully.

"Right there," Joseph whispered, so Julien stopped.

"You will answer, cur," the alfar spat.

"Will I, though?"

Without warning, a bullet shattered the staff in the alfar's hand, bursting the center of the wood into splinters and knocking the remnants from his grip. The others drew their weapons instantly, but after the second it took to reset the bolt action on Joseph's rifle, one of them was thrown backward, the hole in his chest spattering blood onto his neighbor as he hit the ground.

The leader of the alfar snapped orders at his guards, commanding them forward, and one of the men still standing disappeared into the trees, another staying between his master and the direction of the bullets, and the last rushing for Julien himself.

Back on Lochlann, stripped of his weapons, Julien wouldn't have liked his chances against an alfar one on one even when he wasn't wounded—but this wasn't Lochlann. He narrowly avoided the edge of the soldier's silver blade in time to pull the Colt from the back of his belt, and he fired it into the other man's gut as he drew close. The alfar stumbled, his gloved hand moving to cover the injury, and he looked down at himself in pained confusion for the brief moment while Julien aimed again—then he fell, seeping blood from his temple into the dirt.

Julien started after the others as they fled into the woods, but the sound of large wings made him stop in his tracks. He was knocked to the side by the weight of the creature hitting him, slamming his already aching body against a thick tree. The demon bared its teeth to snarl at Julien, but as it reached for him, a loud bang exploded so close that it made the blond's ears ring. White smoke billowed from somewhere in the grass nearby, and as it spread, Julien's eyes and lungs began to burn. Tear gas. Antony coughed on the ground beside him, the demon disappeared into the mist, and Julien squinted in the thickening air to find the source of the canister.

Another deep boom sounded as Julien took a step forward, and he had to move back half a step to avoid the collapse of an alfar guard at his feet. Even through the smoke, he could see the bloody hole in the center of his chest.

Noah appeared at his side with his hands splayed in front of him, holding steady a surrounding sphere of clear air that softened the pain in Julien's chest as it was shared with him. He shared a frowning, confused look with the hunter, but his attention was focused on finding the right incantation to blow the smoke away. Antony grabbed for Julien's legs, so he swung the tranq rifle from his back and fired a dart into his brother's neck, dropping him back to the ground before he could do any more damage. Just ahead of them, Julien spotted the two remaining alfar, both shielding their faces from the gas.

"Prince Agvithr," the guard with the heavy shield said, his hand already on the leader's shoulder, "we must fall back!"

"Where the fuck are Laurent and Joseph?" Julien called to Noah, his own voice ragged, but the witch only gave him a flustered, unknowing wave of his hands.

Through the slowly thinning mist, another figure appeared, holding the launcher and wearing a heavy gas mask over their face. Wavy, dirty blond hair was tied up in a ponytail between the straps of the mask, and the strange woman wore a beaten-up rucksack over their long coat. A nearby demon was the next victim of the gas launcher; the canister thumped heavily into the creature's chest as the newcomer fired, forcing it to stumble backward. Then the launcher itself hit the ground, abandoned, as the stranger ran full tilt toward the demon, using its own leg as a jumping point onto its back. The woman kept enough momentum to fling her body past the creature with one arm around its neck, dragging it down to the ground in a flailing of limbs and feathers, and in one fluid motion, she pulled a long knife from her boot and buried it in the demon's heart, causing a shriek and swift crumbling of ash. Julien only knew one person who moved like that. Anik.

Beside Julien, Noah had frozen, both of them staring at the woman as she rose.

"Who the fuck is that?" Noah asked.

A beat passed before Julien could answer. "That's my sister."

Noah whipped around to give the hunter an incredulous look. "Your fucking *what?*"

The woman swung an arm to wave them over, her shouting voice muffled by her mask. "Aweille, bibitte! On a du travail!"

"For fuck's sake," Julien grunted. "Come on," he said to Noah, and they moved deeper into the trees together, following the woman's shape through the smoke. There was no sign of the alfar—the leader must have taken his guard's advice. In a small clearing, Joseph had Edouard over one shoulder and Hugo under the other arm, and Laurent fired a shot into an approaching demon's heart. He bent to pick Antony up in a fireman's carry and then paused when he saw Arnaud's bulky body still lying in the grass, so Noah gave a soft grunt and lifted him by magic instead.

Anik snapped at them to get to the car, and she led the way quickly through the park to where a beaten-down van sat at the farthest end of the lot from the streetlight. Julien's unconscious brothers were piled unceremoniously into the van as she opened the door, and then the others climbed in as well, Joseph taking the front seat and leaving Julien, Laurent, and Noah to balance themselves in the cluttered rear. Anik slammed the driver door shut as she fell into the seat and pulled her mask from her face and her bag from her back, almost smacking Laurent in the face with them as she chucked them behind her.

Julien steadied himself on the back of her seat as she peeled out of the parking lot and away from Mont Royal. "Anik," he said, his throat still raw from the gas, "what the hell are you doing here?"

"Saving your asses, it looks like, bibitte," she answered with a grin thrown over her shoulder.

Laurent knelt on the floor of the van to check each of his brothers in turn—every one had a dart stuck neatly into one side of their neck. Anik must have done it—but Julien had no idea when she'd managed it.

"They won't be out long," Laurent said. He stopped to cough—his eyes looked just as red as Julien's felt. "We need to get them somewhere Noah can work on them. They seemed placid once the staff was broken; let's hope they stay that way."

"There's no real danger in going back to the house now," Joseph said. "We haven't had an outright attack yet. It doesn't seem likely. Here," he added, gesturing for the woman to make a turn, and she sucked her teeth at him.

"I know how to get to the fucking house, Joseph."

Once they reached the house, after a quick check for pedestrian witnesses, they hauled their brothers inside and got them into the basement. They strapped Edouard to the table first and shut the others in a spare room, bound with rope.

Julien laid a hand on Noah's shoulder as they stood at the foot of the stairs. "Don't overdo it," he said softly, the extent of the weariness in the witch's face not lost on him. "We'll keep things safe upstairs."

"I'm on it," Noah said with false cheer in his voice, but when Julien tried to question him, he shooed the hunter away and turned toward the door where Edouard lay waiting.

Julien found Joseph, Laurent, and Anik still standing in the upstairs hallway, and when he joined them, the woman slung an arm around his neck to kiss his cheek. He smiled, just a little—it was a relief to see her again. She was older than when he last saw her, and she had a few aging scars on her chin, but she had the same bright green eyes he remembered.

"Where the hell have you been?" he asked, and she grinned at him.

"Wherever the hell I feel like."

"I thought you were dead."

She let out a scoffing puff of air. "Father should be so lucky. Besides," she added, reaching up to poke at the strap of his patch, "you look like you've taken more damage than I have."

"Long story."

"I'll hear it tomorrow," she said as she released him. "You ought to go to bed; you look beat to shit." She glanced over at the others and tilted her head toward the stairs. "You think I'd be allowed to crash on one of the bunks?"

"Of course," Laurent said immediately.

"You're welcome here, Anik," Joseph assured her. "And we could all use sleep. I'll take the first watch."

Julien parted with his siblings at the top of the stairs, feeling slightly guilty for leaving Noah to work while he slept—but his injuries were beginning to slow him down. He wouldn't be any use if he didn't rest. So he told himself that Joseph would be there in case of any emergency and allowed himself to fall into bed.

Noah barely made it back upstairs—Hugo had to help him from the basement and deposit him at Julien's bedroom door. The sun had been up for some time, but Hugo was the last one to be set free, and now it was finished. The witch's arms were wet with oil up to his elbows, and the front of his shirt was damp and stained with red chalk. But it was done. Noah had sent each brother away one by one. Edouard had barely looked at him on his way out, Arnaud had at least given him awkward thanks, and Antony had somehow still had the energy to snipe at him from the doorway—but Noah's reward for his patience had been the way Hugo blushed and stumbled once he realized what the spell had entailed. Even now, standing by Julien's room, he wouldn't quite look Noah in the face.

"So let me ask you," he whispered, leaning in conspiratorially close. "Does this...does it make me a little gay?"

"I don't think it's contagious, Hugo; you're good," Noah said. "Good night." He gave the hunter's arm a light pat and pushed the door open, stripping his shirt off as he went and half-heartedly wiping the oil from his arms with it. He crawled into bed beside Julien, laid his head against the blond's shoulder, and passed right the hell out.

When he woke up, Julien's thick arm was draped around him, keeping him warm and close against the hunter's chest. Noah felt like death—his mouth was dry, his body ached, and his eyelids were heavy, but he leaned up enough to check the clock on the nightstand anyway. The middle of the day already. He'd positioned the portal spell's totems in precise places around the city the day before; the longer he waited to use them, the greater the chance they would be moved, disrupted, or destroyed. They needed to make this happen today.

Julien grunted in protest at the witch's movement and pulled him back down to the mattress, and Noah didn't have the heart to fight the embrace. He let the blond kiss his temple and settled back into his pillow before he spoke.

"So why didn't you ever mention you have a sister?"

Julien didn't open his eyes as he murmured, "I haven't mentioned a lot of things."

"This feels like kind of a big one, Julien."

The hunter sighed and gave a one-shouldered shrug as he finally leaned back enough to look the younger man in the face. "It isn't a story that will surprise you. Anik was born right after me—the first daughter in the family. Father never seemed like he wanted her. Tried to say she shouldn't be trained. So one of my uncles took her and did it instead. As far as I know, nobody's heard from her for years. She sort of cut herself off—understandably."

Noah frowned faintly. "We really need to work on your communication of important information."

"It didn't seem important. I'll draw you a family tree sometime if you want."

Noah sighed and tucked his head under Julien's chin. It had taken months before the hunter had even mentioned he had brothers, and over a year before Noah heard any of their names, so he guessed it wasn't a shock that there was even more he didn't know. Maybe he would take Julien up on the family tree—but he let it go for now. "So what's the next step, here?"

"Now that we know where the portal is, the staff is broken, and everyone is back, the next step probably needs to be killing the alfar and his last guard. Then you can close the portal, and we can be done with this whole business."

"You think that's going to be easy?"

"I've handled worse odds than eight-on-two."

Noah snorted against Julien's collarbone. "I mean, it's kind of eight on however-many-demons-he's-let-out-already, isn't it?"

The blond's hand pressed a little tighter into Noah's back. "We only have to kill the alfar and hold out long enough for you to finish the spell. The rest will be up to the others."

Noah softened, allowing his own fingers to curl into the hunter's chest. "I guess so."

"Noah," Julien said, his voice more subdued as he leaned back to cup the witch's cheek. "I want you to be careful, no matter how things play out. You've been spreading yourself thin lately. Don't think I don't see it."

He smiled faintly and turned enough to nuzzle into his touch. "I know. But what else can I do? The demons probably aren't going to take a few days off to let me get some sleep."

Julilen huffed out a short sigh. "I know, but—just...be careful." He pressed a kiss to Noah's cheek, then his neck, and over his bare shoulder, squeezing him almost tight enough to hurt. "Now that I have you, I want...to know what this life with you is like when we're *not* at war with someone."

Noah's cheeks burned so hot he was grateful Julien couldn't see them. Even when he'd spent his time daydreaming about the hunter in his shitty apartment, the Julien in his imaginings never said things like that to him. He maneuvered his hands up between them to take the blond's face in them and leaned in to kiss him, his heart giving a small flutter at the pleased sound that formed in the other man's throat. Julien gripped the back of the witch's shirt to pull him closer, and Noah jumped, smiling through the kiss as he felt the hard press of the other man against him.

"Doesn't take much for you, does it?" Noah murmured against the blond's lips, and Julien grunted.

"It's been a little while," he grumbled.

"Poor thing," Noah purred. He slid deft fingers under the waistband of the hunter's boxers, taking a sharp inhale as the velvet skin of Julien's cock ran smoothly under his fingertips. "You are still injured," the witch went on, giving the other man a long, firm squeeze. He swung a leg over Julien so that he could climb over him and stand, then took his time tugging his own shirt up over his head and dropping it to the floor. He tucked his thumbs into his underwear and eased them down, a smirk touching his lips at the admiring rake of the blond's eyes over his body.

Noah tossed the blanket aside and ran his palms up the hunter's scarred chest as he settled comfortably in his lap, then he leaned down to nip at Julien's earlobe. "Why don't you just let me take care of you?"

"Noah, is this—" Julien hissed a breath through clenched teeth as the witch rolled his hips against him, fingertips teasing the head of his dick through his boxers. "Is this the time—you need rest," he sighed, but when Noah bent down and softly bit one of his nipples, Julien's hips twitched upward, and his argument died.

"I haven't gotten to be with you for days," Noah said as he rose, splaying his fingers on Julien's stomach and arching his back in a slow, purposeful grind. "I've missed having you inside of me."

Julien's cheeks flushed a delicious pink, and Noah couldn't help catching his bottom lip in a grin. Nothing was more satisfying than seeing shyness on the hunter's normally hard, stoic face.

"I'm going to need a minute," Noah said apologetically, lifting his hips just enough to more effectively reach behind him. He whispered the incantation that made Julien's prick jump in anticipation, and the witch's low chuckle became a soft, whimpering sigh as he slid a finger inside himself. He leaned his weight on one arm, balancing over Julien as he worked himself open with slow, even movements.

The blond exhaled what sounded like appreciative French, but when his calloused hand wrapped around Noah's erection, the witch tutted at him and pinned his wrists to the mattress with an easy spell.

"Can't have you overexerting yourself," Noah said with a sly smile. "You just be patient, and I'll fuck you when I'm good and ready."

"Nom de dieu," Julien whispered, and he swallowed hard, seeming unable to draw his gaze from the witch's parted, panting lips.

Noah felt the pulse of Julien's cock, straining against the fabric of his boxers, as he slipped another finger into himself with a longing whine. He let the hunter watch him, rocking his hips back into his hand and allowing his breath to hitch as his fingertips touched his favorite spot with practiced ease. He rolled forward, and a moan fell from his lips at the heat of the other man and the soft friction of his underwear.

"This isn't enough," Noah breathed against the hunter's lips. He finally pulled his fingers free and sat back to pull the cotton barrier between them down Julien's hips and out of the way, then gave the blond's dick a few strokes with his slicked hand. He lifted himself on his knees and sank down again, a slow, satisfied sigh on his lips as the hunter filled him. He allowed himself to settle for a moment, supporting himself with his hands on Julien's stomach, and he gave a soft moan of gratification.

He wet his lips and looked down into the blond's remaining hazel eye. "That's what I wanted," he whispered, and when he began to move, Julien's arms fought the hold of the spell immediately. Noah showed mercy and released him, relishing the touch of the other man's rough hands on his sides and hips. He set his own pace, grinding down against Julien with an eagerness that left both of them breathless and caused the old bed to creak in rhythmic protest. He put one hand on his own erection, stroking and gasping with each push of the larger man inside him.

"Fuck, Julien," the witch whimpered, "I love the way you fill me up."

The blond's breath fell out of him, and Noah licked his lips in amusement at the dark flush in the other man's cheeks. When his moans grew too wanton, he felt vaguely aware of Julien's grip tightening on him—a warning reminder that they were in a very crowded house. He pulled his lips between his teeth to keep his cries inside, and when that wasn't sufficient, he smothered the sound with his free hand, breath coming hard through his nose as he rode the man underneath him. Julien's body clenched, and Noah went faster, his hand keeping pace until he felt himself tighten and release, spilling hot stripes across the hunter's belly.

His strength went out, but Julien's didn't; he pressed his heels into the mattress and almost lifted Noah from the bed, keeping him supported with strong hands on his waist. Noah pressed his other hand over his mouth and squeezed his eyes shut, shivering while Julien thrust into him, just as hard and demanding as Noah himself had been, using the witch's body until his own orgasm finally brought a rough, tight growl from him.

Noah dropped down against Julien's chest, his limbs limp and his heart pounding, rising and falling with each ragged breath of the man beneath him.

"You're going to kill me," Julien rumbled softly, and Noah smiled and let blond chest hair tickle his nose as he nuzzled closer.

"There are worse ways to go."

26

By the time Noah had showered and made his way downstairs, there was more movement around the house—the brothers were beginning to stir, and soon things would be business and doom again. He just wanted some coffee and breakfast before that happened.

He found Anik in the kitchen, standing in front of the open fridge with the milk jug lifted above her head and the corner of the open bag in her mouth as she took a few loud gulps from the plastic teat. A lit cigarette drifted smoke toward the ceiling from her free hand. She still had yesterday's clothes on, but her dirty blonde hair was loose, falling in clumpy waves down a little past her shoulders. The woman gave a heavy sigh as she dropped the jug noisily back onto the fridge shelf and wiped a stray drop from her chin with the ball of her hand.

"Hey, you!" she called, far too loudly for someone standing as close to Noah as she was. "That was magic last night, right? You're a witch."

Noah fought the urge to take a step back. "Yeah."

"Sa coche!" the woman laughed. "I haven't met a friendly witch in a while. How'd you get caught up with these assholes?"

"Uh," Noah began uncertainly. "Well, I got caught up with one asshole, and he came with family."

She watched him for a few beats, then sucked her teeth and nodded. "Julien, huh? C'est-tu ton chum?"

His eyebrows lifted in surprise. Noah's French was pretty abysmal, but even he knew the word for boyfriend. "How'd you know?"

Anik snorted and took a drag from her cigarette, holding the smoke in while she spoke. "I tried telling Father that the more sons you have, the more likely they'll be gay." She turned her face away from him to exhale. "C'est vrai. They did studies." A smirk touched her lips as she gave the witch a slow look up and down. "And Julien always liked brunettes."

"Anik," Edouard scolded sharply from the doorway, and they both turned to look at him. Noah expected some resistance to the apparent black sheep of the family being suddenly in the kitchen, but the oldest Fournier brother only sucked his teeth at Anik and elbowed her out of the way of the fridge. "Put that out in the house."

"Wouldn't want to hurt the resale value of this fucking shack," Anik muttered. She leaned over to snuff out her cigarette in the sink, which Edouard didn't seem to love, then took an apple from a nearby basket and hopped up to sit on the counter. "So what's the sitrep, grand frère?" she asked with her mouth full of fruit. "Haven't seen creatures like those before. Hope the others come back for their dead, or there'll be a fun report on the news this morning."

Edouard let out a small sigh. He hadn't looked Noah in the face since he entered—he seemed to be pretending the witch didn't exist, which suited Noah just fine. These handjobs were worth their weight in—*don't finish that thought*, Noah cut himself off, his nose scrunching a little as he shook his head.

"There's a lot to explain," Edouard said. "Once the others are awake, we'll discuss our next move."

The group gathered around the war table seemed more subdued than before. Noah had sat quietly while Anik was brought up to speed by her brothers, and now Joseph and Antony stood watch at the front and back doors while a final plan was formed. Antony had objected to being sent away, but Edouard had snapped some French at him that seemed to douse his temper. Antony had still frowned at Noah on his way out, but his hate seemed more subdued now, at least.

The room had an air of finality that made the witch's skin itch. Julien looked steady on his feet, but Noah could tell he occasionally leaned forward to rest his weight against the edge of the table. Noah's magic could help him, and he definitely looked better than anyone who'd been shot multiple times in the last few days had any right to, but it would have been nice to have Airmed with them. He ought to have tried to learn more from her while he could.

"We know the alfar goes to the lake at night," Edouard was saying. Noah snapped back to the present, but even as Edouard scanned the faces at the table, he seemed to skip right over the young witch. "We know that without the staff, he can't control us again. And we know that they're down by three. So we should only have to deal with the leader and his guard."

"And the number of demons around," Laurent pointed out. He wouldn't even turn his head toward Noah's end of the table, let alone look him in the face. "We have no way of knowing if the ones we've killed have even put a dent in them."

"This can't go on any longer," Edouard sighed. "The spell to close the portal is ready?" he asked, clearly directing it at Julien so he wouldn't have to address Noah himself.

"Ouais," Julien confirmed, "but Noah needs to be at the site to do it."

"Then we'll do what we can," the older brother answered with a frown on his scarred lips. "This has to be the final push. The alfar leader is the primary target, but our main objective is to keep Noah safe until the spell is complete." He paused to look each of his brothers in the face. "À tout prix, c'est-tu clair?"

The others nodded grimly, and Edouard turned his attention to Anik, who stood silent near the door. "Can we count on your help?"

"When you ask so nicely," she snorted. "Sure. I'll bust some demons open."

"We move out tonight," Edouard continued. "Everyone get some food and get some rest. I want all of you sharp—no fuck ups. Now piss off," he finished.

While the brothers dispersed, some heading to the kitchen and others upstairs to their rooms, Noah hung back, lurking in the doorway with his arms held across his stomach. All of them—every single one of them planned to fight for as long as it took tonight. It wasn't for Noah's sake, he knew—it was because he was the key to closing the portal and putting an end to the invasion. Even so, Noah felt sick. If the spell did turn out to be too difficult—if it was something he just *couldn't do*, or even if he took too long to do it—he sighed. At least it probably wouldn't be guilt he would have to live with for long.

He missed Sabin.

"So tell me," Anik said from a little way down the hall, her elbow bent to lean against Julien's shoulder, "how pissed was Edouard when you told him you're fucking a witch boy?"

"Nine out of ten."

"Did he do that little eye twitch he does?"

Julien snorted softly. "He did."

"Tell me you've been loudly fucking this whole time. Like, every single night you've been here."

"No," he countered immediately, though Noah noticed the faint flush of embarrassment in his face.

"Shame."

Julien looked over at his sister and reached up to give the end of her hair a playful tug. "Are you going to tell me where you've been?"

"You don't want to hear it. You know how it is. Same shit, different day. Lots of monsters, lots of running, blood, blah, blah. Same as you, I bet. With fewer cute witch boys—he got any brothers?"

"I don't think so," Julien answered dryly, and Noah managed a smile as Anik turned back to look at him.

"Sorry," he offered.

"C'est de valeur," Anik said. "Well, if we don't die tonight, I can worry about getting laid again." She thumped Julien on the shoulder and left him in the hallway, taking the stairs two noisy steps at a time back to the bunk room.

When Julien opened his mouth to speak, Noah cut him off.

"I'm—gonna try to get some more sleep. Before...you know," he finished, a little more weakly.

Julien hesitated, but then he nodded. "I'll join you soon."

Noah didn't quite smile at him on his way by, and he shut himself in Julien's room and curled his legs under him on the bed, his eyes on the silver inlaid dogs reclining on the box nearby. Sabin was in

Antarctica, fighting his own demons and mounting a daring rescue. He was in just as much danger as Noah—probably more. But he had his friends. He was smart, and capable, and he'd done amazing things already. Noah hadn't allowed himself to think too much about the situation Sabin was in; he just trusted in the universe that things would turn out all right. Sabin would be fine. He had to be fine. And Noah would be fine too. He had Julien and the others, whether they all liked him or not.

But faced with finally performing the spell that had exhausted him with prep work for days while the man he loved and his entire family fought a potential horde of demons and an Alfar prince, Noah suddenly felt very alone.

He pulled a pad of paper from the bedside table and held it on his knee with the pen poised over the first line, but he couldn't make his hand move. He took a slow breath, trying to still the shameful tremble he felt in it, and then put ink to paper.

Sabin,

Tonight we're going to close the portal. The spell is in place, and I have everything ready—so we have to do it now, before things get worse. We have a plan, and everything should go smoothly. We even have a new person with us. I found out Julien has a sister. You'll like her.

I don't know if you'll even have time to read this. Things must be crazy where you are. I just wanted to send a note before we left. I hope you're getting along with your friends and not pushing yourself too hard. Remember that rest is just as important as work. But I know you're doing your best. You always do your best. I'm so proud of who you've grown into. I wish I'd been there for more of it.

I'm going to take my own advice and have a nap. But I just wanted to write you. I miss you. I'll write you again when this is over. I hope it's over for you soon, too. Please take care of yourself and don't forget to eat more than junk. Just because you're a bunch of teenagers out on your own doesn't mean you don't need vegetables.

I'm going to see you again before you know it. Remember to do your stretches; they really do help you focus. Be good.

So much love,

Noah

He folded the paper, stuffed it into the box, and held the lid shut with both hands, squeezing the wood tight to still the shaking in his fingers. He had to stop this. The spell had to get done—and Noah was the only one who could do it. So he'd do it whether he was afraid or not.

When he finally unclenched his fingers from the box, he took a deep breath, then stepped out into the hallway and headed quietly for the bathroom. He ran some cold water over his face, shook out his hands, and gave one last huff. It had to get done.

He opened the door and almost slammed face first into Laurent, who darted backwards as if Noah might be venomous.

"Pardon," he said immediately, lifting his hands.

"Sorry," Noah answered. He edged to the side to scoot by, but when Laurent's eyes followed him and he seemed to want to speak, the witch paused.

"You don't look well," the hunter offered after a moment.

Noah knew his smile wasn't convincing, but he tried anyway. "I'm good. Just...a lot on the line tonight. Trying to stay focused, you know?"

"We're all depending on you. If the portal stays open, it won't matter how many demons we kill. They will find a way to keep coming."

"Yeah; no pressure."

Laurent's brow lifted slightly, as though he realized what he'd said. "Ah, I mean...c'est pas si tant pire," he offered in a more gentle voice. "All of us will be there, so that you only need to focus on the spell."

"While you guys fucking die maybe." Noah sighed, then shook his head. "Sorry. I shouldn't say things like that."

"Is that your worry?" Laurent tilted his head and paused before continuing, seeming to struggle slightly to force his words out. "Noah—we do this every day. Not on this scale, perhaps, but not with so many of us, either. We know what's at stake. But for us, it's..." He gave a small shrug. "It's simply what we do. It's...natural to be afraid. But you can't let it get to you. I've seen you do incredible things. Tonight you have a job to do. We will do ours, so...you do what you're good at, and let us handle the rest."

He put a warm hand on the witch's shoulder, and Noah stared up at him with a faint frown, watching the hunter's brown eyes until he seemed to realize what was happening and backed away with an awkward clearing of his throat.

"Anyway, I mean to say that you should get some rest," he added with his eyes on the floor.

"Thanks, Laurent," Noah said quietly, a small smile finding its way onto his face. "You didn't strike me as the pep talk type."

"Ah," the hunter grunted, scratching at the short hair at the back of his head, "l'affaire c'est que...you've helped me. I don't want you to feel...unwelcome. By me. From me. Does that make sense?"

Noah snorted softly and nodded. "Yeah."

"So—thank you. I'm...going to—" He gestured vaguely toward the bathroom door, so Noah smiled and waved him on.

Noah's heart felt a little lighter on his way back to the bedroom. He might even get some sleep.

Julien sat on one of the long benches in the basement armory, thankful for the silence as he methodically broke down the weapons he planned to use that night. The familiar, sweet smell of the oil settled his mind, and his hands worked from memory to clean each piece of steel and set it aside. He needed to be focused. They weren't going to get a second chance.

Something moved at the edge of his vision, and when he turned his head, he was on his feet—the Alfar leader was standing near the bolted armory door. His black eyes skimmed right over Julien on their quick examination of the room. Julien didn't hesitate—he snatched up one of the guns he'd laid aside and fired it directly at the alfar's chest, but the bullet passed through him without resistance and buried itself in the far wall.

"You didn't think I'd *actually* come," the alfar said dryly. An illusion? It shouldn't have been possible—the house had more protections and wards on it than Julien could hope to list, even before Noah had gotten to it.

The man approached him with an easy gait, eyes flicking swiftly up and down the hunter's frame as he drew close. Julien didn't know how to fight an illusion—but the alfar didn't look at him like someone who was about to attack. He didn't look like much of a warrior at all, actually, now that Julien could see him up close. He was clean and well-groomed, with a slim build. His clothes were of finer cloth than Julien had seen any of the alfar wear, and they were embellished with delicate gold patterns at the sleeves, which were far too loose for someone who expected to fight. His black hair was held back from his face by a pair of braids on each side of his head, each strung with silver and tied with dark red ribbon into the silver comb at the crown of his head, the rest of his mass of black waves hanging loose to his waist. His long ears were pierced three times each, with thin chains linking the space between the carved hoops. He even had dark smudges of kohl on his eyes. This wasn't a person who was going to get his hands dirty.

"Who are you?" the alfar asked plainly, his voice low and steady.

Julien paused for a beat. "What?"

"Who *are* you?" he repeated with a slight furrow of his brow. "What sort of man can resist the will of the gambanteinn?"

"That one surprise you, did it?" Julien sneered. He *didn't* say that it had been just as much a surprise to him.

The alfar didn't seem offended by the hunter's tone. His eyes followed the lines of Julien's face, and he moved a step closer. As he lifted one hand, Julien recoiled, but the alfar actually shushed him gently, as if he was a frightened animal. Julien scolded himself for retreating from a phantom—until the alfar's grey fingers brushed a very real touch over the strap of the hunter's eyepatch. But when Julien tried to swat him away, his hand passed through the alfar's wrist like there he was a ghost. Was he here or wasn't he?

"This is a fine gift," the alfar murmured. "How did you come to possess it?"

"Just lucky, I guess," Julien grumbled. Should he attack again? Call out for the others? "What do you want?"

"The sort of man who hunts demons, and who claims boons from the Ævintýri," the alfar went on, almost to himself. His fingertips trailed down the hunter's scruffy jaw, making Julien's skin crawl. "An unexpected breed."

"Isn't it rude to just walk into someone's house and start asking questions?"

"Demanding," the alfar muttered quietly. The chains in his ears made a soft sound as he tilted his head. "I'll forgive ignorance. But only once," he added, slightly lower. "You address Agvithr oðlingr, regent of the city of Murias and son of King Huldrekall of the Norðrvegr. Now," he continued, as indulgently as if he were speaking to a small child, "tell me who you are, mannligr, so that we may better understand one another."

Julien watched the alfar's black eyes warily. So he was a prince. That didn't make him inherently more of a threat, but it certainly didn't make him less of one. "What is there to understand? You're the monster—and I'm the hunter. That's all I need to understand."

Agvithr's eyes narrowed faintly, and he leaned so close to Julien's face that the hunter arched his back to retreat. "You're going to make me cross," he warned, softly. He let his gaze drift down the blond's body and back to his face. "You have the bearing of a warrior," he said, and he began to take slow steps around the hunter, circling him with the serenity of an appraising predator. Julien turned his head to keep eyes on him, but the alfar still made no move to threaten him. "And some manner of magic about you. An intriguing combination in a man."

"Are you done?"

The prince came to a stop in front of Julien, and he leaned his weight on one hip as he folded his arms, unconcerned. "You've left me bereft of servants, *hunter*," he mused. "But I see your value. Perhaps you can be made to appreciate mine. These demons are useless—barely able to walk this plane at all but with my help. They portend nothing but chaos and death for your kind; surely you see this?"

"Strange talk from someone opening the door for them every night."

"I have my role to play. When the smoke clears, and my father sees the *agonizing* foolishness of this alliance he's made, we will have no further use for the creatures. The Alfar will crush them, and humanity will suffer their primitive appetites no more. The opportunity will come for men of substance to find their place in the new world."

Julien's lip curled. "Are you trying to offer me a *job*?"

"A position of power," he clarified. Agvithr stepped closer again and took hold of the hunter's chin, keeping him in place with a stronger grip than Julien expected. He dropped his voice as he moved to speak near the blond's ear. "A buck like you could be of great use to me, and you would find me a more than charitable master."

Julien knew, somewhere in the back of his mind, that if he went along with what the alfar wanted, he would have the chance to go with him, get close, find their camp, maybe even to kill this prince and his guard without a ruckus—but the bubbling of anger in his gut made his mouth faster than his head.

"Fuck yourself."

The alfar paused, looking down into Julien's face with black, empty eyes. Then he smiled, showing sharp teeth, and took a step back. "A man's pride is often his fall, mannligr. Remember that you refused me when the end comes."

With a flicker that put a tingle in Julien's skin, Agvithr was gone, and though Julien prowled the perimeter of the armory, he could neither see nor sense any sign of the intruder. He didn't like that kind of magic at all. It was a good thing they planned to make their move tonight.

27

The trees surrounding the Lac-aux-Castors stood just dense enough that Julien and his siblings approached unseen, each settling close to the ground as Joseph stretched prone in the damp grass. He leaned on his elbows and looked through the lens of his scope, inching to one side and then the other as he scanned the lake.

"Lots of demons," he muttered, barely loud enough to be heard by the others. "I count forty, maybe. They aren't even trying to hide."

"They know we're coming," Arnaud grumbled. "If we just charge them, we'll be overrun."

"Can we lead them away somehow?" Hugo whispered. "Draw them out, expose the leader, and leave Noah room to do the spell."

"Unlikely," Laurent answered. "Even if they haven't figured out that we mean to close the portal, they won't abandon the person they're there to guard."

Everyone turned to look at Edouard, who sat hunkered in the grass with a pensive frown on his face. "Then we need a distraction," he said after a pause. His gaze touched each of his siblings in turn. "A first wave. To throw them off guard and allow Noah to move in."

A stony silence passed over them, but when Julien looked back at Noah, the witch's brow was furrowed in confusion.

"Why is everybody making that face?" he hissed softly, but no one turned to answer him.

"I will take lead," Edouard went on. "Joseph will remain here. I'll need two with me, and the rest of you will hang back until a way opens and stay with Noah until the job is done." He looked around at his frowning siblings. "Who is coming with me?"

Julien spoke up immediately. "I am."

"And me," Arnaud added.

Julien glanced sidelong at him and gave him a brief nod.

"I don't like the vibe of this conversation," Noah said uneasily.

"They're volunteering for the suicide run," Anik clarified, and the witch's eyes cut up to Julien.

"Are you serious? Why you?"

"I should let someone else go instead?"

Noah cringed. "That's not what I—"

"Julien and Arnaud are the strongest," Laurent said, though the suggestion made Antony snort. "They'll have the best chance going in first."

"The best *chance*?" Noah whispered. He gripped Julien's sleeve and shook it so hard that the hunter wobbled. "Julien—"

"Noah, it's all right," he interrupted, but the worry in the witch's brown eyes put a pit in his stomach. "Noah," he tried again a little more quietly, turning the smaller man slightly away from the others. "You need to focus, and so do I. The others will take care of you."

"Who's going to take care of *you*?"

Julien sighed through his nose. "I haven't fought all this way just to die now. You trust me, don't you?"

Noah gripped him tighter and glared down at the grass. "That isn't fair."

Julien cupped Noah's cheek and drew his face upward again, and—despite the tension in his gut reminding him that his family was a foot away—he pressed a long, soft kiss to the witch's lips, until he felt him melt, just a little. Noah's fingers were still clenched in Julien's sleeve as he moved back, but his accusing frown and changed to one of resignation.

"I'm going to come back to you," Julien said gently, and Noah managed a small smile.

"You'd better."

Noah seemed to realize they were being watched, so he subtly scooted a little farther away from Julien in the grass.

"Finished?" Edouard asked dryly over Anik's snickering.

Julien fought the heat in his cheeks with a tight frown.

"Good. Let's move before we're spotted. You all know your roles. Get it done."

As Julien began to follow his brothers through the trees, he heard Antony's hushed, sneering voice.

"Don't get any ideas and think you can try something just because your boyfriend's gone."

"Oh my god," Noah snapped, clearly struggling to stay quiet, "I would literally rather die a virgin than touch your dick again, so will you shut the fuck up?"

Julien caught the casual five that Noah exchanged with Anik as they moved out and felt a small smile pull at his lips. He was going to be in good hands.

Edouard led the way around the edge of the treeline, gaining slow ground on the exposed group of demons filling the courtyard beside the lake. They didn't have long before they would be noticed—but it was their job to be noticed. The longer the attention stayed on them, the better chance Noah had.

The demons at the fringe of the lake caught their scent the moment they left the safety of the surrounding trees. Creatures shaped like men turned on them, just as savage as the ones that looked like beasts. Arnaud was a battering ram—knocking his way through the courtyard and throwing demons to the ground whenever he could get a grip on them. Bodies turned to ash in his wake, and dark clouds appeared where demons once stood with every deafening report of Edouard's shotgun. Julien didn't have the luxury of acknowledging his lingering injuries; he forced himself into the thick of the conflict and emptied the bullets from both of his pistols, each one finding a home in demon flesh if not a demon heart. There was little chance for him to stop to reload, so when his ammunition was spent, he was forced to rely on his sanctified knife.

He was slammed to the ground by a demon with limbs longer than its body, all black skin and sharp teeth. It got hold of Julien's arm and tore away some skin even through the sleeve of his coat, but when the hunter regained solid footing, the creature died just as simply as the rest.

Julien's body ached and his lungs burned, but there was no time for him to slow down. He lost track of everything except the enemy in front of him. The next move. The next kill.

Then a sound reached his ears, piercing through the deafness of his focus like a bullet. Across the courtyard, Edouard was on the ground—and it was his cry that broke through the clamor of battle. The Alfar soldier stood over him, the bottom silver edge of his shield dripping with blood. Edouard tried to pull himself backward, but his hands seemed to give way under him, unable to pull the weight of his crushed leg. His shotgun had fallen well out of his reach. As the alfar raised his sword, Julien rushed for him with a cry of rage so loud that the soldier's hand stilled. Julien's shoulder hit the alfar's bloody shield, knocking him off balance and forcing him to stumble back from Edouard's helpless position. Now facing an alfar in armor and bearing a heavy shield and sword, Julien glanced down at his knife and suddenly wished he had found the time to reload.

The alfar didn't have any sneers or taunts for him—unlike his master, this man was a warrior from head to foot. He lunged for Julien, only narrowly missing the hunter with the thrust of his sword. Julien didn't have much recourse—even if he blocked the alfar's blows, he wouldn't be able to absorb many sword swings without leverage. His best chance would be to displace the blade, move in close, inside the shield—but he'd be lucky to have one chance to hit a fatal spot.

One chance was better than none. Edouard needed attention before he bled out on the concrete, and Arnaud was still busy with the mass of demons surrounding them.

Julien took the hit of the alfar's next strike on the narrow guard of his knife, but the bones in his arm vibrated under the impact, and the soldier didn't give him space to breathe before swinging again. The edge of the blade caught the hunter's already suffering shoulder despite his defense, dropping him to the ground hard on one knee. Julien tried to push forward, boot scraping on the cement, and he hauled himself to his feet just as the alfar prepared to thrust again. The soldier's guard was up—he held his shield tight in at his side, sword arm drawing back, black eyes sharply focused on his target. He'd left no openings for Julien to take advantage of. Except one.

Julien took a swift step closer and swung his foot with as much force as he could muster, slamming his boot into the bloody bottom of the alfar's shield and sending it upward to connect with his jaw. The alfar stumbled backward, blood already pouring from his mouth and chin where the silver rim had connected, and with a harsh growl, the soldier threw the shield to the ground and took hold of his sword with both hands, pausing only long enough to spit out blood and a knocked-loose tooth.

As the alfar charged him, Julien heard Edouard's rough voice call his name, and he risked glancing over at his brother and found the shotgun being tossed to him. A trail of blood stained the concrete where Edouard had dragged himself to his weapon, and the throw almost wasn't strong enough to reach him, but Julien caught the gun by the receiver, pressed the stock firmly against his shoulder, and fired.

The alfar stopped, his armor peppered with shot, but he was still standing—so Julien fired again. This time, the tip of the soldier's sword dropped against the cement with a dull ringing sound, then clattered to the ground along with its wielder, who fell in a loose heap beside it. Julien moved in to kick away the weapon and emptied his third and last shell into the alfar's chest, causing a jerk in his torso as bubbling blood poured from his lips.

A strained, screaming voice carried over the courtyard and the hateful growls of demons. "Brynjarr!"

Before Julien could focus on the source, he was blown backward by something he couldn't see pounding into his chest. He flew across the concrete in painful rolls, only stopping when he hit the back of a massive demon's legs. He flailed in an attempt to turn upright again, but as he found his footing, the demon that had turned on him suddenly pulled back—or seemed to *be* pulled back. Its claws scratched at the ground, but it was dragged toward the lake along with the others surrounding it. One by one, the demons lost their hold on the earth, each sliding across the courtyard and disappearing under the water of the lake. Julien felt himself drifting forward as well—the same deep-rooted pull he'd noticed when he'd first found the portal.

Across the quickly-emptying plaza, Julien spotted Edouard struggling to fight the drag that tore at the demons, so he forced himself to move. He crossed the yard, ducking to avoid being hit by the curling horns of a woman's body that flew by him, and he sat behind Edouard and held onto both of his brother's arms. He had to brace his feet against the raised edge of the lake to keep from letting them both tumble in, but after barely a minute had passed, the air went still again. Julien allowed himself a breath, then looked around.

The courtyard was empty. Only Arnaud still stood near, staring over at them with a confused frown that Julien was sure matched his own. All three of them turned to squint across the lake, where Noah and the others stood at the edge of the water. From this distance, Julien couldn't hear what they were saying, but he saw the angry, impatient wave of Antony's arms, followed by Noah moving close to the rim of the lake and raising his hands again. Julien could faintly make out the sound of the witch's incantation, and when a heavy, bone-rattling pulse shook the surface of the lake, Noah collapsed. Laurent caught him under the arms before he could hit the ground and helped him stay standing, and Anik waved across the water at Julien and shouted something he couldn't hear but assumed was insulting.

"What the fuck just happened?" Arnaud asked as he approached at a limp, but his expression fell when he crouched beside his older brother. "Oh, hell, Edouard," he sighed.

Julien didn't speak. Edouard's right leg was almost completely severed at the knee, and blood leaked from him into a broad, shallow stain on the concrete. He was still breathing, but even with Arnaud tying his belt around his brother's thigh as a tourniquet, Edouard had almost completely lost consciousness by the time Noah reached them and was able to offer any real triage.

Leaving Edouard to the witch's magic, Julien heaved himself back up to standing and scanned the plaza in search of the prince. Whether it was Noah's spell that had drawn the demons back to their infernal home or not, they still hadn't found their main target. Julien expected that they would have to search for him, that he would go into hiding now that he was on his own—but Julien spotted him kneeling on the ground beside the body of his guard.

The prince's shoulders were slumped forward as if they were weighing him down, and his hands hung at his sides, knuckles resting against the bloody cement. Julien approached with caution, edging his way toward the remaining alfar's still form. The guard's torso had been mangled despite the protection of his armor, and one arm lay outstretched, bloody fingers curled slightly in the limp stillness of death.

"Finish the job, mannligr," the prince said, so softly Julien barely heard him. His voice was rough, as if he could barely get words through his throat.

Julien hesitated. When Agvithr raised his black eyes to the hunter, they seemed somehow even emptier than before. His cheek was stained with a smear of blood that matched the red droplets on the soldier's fingertips.

"Do what you came here to do."

With a faint crease in his brow, Julien drew closer, bending to scoop the discarded sword from the ground as he circled to the alfar's back. He didn't even look at the hunter; he'd returned his attention to the man lying before him. This person wasn't the same contemptuous prince that had appeared in the armory last night—not anymore. The least Julien could do was make it quick. But as he lifted the blade, steadying his grip in preparation, Noah's shout from nearby stopped him.

"What are you *doing*?" the witch cried, half stumbling across the stained concrete to close the distance between them.

"Noah—"

"You can't! Look at him!"

"*Noah*," Julien tried again, but the witch shoved him with both hands, forcing him to take a step back.

"Being our enemy doesn't stop him from being a person. Isn't it better *not* to kill people if you don't have to? He's all alone now—he's not a threat."

"That's definitely not true," the blond grumbled.

Noah wasn't listening. He moved in front of the prince and knelt down at a respectful distance, pausing a moment before he spoke. "There doesn't have to be any more violence," he tried.

"This is enough, is it?" the prince answered without looking at him. "Now it's enough."

"It is if you let it be. We didn't start this war—but you can help us end it."

"Help you?" the alfar sneered, his hands tightening into fists, and Julien moved to stand between him and Noah.

"It's your choice," Julien said, glancing over his shoulder as Arnaud and Antony approached from behind. "Surrender now, or die here. I do have a preference," he added with a faint scowl on his lips.

The prince was silent for a few moments, his gaze on the blood seeping into the fabric of his tunic where it pooled on the ground. Then he stood with graceful fluidity and looked into Julien's face. "A human should know his place when addressing his betters." He raised his voice slightly to be heard by the others. "I am Agvithr oðlingr, son of King Huldrekall, and I will be treated in accordance with my station."

Antony scoffed. "Big talk from the only creature left alive."

Agvithr kept his black eyes on Julien. "My general deserves to rest in the earth of the Norðrvegr. If nothing else, humans understand proper conduct of war, yes? Provisions will be made for my return home with him, and in the meantime, I shall surrender myself to your custody."

"Is this guy fucking serious?" Antony said, but Arnaud snapped a curse at him that shut him up.

Noah rose and moved forward to touch Julien's sleeve. "We should at least find out what Lugh wants us to do," he said quietly.

Julien took a slow breath and exhaled it in a sigh through his nose, but he couldn't argue. Killing someone who was attacking you was one thing—and executing a surrendering prince was another.

"Fine," he said. "We'll make arrangements as soon as we know what to do with you."

"I expect satisfactory conditions," Agvithr answered flatly. He leaned to one side to peer around Julien at the rest of the gathered family. "Now, if the victors would kindly get a move on—I need to secure my general and prepare him for the trip."

"Edouard needs a hospital," Noah said. "I've gotten him stable for now, but...he's going to lose his leg. That's not something I can handle."

Julien frowned over at the prince. "But you can. Can't you?"

Agvithr touched his fingertips to his own chest, recoiling slightly as if he didn't think Julien could possibly be talking to him. "Me? You're not serious."

"It was your general who crippled him," Julien growled, and the prince snorted.

"Is that wound not avenged by *murder*? I owe you and your family nothing, and I hope the wretched thing dies of the gigt." He waved the hunter away as though shooing a small child. "Away with you. I shall find my way to your hovel and await your return like an obedient captive."

Without waiting for Julien's reply, Agvithr turned his back on them, bending to run slow fingers through the air above the soldier's body and draw it upward from the ground. The man's arms and legs hung lifeless as he was carried, and after a moment, even Julien lost sight of them—both prince and corpse vanished from the courtyard.

"Tabarnak," Antony spat. "What are we supposed to do about all this?" He spread his arms, indicating the amount of blood on the ground around them.

"I can...I can clean it," Noah offered, though Julien could hear the exhaustion in his voice.

"Mon râleur, are you sure?" he asked with a frown, and Noah waved him off.

"This is it, right? We did it." The witch smiled sleepily up at him. "Just...leave somebody here to carry me back, and then I can sleep for a week. Take care of Edouard and the prince."

"I'll stay with him," Laurent offered from Edouard's side. "Joseph will want to stay with Edouard, and the rest of you are injured as well."

Julien grunted uncertainly, taking in the unsteadiness of Noah's posture, but he finally nodded. He didn't doubt for a second that Agvithr would be able to get past their wards without being let in, and the less time the prince was left alone, the better.

28

"It's been *two days*," Ciaran growled, pacing the dirt near the campfire while his brothers ate their breakfast. "Are we moving on Findias or are we not?"

"It's *only* been two days," Cethen pointed out. "Brathair, I know you're worried about Trent, but—"

"But what? But I should be patient? But I should take Rathgeirr's word for it that this Alfar is good and trust that Trent isn't dead, or being tortured, or—" He shut his mouth and scowled at the ground, unwilling to voice the insidious possibility that had wormed its way into the back of his brain—that Trent was, in fact, being taken care of *very* well. Perhaps even...better.

Ciaran snorted, forcing anger to replace his worry as Cu leaned back to look at him.

"We're already doing good work taking out their remaining patrols," his brother said. "We're getting closer to the city than the Ard Rí would like, in fact, I think," he added. "We need to be cautious—we lost a lot of men taking Falias. We're more outnumbered than ever."

"And they're still getting their feet back under them! Why are we giving them time to rally?"

"Brathair," Cethen sighed, "you know better. We'll get him back, but you have to use your head."

"He means think about it," Cu said with a barking laugh, "not try to ram the city walls."

Ciaran echoed his laugh in a mocking tone and cuffed him on the back of the head, which didn't stop his brother's laughter. "Get your gear. We need to start moving." He stalked away from the fire, scooping up his shillelagh and shield and calling to catch the attention of the rest of his men as he went.

When he passed the medical tents, meaning to ask Airmed for another bit of salve for the ribs he'd bruised the day before, he caught sight of her in one of the spotty groups of trees nearby, speaking closely with someone. Ciaran paused, frowning as he leaned around the tent to get a better look. Rathgeirr stood in front of her, one hand's fingers laced with Airmed's and the other gently caressing her cheek. His lips moved—Ciaran couldn't hear the soft words exchanged, but he saw the tired, accepting smile on his sister's face. She leaned up on tiptoe and met the alfar's kiss as he lowered his head, her fingers curling into the fur of his cloak at his shoulder.

Ciaran stared, eyebrows raised, until Rathgeirr pulled away with one more light brush of his thumb over Airmed's jaw and turned back toward the camp. Then he turned on his heel and took swift steps to the front of the tent, barely managing to duck inside the flap before the young alfar turned the corner and passed him by. The sneaky little shit.

He almost bumped into Airmed on his way out, but upon seeing the bright look in her eyes as she smiled up at him, he let his shoulders slump and his irritation deflate. He took the little jar of salve she gave him, touched her hair and kissed her forehead, then smiled at her and left the tent.

Rathgeirr wouldn't look at him as they gathered to discuss the plan for the day, but Ciaran could see the smile he was trying to hide.

"What's there to be so happy about this morning, lad?" he asked, and Rathgeirr jumped at being addressed.

"N-Nothing," the alfar insisted too quickly, focusing instead on checking the security of his scabbard's buckle as he forced his face into a stern frown.

Ciaran gave a skeptical hum and lowered his voice as he leaned in a little closer. "I'll tell her she's nothing worth smiling about, then, shall I?"

Rathgeirr's hands went still as he whipped wide, black eyes up to the fairy's face. "I...Ciaran, I never—I only—you see—"

"Ach; enough." Ciaran gave the other man's shoulder a firm squeeze. "You're a good lad. Don't let me think otherwise going forward, eh?"

"Y-Yes," Rathgeirr agreed, nodding vigorously. "Yes. Of course."

Ciaran gave the alfar's arm another swift pat and tilted his head toward the others, not waiting for him before moving on himself. Anyone who could put that sort of light in his sister's face deserved a shot at it, he supposed.

Hathuwulf hadn't come out of his room all morning. Trent was put to work around the house today rather than in the city—a mercy, since his back still hurt so badly that he frequently had to stop his chore and remember to breathe. He'd tried to go into the prince's room to do his cleaning, but the door was locked, and Trent's knock got no answer. Skathi had allowed him to fold the household's linens, which was about the easiest job he could ask for, he guessed.

The prince finally emerged around the middle of the day and called immediately for Kothran, the alfar he'd met with when they first arrived—Trent assumed he was an official of some kind, but he couldn't pretend to have a real grasp on Alfar government. Hathuwulf took the older man into his room and shut the door, so Trent followed, pressing his ear to the narrow gap between the wood of the door and its frame.

Hathuwulf's steady voice spoke first. "I plan to negotiate with the Hákonungur of the Ævintýri."

"...Negotiate, Yðar Hátign?" Kothran asked, sounding more than a little uncertain. "Negotiate what?"

"Peace, of course. A surrender."

"*Surrender*, herra?" The man said it like it was a curse. "I know the loss of Falias is no small matter, but even so, our forces—"

"I'm not concerned with the strength of our forces," the prince cut him off, "but with the survival of our people. I will not allow this war to continue. I will not let my father lead us to ruin for the sake of his own vainglory. So I will ask the Ævintýri their terms."

Trent smiled, his hands relaxing just slightly where they were flattened against the door. Hathuwulf *had* been convinced.

"Yðar Hátign," Kothran tried to argue, but he stopped short. Trent didn't have to see to know the look the prince must be giving him— Trent himself had shut up under that black gaze more than once.

"Send an emissary to the Hákonungur," Hathuwulf said evenly. "With this letter. I will meet with him, if he will see me."

"...Yes, herra," Kothran reluctantly agreed, and at the sound of his footsteps, Trent retreated from the door as silently as he could.

He kept to his room, folding sheets with mechanical routine now, but he craned his neck to see through the doorway as a new alfar appeared in the house. Kothran passed him a rolled parchment sealed with a wax insignia and sent him out, lingering in the front hall just long enough to give a low, weary sigh before returning to his duties.

It was all Trent could do not to rush back into Hathuwulf's room. He'd believed him. He'd listened. He was going to stop the war. A frown grew slowly on his face, and his hands stopped their work, lowering the unfolded wool back onto the pile. But just stopping the war wouldn't help the slaves.

Trent left his laundry behind and went to find Skathi, to tell her what he'd heard, that even Prince Hathuwulf knew now that the humans ruled the outside world—but she just scolded him for eavesdropping and told him not to put words in the prince's mouth. Jensi and Keldan wouldn't listen to him, either. Jensi just laughed at him, and Keldan quietly said they all ought to get back to work.

Trent had never folded sheets angrily before, but he did now, slapping them onto the stack despite how painful the movements made the welts on his back. These people—didn't any of them have any fight in them? He took a deep breath and shook his head. He couldn't put the blame on them. If he'd grown up on this island, he wouldn't be any different. He hadn't even wanted to go against his own asshole father, let alone an entire system he knew no alternative to.

He was in the kitchen with the others, eating his midday bowl of porridge and dried fish—only slightly less satisfying than his *morning* bowl of porridge and dried fish—when the messenger returned to the house. Skathi hissed at him as he got up to peek out into the front hall, but he ignored her.

"The Ævintýri will discuss terms," the man said, and Kothran nodded with weary acceptance obvious on his face.

Hathuwulf appeared at his side, and the messenger gave a sudden, deep bow, as if he hadn't expected to see the prince in his own home.

"What else?"

The messenger straightened, but still didn't dare lift his gaze to Hathuwulf's face. "The Hákonungur agrees to a meeting outside the walls of Findias—at the suðurdalur. He says he will wait for your arrival."

Hathuwulf nodded and dismissed him, immediately holding up a hand to stop the coming objection from Kothran. "Ready my horse. Arm two men *only* as my escort."

As the other man hurried away, the prince turned his eyes toward the kitchen doorway, where Trent froze. Hathuwulf beckoned him out with a calm gesture, so Trent inched out to stand in front of him, not afraid to raise his eyes to the other man's face now.

"You will come," Hathuwulf said. "A reminder that I still control something precious to one of the Ævintýri. And," he added as Trent's brow furrowed, "if their terms are agreeable—a show of good faith."

"What does that mean?"

"If we can come to an agreement, I will release you. So that you may return to the man who is *not* your master," he finished dryly.

Trent couldn't help his soft laugh. "You mean it?"

The prince subtly arched an eyebrow at him. "I don't say things I don't mean. But." He tilted his head slightly, seeming to study the boy's face. "You would be...welcome to stay."

"You're asking me to choose between freedom and slavery."

"I would like to keep someone like you—who knows the outside. And...I owe you a debt," he added, these words seeming a little harder to get out. "I think you would find your life here very much unlike being a slave, were you to remain."

Trent shook his head. "I appreciate...what you're saying, I guess, but...even if I *was* okay with being a slave, even if it is in name only— I can't stay here. Ciaran is waiting for me. He's probably *really* pissed at me, but he's waiting for me anyway."

"He's your lover."

Now Trent dropped his eyes to the ground. "Yes," he confirmed, the heat in his face spreading up his ears.

"I see." Hathuwulf let out a light exhale through his nose and lifted a hand toward the door as a heavy knock thumped against it, sounding the readiness of his mount. "Then let's return you to him."

Ciaran sat on horseback with one brother at each side, keeping his place behind the three kings as they waited for the appearance of the alfar prince. He itched to ride ahead, to scale the city wall, to burn every hiding place until Hathuwulf was forced to cower in the dirt. But now he was coming to them. So Ciaran waited.

The prince's buckskin horse and its rider appeared over the ridge of the valley, flanked by two others, who followed him at an easy pace down the field. Ciaran's grip on his reins tightened. Sat in front of the prince, riding with the alfar's sure hand on his stomach, was Trent, wearing the blue tunic of a slave. He looked healthy, though he seemed to wince some at the movement of the animal beneath him as they approached. It took Cethen's gentle, sympathetic tutting to keep Ciaran in his place—he could barely stand even the moments it took the prince to reach them.

"Tánaise Hathuwulf Stöðugan Huldusson," Mac Cuill greeted him as the horse slowed to a stop a fair distance from them. He offered a subtle dip of his head in place of a bow, which the alfar returned.

"Hákonungur Éthur Mac Cuill. I thank you for meeting with me. The Tuatha De Danann are worthy enemies; I hope to find them reasonable, as well. Name the terms that will bring an end to this conflict."

Ciaran was hardly listening. He focused on Trent's face, and the boy offered him a weak, apologetic smile. Ciaran wanted to reach for him, snatch him from the alfar's arms and steal him away back to camp—but he bit the inside of his cheek and held still. Why was he here? And why did the prince hold onto him that way?

"The disarming of the Lochlannan forces," Mac Cuill began, "the surrender of the remaining cities to the rulership of the Tuath De, the recalling of any dispatched ships, and éraic for each man killed."

The prince's lip curled almost imperceptibly. "You expect me to pay the wergild for the deaths of my attackers? After they've stolen my horses and burned my fields?"

"The Lochlannan are the aggressors in this war," Mac Cuill countered.

"I feel very much like the aggressor these past days, fleeing my own city and feeding starving refugees," the prince returned flatly. "I am amenable to disarmament and *mutual* aid following the cessation of hostilities, but the Alfar have ruled the island of the Norðrvegr since the time of Ymir, and that will not change while I guard her shores."

"Then perhaps King Huldrekall should have stayed home to defend them himself."

Ciaran saw Hathuwulf's fingers clench ever so slightly into Trent's shirt, causing the boy to peek up at his face with a frown of concern. The fairy edged forward in his saddle. *Don't look at him like that.*

"My interests," Hathuwulf began after a pause, his voice low and steady, "lie with protecting the lives of my people. I trusted that yours were the same. If that is not the case, and the Tuatha De Danann feed only their pride, then we have nothing further to discuss." Black eyes flicked over to Ciaran as he added, "And we have nothing to exchange." He urged his horse back a step, the animal nickering as it turned to head back up the valley hill.

"Mac soith," Ciaran growled, kicking his horse into motion to lurch after the retreating prince.

"Cian—" Cethen called, but with the tone of a master whose dog had already slipped its leash. He only had time to exchange a brief glance with Cu before he snorted and followed their brother up the hill.

Ciaran lifted from the saddle to better steady himself, the grip of his shillelagh already in his palm, and when the first of the prince's guards turned to him, he swung. He caught the startled alfar in the shoulder and toppled him from his horse, passing him by as he raced for the prince himself. Hathuwulf saw him coming and turned, tucking Trent under his arm and behind him as his silver sword flashed from its scabbard to block the fairy's next blow.

"Release him!" Ciaran shouted, circling the prince's horse and glancing to the remaining guard, whose bow fell uselessly to the ground, dropped the moment Cu's slung stone broke the bones in the alfar's hand. He gave a sudden, low gurgle as Cethen's spear shaft locked around the front of his neck, and he was pinned to the fairy's chest, his one good hand pulling at the wood. Behind him, Cu had the fallen guard under his boot, the point of his sword held steadily at the back of the alfar's neck.

Hathuwulf's sharp eyes never left Ciaran's, his sword ready in his hand. He kept Trent pinned protectively at his side and matched the prowling pace of the fairy's horse. "The Ævintýri understand keeping spoils of war," he said with a slight sneer, showing his sharp teeth.

"He isn't spoils!" Ciaran snapped. He wanted to crush this alfar's skull—but he didn't dare swing again with Trent there. "He isn't your *bargaining chip*! He's a person!"

"Tell your king that lives are not for bargaining with!" Hathuwulf held firm, refusing to back away when Ciaran drew near.

"Release him," the fairy said again, lower this time—more dangerous. "If he takes one step back into the city with you, I'll burn it to the ground just like Falias—and I'll follow you to Murias, and to Gorias, and to the edge of the sea, and I will drown you in the blood of all the men it took to reach you."

Trent wriggled under the alfar's grip, and he righted himself with a huff as he pushed Hathuwulf's arm away from him to look Ciaran in the face. "Stop it," he begged. He leaned forward in the saddle, and the prince made no move to contain him. "Hathuwulf came here to make peace!"

"Hath—" Ciaran stopped, letting his shillelagh point to the ground as the strength of his arm failed him. So the Crown Prince of the Alfar was...simply "Hathuwulf" to Trent? He looked into the prince's dark eyes as the other man mirrored him, warily lowering his own weapon.

"Did you guys come here to put a stop to this war or didn't you?" Trent went on, the scowl on his lips shooting straight into Ciaran's gut. "I thought this was about protecting the rest of the world, not taking over the island! Tell whichever bearded asshole over there is in charge that nobody else needs to die." He turned to look unabashed into the prince's face, far too close and far too comfortable for Ciaran to bear. "And you—you thought you weren't going to have to make concessions? That the fairies would just leave because you told them to? *Your* dad started this—you have to fix it."

The alfar's eyes focused on Trent's, and he let a few beats of silence pass, as though he wasn't concerned with Ciaran's presence at all. "Yes," he said finally, so softly Ciaran almost couldn't hear it. Then he looked back up to the fairy. "Release my guards. I will negotiate."

"Give him to me," Ciaran answered, but the prince held his gaze as he took the boy safely by the waist again.

"When an agreement is reached."

His grip tightened instinctively around his weapon. "I said—"

"Ciaran," Trent cut in. "I'm *fine*. Please."

Ciaran stared at him with a sick feeling in his chest. Trent was fine. Fine in the Crown Prince's house. Fine on his horse—fine in his arms. What had happened in the short days he'd been gone? He forced his face into a hard frown and pulled the reins to steer his horse back toward where the three kings waited, looking on in anxious anticipation—no doubt hoping that Ciaran would simply follow through and kill the prince for them. It would be a lie to say he didn't want to.

"Lig dóibh dul," he called to his brothers, who allowed the alfar to breathe again, and then he turned his frown on their prince. "Then come. *Negotiate*."

Hathuwulf followed the fairies down the hill with Trent riding easily in front of him, and Ciaran dutifully apologized when Mac Cuill made a show of scolding him for daring to attack the prince during peace talks.

"I will capitulate to paying half the wergild for each man lost," the alfar said, "but no more. And I will allow my forces to be disarmed— provided the Tuatha De Danann lay no claim upon any part of my island."

"It is customary—" Mac Cuill began, but Ciaran interrupted from behind him with a snort of irritation and leaned his stacked elbows on the pommel of his saddle.

"You think anyone really *wants* to live here with them? Which of the Tuath De will you leave behind to hold your new land?"

The High King narrowed his eyes at him, but then looked back to his brothers. After a moment, he let out a magnanimous sigh and shifted in his saddle as he returned his attention to the prince. "The Alfar will retain sovereignty of the island," he agreed.

"Ard Rí," Ciaran spoke up again, earning himself another sharp look. His eyes were on Trent, who still watched him with guilt written on his face. "If I might make a suggestion. It hardly seems right to have come all this way saying we're protecting the world of men, only to leave so many to a fate like this," he finished with a quick gesture in the boy's direction. "The Alfar should agree to free their slaves."

Mac Cuill's bushy eyebrows lifted, and he looked to Hathuwulf with a slightly amused smile on his lips. "I agree. What says the tánaise?"

The prince locked his black eyes on Ciaran. "The Norðrvegr has existed this way for millennia; her entire economy, our *agriculture*—"

"Any kingdom that cannot support itself except on the backs of slaves deserves to fall," Ciaran snapped, and Hathuwulf's stoic mask faltered.

"That the Tuatha De Danann would make such demands on the pretense of peace—"

Trent turned in his seat and fastened his fingers in the prince's cloak, stopping him before his voice became any angrier. He spoke quietly to him, but though Ciaran strained, he couldn't hear. Hathuwulf listened with his brow furrowed, mouth set into a thin line as he stared at the ground. When he looked back to the boy's face, his own expression had softened, just slightly, and he lifted his head to address the High King.

"The humans of the Norðrvegr will be free," he agreed with a small nod.

Even though that was the answer he wanted, Ciaran's stomach hurt to think that Trent had been the one to convince him with a familiar touch to the arm and some softly-spoken words.

"And the dispatched ships?" Mac Cuill asked.

"I cannot control my father," Hathuwulf admitted. "But as Mjötuðr, you have my assurance of cooperation as far as my dominion extends—and in Konungr Huldrekall's absence, that is the entirety of the Norðrvegr herself."

"We can trust that this agreement will be upheld upon his return, as well?"

Hathuwulf didn't hesitate. "When my father returns, you will find the Konungr receptive to negotiation," he promised.

"Then our scribes will draw up a treaty for your signature," Mac Cuill agreed, "and we will commence the disarmament."

The prince nodded, and after a moment's pause, he dismounted. He offered his grey hand to Trent, and when the boy took it, he helped ease him down from the horse with a gentle, steadying touch to his waist. The alfar said something to him that Ciaran couldn't hear, and when Trent shook his head, a faint hint of a resigned smile touched Hathuwulf's lips, and he laid a hand on the boy's hair. Then he took a step back and gestured toward the fairies. Trent only waited long enough to offer the prince a nod before crossing the distance between the groups, fingers fidgeting in front of him as he approached Ciaran like he expected to be grounded.

Ciaran dropped from his own horse and snatched Trent into his arms, clutching the boy to him with a hand in his hair. He buried his face in Trent's shoulder, trying to fill his lungs with his scent. Trent tensed and hissed in pain immediately, gripping the buckles of Ciaran's armor at his sides, and the fairy pulled back with instant fury in his chest. His back. There could be only one cause for a human's back to be injured in an alfar's care.

"He didn't do it," Trent whispered before Ciaran could ask, and he held on tight when the fairy moved to get by him. "It wasn't his fault. Please."

Ciaran looked down into Trent's face, his brown eyes wide and his mouth set tight. Defending him. Pleading. For him. While Ciaran was sick to death with worry these past few days, Trent had been...what? Making friends with his captor? More than friends? The pit that had been growing in his stomach since Trent had first arrived with Hathuwulf was now almost too heavy to bear.

"Take me back," Trent said softly. "Take me home."

Ciaran forced a calm breath through his lungs and only released Trent long enough to help him up onto the horse, then mounted behind him. He excused himself from the Ard Rí's presence while the leaders came together to oversee the writing of the treaty, and he urged his horse as fast as he dared out of the valley and back toward the camp. Trent's ill-fitting blue tunic was loose enough at the collar to show the narrow ends of raised red welts on his upper back. He'd been whipped. Punished like slave. That's what Hathuwulf hadn't done. He let his fingers spread where he held Trent at his stomach, wishing he could pull him closer.

29

At the camp, Ciaran left his horse to the nearest servant and near carried Trent back to his tent, urging him to a seat on the furs inside. As soon as the flap fell closed, Ciaran's hands were on him, pulling swiftly but carefully at his tunic. Trent let him pull it off, and when Ciaran went right back out of the tent again, Trent saw him throw the blue shirt onto the closest fire. He barely let the flap close again behind him before he was on top of Trent, cradling the back of his neck with a firm, gentle hand and not allowing him to drop far enough for his injured back to touch the ground. Trent let out a small sound of surprise, his elbows going back to help support him. Ciaran's kiss was devouring and hot, and Trent didn't bother trying to fight the stirring in his belly. Having Ciaran here at last, warm and solid on top of him, the touch of his fingers drawing familiar shivers from him, melted away the tension and uncertainty of the last few days.

Ciaran pulled him up to sitting again, and Trent's hands moved without prompting, working loose the buckles at Ciaran's sides. His chestpiece was fast discarded at the edge of the bedding, his belt and weapon abandoned. When Ciaran's fingers began to tug at the tie of Trent's trousers, he leaned back on instinct and instantly regretted it as he put weight on his back. The fairy tutted affectionately at him and lifted him easily into his arms, pulling off his glasses for him and setting them safely aside. He settled Trent on his lap and leaned in to taste the skin at the hollow of his throat, a quiet sound of satisfaction rumbling in his own chest. He let his fingertips run down Trent's arms and raised his hands to his lips, brushing warm, savoring kisses over his knuckles, then up one arm and then the other, guiding each up and around his own shoulders in turn. His palms were hot on Trent's waist and his lips were eager as they moved over his chest, as if he didn't want to miss a single inch of skin.

Trent's fingers curled against the fairy's back, and when Ciaran's mouth found his nipple, he took a sharp breath and rocked his hips forward, longing to feel the other man's erection against his. Ciaran gave a soft groan of appreciation and set his hand to work on his lover's trousers again, exposing him to the chill air for just a moment before enclosing him in a firm grip. Trent let his head fall forward to rest on the fairy's shoulder, goosebumps prickling on his skin as the other man tugged him a little closer. He wanted to say something to him—to apologize, maybe, or to tell him how much he'd missed him, or to explain why he'd gone—but then Ciaran's fingers were in his hair, urging him back, and the heated look in those green eyes silenced him even before the fairy's kiss did.

Ciaran's tongue parted Trent's lips and took over his mouth, stealing the younger man's breath and taking it for himself. He ran his thumb over the quickly dampening slit of Trent's cock to draw a shuddering whine from him, then eased him from his lap. He reluctantly broke the kiss and turned Trent onto his stomach so that his back wouldn't touch the ground again, but then he paused. His fingertips barely skimmed Trent's shoulders and down his waist, lingering at his sides. Trent turned his head to look back at him, and his heart dropped at the look on the other man's face. There wasn't anger there now, or hate, or even bitterness—it was guilt.

"Ciaran, it—"

The fairy bent over him and cut him off with another kiss, muffling his protest. He laid a warm palm at the small of his back as he rose, then took him by the hips and shifted him up onto his knees in one motion. Trent gave a soft whimper of embarrassment as Ciaran exposed him, tugging his trousers down to bunch around his knees and running his hands over the now bare skin. He didn't feel shy around Ciaran anymore, really—but being in this position felt exceptionally defenseless.

He tightened his fingers in the blanket near his head for security, but the moment Ciaran's thumb brushed him, his breath hitched and his back arched on instinct. He lifted up just enough to reach toward his bag, which still laid crumpled in the corner of the tent, and retrieve the small bottle of clear gel. Ciaran reached over him to take it from him, the thick shaft of his dick pressing achingly hard against Trent's ass as he leaned. Trent whimpered and pushed back against him, causing the fairy to grab tightly to his hip with a strained groan. He ran slicked fingers over the boy beneath him, melting him into the blankets with practiced ease. Trent's cheek and chest pressed against the soft fur, fingers splayed to steady himself, and when Ciaran's fingers slipped inside of him, he couldn't help letting his legs slip a little farther apart.

Ciaran supported himself on one hand so that he could reach to kiss the back of Trent's shoulder, his soft whispers sending a shiver across the boy's skin. Trent bucked against the fairy as he subtly crooked a finger inside him, unable to keep his voice quiet. He didn't want to wait—he wanted Ciaran on him, over him, in him—but he barely had the breath to tell him so.

As if reading his mind, Ciaran slowly pulled his fingers free and shifted forward, guiding himself to press against Trent's entrance and then resting a steadying hand on the boy's hip as he pushed deep into him. He only gave Trent a moment of shuddering to adjust before he began to move, slowly withdrawing the length of his cock and sinking it back inside at a pace that quickly grew insistent.

Trent fought for stability against the roll of the fairy's hips, reaching back for him and gripping the hair at the back of Ciaran's head as he dropped down to his elbow. He laid as close to Trent as he dared, seemingly unwilling to let any part of him touch the boy's injured back, but Trent was pretty sure he wouldn't have felt it anyway—his head swam from the overwhelming pressure of the other man inside him and the familiar sound of his panting breath.

He turned his head to catch the fairy's lips in a kiss and cried out at the fervent thrust the affection caused, and when Ciaran reached under him to stroke him, he almost finished at the first touch. He tried to hold back for the sake of his dignity, but Ciaran knew precisely how to squeeze him, and he knew just the right angle to hit the spot inside that turned his limbs to jelly. So when Ciaran whispered Trent's name against his cheek, he came, the half-strangled moan catching in his throat as he spilled his orgasm onto the blanket beneath him. Ciaran pushed himself upright and took a firm hold of Trent's ass with both hands, hauling him higher up on weak knees so that he could finish at his own hard pace.

It was all Trent could do to keep from lurching forward into the back of the tent; he didn't have the strength left to grip too tightly to the blankets, but Ciaran's body was just as eager as his own. Within a few more thrusts, the fairy gave a low, panting growl, and Trent felt the tight clamping of his fingers, the stilling of his hips, and the pulsing of his cock as he finished inside him. He steadied himself for a few moments before easing himself free of his lover and dropping down onto the furs beside him.

Their heaving breaths and sweat-damp bodies had made the air in the tent warm despite the cold wind outside, but neither of them minded. Ciaran gathered Trent to him and laid his cheek on the boy's hair, breathing deeply, as if he still hadn't had enough of his scent. Trent smiled, his fingers curling against the fairy's chest. He flinched a little when his fingers brushed one of the welts near his shoulder, and Ciaran leaned back to look down at him, seeming to study his face with a tense anxiety Trent had never seen before.

"Does it hurt you?" Ciaran asked. "Shall I fetch Airmed?"

"It's okay," Trent answered, mostly honestly. "It's...a couple days old now, and they did treat it. It's just tender."

Ciaran opened his mouth to speak, then seemed to stop himself, letting his hand rest gently at the side of Trent's neck as he leaned forward to allow their foreheads to touch. Trent flattened his hands against the fairy's chest and listened to his unsteady breath, the tension that had been settled deep in his own shoulders for days all but gone now that he was in Ciaran's arms again.

"I'm okay," Trent promised him. "Hathuwulf is good, really—I didn't have it so bad while I was gone."

The second he said Hathuwulf's name, the fairy's fingers tightened, and his brow furrowed against Trent's. Ciaran's voice was quiet and haggard when he spoke again.

"Did he touch you?"

Trent went still, and he frowned as he pulled back far enough to see the tortured look on his lover's face. *That* was what he was worried about? Trent was in danger of being killed from the second he'd left the camp. He was enslaved and whipped. He was lucky to have been returned to Ciaran without a fuss—and the fairy was worried that he might have *cheated?* Or that someone else might have laid hands on what was his? Was that why he'd been so eager to get Trent back into bed—to lay his claim?

"Did he touch you?" Ciaran pressed. "A mhuirnín, please—"

"Are you serious? You're asking if I *fucked* him? I could have died!"

The fairy huffed at him. "Well I can see that you're not *dead*," he sighed. "But I can't see if he—" He stopped and pressed his lips together to swallow, dropping his eyes from Trent's face to his chest. "You were his *property*, or he thought so, and...if I'd failed to protect you from that, I..." Ciaran shook his head. "I'm sorry. I don't mean to say—I'm not—trying to accuse you of anything, I only...his name leaves your lips so easily—"

Trent softened a little as the depth of the other man's suffering became clearer on his face. This wasn't about cheating. "He didn't touch me," he said, as gently as he could. "It wasn't like that at all."

Ciaran's whole body seemed to slump with relief. "Trent," he murmured in a weary voice. "The way he looked at you, and how comfortable you seemed with him, after just a few days—a man who should have been your enemy, and instead..."

"Stop," Trent whispered. He touched Ciaran's jaw and leaned in to close the gap for him, holding the fairy in a long, breathless kiss. He pulled back to look the other man in the eyes and saw the uncertainty lingering there, and his chest felt warm. "He's not a cruel person," he said, "and he listened when I talked to him about the war. We got along, I guess, but I wouldn't even call him a *friend*, just..." He gave a small shrug. "I...respect him. And maybe he thinks a little differently about humans than he did before."

Ciaran's lips curled into a faint smile at last. "You're older than I left you," he said softly.

Trent frowned. "What does that mean?"

"*You* did this," he answered. He ran a gentle hand over Trent's hair. "You brought peace here. And you're surely the reason the prince agreed to free the Alfar's slaves. I was just trying to keep you safe, but...it was wrong of me to hold you back. I hope you can forgive me," he added softly, his thumb brushing Trent's cheek by his ear. "For not seeing clearly all that you're capable of."

Trent stared at him, heart thumping heavily in his chest and a flush rising quickly up his neck and over his face. He managed to swallow down the worst of his embarrassment before speaking. "I—don't say stupid things," he grumbled, shoving lightly at the fairy's chest.

Ciaran only smiled, refusing to be moved, and he pulled Trent closer again to kiss him despite the boy's wriggling. "I was worrying about you for days, you little shite," he went on, hauling the smaller man over on top of him with an easy grip around his waist. "The least you can do is let me praise you."

Trent fought the fairy's hold but gave up after a few moments, slumping down against him with a faint scowl as Ciaran patted his head.

"There's a good lad."

"Yeah, thanks; I managed to go a few days without supervision and not die. Good for me."

"Good for us both," Ciaran chuckled. "I'm still not entirely clear on this spell situation we're in, but I'm fairly sure that if you die, I die—so I'm more than a mite glad to see you home safe."

Trent pinched one of the fairy's nipples so hard that he yelped, but he was laughing as he set the boy free and sat up himself. Trent leaned over to find his last remaining shirt rumpled under Ciaran's discarded belt and pulled it over his head with a huff, then gingerly laid on his back just long enough to pull his pants back up. Ciaran caught him when he sat up again, both hands on his cheeks, and placed another deep kiss on his lips.

"I love you, a mhuirnín. I'm proud of you."

Trent finally gave in, letting a sigh escape through his nose as he took a light hold of Ciaran's wrist. "I love you," he admitted in return. "And I'm...glad everything worked out the way it did. Before anyone else had to get hurt."

"Maybe they'll build a statue of you."

"Oh my god, shut up." He shoved Ciaran away from him by the face and only winced a little as he climbed out of the tent to go clean himself up.

30

By the time Noah was conscious again, the brothers had already changed guard in the basement twice. Joseph called and said he'd told the staff at the hospital that Edouard had been the victim of a hit and run. He was sleeping now, but Noah's assessment had been correct—his right leg had been amputated above the knee. He would need to be in the hospital for a few days, at least. Arnaud, Laurent, and Hugo took turns going to visit him, but Julien refused to leave the house as long as Agvithr was in it.

The Alfar prince didn't seem to have anything to say to any of them. Noah brought food and drink down to the basement for him, but he sat still in the metal chair in the corner of the room, not even acknowledging the plate Noah set down. The guard's body had been cleaned thoroughly and covered with a sheer, shimmering barrier of magic—to keep it from decaying until he could be buried, Noah guessed. But he'd seen the kind of magic this alfar could do; there was no chance he was focusing this hard just to maintain such a barrier. Noah was being ignored.

"I know it won't mean much," the witch offered quietly as he neared the door, "but I really am sorry for your loss. I wish no one had had to die."

He waited while the prince took another slow, silent breath

without moving, and then he left him.

Julien met Noah outside the door. "Has he said anything?"

He shook his head. "I don't think he wants to talk to me. I don't blame him. *You* definitely shouldn't go in there."

"I didn't plan on it. What do we do with him, now that we have him? How are we supposed to get him back home?"

Noah sighed lightly and looked down at the floor with his hands on his hips. "The only thing I can think to do is try to ask Sabin. He and Lugh were going to the same place, at least. I'll write a note." As he climbed the stairs again, he muttered, "We really need to get Lugh a cell phone or something."

He tore a page from one of his notebooks in Julien's room and sat down at the desk to write.

Sabin—is Lugh with you? We have an Alfar here who is apparently a prince. He surrendered and wants to go home. Will you see if Lugh can come pick him up or something? We don't have any way to get him back to Lochlann. Please tell me everything is ok with you.

Much love,

Noah

When he opened the box to send the message, he paused at the sight of a slip of paper inside, then snatched it up. Sabin's handwriting—but not much information. *I'll see you soon.*

Noah gave a soft exhale. "You'd better," he murmured, then shut his own note inside the small chest and watched the silver dogs slip back onto their bellies.

He listened on the bed for the soft snick of the moving box, and his fingers fumbled in his haste to open it when the sound of a reply finally popped in the quiet room.

Lugh said he'll come back to collect him. We're a few hours away from New Zealand, and we'll take the fairy road back to Montreal. He says don't meet us at the tower. We'll come to you.

Noah heaved out the air in his lungs. Sabin was safe. He was coming home.

The next few hours were misery—Noah waited on the bed with his fingers drumming on his stomach, then began to linger in the front hall and listen for sounds from outside, and finally stepped fully out of the house and planted himself on the front stoop. His heels tapped on the stone, fingers laced and pressed between his knees, until at last, a familiar figure appeared at the end of the street. Noah shot to his feet and rushed down the sidewalk, shouldering his way past Lugh's broad frame and latching onto Sabin just too late to hear his panicked yelp of "Wait—"

As soon as Noah gripped him, the boy winced and swore, so Noah took him by the shoulders instead for inspection. "I'm so sorry—are you okay? God, look at you." He touched Sabin's chin to turn his face, examining the yellowing bruise on his cheek, but the boy scoffed softly and brushed him away, focusing on pressing a firm hand to a spot on his chest.

"We just finished a huge demon war, okay? We're all a bit scuffed."

"Then you need lots of rest," Noah insisted, barely acknowledging the other boys or the fairy general as he dragged Sabin by the hand back toward the house. Julien was in the doorway now, waving the rest of the gathering inside while Noah ushered his young charge up the stairs and into the bedroom.

Noah's hands shook as he gathered his supplies to tend to Sabin's injuries, and he had to make himself take a steady breath. He was here now. He was safe. Noah forced a calmness he didn't feel into his voice as he caught Sabin up on what he'd missed, but the facade crumbled when he helped the boy out of his shirt to tend his hidden bruises. One side of his chest was nothing but a nebula of red and purple. Noah swallowed to keep down the tears that welled up in his eyes, but when he looked up into Sabin's face, the boy was smiling.

"Did you know that magic fur you gave me stops bullets?"

"You got *shot?*" Without waiting for the answer, Noah turned to dig back in his bag for a more potent salve. He barely had enough attention for conversation after that—he answered Sabin's questions while he worked, but his focus was on the boy's broken skin, his mind running wild with terrible visions of what he must have gone through. It wasn't until Sabin's voice got softer that Noah finally paused.

"I really hated that letter you sent me."

Noah kept his eyes on the young witch's broken skin. "I'm sorry," he said, a little mechanically. He wasn't going to keep it together if he looked into Sabin's face now.

"That's not the sort of apology I want. Seriously, Noah," Sabin pressed, and Noah had no choice but to peek up at him. "You were writing me a goodbye letter?" The boy glared at him with a frown barely softened by the redness touching his eyes, and Noah pulled back from him in shame.

"I...didn't know what was going to happen," Noah admitted through a tight throat. He looked down at his hands and wrung his oiled fingers. He'd been too obvious—let his anxieties seep through despite his intentions. "I wanted to...I didn't want you to be worried about me. But I was scared," he admitted in a softer voice. "I was trying not to show it, but I guess...I didn't do such a good job."

Sabin was silent for a few agonizing seconds, and Noah kept his eyes lowered. Then Sabin snorted. "You're really the worst liar I've ever met, so I don't know why you even tried."

"I was treating you like a kid again," Noah murmured. He risked a guilty look up at the boy and sighed lightly under his mildly teasing gaze. "I was trying to hide the truth from you. But...you're not a kid anymore. I should have known better." His brow furrowed. "But it's hard not to want to shield you from...everything, you know? I'm sorry."

Sabin shook his head with a small, weak laugh. "You know," he began quietly, "it wasn't until I'd been at Haven for a while that I realized how *much* you'd been shielding me. When I realized that you were giving up our heating to buy me textbooks. How sometimes I'd hear your stomach growling after I'd had a proper meal. I guess lying to a kid is much easier."

Noah reached out for his hands and clutched them tighter than he meant to. "I never meant it to be like lying to you," he insisted. "Just—a kid should be a kid, and you'd already had it so tough, I just wanted to—"

"I'm not mad you were lying," Sabin assured him, and Noah exhaled with relief as the boy gave his hands a gentle squeeze. "I just don't want you to think you have to give everything up for me." He tilted his head to catch Noah's teary gaze. "We can, like...make sure the heat's on together, now. Or something," he added with an awkward shrug.

Noah managed a quiet laugh, and he released Sabin's hands to wipe at his eyes with the back of one wrist. "Deal," he said with a nod.

It was relaxing just to chat together as Noah finished slathering up the boy's bruises and cuts—and they had all the time in the world now.

A sharp knock on the door interrupted them, and Laurent leaned into the room. "Uh, Noah—one of the people in the other room is missing an arm. Or most of one. There's a lot of blood on him. Don't know if it's still bleeding."

"What?" Noah wiped his hands on his jeans and rose from the bed to snatch up his bag from the floor nearby. "Why didn't anybody tell me someone lost an *arm*?" He squeezed past Laurent in a hurry and jogged down the hallway to the open bunk room door.

The boys had spilled all over the beds in various states of exhaustion—and they'd gained a few new additions, including one with a set of large, black wings and horns that curled close to his ears. That must be Cole. But the man who drew Noah's attention, lying in one of the lower bunks in bloodstained clothing, was an adult. Noah set down his bag and knelt on the floor, focused on getting the stranger's stiff, browned shirt away from his skin so he could get a better look at the injuries beneath. A boy with long, strawberry blond hair helped him strip off the fabric and tossed it aside for him.

"Is this all *his* blood?" Noah asked, and the man gave a faint, wry smile.

"It's really not as bad as it looks," he answered. "Someone's already tended to it."

The man's arm had been severed between the shoulder and elbow, and while the wound looked fresh, it seemed to have been sealed— almost cauterized. Whatever had happened, the man had lost a good amount of his blood. He was pale and clammy, and his hair was slicked back from his face with sweat. Noah leaned over the bed to check him for fever and hesitated as he met the stranger's eyes. *Was* this a stranger? His voice, quiet and weary, tickled the back of Noah's mind.

He didn't feel hot, and none of his wounds seemed to be open, but Noah had no doubt his body was in shock. So he plucked a small glass vial from his bag and unscrewed the cap, then shifted to help the man raise his head to drink.

"This should help you rest. Just take it easy."

His hand shook while he drained the tonic, and he seemed grateful to rest his head back on the pillow when Noah released him. The witch still had a frown on his face as he tucked the empty bottle back in his bag.

Milo hovered over Noah's shoulder with concern etched in his brow. "Don't you think you should go to the hospital, Mr. Shipton?"

Noah froze with his hand still in the bag at the sound of the man's name. Shipton.

"I don't think the hospital will do much more than rest will," Shipton answered. "And having to explain how I lost a whole arm will be another issue I don't have the energy for."

Noah's fingers curled into tight fists as he eased his hands back to his knees, and he didn't look back at the man in the bed as he slowly pushed up to his feet, bag in hand. He did know this man. But now wasn't the time.

"Anyone else injured?" he asked, turning his back on the man in the bed.

Every one of the boys had at least some cuts and bruises, so Noah pasted on bandages or smoothed oils onto each of them in turn. While he was finishing patching up the large, silent boy, Cole leaned down close to him to catch his eye.

"Um, excuse me," the boy began, so Noah gave the burly boy's wrist a pat to indicate he was done. "I'm not hurt, but I was wondering if you could help with this?" Cole held open the unzipped top half of the winter coat he still wore, exposing the golden collar attached to the other end of the matching chain in his hand.

"Oh, Jesus," Noah said, immediately reaching for the collar to lift it from the boy's neck and peer at it. He almost bumped into Bastian as he drew close, the blond was so eager to look along with him. "Is it magic? This might be a problem for a saw, not for me."

"I don't think it's magic," Cole answered, and he lifted the end of the chain to show where the end link had been twisted free. "Do you have a saw, then?" he asked with a light laugh.

"I'm sure," Noah said, finding a matching smile on his lips. He glanced over his shoulder and waved Laurent over, and the hunter gestured for Cole to follow him. The boy swatted Bastian's rear with the end of the chain on his way out, making the blond jump. He tried to follow, but Cole gave him a small, staying wave and a smile, so he stayed back.

On their way out, Noah heard Laurent ask, "Is that *real* gold?"

"Hey," Bastian started quietly, drawing Noah's attention back to him. "I really appreciate everything you and the others have done for us. I'm sure it didn't seem that way when we were last here, and I'm really sorry for that." The boy hesitated, eyes flicking down to the floor before meeting Noah's gaze again. "I know you've already given us a lot, but do you think you might have a spare change of clothes for Cole? He's, uh...the clothes he has now...he just needs something to change into."

Noah softened a little. This boy had grown up some since he'd been here last. "It sounds like we have a lot to thank you guys for," Noah answered gently. "I'm happy to help. I'll find some things for him."

"Thank you," Bastian said earnestly, though he still wrung his hands and glanced toward the door. "Really."

"You guys get some rest, okay? We'll have some dinner soon." Noah gave Bastian's arm a reassuring squeeze, and he risked a glance at the man in the bed before scooping up his things and heading for the door. He wished Shipton had bled more.

31

Julien led Lugh down the basement stairs and to the door containing their unhappy guest.

"He said his name is Agvithr. He's the one who was opening the portal every night. You sure you want to just take him back?"

"My inclination is not to," Lugh admitted. "Him or his father. But acting on that inclination could lead to a more drawn-out war—one that may spill beyond their island to mine. The demon has no recourse without the Alfar's aid, so I don't anticipate any continuing trouble on that front. Huldrekall lost one son to this war already—we shall see how he feels about keeping the others when we return to Lochlann."

"What does that mean?"

"A king with no heirs has greater concerns than making war on other nations. Even an ageless ruler must secure his legacy against unforeseen ends. Without an heir, that means dealing with endless squabbling and conspiracy. Huldrekall will either stand down, or he'll end up with his hands full."

Julien glanced toward Hugo standing guard and found a frown matching his own. Probably better to keep the possibility of Lugh murdering their captive from Noah. He looked back up into the tall fairy's face. "What about when it's all done? You'll go back to Tír na nÓg ?"

"I'll go home," Lugh corrected. "But home is not Tír na nÓg . I've had my fill of politics for this century."

"Then...I'm not likely to see you again, am I?"

When Lugh glanced down at him with one eyebrow faintly ticked, Julien grimaced and cleared his throat, suddenly aware of how he'd sounded.

"I'm sure our paths will cross again, mo chara," the fairy said, giving Julien a light clap on the shoulder that still made him lurch. "Let's have this prince."

Julien nodded, glad to turn away from him, and he tapped Hugo's arm to urge him away from the metal door.

"I don't think he's had anything to eat or drink," Julien said as he unlocked the door. "But he hasn't given us any trouble, either."

"If he behaves himself going forward, he may even make it home," the fairy said dryly.

Julien hauled the door open and let Lugh inside. As expected, the food Noah had brought sat untouched on the table, and the alfar didn't seem to have moved from his place at the far side of the room. His eyes lifted to Lugh as he filled the doorway.

"Agvithr oðlingr," the fairy greeted him—notably without a hint of deference. "I am Lugh Lámfada, Ollamh Érenn of the Tuatha Dé Danann. The demon Ashmodai has been defeated, and King Huldrekall has surrendered to me. This war is over."

"It's about time," Agvithr sighed, and he pushed himself up with hands on his knees. He paused a moment to brush the hem of his tunic and straighten his shoulders before looking up into Lugh's face. "My father isn't dead, then?"

"No."

The prince gave a small snort. "Shame. After all this, he'll still end up starving the ravens." He gestured toward the body on the table. "My general is to be returned home with me."

Lugh's eyes flicked over the corpse, and he gave a brief nod. "Agreed."

The door at the top of the stairs swung open with a faint creak, drawing Julien's attention back to the corridor. Laurent was guiding one of the boys into the basement—the demon. His black-feathered wings filled the stairwell, and as he reached the bottom step, he scanned the room with wide, dark eyes set in a porcelain face and framed by curling horns. He smiled cheerfully at the waiting men and let Laurent go past him into the armory.

Laurent reappeared a moment later with a handsaw, and the curious furrow in Julien's brow lifted in surprise as the demon shed his heavy parka. It took him a few awkward seconds to untangle his wings from the coat, during which the scant nature of the clothes beneath became embarrassingly apparent. It was more like a robe or a dressing gown than real clothing—just dark teal fabric draped over narrow shoulders and cinched at the waist, leaving the boy's legs exposed by body-length slits at the sides. He held the end of a gold chain attached to a collar around his neck, which he shifted away from his skin with a small wince of discomfort.

Hell was a very different place from what Julien had imagined it was.

Laurent had stopped his approach mid-step, the handsaw hanging at his side. After a heavy, awkward pause, the demon gently jangled his chain at the staring hunter, and Laurent seemed to remember himself.

"Here," he said in what seemed to Julien a strangely tight voice, and the demon followed him back through the door into the armory.

Julien glanced over his shoulder at Lugh before moving to the door himself, Hugo right at his side, just in time to see the demon lower himself onto one of the low metal benches. He bent close to the edge with wings held aloft so that Laurent could steady the metal around his neck before touching it with the saw, silky fabric falling away from slender white thighs as he settled. Laurent didn't move for what felt like too long. The demon's black eyes turned up to him, and heavy lashes blinked slowly as a small, sympathetic smile touched his lips.

"Ready when you are," the demon murmured, and Laurent again started back to reality.

With a focused frown, Laurent began to saw, the heavy, scraping vibration filling the room. He made quick work of the collar—it snapped away from the demon's pale throat after only a minute or so of fervent sawing, and when it clanked to the floor, the boy rose with a bright smile as he touched his newly-free neck with his fingertips.

"Thanks! You can keep that, in case it is real."

Laurent only nodded, and the demon excused himself, brushing past Julien with another friendly smile and scooping up his abandoned parka on his way back up the stairs. Julien watched him go, then exchanged a look with Lugh, who gave a small shrug. Agvithr stood in the doorway now, watching the demon's exit. The alfar snorted.

"They didn't send *me* any ones like that."

Lugh turned to look down at him. "Your father is waiting."

Agvithr glanced back into the room, and with a soft hum and a gesture, lifted the body of his slain general from the table and carried it along with him while he followed the fairy up and out of the basement.

Julien spared one more look between his brothers, but it was impossible to tell which of the three of them was most uncomfortable. Finally, Julien broke away from the tense silence and took the basement steps two at a time back into the main hall.

Noah was happy to spend the time before dinner just talking with Sabin, but he couldn't shake the prickling anger at the back of his neck. He'd smiled and chatted with Cole when he brought a change of clothes for him, and he'd said goodbye to Lugh and unsuccessfully attempted to speak to Agvithr one last time—but something sick built inside of him all the while.

When Hugo shouted up the stairs that dinner was ready, Noah let Sabin out ahead of him and watched the other boys file out of the bunk room down the hall. They all talked and laughed, the relief among the young men palpable after the friction of their last visit. But Noah couldn't share their cheer.

In the main hall of the house, while the group filtered into the dining room, Noah hung back, his eyes on the back of the one-armed man. Shipton had been given a change of clothes, too, and he'd been washed clean of blood, but he still walked unsteadily.

"Hey," Noah spoke up before he could round the corner to the kitchen. "Do you have a second?"

Shipton paused to look back at him. He urged the redhead next to him into the kitchen with the others, and once he was alone with Noah in the corridor, he followed the witch through the open study door. Noah stood silent while Shipton passed him, then slowly shut the door and leaned against it with his hands still squeezing tight on the knob behind him.

Shipton slid his remaining hand into his pants pocket and looked evenly across at Noah. He looked a bit lopsided with just the one arm—but Noah still recognized his casual, haughty stance. The careful slick of his hair. He'd seen it in his own apartment, years ago. Shipton had been younger, then. So had Noah. Younger, and dumber. More gullible. He'd listened like an idiot while Shipton poured promises into his ear. Assurances. Every word had been a lie.

"So," the man started, "how have you been, Mr. Clark? Didn't expect to see you on the other side of the country."

The easy tone in his voice churned Noah's insides. Before he knew what he was doing, he'd thrown out his hands, sending Shipton crashing ungracefully across the surface of the desk and pinning him upside down against the far wall. The man grimaced, taking sharp, pained breaths, but his suffering couldn't reach the witch who held him.

"You—you *liar!*" Noah shouted, hating the catch in his voice. "You fucking—snake! You told me he'd be safe! You told me this would be best for him!"

Shipton cringed at the pressure keeping him suspended, his grey eyes watching Noah with what might have been resignation. But he stayed silent.

"Nothing?" Noah huffed out a scoff. "Nothing at all? You stole him from me! You ruined his childhood and almost got him killed, and you don't even have anything to fucking say?"

Shipton's chin tilted upward just slightly, and when he finally spoke, it was through gritted teeth. "I don't think there's anything I could say that you would want to hear."

"You—" Noah scowled across the room at him, his fingers tightening at his sides. The little grunt of pain from the man he held didn't move him. "How many children's lives did you destroy?" He couldn't keep the ache or rising tears out of his own voice. "I was the only family he had, and you just—"

Behind him, the study door slammed open, and Noah heard the footsteps of people behind him but kept his eyes on Shipton's tight-jawed face.

"Noah," Julien called sharply. "What are you doing?"

"What he deserves!" the witch snapped back. "This—he showed up and said he was from some special program, where—where Sabin would be safe, where he'd be taken care of and taught, not—not—not thrown in front of monsters with a bunch of fucking kids! *Kids!*" he spat, his voice ragged as he stared at the man on the wall.

Something touched Noah's balled fist, and he jumped. Sabin was next to him, gently squeezing Noah's hand in both of his and looking up at him with a quiet frown.

"You said not to use this on people," the young witch murmured, so quietly that Noah ached.

"But it's all his fault," Noah protested, hurt and anger almost choking him. It felt like a lie. It wasn't Shipton's fault. Not really.

"Hurting him won't fix that." Sabin eased Noah's tight fingers apart and laced them with his own. "He helped us, too. We couldn't have gotten to Ashmodai without him. Noah, please," he added softly. "I don't want you to do this."

Noah hesitated, guilt filling him so full he could barely breathe. He let Shipton drop to the floor in a heap and squeezed Sabin's hand, unable to hold in his small hiccup as he wiped uselessly at his eyes. "I'm sorry."

Sabin let out his held breath and pulled Noah's head to his shoulder, allowing the older witch to catch him in a hug Noah hoped was tight enough to convince him he'd never let go again.

The boy with the red hair edged by them and lifted Shipton to his feet by his one good arm, pulling it over his shoulders to help him out. "You deserved that, you know," he muttered, and Shipton snorted softly.

"Yeah," Noah barely heard him agree from the hall. At least he knew it.

He was reluctant to pull back from Sabin, but when Julien lightly touched his elbow, Noah slowly eased his grip.

"Do you want me to just bring some food upstairs for you?"

Noah didn't quite manage a smile, but he nodded and wiped at the fading tears on his cheeks. "That...would be good." He gave Sabin's shoulders one more squeeze, urged him toward the kitchen with the others, and retreated upstairs to Julien's bedroom. He wasn't helping Sabin by being this way. If the boy was prepared to let go and move on, then Noah owed it to him to do the same, didn't he?

32

Julien was out a place to sleep again. With Sabin back, he would have to give up his spot in his own bedroom to make room for the pair of witches. He didn't mind—though Noah seemed to be working through some guilt about his young friend's absence, he was obviously ecstatic to have him home safe. Julien would happily change his sleeping arrangements to give them time to catch up. Even if the bunk room was more than a little crowded now.

The boys had paired off much the same as they had the last time they were here—with the new additions taking their places with their chosen partners. Julien guessed when you put a bunch of teenagers in an isolated bunker together for long enough, it was bound to happen. He just hoped they were all polite enough to keep it to themselves as long as he was sharing the room with them.

Julien managed to fall into a light, wary sleep despite the number of people around him—he knew, rationally, that the major threat was over. Even if he hadn't seen the portal close himself, Lugh saying that the matter was dealt with was enough for him. But it was still hard to relax after so many weeks on edge. He would feel better after these boys all went wherever they were going. The less time a demon spent in his house, the better—if he was still here when Edouard came home, it would be a fight for sure. Julien had already had to talk

Antony down more than once. And the boy seemed to be making Laurent exceptionally uncomfortable for some reason. The sooner they were on their way, the better.

The small click of the door shot Julien's eye open. No light came in from the dark hallway, but he heard quiet footsteps on the wooden floor and tracked the movement of the shadow that entered. The figure paused at one of the bunks and reached down to pat the lower bed's occupant, and after a quick exchange of hissing whispers, climbed in himself.

These fucking kids—

He stopped himself before he sat up. The only one who wasn't in here already was Sabin. And the one in the bunk he'd just slipped into—that was the one Noah had threatened before. The one with the tattoos. They hadn't seemed friendly before, but that had clearly changed.

Julien listened in silence for a while, but the boys whispered too softly for him to make much out. Sometimes the brief silences told him more than the whispering.

The room went fully quiet after some time, and Julien finally fell asleep. Sabin was nowhere to be seen when he woke up in the morning, and neither was the other one. A few of the beds were still filled, but faint noise from downstairs told him some of the guests had already started the day. He reached under the bunk where he'd left his phone and patch, then paused as he felt nothing but the screen of his phone. He bent down to look under the mattress. His patch was missing.

Not much of a mystery what probably happened there.

Julien stepped quietly out of the bunk room, slipping past the boys who were still sleeping, and knocked on his own bedroom door. When he got no answer, he peeked inside and found the bed empty. Chatting voices drifted upstairs from the hall, so Julien made his way down and into the kitchen, where Noah stood in front of a steaming pan with a large mixing bowl in one arm. The witch looked over his shoulder at Julien with a bright smile.

"Good morning!"

"Is it?" Julien grunted as he approached. "What are you doing?"

"Pancakes," Noah explained with a gesture toward the bubbling blobs on the pan.

"That's domestic."

Noah smiled. "Misplace your eyepatch?"

"About that," he snorted. "Did Sabin talk to you about that kid from before? The one you wanted to murder?"

"Yeah," Noah said as he flipped over the pair of pancakes. "Sabin said he'd been better since they left—why?" His brow furrowed with suspicion. "Did he do something?"

"Well, no. But...I think they've gotten more than friendly."

"What does that mean?"

Julien hesitated, not sure how to phrase what that meant in a way more delicate than he already had. "Last night, someone came into the room and got in bed with him. Unless you think it was one of my brothers, it must have been Sabin."

Noah went briefly still halfway to lifting a pancake onto the waiting plate, then carried on scooping the other one out of the pan. "Oh."

The hunter's heart grew tight in his chest. "Noah, he must have—"

He waved him away. "I know. Everything has been so crazy, and they only got back last night—" Noah offered him a smile that Julien half believed. "It's fine. But what does that have to do with your eyepatch?"

Julien stared flatly at him. "I just told you Sabin came into the room I was in last night. Three guesses."

"Don't hurt him."

"No promises." Julien smiled faintly and bent to kiss Noah's forehead, then turned to leave him to his cooking.

In the doorway to the hall, he collided with a smaller body and looked down to see Sabin stumbling a step back from him. The young witch looked up at him, one hand holding the side of his half-shaved head to keep Julien's slightly-t00-large eyepatch in place.

"Morning!"

Julien stared at him. "What do you think you're doing with that?"

Sabin gave a dramatic sigh. "Why does everyone keep asking me that? I'm looking for pirate treasure, *obviously*."

"Playtime's over." Julien held out a hand and twitched his fingers forward, waiting.

"It's a mutiny, is it?" the witch shouted too loudly, moving back into a wide stance and putting up his dukes. "There's only room for one captain on this ship!"

Julien inhaled slowly and ran his tongue over his bottom teeth, but he didn't move his extended hand.

"I'll have you thrown in the brig if you lay a hand on me!" Sabin circled his fists in front of him with his chin jut out—but as soon as Julien's foot scuffed on the wood, the witch scrambled so suddenly he almost had to catch himself on his hands on his way down the hall.

Julien shot forward and snatched him by the back of his shirt collar, stopping him short in a flail of limbs. Sabin struggled and cried mutiny, and once he caught Julien in the side of the head with a swinging arm, the hunter hauled him up like a wriggling cat and caught him in both arms, turning him upside down and giving one solid shake so that the eyepatch slipped off onto the floor.

"I'm so glad you two are getting along," Noah spoke up from the doorway, and both Julien and Sabin froze to look at him.

Sabin gave one last wiggle, and Julien dropped him to the floor more gently than he wanted to, then bent to scoop up his eyepatch before the witch could make off with it again.

"He started it," Sabin blatantly lied as he stood and dusted off the seat of his jeans.

"Come help me with pancakes," Noah said, urging Sabin to follow him with a small wave of his spatula.

Julien fixed his eyepatch back over his head as Sabin straightened beside him. The boy dug into his pocket, then held out a closed fist as if he had something to give. Julien was wary, but he held out his hand, and Sabin slapped a small, soft object into it.

"Some booty for ye," he said, a sly smirk on his face as he swung around on one foot and followed Noah into the kitchen.

Julien looked down at his gift—a keychain of a google-eyed kiwi bird wearing a t-shirt that said "I ♥ New Zealand." He closed his hand around it again and sighed, already weary down to his bones imagining the future in store for him.

Noah hurried across the room to flip his swiftly browning pancakes, and Sabin hopped up to sit on the counter nearby. It warmed Noah's heart to see him there, leaning on his hands like a little kid. He was twice the size he was the last time they'd eaten pancakes together, but hearing the soft sound of his heels against the cabinet doors made it seem like no time had passed at all.

Sabin was eager to talk about his adventure around mouthfuls of pancake—dotted with chunks of Reese's cups stolen from Julien's duffel. He regaled Noah with tales of hikes across New Zealand, battles with giant monsters, Alfar, and demons on a snowy tundra, and a sea voyage back to civilization. Some of it was hard to believe. A few times, Noah had to block out the mental images of the dangerous things Sabin casually described, but the young witch's pride at having stood his ground in the face of Hell itself put a smile on Noah's face.

The boys and the Fournier brothers still at home passed through to collect their plates—with the exception of the redhead, Alistair, who looked down his nose at the offered carbohydrates and took an apple from the counter instead. He still took a plate for Shipton, which Noah briefly considered poisoning. Anik seemed to have made friends with all of them already—her voice rose from the dining room louder than most. Noah chatted with some of the others as they came and went, but out of the corner of his eye, he caught Sabin's foot reaching out to tap the outside of Berlin's thigh as the tattooed boy approached. Berlin muttered a quick thanks with his eyes on the floor, only flicking a quick glance up at Sabin as he took his serving of pancakes. Noah thought he saw a hint of a smile on the other boy's lips as he turned away with plate in hand.

"You all really do seem to be getting along better now," Noah said once everyone else had been fed. "That's great."

"It's a relief," Sabin admitted. "I was about ready to jump in the ocean. Now I guess we all have to figure out what we do next."

"And Berlin hasn't been giving you any more trouble, right? You guys seem almost friendly now."

"You think so?" Sabin's gaze was on his empty plate as he dropped from the counter to place it in the sink. "Well, it's definitely better than it was. And that's what matters, right?" Before Noah could reply, Sabin jerked a thumb over his shoulder toward the door. "I'm going to go round up the dishes from the others; gimme a sec."

Then he was gone, and Noah gave a soft sigh through his nose as he set down his spatula and leaned his hip against the counter.

******

After breakfast had been cleaned up, and the various young men had begun to splinter off around the house, Noah caught Sabin on his way upstairs.

"Why don't we get out of here?" he asked, smiling at the curious tilt of the boy's head. "We can go see the city. Between the two of us, we might even know enough French to get by."

"Are there things to do other than smoke and drink wine?"

"There's a botanical garden, and—oh, there's actually this cool thing I saw while we were out one night. It's like a big ball that lights up all rainbow-colored. Julien says it's actually a science museum? I wanted to go. If...that sounds fun to you." Noah hoped his hesitation didn't show on his face. If Sabin didn't want to talk about his romantic life, that was up to him—he just hoped they hadn't grown farther apart than he thought.

"Man, I don't care what we do," Sabin answered with a chuckle. "Just the idea that I can go out whenever I want is enough. Even if we did just go smoking and wine tasting."

"Well wherever we go, on the way back we can stop and get a drink. I didn't get to buy you one on your birthday."

"I actually got to have my first legal beer already. While we were at the monastery Berlin took me to—" He stopped short and tried to casually wave away his mistake. "I mean, some of us went to this pub. Berlin showed us where it was."

"Oh," Noah said softly. He brightened his smile with some effort. "That's great. Well," he went on right away, "I can't guarantee anything in Quebec will be as good as German monastery beer, but maybe we can find a maple syrup shot or something."

Sabin paused, glancing between Noah's eyes as if he expected to be interrogated as he let out a small, awkward laugh. "I'm...gonna go take a shower before we go." With that, the boy took off up the stairs in a clamor of feet on wooden steps, leaving Noah to slump against the wall and sigh. This was going to be difficult.

He put on a smile as they left the house, but he soon didn't have to force it. Being out in the city with Sabin, exploring the museum, and just walking on the street together, talking about nothing and laughing—it felt like no time at all had passed. Noah held Sabin's hand without thinking to lead him to this or that exhibit, and the boy never fought him or tried to shake off his touch.

When they'd exhausted the museum's offerings, they walked along the river until they found a promising-looking place to get a drink. They took their places at the bar, and Noah offered Sabin the small menu of specialty cocktails while they waited for the bartender to get to them.

"Montreal has an official cocktail?" Sabin asked with a slight sneer. "That's so fucking French. I bet it's disgusting."

"Should we get one?"

"Oh, definitely."

"Shot first," Noah advised. "In case it's awful. We'll care less."

Noah smiled and did his best to communicate in French once the bartender approached, but, luckily, the man took pity on him and answered in English. Sabin hesitated for half a second before requesting scotch as his first shot, which Noah guessed would be a mistake but didn't argue with. He ordered vodka for himself, and one of the cocktails—which, in true pretentious fashion, was just called a *Montreal.*

"This isn't permission for you to start drinking all the time," Noah pointed out as he lifted his shot glass and clinked it softly against Sabin's. "But happy late birthday." He downed the liquor with a faint grimace and thunked the glass back onto the bar, snorting softly as Sabin coughed through his own.

"It's so weird seeing you take a shot," Sabin said once he'd sufficiently cleared his throat.

"I'm an old pro," Noah said with a wink that made them both laugh.

The martini glass placed in front of them a moment later was filled with a dark amber liquid, which Noah bravely tasted first. It was bitter and way too strong. He couldn't keep a straight face as he scooted the drink across to Sabin, but he did enjoy the dramatic gag the boy gave after his sip.

"Fucking French," Sabin snorted, and they both hid their laughter from the bartender as well as they could as Noah waved him over again to order another round. This time, Sabin tried to play off asking Noah for his recommendation rather than admit the scotch had been a little much for him, so Noah ordered them both peach schnapps instead. It went down easier, and they followed up with beers—which Sabin only smacked his lips at for the first few sips.

Noah smiled. He was still soft on the inside after all.

After a minute or so of quiet, Sabin looked down into his glass and turned it in a slow circle with his fingertips. "So," he began, "how did you know that you liked Julien?"

"Have you *seen* him?" Noah answered before he could stop himself, and he touched his lips with the back of his hand to hide his snort of laughter. "Sorry. You mean *like* like." He leaned an elbow on the bar. "Well. It started just because he let me come hunting with him, and I got to learn about all these creatures I'd only read about in books and never even knew if they were real or not before, you know? I got so many cool components," he added earnestly. "And whenever we were around something dangerous, he protected me. And not in a macho, you shouldn't be here kind of way—just..." Noah trailed off for a moment, smiling down into his beer. "He always protects people. He's always throwing himself under buses for people. One time literally. The point is, he always steps up, and he never complains. I knew that someone like that might...be willing to always step up for me, too."

Sabin gave a faked dry heave, but he had a smile on his face as Noah looked back up. "I'm sorry I asked."

Noah's smile turned sly, and he raised his eyebrows as he ran a casual fingertip around the rim of his glass. "How did you know you liked Berlin?"

The boy snorted into his next drink, spilling beer down the front of his shirt. He swore as he wiped at himself with the nearest bar napkin, keeping his eyes lowered. "Look, Noah," he began, but the explanation stopped there—he just frowned and awkwardly rubbed at the same damp spot on his shirt, seeming unable to find the words to continue.

Noah leaned over to him and reached out, cupping his cheeks in both hands and gently urging it upward so he could meet the boy's eyes. "Sabin. You don't have to tell me every single thing about your life. I'm never going to judge you for your decisions. You're a smart, brave, amazing man. I just want you to trust me enough that you *want* to share the big stuff. You know?"

Sabin rolled his eyes—the same way he always did when Noah complimented him—but he took a deep breath and let it out as Noah released him. He shook his head, his brow furrowed in what looked like guilt. "You know, Berlin actually told me the same thing—that I should just trust you not to get mad. If you can believe it."

"Maybe he does have more than two brain cells to rub together," Noah said, but he immediately shushed himself. "Sorry—sorry. I'm sure he's great. Go on."

"Well... I think we're gonna try to make something work. But I know you don't like him, so...I don't know. I guess it was hard to tell you."

"Sabin," Noah sighed. His own guilt settled in his stomach. What had he done to make Sabin feel comfortable talking to him? If he'd hidden it forever, it would have been on Noah. "Listen. All I know about this kid is that he insulted you. If he's apologized for that and you're satisfied, and you don't think he's going to do it again, then...the rest isn't really my business. I don't *not like him*. I don't even know him."

Sabin stared flatly at him. "You told him you were going to turn him inside out."

"He called you a mean name," Noah pointed out with a frown.

Sabin laughed, seeming more relaxed now. "Who knows? Maybe a good threat now and then will keep him in line. He's definitely got his flaws, but I've also seen him do the stupidest stuff to keep other people safe. Even if he doesn't like someone. Even if he knows he'll get hurt, he still..." Sabin paused, then snorted, obviously realizing his reason and Noah's were exactly the same. "That, and he's a surprising wealth of information when it comes to Catholic bullshit," he said more matter-of-factly, talking into his glass as he took another drink of beer. "And he has a good scream."

"I guess something has to keep him in line," Noah chuckled.

"I'll keep him in line if you keep Julien in line."

"Deal," Noah agreed before taking another drink.

"Berlin actually thinks Julien is pretty cool. For *some* reason," Sabin added dryly. "He said that he would like the sort of work Julien does. I told him already that I'm going wherever you're going, and the rest is up to him. But, if he wanted to come..." He stalled awkwardly, glancing down into his beer before peeking up at Noah's face.

Noah gave the boy his most reassuring smile. "I'm sure Julien could use some more muscle around sometimes."

Sabin allowed himself a brief, honest smile, then lifted his beer to his lips. "So how upset *would* you be if I told you details?"

"Pretty sure I *just* told you you don't need to tell me every single thing," Noah said in a rush. He paused to take a deep breath, correcting himself but not looking Sabin in the face. "Sex is natural, and healthy, and I am here if you ever have any problems you want to talk about, but it is also...none of my business."

"Does that mean you *won't* look at this rash for me?"

Noah's head whipped around. "He gave you a *rash*?"

Sabin laughed so earnestly that Noah's shoulders relaxed, and he smiled as he watched the boy drain his beer and lift a hand to the bartender to ask for another.

"Don't get ahead of yourself, cowboy," Noah said, though he also took a sip from the additional beer placed in front of him. "We don't have a lot of money."

"I still have Julien's card. That's, like, free money."

"No it's not! Julien doesn't have any money either!" Noah took another drink from his glass, then frowned pensively down at it. "Just...I'll take care of it. Don't worry."

Sabin eyed Noah with suspicion but didn't question him. They just enjoyed sitting together, Sabin much more open to telling every detail about his adventure now that he didn't have to pretend Berlin hadn't been there. He asked questions about the portal in the city, and they shared their mutual experience of Lugh purposely taunting their boyfriends.

When it was time to leave, Noah tried to get Sabin to go out ahead of him, but the young witch stayed right by him, watching over his shoulder as Noah neatly folded a clean bar napkin. He sharpened the crease with a pass of his palm, and as he did, the white paper changed into a crisp, peach-colored bill marked with the number fifty. The old man on it seemed to be staring out at Noah with as much scolding shame as Noah felt himself, but he smiled as he waved at the bartender and tucked the bill under his empty glass for collection.

Sabin kept it together until they were out the door, but then he erupted into cackling laughter, shaking Noah's elbow with both hands. "Julien doesn't have any money, so stealing is the answer? Holy shit." He heaved to breathe and wiped a fake tear from his eye. "That was amazing. Show me how to do that."

"Absolutely not." Noah hooked his arm in Sabin's and started down the street with purpose, as if he could outrun the conversation. "It's only for emergencies."

"Like *shots*?" More laughter fell out of the young witch, and he held his stomach as if it had started to hurt.

Noah sighed. "When we get home," he said loudly, over the top of Sabin's cackling, "we are going to meditate on the nature of need versus want." He tried to keep a straight face, but when he glanced over at the boy's smiling face, he felt a warmth settle over him that brought a matching smile to his lips.

33

The fairies held up their end of the treaty—as soon as Hathuwulf had delivered what looked to Trent like a massive pile of silver junk but Ciaran assured him was the promised wergild, or death price, of each slain man, the Tuath Dé began to lend their soldiers to the reconstruction of Falias. Servants joined the human farmers in clearing the burned land for replanting, and Airmed offered her help to the alfar healers.

The only thing there had been no progress on was the slavery issue. Ciaran argued against Trent even leaving their tent again, let alone the fairy camp, but with the fighting finished, there was nothing to keep him from walking right into the city along with the other foreigners to the island. The ramparts were left open, though still guarded, to allow easy passage for anyone moving supplies, so Ciaran begrudgingly rode through the broad gate with Trent in the saddle in front of him.

The city was a wreck; many buildings still stood, but hardly any had survived without damage. The market had been turned upside down, and the stable was still only a pile of cinders. The attack on the island had only lasted a few days—but Trent suspected the damage would take a lot longer to undo.

Ciaran hitched his horse outside the grounds of the Great Hall and presented himself to the guard at the door, who held up a hand to stop them going any further.

"The Crown Prince is in meeting with the Jarlar," the alfar said. "He is not taking audience."

"Then we'll wait," Trent said before Ciaran could answer.

The fairy looked over at him. "Will we?"

"Yes, we will. Unless you think one of your leaders is going to be the pushy one about making sure this part of the treaty actually happens?"

"Aye, not likely." Ciaran puffed out his cheeks and shrugged with his hands on his hips. "Waiting it is, then, I suppose."

The alfar guard didn't seem pleased about the way the pair lingered, quietly chatting and occasionally sniping at each other. But eventually the door to the Great Hall swung open, and a number of finely-dressed alfar filed out, some with deeper scowls than others. The last to appear in the entrance was Kothran, the prince's head of household. He paused when Trent approached him, but instead of objecting to the boy's presence, he merely sighed.

"I have been told to allow you access to his highness," he said, barely concealing the distaste in his voice. "Come if you must." He gave Ciaran a quick glance up and down, apparently finding him acceptable, and turned back into the Great Hall without waiting for them to follow.

Ciaran snorted his displeasure, but he let Trent lead the way into the hall. Hathuwulf sat at the far end of one of the long tables, just in front of the pair of empty thrones on the dais. Sheafs of paper lay around him, some tightly bound and others haphazardly piled. The prince tilted his head back to drain the last liquid from his carved silver cup and let it thunk back onto the heavy wooden table with a soft grunt. When he turned his eyes to the door, he seemed ready to dismiss any new visitors, but when he spotted Trent, his expression changed. He nodded his acceptance to Kothran and gestured to the bench across from him, inviting both Trent and Ciaran to sit. He looked tired, and significantly less princely than when Trent had first met him.

"I know why you've come," he said as they settled. He began to gather some of the parchment and tap it into a neater stack. "But these things take time."

"Do they?" Trent asked. "It seems like a pretty simple thing to say, 'hey, you're not slaves anymore.'"

"Doesn't it," the prince answered dryly. He set down his papers and tapped them lightly with one grey hand. "Every landowner in The Norðrvegr is about to be deprived of an appreciable amount of his property. They must all be compensated, or we risk either noncompliance or insurrection. There is significantly more *counting* involved in emancipation than I suspect you realize. In addition, hundreds of men and women are about to be set loose homeless on the island with not a single possession or means of life to their name—what shall I do with them? Without support and subsidy, what remains of our cities will be overrun with starving vagrants and we will *still* not have enough labor to till our fields. And, perhaps most importantly, I cannot legally enact this measure at all until my father returns—all I can do is prepare for the ramifications. So," he added with weary finality, "these things take time."

Trent skimmed the papers on the table with a frown. "Is there anything I can do to help?"

Hathwulf allowed himself a small exhale of amusement. "Not unless you happen to be exceptionally good with finances."

Trent paused. A beat passed, and then he looked up into the prince's face, a quiet, unintentional laugh falling from him. "Actually, I am."

Before the prince could respond, the door swung open with a loud creak and thud, and Kothran reappeared in the Great Hall.

"Yðar hátign," he said in a rush, "a ship approaches Falias from the South—the lookout claims it is Lugh Lámfada. It will land any moment!"

Hathuwulf's face fell into its prior, public sternness, and he rose from his seat without a word. He picked up his shield, bow, and quiver from where they lay near the door and strapped them swiftly to their places, then stalked from the hall. By the time Ciaran and Trent got out after him, all they saw was the dark tail of his buckskin horse disappearing at a gallop down the street.

"Well," Ciaran said, "let's go see if it's good news or bad." He helped Trent up onto the saddle with him and took off after the prince.

Word had apparently spread fast—they were soon joined by other fairies and alfar on horseback, all making their way toward the rocky shore to get a look at the incoming ship. Trent recognized the ox skull at the bow of the ship right away, and they arrived on the cliffs just in time to see the vessel slide onto the dark sand. Lugh wasn't alone. Two fairy soldiers stood at either end of the ship, and between them, a pair of alfar bound in chains sat grimly on the center bench. One of them could only be King Huldrekall—Trent had only seen him once, and that had been enough to burn that hateful scowl into his memory forever—but he didn't know the other.

Lugh and the guards escorted the king and the other important-looking prisoner from the ship with what Trent thought was probably more dignity than they deserved, and two other alfar were permitted to approach. They carried between them a cloth-covered burden hefted gently from the ship. A body.

Hathuwulf waited on the bank, his horse fidgeting beneath him, but he dismounted when Lugh approached him. Trent leaned forward against the pommel to try to hear better.

The prince spoke first. "I am Hathuwulf Huldusson, Mjötuðr of The Norðrvegr. I am at the service of the Ollamh Érenn."

Lugh acknowledged him with a brief nod. "King Huldrekall has conceded his defeat," he said loud enough for everyone gathered to hear. "The demon Ashmodai is vanquished, and the matter is no more. The remaining Lochlannan soldiers will be returned home upon the arrival of my ships," he went on just a little quieter, his eyes on Hathuwulf alone now.

"The Tuatha De Danann are generous in victory," the prince replied, and Lugh tilted his head slightly as he looked at him.

"So we are."

The High King and his brothers arrived and rode down the bank to meet their general, but Hathuwulf didn't give them time to speak.

"May I request the witness of the Ævintýri?"

The fairies paused, and Lugh's eyebrows raised faintly. He exchanged a brief glance with the kings before nodding.

"I will witness," he said.

"Witness what?" Trent whispered over his shoulder, but Ciaran was staring down at the beach with a curious frown.

Hathuwulf moved from his horse to stand in front of his father. With a glance, he commanded one of the standing fairies to unfasten the silver chains holding the king, and he gave Huldrekall a moment to rub at his wrists and shake free the weight of his bondage.

"Huldrekall Eiðsson," the prince said, his voice clear and steady over the soft wash of the waves, "you have allowed the people of The Norðrvegr to pay the cost of your vanity. You are not a man's equal and not a man at heart."

A hush fell over the gathered alfar and fairies alike, and Huldrekall's face twisted with fury. The still-bound man next to him took a broad sidestep to distance himself from the conversation, his lips pursed and his eyes on the dark sand.

"I am as much a man as you," the king growled in return.

Hathuwulf nodded, as though expecting this response, and he turned to face the alfar soldiers and nobles assembled along the cliff with a fierce shout. "Hólmganga!"

Many of the alfar called out in response, but Trent couldn't tell if it was an agreement or not. He shifted in the saddle to look back at Ciaran.

"What the hell is happening? What's Hólmganga?"

"It's a duel," Ciaran answered in a low voice. "He's going to fight his father for the crown."

Trent had to push through a thick, murmuring crowd to get close enough to see the open arena, but Ciaran helped him shoulder his way in. Six tall stone spires marked the boundaries of the clearing, and Hathuwulf stood at one end, facing King Huldrekall at the other. Both of them held round shields and longswords, and their faces had been marked with kohl—the king's eyes and forehead had been entirely blackened, and Hathuwulf wore five thick lines down his nose and cheeks to his chin, as if painted there by a single swipe of the hand. But while Huldrekall seemed as if he might bite, gnashing his teeth and spitting into the ground, Hathuwulf stood still, his dark eyes focused and his expression calm. How long had he been planning to do this?

Lugh stood between them, arms folded, and he glanced between the two men. "The fight must remain within the circle," he began evenly, as if he oversaw royal duels all the time. "To step outside is to acknowledge defeat. To kill within is to claim victory. Let it be done," he finished, and he stepped back into the space that opened for him between two of the stones. The other alfar prisoner from the boat stood beside him, unchained now and watching the prince with keen interest.

Trent's breath went just as silent as the men around him. Huldrekall lunged first, a shout of rage ripping from his throat as his sword slammed into the prince's shield. It was hard to even tell what was happening—both men moved faster than Trent could keep up with. Every strike rang loud in the cold air, and the king's growling yells put a shiver in Trent's skin. Hathuwulf stumbled once when his father's sword cut into the meat of his leg, but he pushed back, his own roar shaking Trent's bones as his next blow split the king's shield. When Huldrekall tossed it aside, Hathuwulf matched him, discarding his own protection and instead taking his sword in both hands.

Father and son seemed distressingly evenly matched—both men were bleeding within minutes, and both took heavy breaths in the scant seconds between strikes. But in a movement Trent could barely follow, Hathuwulf dropped his body low to dodge a swing, turned, and slid the edge of his sword along the backs of the king's knees. Huldrekall's legs failed, and he crumpled to the ground on hands and knees. He tried to rise and faltered, allowing the prince time to stand beside him.

Without hesitation, Hathuwulf raised his sword above his head and heaved it down, the blade slicing easily through the spine and muscle of King Huldrekall's neck to bury itself in the grass. The severed head rolled toward the edge of the arena to the feet of the alfar who stood beside Lugh, and his lip curled into an almost imperceptible sneer. He put one boot on Huldrekall's head and shoved it disdainfully back into the circle, then gave a soft snort and offered Hathuwulf a small bow of his head.

"Victory is sealed and witnessed," Lugh shouted, and the alfar and fairies in the crowd erupted into whoops and cries so loud that Trent flinched. His stomach lurched at the sight of dark blood still pouring from the now empty neck of the king—or, Trent guessed, the former king.

Hathuwulf stood tall at the center of the circle, clearly trying not to appear too out of breath. From the mass of people surrounding Lugh, an alfar in a fine robe stepped forward, and Hathuwulf knelt to allow him to place the heavy silver crown upon his head.

"Konungr Hathuwulf Stöðugan!" the official cried as the new king rose, his voice almost overwhelmed by the shouts of the crowd.

Trent realized he'd been squeezing Ciaran's hand so tightly that now it stung to ease his fingers free. As Hathuwulf turned slowly to pass his eyes over the gathered spectators, his gaze paused on Trent just long enough to acknowledge the smile of relief on the boy's face.

34

There was no fancy coronation for Hathuwulf. There was no party. Not even a funeral for the former king. Crowning King Hathuwulf with his father's corpse at his feet was apparently sufficient ritual for the Alfar. The one who had been brought back with the king was apparently Agvithr, Hathuwulf's younger brother, who—luckily— seemed to have precisely zero interest in attempting to pursue the throne for himself and only wanted to return to his home city of Murias and carry on as if the war had never happened. His third brother had been killed in battle, Trent heard. Other people would be promoted to leadership of Gorias and Findias, since now they were down one prince and Hathuwulf would live in the capital city full time.

Now the war recovery could begin in earnest. As Hathuwulf had promised, the fairies found the new king receptive to peace. Trent wanted to see him, to offer what help he could give, but now that he was King Hathuwulf, and not just Prince Hathuwulf, it felt silly to think Trent could just ask to talk to him.

He wasn't much use with the restoration of Falias itself, either— not when he was surrounded by Alfar and fairies with three times his strength. He helped Airmed when she asked, but even that was busy work. The fairies' magic was enough to heal the wounded now that there were no fresh patients coming in.

By the afternoon, Trent had apparently looked across the distance toward Falias enough that Ciaran sighed and hauled him up to his feet in the middle of rolling a bandage.

"Come on then," the fairy grumped as Trent looked at him in confusion. "Let's go see him."

"What? Why?"

"Because you've been slouching around here like a dog that's lost its master. I'm sure the new king will have some paperwork for you to do, if you ask."

Trent pulled his arm free as Ciaran tried to lead him on. "Since when are you *encouraging* me to be in the same room as Hathuwulf?"

"Someone in his position is far too busy to have an affair," Ciaran answered with a faint smirk. "But mostly, I can't bear to see you mope. Come along. At worst we'll be turned away."

Trent smiled, and he turned to drop his half-rolled bandage back into the basket before following Ciaran away toward the horses. He waited for Ciaran to mount himself, then accepted his hand up behind him.

Rathgeirr approached them before they could move, leading his own horse by the reins, and he stopped when Trent and Ciaran looked down at him. His face seemed to be a slightly paler grey than usual, and he didn't smile.

"Are you going into Falias?" he asked, his voice subdued.

Ciaran nodded. "To see the king, aye."

"May I ride with you?"

Ciaran exchanged a brief glance with Trent before he answered. "Of course, lad. What's amiss?"

"I...have business in the city. I would be glad for company." He lifted himself up onto the horse and started off ahead of them, so Ciaran urged his horse into a trot to catch up.

They rode in silence for a minute or two, Trent glancing over at Rathgeirr's solemn face and nudging Ciaran's shoulder to draw attention to it. The fairy cleared his throat softly.

"Have you seen Gunvard or your brother, since the ships have returned?" he asked, but Rathgeirr kept his gaze forward.

"No," he answered softly. "They didn't come back."

Trent frowned across at him, a faint ache in his own chest. "Didn't come back?"

Rathgeirr hummed a faint agreement. "Perhaps it's for the best." He spurred his horse a little faster, and Ciaran followed, all the way to the ramparts of Falias.

The alfar didn't seem to have anything else to say, but when the three of them dismounted near the Great Hall, Rathgeirr put himself between his companions and the door. He hesitated, black eyes glancing between their faces.

"I want to thank you," he said. "Both of you. For trusting me. And for...being my friends." With his lips pressed into a tight line, he nodded once, then turned and approached the guard at the door to the Great Hall. He gave his name and was allowed inside as the guard turned his gaze on Trent and Ciaran. He waved them forward as well—he must have recognized them.

Trent looked up at Ciaran with a furrowed brow, but the fairy's expression had turned grim.

"Let's go in, a mhuirnín," he said, one hand on the small of Trent's back to urge him inside.

The Great Hall was loud with overlapping voices as they stepped into the entryway. Another pair of guards stood watch at the inner door, but they didn't try to stop the new arrivals. The long tables' benches were full of men who shouted over and at each other, some on their feet to point accusing fingers at the others across from them. Hathuwulf was at the end of the hall, seated in the larger of the two thrones on the raised platform. He looked out across the room with stoic patience on his face, though Kothran at his side shifted on his feet as though he might shout himself at any moment. Trent wondered if the crown on Hathuwulf's brow felt as heavy as it looked.

Rathgeirr crossed the hall with purpose in his stride, making his way down the narrow aisle at the center of the room until he stood at the base of the king's platform. He dropped to one knee and lowered his head, not lifting it even when Hathuwulf shifted forward in his seat and raised one hand slightly from the arm of his throne.

Silence washed over the room in an instant from the simple gesture, and the men on their feet took their places again with dutiful swiftness, all eyes turning to the end of the hall.

"Rathgeirr Gunvardsson," Hathuwulf said evenly. "Etiquette dictates I offer my sorrow for the loss of your father and brother, but I find it difficult to console the collaborator before me."

Trent grabbed onto Ciaran's sleeve reflexively, but he kept his eyes on Rathgeirr. A collaborator—that's what Rathgeirr was to his people now. Of course. He moved along the edge of the hall to get a little closer.

"Yðar Hátign. I have no defense. I did only as my heart dictated—I wished for peace and acted as I thought was right. I accept responsibility for my part in the damage done to our home."

"So you've come to ask for mercy, then?"

"I expect none," Rathgeirr answered immediately. His fingertips tensed against the wood floor where his hand supported him. "I raised my weapon against the people of the Norðrvegr, and whether there was anger in my heart or pain, the outcome was the same. I know and accept the judgment of the king."

Hathuwulf watched him in silence for a moment, dark eyes faintly narrowed. "On your feet, Gunvardsson. Let your king look you in the face."

Rathgeirr did as he was told, standing up straight and lifting his chin but not his eyes. He was clearly trying to keep steady—but if Trent could see the faint tremble in his closed fists, Hathuwulf must have seen it, too.

"By rights, I could put your head on a post outside this very hall," Hathuwulf said, and Rathgeirr visibly swallowed.

"Yes, Yðar Hátign."

"You have made a place for yourself among the Ævintýri. You could have stayed hidden and slipped away on one of their ships, and so avoided the wrath of the island you betrayed."

"Yes, Yðar Hátign," Rathgeirr said again, slightly more strained now. "But I—though it will not save me, I—wish to say that I...love our home deeply, and fought only against the bloodlust of Konungr Huldrekall. I have seen the world of men, and I wished—I wished to help preserve it," he finished before his voice grew too unsteady.

Hathuwulf tilted his head, brow lowering into a pensive frown. After a few tense seconds, he spoke again. "You are now the last of your line, Gunvardsson. In consideration of this, I find it prudent to open the issue to the court—if anyone here will speak for you."

The silence in the hall was so heavy it almost crushed Trent to the ground. Rathgeirr didn't move—and neither did anyone else. Trent looked up at Ciaran in desperation, but the fairy subtly shook his head. Even if he had spoken up, what would it matter to Hathuwulf? From his perspective, Rathgeirr was a traitor. He'd literally let the enemy into their gates. A cry for mercy from one of the enemies themselves would be meaningless.

"I want to speak for him," Trent spoke up before he could stop himself, his voice uncomfortably loud in the long hall. He shrunk slightly under the harsh faces of the alfar around him, but he tried to look only at Hathuwulf.

"A human holds no sway in this court," an older man across the room snapped. "Let alone the human pet of one of the Ævintýri."

Trent's fingers tightened in Ciaran's sleeve to still him before he could bite back, and Hathuwulf let a beat of silence pass before lifting his fingers in a subtle gesture allowing Trent to continue.

"Rathgeirr is my friend," Trent said. "He's a good person, and he just wanted to stop things from getting out of control. Just like you did. Yðar Hátign," he added in an awful approximation of the language, and he tried to give as natural a low bow as he was capable of. It wasn't graceful.

Hathuwulf took a single slow breath before speaking. "A human holds no sway in this court," he agreed. His eyes scanned the nobles in the hall. "Yet truth must. Rathgeirr Gunvardsson," he went on, focusing on the young alfar in front of him. "Given that you are the sole remaining survivor of your family, and in recognition of the honor you've shown in presenting yourself to me today—your king grants you mercy."

Rathgeirr's shoulders seemed somehow more tense at this news when Trent straightened to look up at him.

"Instead of execution," Hathuwulf went on, "you are hereby named Ósnertanlegur, for a period of no less than five years. Your father's estate will be relinquished to the crown, and you will pay your debt to the Norðrvegr in sweat." The king's voice dropped into a low promise. "You have until the end of your servitude to convince me that you can be more loyal to the current king of the Norðrvegr than you were its last."

Rathgeirr fell into a deep bow, hands tight at his sides. "I am...humbled, Yðar Hátign. I will not disappoint you."

"My steward will see to your father's estate," Hathuwulf said, and Kothran gave a brief nod. "You will be outside the borders of my cities before dusk, and you will report to the outpost at Dolgrveginn at dawn tomorrow."

"Yes, Yðar Hátign." Rathgeirr dipped just a bit lower, then took a step backward before turning to leave the hall.

Ciaran started after him straight away, but Trent lingered, hoping to catch Hathuwulf's eye. The king turned his head to say something to Kothran, then called to a noble Trent didn't recognize and started up the noise of argument again. He was too busy to talk to Trent—of course he was. Trent wasn't a servant in his house anymore, and Hathuwulf wasn't just a prince anymore. The treaty was signed; the demon portal was closed; the war was over. Things were going to move forward now.

Trent turned from the throne and followed Ciaran outside, where Rathgeirr had already mounted his horse. He turned the animal and kicked it into a run before Ciaran could pull his reins free of the post. Ciaran pulled himself into the saddle and reached down, but when Trent moved to take his hand, the sharp clearing of a throat behind him made him pause.

Kothran was in the doorway, hands folded in front of him and cold eyes on Trent's face. He waited for the boy to turn fully back to him, then straightened his shoulders just so he could look down his nose at him a little more deeply.

"Konungr Hathuwulf requests your presence at his residence tonight. You will be expected at sunset."

"Uh. Okay," Trent answered. He opened his mouth to ask why, but Kothran was already gone, so he took Ciaran's hand up and held onto the sides of the fairy's tunic as the horse began to move.

"He's asking for you at night, now?" Ciaran grumbled, his words half hidden by the wind. Trent didn't give him the satisfaction of replying.

Back at the camp, they arrived just in time to see Airmed explode out of the medical tent in a dramatic flap of canvas. Rathgeirr was waiting for her, and she hit him so hard that he stumbled back as her arms tightened around his neck. Her feet left the ground with his supporting arms around her waist, and as Trent and Ciaran dismounted to approach them, Airmed's soft, hiccuping breaths escaped from where her face was hidden in the fur of Rathgeirr's cloak. When he set her back on the ground, she pulled back only enough to take his face in her hands and kiss him.

Trent glanced sidelong at Ciaran, expecting some kind of objection—but he watched the pair with crossed arms and the faintest crinkle at the corner of his eye.

"He really just walked in there expecting to be executed?" Trent asked, and Ciaran nodded.

"I suppose he did. He's a damn sight more honorable than I am."

"That's a low bar," Trent snorted. Ciaran lightly elbowed him.

Rathgeirr seemed to realize they'd attracted the attention of the people around them; he separated himself from Airmed with awkward stiffness. She wiped at her damp eyes and took him by the front of his cloak, pulling him along with her past the corner of the tent and out of sight.

"Well, I suppose she could do worse," Ciaran said with a chuckle. He tilted his head toward Trent. "He's lucky he had a friend to speak for him."

"Friend might be overstating it," he grumbled, but Ciaran only smiled wider.

"I heard you say it. No take backs."

"Shut up." Trent made his way back to the tent to retrieve the bandages he'd abandoned earlier and focus on rolling them—rather than spending the rest of the day wondering why he'd been summoned to Hathuwulf's house.

Ciaran wanted to come with him when evening came, but Trent refused. He promised he was capable of riding a horse on his own—slowly—at least as far as the city. And whatever Hathuwulf wanted, it definitely wouldn't have been made easier by Ciaran standing in the corner glaring at him. So Trent mounted Ciaran's horse with only a little difficulty and made his way through the fields surrounding Falias.

He knew the way through the city to the royal residence by now, thought it was harder to tell with the charred remains and reconstruction everywhere. He still managed to arrive a little after sunset. Skathi greeted him at the door with a tight hug, which he endured, and she led him straight through the house to Hathuwulf's bedroom.

The king was standing near the fire when Trent was announced and let inside, a bit of parchment with rolled edges in his hand. Without his crown, wearing a simple tunic and robe, he looked more like the man Trent knew. His eyebrows raised just slightly as Trent stepped into the room, but he waited until the door was closed to speak.

"You came."

"You asked," Trent answered with a small shrug. He shifted on his feet and picked awkwardly at the hem of his tunic. Should he be bowing? Should he be more formal now? Hathuwulf had seemed so different in the Great Hall—even sterner than usual. Even now, he seemed more distant, so Trent decided to hedge his bets and give a small, brief bow.

"Earlier," the king began, moving to the table to lay down his parchment, "you came into Falias because of Gunvardsson?" He kept his eyes on the report, fingers splayed across its surface to keep it from rolling back onto itself.

"No," Trent admitted. "That was kind of a coincidence, I guess. I came to try to see if there was...anything I could help you with." When the alfar's gaze lifted to him, Trent tensed a little. "But I guess then I thought that...the King of the Alfar wouldn't want or need some random human giving his opinion."

Hathuwulf paused, then pulled the nearby chair away from the table and sat heavily down into it, looking across the room at Trent with the barest hint of a warm smile on his lips. It heated Trent's cheeks, but he kept a straight face. "I didn't know if you would still have opinions to give to a king," Hathuwulf said gently.

Trent hesitated, and for a few seconds, they held each other's gaze without speaking. Then Trent let a small chuckle slip from him, and he approached the table and pulled out the chair opposite the king to take his own seat. "You haven't even heard half of my opinions yet," he promised, and Hathuwulf exhaled softly through his nose as he slid the parchment across to Trent's waiting hands.

35

The next few days were remarkably quiet, considering how many teenagers were in the house. Everyone was happy to rest and recover—even Julien's brothers didn't seem to have enough energy to keep up their protests. Anik was, perhaps, the most animated. She had infinite energy for chatting and questioning their young guests. Julien took his turn visiting Edouard in the hospital and promised him that the visiting boys wouldn't be staying long. The adult with them had mentioned leaving for California as soon as he was well enough to travel, and Noah had dutifully helped him along with his tonics and herbs, despite his obvious hatred for the man who'd taken Sabin from him years ago. The witch was probably just eager to get him gone.

Julien was eager to have them all gone, if he was honest. Sabin was definitely going to be a permanent fixture from here on out, which Julien would learn to live with—but he wasn't keen on keeping the others around for longer than necessary. Secret government organizations and a literal demon living under his roof were more than he wanted to deal with. After the last few weeks, going back to hunting slimy things that went bump in the night would feel like a vacation.

Luckily, most of the boys seemed to plan to leave when their grownup did—and when the day came, the scene was almost surreal in how normal it was. The four only had a couple of small bags between them, and they stood waiting in the front hall for their car to the airport, looking very much like Shipton was their chaperone on a class trip. The boys had cordial goodbyes for each other, mostly, which seemed like a definite improvement over how they'd been when they first arrived. Julien was content to stay out of the way, but when he noticed Noah following Shipton into the kitchen, he moved to the doorway to listen—if only to make sure Noah didn't do anything he'd regret.

"Mr. Clark," Shipton began quietly, "I wanted to mention before we leave—I would be authorized to send you a small stipend going forward, as technically I'm leaving at least one Haven recruit in your care. If you have bank account information you can give me, or at least an address or PO Box, I could send you money on a monthly basis. To make things easier."

Julien grimaced; even without looking around the edge of the doorway, he knew the scowl that would be on Noah's face, and he heard it in the witch's voice as he spoke.

"Fuck you. I don't want your money. *Now* I'm supposed to believe you give a shit about Sabin's care? We were fine before you showed up, and we'll be more than fine after you're gone," he spat. "I don't want anything else to do with you or your fucking *Haven*."

Just a moment of quiet went by before Shipton answered. "Of course. It was only an offer. I wish you and Sabin well, Mr. Clark."

"Fucking sure you do," Noah sneered.

Julien managed to scoot far enough away from the door that he didn't get bumped into when Noah stalked out, and he let the witch go by and watched him head up the stairs. When Shipton reached the doorway, Julien tapped his knuckles on the other man's remaining arm to draw his attention.

"Listen," he began once Shipton paused and looked at him, "Noah's proud. But when it comes to money, I'm not. We've both been broke as hell for a long time. Can I text you?"

Shipton gave a small snort of amusement that definitely would have made Noah want to punch him in the face. He took a slim leather wallet from his pants pocket and unfolded it, but then he fumbled for a bit, only managing to eke a card partway from one of the front pockets with his thumb before a faint, resigned smile crossed his lips, and he held it out for Julien to take himself. The hunter stuffed immediately into his own pocket just in case Noah was still watching. "Thank you for your family's hospitality, Monsieur Fournier. Please feel free to be in touch." He moved as if his instinct was to offer Julien his hand, then realized the great majority of his right arm was missing. He paused for a single awkward second, then reached out with his left hand instead just as one of the boys called from the window that their cab had arrived. Julien accepted the brief handshake with a nod.

Shipton followed his class out the front door after another quick round of goodbyes—from everyone except the slender redhead—and in a moment, Julien was left standing in the entry with Sabin, Berlin, an angel, and a demon. Julien couldn't remember their names. They hadn't said anything yet about leaving, but they'd want to be gone before Edouard set foot in the house again.

When Julien got the call that Joseph would be bringing Edouard home that afternoon, both boys—though Julien was hesitant to call them that—seemed to understand that their welcome had been stretched to its limit. Sabin gave the small demon as genuine a goodbye as Julien suspected the little punk was capable of, and when Berlin squeezed the blond boy tight, grunted out a threat that his friend had better not disappear on him, and wiped roughly at his face as he stepped back, Noah was watching him with much softer eyes than usual.

With only Sabin and Berlin remaining, and even Anik cuffing Julien on the shoulder that evening to tell him she'd be on her way, it was almost peaceful in the evening. Edouard was put straight to bed and Laurent on nurse duty, and Julien was able to avoid any further conversations with his oldest brother about his lifestyle. It was time for them to go—the less Julien had to listen to Edouard berate him for leaving with *two* witches in tow this time, the better.

Julien came upstairs after Edouard was settled, fully prepared to pack what things he wanted to take from the house and leave that very night. He entered his bedroom to find Noah and Sabin sitting on the bed, cross-legged and facing each other—which seemed to be the usual pose for their "arguments."

"How can you not know?" Noah was asking as Julien came through the door.

Sabin shot the hunter a quick, frowning glance, but then continued to ignore his presence. "Because I don't? It's his life; how am I supposed to know what he wants to do?"

"By *asking him*," Noah pressed. "You already said he mentioned an interest. You want him to come with us, right?"

"I mean—yeah," Sabin admitted.

Julien crouched at the foot of the bed to dig a few things out of his footlocker. "Are we talking about Berlin?"

"Yes," Noah confirmed with a hint of a sigh in his voice. "Sabin, I know you're probably nervous about him, and I know the kinds of things you must be thinking about yourself—don't even try," he added when the boy opened his mouth to protest. "But you have to be able to communicate. It's the only way you two are going to get on the same page and stay there."

"We are on the same page," Sabin grumbled. "I think. And anyway, what about you? I can't just—"

"Can't just assume that I'm okay with you bringing your boyfriend along with us?"

Sabin's face turned a shade of strawberry as soon as Noah uttered the word "boyfriend" that pleased Julien immensely. "But I can't just *assume* he really wants to come, either."

"You just have to be honest with him," Noah pressed, more gently. "Be genuine. Tell him how you're feeling. If he's the right person for you, he'll listen, I promise."

The teenager frowned down at the bed and gave an exceptionally teenage-sounding sigh. "But...what if he—"

"Ah, ça va faire là," Julien said in a grunt as he stood. He pulled the bedroom door open wider and bellowed Berlin's name down the hall. When the boy poked his head out of the bunk room with a curious frown on his face, Julien called, "Do you want to come with us and hunt monsters for a living, or not?"

Berlin shrugged one shoulder, as though the answer was a given. "Yeah."

"Okay. Get your shit."

"Yep," the boy called, already closing the bunk room door again.

Julien turned back into the bedroom and gave a grand gesture toward the hallway with one arm. Both witches were staring at him—Noah with a warm smile, and Sabin with a slight gape of disbelief and embarrassment. The boy quickly scoffed away his show of emotion and turned his face from the hunter as he scratched at the shaved side of his head, but Julien could still see his smile and the touch of red in his cheeks.

"...Okay," Sabin mumbled. "That's cool, I guess."

Hugo gave Noah a hug goodbye as they left, and the others—except for Antony, of course—thanked him and shook his hand. Even Edouard had told Julien to pass on to the witch that "he'd done his duty admirably." It was something.

Now they stood on the sidewalk outside the Fournier house, Sabin and Berlin standing close-but-not-too-close to each other and Noah reaching for Julien's fingers to give them a tender squeeze.

"So," Noah said with a smile, "where to?"

"I always wanted to see Buenos Aires," Sabin suggested, and Julien shot him a tight frown.

"Maybe think smaller, since I've recently come into some debt."

"Man, that sucks for you," Sabin sighed. He looked up at Julien with concern furrowing his brow. "You really ought to be more responsible with your finances."

"Sansdessein," Julien snapped, but Noah distracted him by wrapping his arm fully around the hunter's elbow.

"Before anything else, why don't we go home?" Noah smiled across at the boys. "You can show Berlin the Holy Rosary Cathedral. And I owe you a tattoo," he added with a smile at Sabin.

"Yeah!" Sabin agreed, then immediately tempered his enthusiasm. "Yeah," he said again, slightly more subdued. "That sounds cool."

"It does sound cool," Noah agreed. "But it's far, and we're all out of fairy magic to get us places. It'll have to be a leg at a time."

"Will there be monsters to fight on the way?" Sabin asked with a sidelong glance at Berlin, whose eyebrows lifted in interest."

"Unavoidably," Julien said, and the boys exchanged a quick smile.

Noah hugged the blond's arm a little closer to him, then shifted his bag on his shoulder. "Well—then it's about time we get going."

Julien looked over at the teenagers they'd apparently adopted, then down at the witch beside him. It was going to be better from now on.

36

There were a hundred thousand things to be done on the island, and just about all of them were Hathuwulf's responsibility. Reconstruction was progressing, though slowly, and plans were moving forward. The runes the Alfar wrote in didn't even take long to learn, so Trent didn't have to keep asking the king for phonics lessons.

He suddenly found himself actually able to help. Even if the Jarlar—which he found out was just any kind of landowning noble—weren't willing to take the advice of a human, Hathuwulf was. He listened when Trent presented him with spreadsheets drawn on rolls of parchment and discussed complications and possibilities with him that the new king could pass on to his court. It felt like having work to do—like being useful. There was no magic involved here. These, at last, were problems that Trent could visualize and break down as he grew familiar with the current workings of the island's economy. Once Hathuwulf announced the emancipation, his workload seemed to double—it was time to enact all of the systems and protections they had so carefully planned.

Ciaran was less than pleased at the amount of time Trent was spending at the Great Hall, but he didn't complain—much. And Trent didn't complain at all. The fairy's thinly-veiled jealousy was giving him the best sex of his life, even if it was in an army camp tent.

But the camp was growing smaller. As the rest of the fairy ships arrived, soldiers had begun to break down their temporary homes and prepare for the journey back to Tír na nÓg , and Ciaran was anxious to claim a place on Lugh's ship and "put the whole cursed island behind them," as he said. Trent was too—this was what they'd been trying for since the start, after all. Leave together, travel, be whoever they wanted to be and do whatever they wanted to do—though Ciaran still wasn't too clear on how they were going to afford to be so well-traveled now that he'd lost his magic.

So why did Trent's heart feel heavy as he sat at the broad table in Hathuwulf's bedroom, surrounded by half-unfurled reports, the only sound the crackling of the fire pit as the King of the Alfar read over a letter?

After Trent had been still and quiet for a while, Hathuwulf lifted black eyes over the top of his parchment to look across the table at him. "I've designated an appointment for you," he said evenly, then returned his attention to the letter.

Trent lowered his eyebrows into a frown as he looked up. "A what?"

"A title," the king explained without looking up. "I've already told the Jarlar. Now that every human on the island is free, it only makes sense that I should have a representative in the court. I've named you Hirðmaðr—retainer to the crown."

"That—Hathuwulf, I'm not even from here; just because I know how to—do your taxes, that doesn't mean I'm qualified to—"

"You are the only human who is qualified," the alfar interrupted him. He let his eyes shut for a moment and exhaled softly through his nose—not quite a smile, but close—then leaned forward to lay his parchment on the table. "Precisely because you call me Hathuwulf." He held Trent's gaze long enough that the boy felt like squirming, then casually scooped up the next report in his pile and settled back in his chair. "The office belongs to you regardless, as well as its associated grants," he said. "But I hope you will reconsider your decision to leave The Norðrvegr."

Trent let his gaze drop to the table, his hands laced together in his lap and a twisted feeling in his stomach. "I'll think about it," he promised, though his voice was quiet.

"Hold on," Ciaran said, shaking his head. He pinched the bridge of his nose with two fingers and held up a hand to urge Trent to give him a moment, then dropped his hands to stare across the tent at him. "You're going to have to say that again, lad, because I am positive I didn't hear you correctly the first time. You want to *stay?*"

Trent puffed up a little defensively. "Well—why not? Isn't it better to be somewhere we can be useful, instead of just wandering aimlessly, never knowing how we're going to make it from day to day?"

"No!" Ciaran laughed. "Being useful is the most overrated thing I can think of. And you want to not only stay, but accept a *title* from the king of the Lochlannan?"

Trent sighed. "You're going to have to stop using that word."

"Ach," the fairy scoffed with a wave of his hand. "A title is a *job*, a mhuirnín. You know that, don't you? Why on Earth would you want a *job* when you could have *no job?*"

"Nobody's telling *you* to get a job," Trent pointed out. He shifted forward to put his weight on his hands, leaning in close so that his lips faintly brushed Ciaran's cheek as he murmured, "You'll have all the free time in the world. We can get some horses, and you can go for a ride whenever you want...take long baths...eat whatever you want..."

Ciaran grunted defiantly, though it sounded more petulant than anything. He leaned back enough to look Trent in the face. "You're trying to turn me into a kept man, are you?"

"Why?" Trent asked with a tilt of his head as he laid one hand on the other man's thigh. "Don't you want to be kept?"

"What if—what if your glasses break? We can't exactly pop down the shop and buy you new ones."

Trent stared flatly at him. "Be serious."

The fairy huffed out a grumpy sigh. "I want you to be happy, a mhuirnín. And I'll be happy wherever you are. Just— you're *absolutely sure* this lochlannan isn't trying to fuck you."

"For fuck's sake, Ciaran," Trent groaned, taking him by the back of the neck and pulling him into a long kiss. He let his forehead rest against Ciaran's and smiled despite himself. "Just let me keep you."

Ciaran snorted softly and gathered the younger man to him,

running gentle fingers through his hair. "I suppose I can live with that."

When Ciaran's family was ready to board the ship waiting to return them home, both he and Trent saw them off. Cu and Cethen shook their brother's hand in turn and asked him more than once if he was sure he hadn't been knocked too hard in the head in some battle or other, but they both had smiles on their faces as they made their way down the beach. Airmed wiped rogue tears from her eyes as she held Ciaran around the neck, squeezing him tightly until he awkwardly patted her back in an attempt to get a little more access to air. Then she moved over to Trent and caught him in a similarly suffocating embrace, deftly avoiding the barrier of his outstretched arms.

Ciaran snorted out a soft laugh at the helpless look Trent gave him over Airmed's shoulder. Rathgeirr appeared from behind to stand beside him, and Ciaran didn't have to look at him to know the alfar was watching Airmed.

"May I speak with you?" he asked. His eyes flicked across Ciaran for a second, and the fairy followed his gaze back to where his sister was only just releasing an uncomfortable-looking Trent.

"Sure, lad," Ciaran murmured, and he followed Rathgeirr a short distance away, folding his arms as the alfar moved to stand near a gnarled grey tree.

"You could still go, you know," Ciaran said. "Nobody's likely to follow you."

Rathgeirr shook his head. "It wouldn't be right. I'll stay, I'll pay my debt, and I'll prove my fealty to Konungr Hathuwulf."

"She'd stay with you, if you asked."

"I know," the alfar answered softly. "But I can't let her live the life I will, even if Ævintýri were permitted to stay—I think you've used up all the king's allowances," he added with a brief look over at Trent. He glanced down at the ground then back to Ciaran's face. "Airmed told me that...your father has disowned her?"

"Aye, something like that," Ciaran snorted. "They haven't been on speaking terms since my brother Miach was killed. By my father, you see. He's really a nasty piece of work."

"I see." Rathgeirr hesitated, fingering the string of the bow across his chest as he looked down to where Airmed was gathering her things to be loaded onto the nearest ship. "Then it's you that I must—before I speak to her—" He took a breath and tried again, more firmly this time. "As her eldest brother, it is you I must ask for permission to marry her. If—if she agrees, of course. And when I've cleared my name."

"Marry?" Ciaran echoed, eyebrows raising in surprise. "Are you serious, lad?"

The alfar nodded with his mouth set into a stern line. "I love her."

Ciaran opened his mouth, ready to offer all the regular objections—they didn't know each other very well, they were very different, they shouldn't rush—but each one died on his lips before it could escape, replaced instead with a soft laugh and a resigned shake of his head. He was in no position to give such advice—and why should he? He'd never seen Airmed light up the way she did when the two of them were together—not in a thousand years. He took Rathgeirr by one shoulder and gave him a gentle shake.

"If she'll have you, then I suppose I should count you luckier than any man in Tír na nÓg ."

Rathgeirr brightened, showing his sharp teeth in a broad smile. "Then..."

"Aye, lad. If it's my blessing you're after, consider it given. Good luck with that one. She's more of a handful than you'd suspect."

The alfar was already looking past him toward the shore, almost bursting in his eagerness to be dismissed. He seemed to remember himself and returned his attention back to Ciaran. "Thank you," he said, so earnestly that Ciaran was a little embarrassed. "I'll make her happier than—than—than the happiest woman that's ever been," he finished in a rush, but then his smile faltered. "If...if she will wait."

"That's a question for her," Ciaran pointed out, and Rathgeirr nodded, seeming to steel himself before joining Ciaran on the short walk back to the shore.

Airmed was waiting on the beach, squeezing Trent's hands as she spoke, and the boy caught sight of Ciaran's return and begged him with his eyes—for rescue or death, Ciaran couldn't tell. She smiled at them as they approached, but it was subdued. She reached timidly toward Rathgeirr, then stayed her hand, lacing her fingers together in front of her.

"I...will miss you," she said, and Ciaran had to stop himself from gathering her in his arms like a child. He wished he had pockets to put his hands in.

"Airmed," Rathgeirr began, taking half a step toward her as if hesitant to close the gap, "I will—when my time in service is done, and I can hold my head up again, I—I'll come to you. If you still wish me to, after..."

"I've lost count of how old I am," Airmed interrupted him. "Five years don't mean anything."

They both smiled, relief finally touching their faces, but any further romantic promises were cut off by Lugh's approach.

"The ships are ready."

Airmed looked up at him then back to Rathgeirr with suddenly damp eyes. She latched onto his neck, all propriety forgotten, and Ciaran saw the tremble in her shoulders as the alfar held her.

"Why do you cry, Aintín?" Lugh asked. "It seems dramatic for mere months apart."

"Months?" Airmed echoed as she moved back from Rathgeirr, turning to look up at Lugh with her fingers still tight in the alfar's tunic. "I don't think you—"

"I'll be returning in a year's time to make contact with King Hathuwulf, and in the years following," he explained. "If you wish to accompany me—you so rarely have cause to leave Tír na nÓg . I thought you'd appreciate the fresh air."

Airmed paused a moment as realization crept over her, and then she released Rathgeirr in favor of standing on tiptoe and tugging on her large nephew's shoulders until he bent down far enough for her to press a long, grateful kiss to his cheek. Then she turned back and took Rathgeirr's hands in hers, her smile beaming now despite the wet streaks on her face.

"I'll see you in a year," she said.

He smiled. "In a year."

She bounced on the balls of her feet once or twice, then leaned in and kissed him again, one last time before following Lugh down the rocky beach to his ship. She leaned over the side to wave at them as Lugh guided the ship away, but once the sails were dropped, she and the rest of the fleet soon grew too far away to see.

Rathgeirr turned to face Ciaran and Trent, his faint smile just a little less weary now. "I may not see much of you both in the coming years," he said, "but I will surely have you in my thoughts. I believe that the Norðrvegrwill be made better by you two being here."

"Well," Ciaran chuckled with a sidelong glance at Trent, "better for one of us being here, at least."

37
SEVERAL MONTHS LATER

Trent fastened the brooch of the grey fur cloak that hung down to his knees, pausing to shift the weight more comfortably on his shoulders. Winter had come to The Norðrvegr weeks ago, and Trent would be lying if he said he didn't miss his Canada Goose jacket—but he was adjusting. The fresh goat's milk Skathi brought them weekly helped warm him up in the mornings, and usually came with the unintended addition of a quick tidying-up if the old woman happened to come by when neither Trent nor Ciaran were home to object.

The longhouse that had been built for them on the outskirts of Falias at Hathuwulf's behest wasn't large, but it suited their needs well. Trent didn't need much other than a desk to work at, and it hadn't taken Ciaran long to build a small stable and yard with the silver paid to Trent at the start of every month. A horse had been the next purchase, and then another—so the first one didn't get lonely, Ciaran said. Trent still didn't really like to ride them.

He took a drink and stopped in front of the polished bronze mirror by the wash basin, fingers working easily to pull his hair back from his face into a simple silver clip. The growing length had irritated him at first, but the first time Ciaran had wrapped his hand in it and

314

tugged, he'd decided to keep it. It helped him look at least a little less out of place in the city, as well.

Falias was an entirely different place from the grey, rigid city he'd first seen through the mist. The market stalls were filled with both alfar and humans now, each selling crops, milk and eggs, mead, and any number of other goods side by side. There were no more cowering figures in blue tunics or dresses. It was taking time for some of the alfar to adjust to humans being treated as equals, and would still take some time yet, he suspected, but things were improving thanks to Hathuwulf's swift and uncompromising methods of dealing with antagonists. The fields that fed the whole of the island still grew tall, but now the men and women who tended them did so because they were either paid to or because they owned them outright. Slave quarters had been replaced by homes where families lived and worked. A second school had even been opened—a separate one, for now, but that was something Trent could work on.

Ciaran had already been missing when Trent woke up, as usual, but by the time he made his way outside, the fairy was standing by the entrance to the stable, brushing the neck of his dark bay horse, Bébhinn, and humming softly to her. His long staff already leaned against the nearby fence, strung with caught fish. He turned his head when he heard Trent's steps and smiled at him, his breath white steam in the frigid air. His hair had grown a little long, too, but he was better at braiding it out of his face than Trent was. As Trent approached, Ciaran set his brush on the fence post and wrapped his arms around the smaller man's waist to kiss him, allowing him just enough time to settle into the warmth of his lover's lips before sliding icy hands up beneath his tunic and spreading them across his back. Trent yelped and tried to shove him away, but Ciaran only laughed and kissed him again.

"Give them hell today, a mhuirnín," he murmured with his nose brushing Trent's, and the boy didn't try to fight his smile.

"Try not to nap *all* day," he countered as he pulled back and straightened his cloak.

"Aye sure," the fairy grinned. "I'm seeing Hlífa today—she's promised to make me some cakes with honey. Shall I save you some?"

"A little," Trent agreed begrudgingly. He went into the stable, where Ciaran had already saddled the cream-colored mare Múireann for him—carefully chosen for her even temper and reluctance to gallop—and hefted himself up with only a little awkwardness. The animal nickered as she was urged out of the warm building and nosed at Ciaran's shoulder as they passed him. Trent paused to smile back at the kiss Ciaran threw him, then kneed the horse gently into a trot.

The cold air felt good on his face.

ABOUT THE AUTHOR

T.S. Barnett is the author of The Beast of Birmingham werewolf thriller series, steampunk horror romance A Soul's Worth, dark urban fantasy series The Left-Hand Path, and a number of m/m paranormal romances.

Tess likes to write about what makes people tick, whether that's deeply-rooted emotional issues, childhood trauma, or just plain hedonism. Throw in a heaping helping of action and violence, a sprinkling of steamy bits, and a whisper of wit (with alliteration optional but preferred), and you have her idea of a perfect novel. She believes in telling stories about real people who live in less-real worlds full of werewolves, witches, demons, vampires, and the occasional alien.

Born and bred in the South, Tess started writing young, but began writing real novels while working full time as a legal secretary. When she's not writing, she reads other people's books, plays video games, watches movies, and spends time with her husband and daughter. She hopes her daughter grows into a woman who knows what she wants, grabs it, and gets into significantly less trouble than the women in her mother's novels.

www.hisprincelydelicates.com